Motherless Child

A NOVEL BY

MARIANNE LANGNER ZEITLIN

2012 : ZEPHYR PRESS : BROOKLINE, MASS.

Cover: Detail from "Unfinished 2," an oil painting
by Sarah Longlands, 2001

*type*slowly designed

Zephyr Press acknowledges with gratitude the financial support of the
Massachusetts Cultural Council.

massculturalcouncil.org

Zephyr Press, a non-profit arts and education 501(c)(3) organization,
publishes literary titles that foster a deeper understanding of cultures
and languages. Zephyr Press books are distributed to the trade in the U.S.
and Canada by Consortium Book Sales and Distribution [www.cbsd.com]
and by Small Press Distribution [www.spdbooks.org].

Cataloguing-in publication data is available from the Library of Congress.

Zephyr Press / 50 Kenwood Street / Brookline, MA / 02446
www.zephyrpress.org

For Zvi Zeitlin and his violin

Prologue

At nine-thirty on a cool November morning in 1977, Elizabeth Guaragna picked up a copy of the *New York Times* from the vendor at her subway station and, in anticipation of cramped subway space, opened it to the entertainment section, folded it back in double and turned to go. The announcement that Alfred Rossiter had left the music conglomerate he had founded to open a new agency hit her between the eyes.

"Wait, miss," the vendor called after her, "here's the rest of your change."

Unhearing, Elizabeth ran down the stairs to the downtown subterranean level and squeezed into the last remaining space on a bench. Motes of dust were suspended in the lurid glare from a neon orange juice sign over the newspaper. As an express train thundered past, fear engulfed her and she focused her eyes at the newsprint and accompanying picture. The strong, carved, self-contained face seemed to stare right back. She was gripped by the onset of a familiar, if unidentifiable, pain. Under a two column headline *DEAN OF AMERICAN IMPRESARIOS TO OPEN NEW AGENCY*, the story read:

> Alfred Rossiter, internationally known as "Mr. Music" since his introduction of classical music to radio in its early days, announced today that he will leave Eagle Artists Management to open a new agency.
>
> Rossiter founded Eagle Artists Management in 1928 and developed it, along with the Eagle Broadcasting System and Eagle Records, into the world's largest musical conglomerate. It was a Fortune 500 corporation last year, with over 2.4 billion dollars in earnings.

The news sent shock waves throughout the music world and plummeted the corporation's stocks on Wall Street. The $11.25 drop per share was the biggest one-day change in the history of the company and brought the Dow Jones average down twelve points. "We have regretfully accepted Mr. Rossiter's decision," said Roger Carron, Chief Executive Officer of EAM. Rumors abounded but no explanation for Mr. Rossiter's sudden departure has been confirmed.

Artists under the 80-year-old impresario's management, which include some of the biggest names in the musical pantheon, were also taken by surprise at the announcement. "I was sitting in the Green Room after a concert in Paris when I heard the news," said Abraham Strelski, the renowned tenor. "It came as a shock. Naturally, I cannot comment further until we know more."

One source, who asked to remain anonymous, suggested that Rossiter's relationship with the Board of directors at EAM had become increasingly strained in recent years. Rossiter is known to prefer total artistic, financial, and administrative control. "He's a martinet. If they don't do something his way, heads roll," the source said.

Rossiter, for whom both Rossiter Towers (which houses EAM) and Rossiter Court in the heart of Lincoln Center were named, would not return telephone calls. Efforts to uncover his whereabouts remained fruitless.

The man who was the recipient of the Presidential Medal of Achievement Award, the keys to the cities of New York and Washington, the Alice Peabody Award, and numerous other awards and honorary degrees, has often been called a legend in his own time. In a speech to the National Press Club in Washington earlier this year, the music magnate dismissed such accolades saying: "I had more luck than pluck—was in the right place at the right time."

Reached at his home in Westport, Gregory Mickiewicz, conductor of the New York Symphony Orchestra, summarized what Rossiter's pioneering example has meant to classical music: "More than any other force, he brought music to the people first on recordings, then on radio, then on television; and he brought the people to music by his establishment of organized concert series in every city in the land. I don't know what he has in mind for his new agency, but the man has always been ahead of his time and this new move augurs well for the future of music in America."

Elizabeth lifted the photo of Rossiter closer, then dropped it down again. The unidentifiable pain had now spread throughout her entire being. This, she thought, is a defining moment. Usually one doesn't recognize one at its conception, only in retrospect later, but she recognized it for what it was now. But why? What did it matter?

Though already late for work, she read the article through a second time, then, on a hunch, scoured the "Help Wanted" columns for possible listings.

The following Sunday, after "Impresario for All Seasons" by George Wentworth appeared in the magazine section of the newspaper, she became even more diligent in her search, for the article almost bordered on the worshipful, a distinct departure from Wentworth's usual laconic style.

Within a week, the hunch was rewarded. Several agencies had the job of "Executive Assistant for Concert Manager" prominently displayed and Elizabeth applied to Prestige Personnel the very next day.

Chapter I

". . . well, isn't she here?" The receptionist, identified on her name-plate as Virginia Lavin, had been addressing the applicants, but the young woman in the blue duffle coat was oblivious until she waved the olive card before her.

"Are you Lisa Sullivan? No, stay where you are," she said, lifting her hand in restraint as Elizabeth Guaragna straightened the stuffed canvas bag carelessly looped over her shoulder and started to move forward. Miss Lavin put her reading glasses dangling from a gilt chain back on. "It's not your turn yet. I just wanted to get the names straight in my mind."

Thank heavens, Elizabeth thought, as she returned to the spot next to the water cooler, the woman didn't have the original college transcript before her, for she might have noticed the different print where *Elizabeth Guaragna* had been covered with white correction fluid and *Lisa Sullivan* typed over it. On the photocopy the change was barely noticeable, but still, under the searchlights of the receptionist's revolving eyes, it might have been noticed.

Elizabeth kept her own eyes averted from the inquiring glances around her. Compared to these fashionably groomed New York women in their tweeds and cashmeres, gold chain necklaces entwined like tribal badges just so, she felt like a misplaced schoolgirl who had wandered into the office by mistake. And while they went through the conversational rites—the new Rockefeller Wing, the sweater in Bendel's window, the cholesterol in cheese—glancing at their wristwatches with large, almost pantomimic gestures of impatience, she remained silent and remote.

Her neck began to ache from staring ahead rigidly; the coins she churned in her coat pocket felt wet. For a moment she studied her face in the water cooler. *I have seen the face of my enemy and it is I.* That had been one of her father's expressions, lifted from a Pogo cartoon, but it was as applicable to her as anybody.

And here she was, bold as brass, right in the heart of the enemy's enemy encampment, without the elementary precaution of a name closer to her own that would at least have allowed sonic reflexes to take over.

But what name sounded like *Guaragna*? *Lasagna*, of course, though a laughing matter this was not.

Every now and then the door, on which the name Ruth Pryor was emblazoned in bronze, opened; as one hopeful emerged, another was ushered in by the receptionist. From where she stood, Elizabeth could glimpse the interviewer sitting behind a large oak desk with a sloping maroon felt hat set carefully on her head. She wore the hat as a general might wear gold braid and campaign ribbons: to separate commanders from commanded. Once, over the murmured exchanges going back and forth among the job applicants, her voice was clearly heard to say "We'll let you know" and the women looked at each other with cynical smiles.

As the next name was called, its owner rose, nodding to Elizabeth to take her seat. Elizabeth made a demurring noise, for several of the others who were also standing had arrived earlier. "That's an awful heavy bag you're carrying," the woman said, by way of explanation, but Elizabeth suspected that the real reason was that she regarded her as someone to whom she could afford to be kind.

Nonetheless, she was grateful. Slumped into soft leather, she felt far less conspicuous, and dropped the canvas bag filled with overdue library books and records on the floor with a thud. She stooped to prop it against her legs, her long black hair tumbling over the barrette.

As she pushed it away, her deep-socketed blue eyes came into view, but on one so unprepossessing as a whole, they seemed wasted, as though the product of some genetic miscalculation.

Of course she knew she was all wrong for the job. But it wasn't really a job she was seeking. She already had a reasonably good one at the Lincoln Center Library for which, as a musicologist, she was well-trained, and, by disposition, well-suited.

Elizabeth clutched her arms across her chest trying to keep from rocking to and fro. She had awakened that morning with the certainty that something was dreadfully wrong. Sitting up in alarm, she strained her ears to hear if there was any external cause.

But what burglar in his right mind would ply his trade in that dreary rear-end apartment?

Aunt Ada, that was it. Grabbing the telephone, she dialed directly, and imagined the ringing of the extension phones reverberating from oversized living room up two flights to her aunt's bedroom. *Bzzz, pause, bzzz, pause, bzzz, pause.* Twelve rings, thirteen rings, fourteen. Long distance operators tell you to stop at six, but she hung onto the receiver tightly until at last there was a click and her aunt's cheery "Good morning" flooded her with relief.

But there was nothing wrong at all, in fact she was all aflutter because a student of hers had just won the Trans-Canada piano competition and big doings were ahead for him. Nor was there anything wrong with Tom, to whom Ada had spoken the night before. He was still deep into his research of Gregorian chants and his abbot had called him in especially to commend him. And then her aunt admonished her for calling in prime telephone time. "Let's save everything for Thanksgiving. Can't wait to see you. *A piu tardi, bambina.*"

Shivering uncontrollably, Elizabeth had slid back under the covers, though it was getting late. Not only did the fright not lessen with the telephone call, it intensified. Perhaps she should call in sick.

And then she remembered. She wasn't going to work that day. Nor did the fact she had taken a vacation day to apply for a position she didn't want have anything to do with logic.

So it wasn't something that happened which had put her stomach on red alert, but something that might happen.

A workman, who had been busy measuring the walls behind the reception desk climbed down the ladder to ask the receptionist if A.R. had decided on a color scheme.

The two red impressions over Miss Lavin's nostrils quivered as she slipped off the mauve-framed glasses and sniffed at him. "Come now, Tony, you don't think His Nibs bothers his head with things like that, do you?"

The young man stretched a powered tape measure back and forth, the whirr of the recoiling tape making an angry sound as he complained that he wished *somebody* would. "I still don't know which wall they want down."

"You know Mr. Rossiter'll get around to it soon," Miss Lavin said, chiding him for his impatience with a tsk, tsk, tsk sound. "He's just not sure how many offices he's going to need. And we're waiting to see if we can line up more space on this floor."

He remained unconvinced. "Yeah, but that means waiting until somebody's lease runs out. It may take months."

"But he still wants to get these main offices gussied up, so don't worry. Mr. Rossiter never goes back on his word." With that, she put her glasses back on, indicating the end of the conversation. Reshuffling the agency cards before her discreetly, she looked up from time to time at those seated around her, trying to match vital and educational statistics.

She had short hair, with marcelled waves close to the head—a coiffure again newly fashionable—but Virginia Lavin looked as if she never ceased to wear it that way even when it wasn't. The thin, auburn hair was white at the roots which the harsh, fluorescent light exposed mercilessly, but the queenly receptionist exuded a confidence that suggested she had once been a beauty.

"I remember her when," the woman sitting next to Elizabeth whispered with an upward roll of her eyes. "Quite the *femme fatale*. I used to work for Eagle Management. She and Miss Pryor were part of the old guard with Rossiter from the beginning. They worshipped the ground he walked on. We all did then. Not for nothing do they call him the dean of American impresarios. He began with a shoestring and a prayer, you know." And then she went on to describe how he expanded his empire by gobbling up minor domains right and left. "During the Depression this could be done with barely a burp in the process," she added with a chuckle.

Nothing the woman said about Rossiter was news to Elizabeth, but she was interested in hearing somebody else's point of view.

"They must be very loyal to still be with him."

"Yes, I suppose so," the woman acknowledged grudgingly. "He knew how to get loyalty, all right. By never allowing his right-hand lackey know what his left-hand one was doing. And by keeping absolute power to himself absolutely."

"Why do you think he left Eagle?"

"Rumor has it he didn't like being kicked upstairs to become board chairman instead of being CEO. That couldn't have been easy for such a man. You can't imagine how his every move used to be weighed and analyzed—like they were stock indices on Wall Street. What a comedown now. And like him, these women are starting over again too." Another malicious roll of the eyes. "Still, I suppose it's better than senior citizens' craft classes. But I can't get rid of the feeling they're all 'playing office'—refugees from Our Lady of Compassion

Nursing Home." She broke off abruptly with a groan and pointed to the window. "Would you look at that—It's beginning to snow."

Elizabeth also groaned. Her portable heater was still on the blink; when a northeaster blew her apartment whistled as if the Canadian Pacific Express had decided to detour through it. It was sheer procrastination, but since her father's death, she was lost in memories of the ancient world—or what seemed like the ancient world to her—and found it hard to get herself to do anything. Scooping ravioli straight out of the can with dried up crusts of Italian bread or lying in the unmade bed with the unwashed sheets, she spoke with him all the time, still trying to get things straight, to hang things out, to *enumerare*.

What was memory but a tormenting recapitulation of loss? Her head hung down, weighted by these recapitulations.

Alfred Rossiter had once played a crucial role in that ancient world. In the course of so long a life and broad an empire, he undoubtedly directly or indirectly influenced many lives, but few, she felt sure, as much as hers. And he probably didn't know—or had forgotten if he ever did—of her existence.

The receptionist was staring at both her and the olive card alternately as the workman went over to consult whether they wanted a matte or high gloss for the office between that of Miss Pryor and Rossiter. The ears of the applicants perked up: obviously this would be the office for the lucky candidate. Elizabeth was thankful to the man for creating a diversion for Miss Lavin tucked the card on the bottom of the pile in her hand. She was also thankful that the *Lisa*—her nickname ever since she could remember—was real, in the unlikely event she should ever get on a first-name basis with these people. Since her father wanted no reminder of her namesake, her actual name was reserved for official records only. She had gambled on their not associating that name with Elizabeth, for by now the shortened version had become enough of a commonplace not to arouse any suspicion.

But why worry? Rossiter's age was well-known, obviously he would want a mature woman as his chief *aide-de-camp*, as witness the average age of the other candidates, few of whom were in their thirties, let alone twenties. And even though she had changed the birth date on her application—another paranoid precaution—to add two years to her twenty-six, what hope had she, without any experience except as a librarian specializing in baroque music, against the bravura competition surrounding her? *Bravura!* Even her mind betrayed her—always thinking in musical terms.

But, of course, it was precisely because of her musical background that the Prestige interviewer had agreed to send her here. Otherwise, as had been so gratuitously emphasized, her qualifications were insufficient. "And I like to build faith with my clients," the interviewer said curtly, leaving no doubt as to which client, the job seeker or job provider, she had in mind.

Elizabeth felt trapped as she tugged at her green tartan skirt, and her mouth was sour. She had put this machinery into motion in the hope of getting a glimpse of *him*, but now it was apparent this would be denied her, for Miss Pryor was doing the initial screening, and Rossiter would probably only speak with the final contenders—if at all.

The outer office door clanged open and a tall loose-limbed woman came in, waving a sheet of copy in her hand as her high-heeled pumps echoed on the still-uncarpeted floor. "I've got the release about . . ." she said in a loud voice, removing the cigarette dangling from her mouth, but seeing the crowd behind her, mouthed the final words for Miss Lavin's eyes only. Then the two women began to speak with relish in the kind of exclusive undertones intended, paradoxically, for the benefit of the excluded.

"That one's a nobody," the woman said, loud enough for other presumable nobodies to hear, and blinked her eyelashes. "He couldn't draw flies." She drew deeply on her cigarette. "But this one's different," she pointed to the release which she now handed over for Virginia Lavin's perusal.

Elizabeth wondered who it was who couldn't draw flies or who it was who could—as if artists were furled strips of sticky flypaper, with the most advantaged coated in thickest gloss. Ever since the announcement of Rossiter's new venture, speculation was rife in the music world as to which soloists and conductors would move to his new management or stay with his old one.

George Wentworth had hinted at big switches in musical chairs, but little had been revealed, for his article concerned itself more with Rossiter's past than his future.

These underpinnings of great art both repelled and fascinated Elizabeth: how could something that produced such mingled feelings of exaltation and sadness be reduced to contracts between parties of the first, second and third parts?

Miss Lavin skimmed over the paragraphs of the release while its author watched her closely. If signs of approval were what she was seeking, she sought in vain. The receptionist remained stony-faced, handing the release back when she was finished with a barely perceptible nod.

"Is A.R. here yet?"

"No, Isabel, he won't be here till the afternoon. He had a dental appointment at eleven and I think he's going straight on to lunch with—"

The sentence hung in mid-air as Alfred Rossiter gave the lie to it by striding like a reigning monarch into his realm. The atmosphere of the room changed as though some new chemical substance had been released.

A spike of hair fell from Rossiter's carefully guarded store, but otherwise the legend seemed intact, walking tall and authoritatively, with the vitality of someone half his age—the kind that shines down from the portraits of nineteenth-century empire builders. Glancing perfunctorily at the messages Miss Lavin handed him, he grunted

"Everybody and his cousin wants a job" under his breath and then returned them helter-skelter to her. "They can keep."

"A.R.," Isabel said, handing him the paper now held at her breast like a shield, "here's that release we agreed on yesterday. I rushed it through just as you wished . . ."

"Hmm?" he replied, for he had turned away and caught sight of his audience, sitting silently and hanging on his every word. "Who are all these people?" he asked, turning to Miss Lavin.

Her hand tightened on the eyeglass frame which she held in her hand uncertainly. "They're applicants for—"

"Oh, yes."

Breath had deserted Elizabeth when he entered and she held it as she studied his every move. No, he was not quite the monster she had supposed, with his wind-whipped face, red-veined nose, watery grey eyes. But neither was he—or ever could have been as far as she could visualize—an answer to any maiden's prayer. For a moment he bent over and then headed straight for his office, leaving both release and message slips behind on Miss Lavin's desk.

When he shut the door behind him, Elizabeth's breath returned. She inhaled and shifted her cramped body and legs. Her presence had not been a totally wasted exercise after all. She'd been driven to it perhaps by curiosity, perhaps by assertiveness, perhaps by right. She had managed to see him—that's all she'd really wanted.

Far better to know the precise outlines of your real foe than let phantoms, as they so often had done in the past, run riot.

Chapter II

Although Alfred Rossiter was a household name at the Guaragnas', Elizabeth always knew it was one never to be mentioned. Once she heard Tom caution Chris never to say the name before Dad, and she remembered feeling superior, for nobody had to tell *her* that. "But why shouldn't I?" Chris asked, to which Tom only shrugged his shoulders and answered, "Be-because you sh-shouldn't, that's wh-why."

She suspected Tom himself didn't know why at the time any more than she did, for whatever she absorbed in those days was without the medium of speech. Allusions, innuendoes, rumors, yes; straight talk—no. At one time or another she had deduced (sometimes concurrently) that Rossiter was a savior; Rossiter was an ogre; Rossiter was a bastard; Rossiter was a billionaire; Rossiter was a thief; Rossiter was a lady-killer; Rossiter was the devil's gift to music. About the only thing she knew for sure was that any mention of him would be a gigantic breach of family etiquette.

Chris never did find out why, for that conversation took place the summer of 1958 when he drowned in Lake Couchiching. Chris had been nine then, which meant Elizabeth was only six, but she could still see her father carrying his body to the beach and holding him upside down, as if all the waters of the lake would pour out of him. And then he squatted over him on the ground, trying to breathe his own life into the child while nearby Aunt Ada took the ever-ready string of blue crystal beads from her pocket and knelt down to pray.

She must have blanked out after that. The next thing she recalled was her father sitting on her bed, crying silently, tears running down on his cheeks and falling on the patchwork quilt.

"Thank God, Lisabeta didn't live to see this day," Aunt Ada said, speaking in Italian. "It's like all the heavens have opened up in retribution." Abruptly her father rose and stamped his foot on the floor. "Now don't blame this on her too," she added with an edge of savagery in her voice.

"No, but if she'd been around, perhaps this wouldn't have—"

Through narrowed lids Elizabeth saw him fling out his right hand to show how restricted its use had already become.

They were referring to her mother. Though feigning sleep, Elizabeth was rigid with uncomprehending fear, afraid to hear what they said, afraid not to hear, wanting to blend into the quilt—just another patch of calico red. Her mother had died when she was three years old—everlastingly ignominious as far as the Guaragnas were concerned—for earlier she had abandoned hearth and concert stage to run off with Alfred Rossiter. She had even left her husband owing thirty-seven hours in their baby sitting pool. As a child Elizabeth never knew what a baby-sitting pool meant; thought it a pool where babysitters collectively swam. And she never understood the bit about her having run away. What did it mean she ran off with Rossiter? Like she once ran off with Chris to a Saturday matinee at the movies? If that were so, why didn't she return when the movie was over?

Besides, a person couldn't just run off, could they? Just like that—to nowhere? A person was too connected for that. A person was composed of so many things, of flesh and skin, of thoughts and hopes, of past and present, of people known and unknown, of country known and unknown, of race known and unknown, of ground and air and sky and flowers and trees, a person couldn't just run off to nowhere, could they?

Her earliest fantasies of her mother centered on a Camille-type figure whirling serenely in a summer garden, long golden hair drenched by the gleam of a mellow sun, but with handkerchief held at her mouth to prevent the spread of germs. And she would be whirling alongside her, little Elizabeth and big Elizabeth holding hands, both in matching chiffon gowns, just like the matching mother and daughter outfits her friend Evelyn and her mother wore on their outings to museums and restaurants.

After Chris' death a somewhat more concrete fantasy was added in the form of a china-headed doll which Aunt Ada gave her for her birthday. At first she'd wanted to call it Chris, but somehow she took to calling it . . . Mother. Never Mom or Mama—she never felt on intimate enough terms for that—only Mother.

From the start it was a love/hate relationship. Love because she was Mother . . . hate for having died when she did. For having made her into a half-orphan. For having run off to . . . where? One moment she'd yell at her and throw her across the room—*why can't you talk to me, why can't you tell me something about who you are, why can't you tell me what your skin is like, your hair, your eyes, your teeth, why can't I know about your mother and your father and whether you like your eggs hard-boiled or soft, why can't you tell me something, just something*—the next she'd pick her up, smooth her clothes and tell her how sorry she was. Once she threw her so hard, her china face cracked. Elizabeth was beside herself. She stuck a Band-aid on it and never removed it. And when Aunt Ada wanted to throw it away with other outgrown toys one day, she had grabbed it from her, shouting furiously, "You can't throw Mother away, don't you understand?"

The only thing she actually had of her mother's was a locket, sent after her death, containing a lock of Elizabeth's baby hair in it, on the back of which a photograph of her maternal grandmother was so blurred her features could hardly be distinguished.

What could be distinguished meant nothing, conjured no lurking memory: she could have been anybody's grandmother. She was nothing like Grandma Adelina for instance, with her squinting dark eyes as she bent over the ironing board perpetually fluting the frills of the white organdy dresses Elizabeth wore to communion. Or as she daubed paint on canvas to produce the primitive landscapes which became such family prizes after her death.

The locket, however, provided fuel for more fantasies as she imagined her mother's feel still on its golden surface, imagining that other hand . . .

Was it large, was it small, was it smooth, was it chapped, were the fingernails long and graceful or short and bitten like her own? Particularity was what she craved, blankness was what she got. "Don't you understand, mama, you're not really dead. They're just saying that to fool me. You've got to take better care of yourself, though, so we can meet soon, don't you understand, don't you understand? And then we'll fool *them*."

But her mother remained stubbornly silent. Elizabeth would look at the filigreed tree on the locket where minute particles of dirt were embedded and would picture her pausing from time to time in her whirls around that garden to open it to lay her lips on Elizabeth's hair. And then Elizabeth would touch her own lips to the hair, trying to establish ghostly communion.

For a long time after Elizabeth learned of her mother's flight with Rossiter, she still couldn't relinquish the fantasy, clinging to it as a long distance runner clings to the agony of the last quarter mile.

But eventually it had to go. She didn't know about psychosomatic illness or behavior, but she couldn't help feeling her mother responsible for much of what eventually befell them—dad's tendonitis, Tom's stutter—and, yes, Aunt Ada's declaration notwithstanding, even Chris' death.

Not that Elizabeth ever blamed her for leaving her father. "Away from the keyboard," as Aunt Ada once put it, "artistic temperament does not make for great harmony."

But Tom disagreed. Violently. Mother was to blame, only she.

"How could she condemn us," he had once written from college, "her own flesh and blood, to a lifetime sense of unworthiness? To be unworthy of even a mother's consideration—didn't she know what that would mean? What sanctuary provided by the arms of her lover was worth that? And even when you were just an infant, she was romping in hotel rooms, sneaking into hole and corner restaurants, telephoning in code . . ."

The letter had come *special delivery* in reply to a casual mention in her note that she had celebrated their mother's birthday by treating herself to a double banana split.

Thereafter, such celebrations ceased. No fantasy, she realized, could withstand the imposition of so sordid a burden of facts.

But if she began to actively dislike her mother, Alfred Rossiter became anathema. At least her mother, however later deluded, had by all accounts given her father the seven best years of his life. "Man's love is of man's life a thing apart: 'tis woman's whole existence." Byron could have had her mother in mind when he wrote that: for what she must have perceived as her great love, she had obviously given up a great deal.

But the predatory and pernicious Rossiter?

From what Ada had once confided with a disgusted toss of her head, the gossip columnists at one time were full of stories about him. "First this diva, then that pianist, then the prima ballerina of the *Ballet Russe*. And each one of them discarded or abandoned when inconvenience exceeded appetite."

Elizabeth didn't know how her mother fit into this company of the elect, but was afraid to ask. Although an accomplished flautist, (the flouting flautist, she called her in a private joke) she never made it further than the ranks of the City Center Orchestra. "Perhaps the enormity of her sacrifice—which must have contributed to her early death—served as a stimulus to his jaded appetite," she ventured to Ada in Italian, choosing her words carefully.

Ada shrugged her shoulders in a way which meant "don't ask me."

But Tom had no such doubts. "You s-said a m-mouthful," he piped in. "J-jaded it must have b-been; he'd b-been married when he m-met her; he m-married again after her d-death. I ask you, were their th-three years together worth it?"

They were still living back in Italy when she died in 1955. No note accompanied the locket when it arrived, but Aunt Ada remembered it as one of her mother's most prized possessions. Tom once told her that their father had wanted to throw it away, but Grandma Adelina restrained him. "You *stupido*! You've no right, Dominic, no right. One day you'll regret. Before you know. The days may crawl, but the years fly. Don't make this hurt of today last forever."

From the start Elizabeth wore the locket all the time, but when she saw the scowl it raised on her father's face, she began to hide it inside her dress. Even when she grew older and learned exactly how her mother had behaved, she never ceased to wear it—her only tangible evidence that for one short instant, she had been in her mother's thoughts.

But she never spoke about it. Mother's name, like Alfred Rossiter's, was not one to be uttered. It was a house of silences upon silences, with knowing looks exchanged among the grownups; with the children left to figure everything out for themselves.

After Chris' death, Elizabeth had nobody to figure anything out with, for Tom was six years older than she, and they had never been close. Besides, his stammer made it difficult for him to speak and Elizabeth didn't want to subject him to this humiliation any more than was necessary.

She would try to figure things out by herself, her memory sweeping over the empty landscape of self. Sometimes, upon hearing a Beethoven symphony, or even more, some bars of Chopin, she knew she was getting close to a former habitation, but she could never reach it.

And she could never reach Chris, with whom she had felt so indissolubly bound. Implanted like a bare tree—branches intertwined but roots indiscernible—she grew up with eyes and ears open at all times, in the community of the blind, deaf and stuttering.

Except for music. A very large *except*. Dominic Guaragna was a concert pianist; son of a pianist; brother of a pianist. Her earliest recognizable memories were of lying in bed in the morning and hearing him play a Bach fugue or a Chopin nocturne, as though his life depended on it—as perhaps it did.

And every night when she went to bed, knowing it was her favorite, he would play the *Traumerei* of Schumann.

She would lose herself in the sound, feeling the rhythm of life quicken with each touch of his fingers on the keys. One moment the notes were sunbeams dancing on the wall; the next a November rain with the chill of winter in the air. One moment lifted to the heavens, the next exploding in some crater four stories below the ground.

"But music isn't something delivered whole," he once said at a graduation speech, "with self-contained messages in every bar. No, you have to bring something to it, it unfreezes the imagination if you let it, opening new and unexpected tributaries of awareness."

Dominic could do that for Elizabeth—in the concert hall or an outdoor pavilion or the rehearsal hall—but mostly when she went about her duties around the house, spending time polishing the brass umbrella stand just outside his studio in time to the bright harmonies floating from within.

But if his music unfroze her imagination, it refroze when she heard the sound of the piano lid closing, for away from the piano the god could turn to devil in a heartbeat. Tirade upon tirade. Like a work of art, he could be enjoyed in the concert hall, on a museum wall, or in the pages of a book. But to live with, no. Always expecting everything and everybody to be perfected with just a little more practice, a further stretch of finger on keyboard, a few more drops of blood.

They were living in a house in Toronto with an ornamental widow's watch on the roof, crewel embroidered couches, majolica dishes brought from Italy. At school she was learning of Wolfe's conquest of Montcalm and singing by solfege: *"In Scarlet Town where I was born; there was a fair maid dwelling."* Face pressed at the living room window, eight-year-old Elizabeth watched her father one day walking in a driving rain up Palmerston from College, the ubiquitous stuffed briefcase of music clutched under his left arm, an oversize black umbrella in his right hand threatening to blow inside out with each gust. When she heard his footstep on the veranda, she ran to greet him, her body still advancing at full tilt when he scowled at her and said, "Where's Aunt Ada? Where's Grandma? Aren't they home? Don't tell me dinner's not ready. Do you know how hard I have to work for all of you? What in hell do you people do all day?"

But then there were the other times, like that September afternoon in High Park with the leaves under her patent leather shoes and her pink dress matching both the scar on her knee and the sticky cotton candy pressed onto her face. Over the bandstand a red and white flag blew in the soft breeze; under its festooned roof, men in red uniforms pompously oom-pa-paed the *Maple Leaf Forever* while a joyous throng moved to and fro.

Her father had mimicked the stolid sound of the brass and drums and laughed. "It reminds me of Italy before the war when I used to go to Luigi Borelli's house—he was my first teacher—across the park.

But I loved to walk. In summer, the sun filled the park with watery gold; in winter, the wind whipped the leaves of the great chestnuts and mimosas round my feet. And all the while I was listening in my head to the music I was practicing every step of the way"—he lifted his graceful hand in the air and began to sing, "Dum ta dum ta dum dum, dum ta dum ta dum"—the opening theme of the *Andante* of Beethoven's Fourth Piano Concerto.

"I loved Professor Borelli. In winter he would sit on the hearth rug, eyes staring at the fire, grey hair long and loose—he looked a bit like Paganini—his thin, bony nose sniffing over his snuff box. The smell of the spices was all over the room. *'Falso, falso'*, he would yell whenever I hit a wrong note. Sometimes, he waited until I was through playing and then, only then, would he give me what for. 'You can do it better, you can do it better. *Che cosa si sente?* Here, *solamento un poco*—there, it's Promethean, reach for the stars, give it all you've got.' I guess I never liked playing for anybody else in my whole life as much as I did for him."

For a few minutes they sat in silence while Elizabeth unravelled strands of cotton candy and stuffed it into her mouth. "Do you want another one?" he asked when she finished and threw the paper cone in a trash bin.

"No, I love it, but I always bite into nothing."

Sprays of light splintered the shadows of the maples through their leafy spaces. "You can say that again, little one," he said, suddenly compressing his lips.

For just a short while, a moment snatched from the void, she felt she had glimpsed another man, with no sign of the enchafed soul he had later become.

By the time Elizabeth was born, from all she had heard and gathered, he was no longer at his best. Once he was so enraged at the way Tom played a Czerny exercise that if Tom hadn't pulled his hands away in time, they might have been crushed by the force with which he pulled down the lid. With Chris, the most musical of his children, he showed far greater patience, but after the boy died, he seemed to give up.

He never even tried to teach Elizabeth to play.

There were rationalizations. "I don't believe in forcing children to become superstar trainees—like I was." This last flung from some lugubrious depth at his mother who busied herself at the sink. "And if you don't make it to the top rung—if you remain on the second from the top—you're a failure. They talk about making a career like baking a cake, open the oven once too often and the whole thing falls. Or they say, 'Don't worry, you'll get there.' Where is there? Medicine Hat, Alberta? Like you're on a train with conductors punching holes at every stop. Conductors, yes, they sure punch holes."

The real reason he discouraged her playing, Elizabeth suspected, had no such logic, for it was not only her music he neglected. Even the dutiful good-night kisses, however sporadically given formerly, ceased. Only the nightly gift of the *Traumerei*, the two F notes unerringly aimed at the heart. (She had read somewhere that Schumann once threw himself in the Rhine and had been rescued by some boatmen. She never heard the work without thinking of this. Schumann's wet face, Chris' wet face and her father's wet face all intermingled in her mind's eye.) Her father would regard her from afar, as though to come too close was to court the tragedy that plagued his life.

No statute of limitations was ever devised for his kind of grief. In some sort of flagellant expiation, he seemed to Elizabeth to be nursing it deliberately, keeping it alive, as if to forget for one moment would be to lay himself open to a new onslaught. Grievance was holy, second only to music. But whereas with music he was both slave and master, with grievance he was only slave. Sometimes he would begin to practice the *Emperor* Concerto, but then, remembering that it had originally brought him and her mother together, (she had heard him play it with the Juilliard Orchestra and had shyly come backstage to congratulate him) he would stop abruptly. On several occasions he had refused to play the work in public, even when it meant giving up lucrative engagements.

He kept to himself, becoming more and more of a closed book, pages stuck together from disuse and yellowing in the corners. What little Elizabeth learned was either from his music, by divination, by puzzling omissions, or by ferreting some tidbit from Aunt Ada's carefully concealed hoard.

There were photographs, of course—although even these she only saw after he died. The largest showed him in christening clothes next to the Church of San Severino in Naples, clutched to his mother's satiny bosom, while Grandpa Tomaso, replete with handle bar moustache, stood stiffly to one side, and curly-haired two-year-old Ada stood on the other. On the back in Grandma Adelina's spiky, faded script was written *Dominic Guaragna, nato ll Novembre, 1920.*

A photograph of him at about ten, when he was already known as *Il Guaragniello,* showed a stocky, sprightly child with dark eyes looking at the world. Then there were the flyers when he was first hailed as a *wunderkind,* the Paganini of the piano—the caption under a velvet-suited twelve-year-old simply stated: "The gods have not forgotten the piano," Marcello Besanzoni, *Il Posta,* Roma. Other leaflets were from Carnegie, the Royal Albert, Festival Hall, Massey Hall. One photograph showed him with Ada and her bridegroom in Naples before the war; others with him in the United States in 1946 in front of the old Juilliard School on Claremont Avenue in New York. Photographs of Tom as a baby in Riverside Park, later of Tom and Chris, tumbled from the back page of the album. There were none of Elizabeth.

And there were none of her mother, Elizabeth senior, (who was called Lisabeta by the Guaragnas) although pictures roughly torn down the center bespoke her former presence. So did the occasional hand around the shoulders of one of the children from a beheaded source. So sternly did her father rid himself of every remembrance that Elizabeth grew up without having any idea what her mother looked like. Chris never remembered her and Tom usually clammed up on the subject. Only once did he weaken, that time they walked home together after her first Communion, as though having reached that milestone entitled. "She was s-strange and always s-s-smelled of f-flowers. G-ladioli was her fa-favorite. I remem-member her face g-glowed and her eyes sh-shone that ti-time I saw her with hi-him, but may-maybe it was be-because she was c-crying. I d-don't know."

Tom was the only one with a memory of *him,* him being Alfred Rossiter, the Great Unmentionable. At the time of the fateful meeting, he was president of Eagle Concerts, and chief stockholder of the Eagle Broadcasting System and Eagle Records; among the stable of his artists, some two hundred in all, was an Italian newcomer of increasing renown, one Dominic Guaragna.

Elizabeth had come across the annual issue of *Musical America* of 1951 and was flabbergasted at how the man, like an octopus, snatched in all directions, dominant and supreme.

Dominic had been on tour when his wife went to the annual Christmas bash thrown by the corporation for artists, managers, salesman and staff. There, for the first time, she met Alfred Rossiter and what followed was vague, or not so vague, surmise, depending on who did the surmising.

Wanting to get as far as possible from the scene of this betrayal, Dominic fled to Italy with the children. But as Aunt Ada, speaking in Italian, once said in an argument with him, "A betrayal avenged remains a betrayal, and vengeance only begets vengeance."

The move brought no peace, neither did the loss of self-respect it engendered. It was only after Elizabeth died of a heart attack three

years later that the family left Italy, this time to move to Toronto. After World War II, in which her husband died in Libya, Ada Guaragna
had immigrated there to take up a position at the Royal Conservatory
of Music, and she offered her services to Dominic to help raise the
children.

When Elizabeth turned eighteen, her father gave up his concert
career; the tendonitis he ignored for years had become progressively
worse. The first thing that went was Tchaikovsky's *Piano Concerto
No. 1 in B-flat Minor*; to repeatedly play the octaves became increasingly hazardous.

"It's like walking through a minefield," he cried, throwing the music across the room after he made what he called one of his clinkers.
Beethoven's *Third Piano Concerto* was next to go. Then it was the trills
in the coda of the last movement of Beethoven's *Waldstein Sonata*;
next it was the arpeggios in the scherzo of his *C Major Sonata*.

For a while he joined Ada at the Royal Conservatory, but his heart
wasn't really in teaching. Cancer had closed in on him, he grayed
quickly, appeared dry and sapless, the hands once so firm and graceful grew long and sinewy.

"You know some people are glad when they hear they don't have
much more to live," he said to Ada one night. "I remember when the
doctor told me that it would be five months—my first reaction was
one of relief. Then I started to think in terms of hospices and such,
but my first thought was one of relief".

For the last days he was in a coma in the hospital, but just at the
end, he opened his eyes to speak again of Professor Borelli and "of
running under the chestnuts with the dew still on the ground . . . the
Appassionata alive in my fingers. That trill there, why it's a trembling
of the soul, Dominic, play it that way, play it that way."

Chapter III

"Frankly, Miss Sullivan, I think Mr. Rossiter is making a mistake. Nothing personal, of course, but you've hardly any office experience at all."

Ruth Pryor glanced down at the olive green card from Prestige Personnel and tightened her lips. From where Elizabeth was sitting she could also see the photostat of her name-altered college transcript, as well as several inter-office memos.

The woman sat brooding over these, her face sagging as though pebbles inserted in her cheeks were dragging them down. This was in marked contrast to the containment in evidence elsewhere: a rotundity hermetically trussed by underwire and latex extending to the furthest recesses of her mind. "There are women who have applied for this job with fifteen years of experience in the music field. Every phase from booking Community Concerts to personal representation of artists. Have you any idea why Mr. Rossiter should have selected you?"

Elizabeth bowed her head in turmoil. Although Miss Pryor had greeted her with a spurious joviality when she arrived, it was clear she was angry. Thanks to Rossiter's whim, she was compelled to consider a waif who ordinarily would be beneath her notice. A cash register rested where her heart should have been; qualifications like Elizabeth's did not promise an uninterrupted progression of cash flow.

A run in Elizabeth's panty hose began its crawl down her right leg, like a man-made insect of the disease-carrying kind. Had she known she would again be entering these hallowed precincts, she would have taken more trouble with her appearance, but having overslept that morning, she had jumped into the same frayed shirt and green tartan skirt she had worn the previous day. She could feel distaste gathering force from the tip of the plume on Miss Pryor's maroon felt hat to her matching fingernails as she again expressed her indignation.

"Why choose somebody who has to start from square one?"

"Luck of the draw, I suppose" Elizabeth said, hiding her own chewed-down nails in her fists.

"Nothing of the kind," Miss Pryor said. "As soon say he'd sell Manhattan island back to the Indians for twenty-four dollars. It must be for some other reason. What could it be?"

"I really don't know," Elizabeth said, shaking her head, "it's as much of a surprise for me too."

As a matter of fact, never having entertained the possibility, it was more, much more. First of all, if she hadn't overslept, she would never have received the call. It came just as she was leaving the apartment, for she had not given them the number of the Lincoln Center Library—ostensibly because it would have been indiscreet for her to receive a call where she was still gainfully employed, but in fact because of the switch of names.

With its slight Irish brogue, Miss Pryor's voice was easily recognizable and Elizabeth's diaphragm had contracted in fear when she heard it, her first thought being that they had discovered her deception and were about to . . .

What? They couldn't prosecute her for a false moniker, could they?

Now, finding that the job was being offered to her, she was dumbfounded. It was the last thing she expected following the cursory interview Alfred Rossiter had given her the day before.

She had come into his office with her heart thudding so hard that she leaned against the jamb of the doorway to steady herself and forced herself to think of non-essentials, like how well, for instance, the off-yellow walls and Persian rug were color-coordinated with the Turner painting—and the fact it was an original Turner and not a reproduction.

The room was not like an office at all. There was a bookcase containing music manuscripts, a set of *Grove's Dictionary of Musicians*, and leather-bound biographies of composers. In a corner was the famous burled walnut stand-up desk that George Wentworth had so lengthily described in his article, as if the fact that Rossiter stood to do his paper work were the secret of his success. On the desk a vase of freshly-cut anemones embedded in wispy fronds stood on the edge of the gold-tooled blotter, the ruby petals reflected in the highly polished wood veneer. On the other side of the room several books lay on a circular table under a lamp with a shade made of antique music parchment.

She had been startled out of her reflections by the sound of his gruff voice as he harrumphed noisily. "Well, don't just stand there, girl, come in and sit down." His skin, which had seemed so ruddy when she first saw him, was bloodless upon closer inspection, rising out of the starched collar in leather ripples. With the wave of an impatient hand he indicated the cane-backed chair facing him.

Was this really happening, she asked herself, still unmoving, was it? Could the unthinkable of less than a week earlier not only be thought but acted out and realized? Nevertheless, she was damned if she was going to be cowed by him. Tautening her arms to keep from visibly shaking, she forced her feet forward briskly, and sat down.

For a moment creature studied creature across the four feet of emptiness between them, while the ormolu clock on the wall ticked noisily. No chair or table from which she could at least partially hide separated them. As he opened his mouth to speak (but shut it quickly again), she was reminded of an earthquake the previous summer, when she watched the window sill in front of her desk crack open and gobble the paper clips lying on it. Above her the chandelier had swung to and fro, the tinkling of its crystals scarcely heard amidst the crash of books and bric-a-brac from across the room.

Nothing is safe. Lakes gobble, people gobble, window sills gobble. Even within the safety of your own home the walls can crumble and crush you to death. *Mama,* she had cried out to her surprise—not, for her, the more logical saviors *Aunt Ada* or *granma* or *papa* . . . *Mama.*

But mystique is thicker than logic. No matter what she did, no matter where her impulses took her, her blank-faced mother would always take precedence, watching and warning her that all things come to naught in the end. And this from a mother she never knew, from a mother who ran off with a shadowy figure who had always loomed in her mind like a black-hearted giant standing foursquare in a doorway, shutting out the light from behind.

And here that giant was sitting across from her knee-to- knee, elegantly swathed in grey slacks and a monogrammed shirt, a jaunty scarlet tie vainly trying to divert attention from the loose folds of the neck it so tightly encircled.

But not, *blast him,* tightly enough. The atmosphere between them seemed to solidify in the silence and he looked at her blankly, as if not quite remembering what she was doing there. In any case, instead of conducting an interview, he launched into a speech about the new agency he was trying to build. "We hope to learn by the mistakes we made with the last one. Began to be like a supermarket with pianists down this aisle, fiddlers down that one, *basso profundos* next to the check-out counter. And double couponing on cellists and violists. Everybody thinks the old codger's lost all his marbles and doesn't know what he's doing. They regard us as a waxwork museum." He gave her a piercing look. "And you too probably. How old *are* you anyway?"

Each beat of her blood doubled its measured pace. "Twenty—er—eight."

He looked hard at her. "Sullivan, eh?" he said. "You don't look Irish . . . Still, who's to say what constitutes—" Raising his feet, he placed them on the crewel footstool in front of him. "Tell me why you think you qualify for this job."

"I don't," she said curtly, wishing she had the guts to add: *And I wouldn't want it if I did.* Seeing his puzzlement at her reply, she clasped the arms of her chair. "But I care about music."

"And you think caring about music is enough?"

"According to that article by George Wentworth, that is what you claimed was most important."

"Do you believe everything you read?"

"Hardly anything, as a matter of fact. But are you saying that caring about music is not important?"

"No, I'm not." A brief shadow passed across his face. "If it were only music per se that concerned us it would be one thing. But it's the executants of music we have to deal with here. Do you know what they're like? The very qualities which make for musical propensity—tunnel vision, razor sharp sensitivity, obsessional passion—make these people hell to deal with."

"Yes, but look at what *they* have to deal with."

"Like what, for instance?"

"Like—" She shut her eyes. "Like Mozart having to dance round the flat with Constanza in order to stay warm."

"Believe it or not that was before my time. I'm talking about today."

Elizabeth drew herself up, determined not to let the man's amused smile disconcert her. "All right, then, like vicious critics for starters, and empty houses and socked-in airplanes and"—this with a glare—"predatory managers."

He held up his hand. "Whew! Are you quite finished? Sounds like somebody's been filling your head with rubbish."

"Maybe, but one man's rubbish is another man's—"

". . . wisdom?"

"Precisely. Well, isn't that true?"

"To a degree. A very small one."

"So you say. But it's obviously a matter of opinion. And if one is going to run the kind of humane agency you claim to want, it would seem to me that considering what you call the *executants'* point of view would be of prime importance."

"No doubt, but there are other considerations."

"The rest is logistics and any competent person could do that."

"Don't underestimate the complexity of what you dismiss as logistics. A word of advice: always read the fine print, therein lies the crux of the matter. Moreover, it may come as a surprise, but er . . . *performers* aren't the only ones that know music."

"Maybe not. But *artists* are the only ones that know it—" she cast for a phrase—"in the biblical sense."

As soon as the words were out, she regretted them. She had meant *biblical* in a spiritual connotation but immediately realized the unintended double entendre. In any case, faced with his supreme presence, such thoughts were obviously not far from her mind. Besides, it wasn't so far off the mark anyway. When her father played the piano, it was a case of requited love all the way. *Had* played, *had* played—she still needed to remind herself that. In Rossiter's sudden silence, she began to rise, thinking she'd had the last word and the interview was at an end.

But he waved her back to her seat. "What an extraordinary way of putting it." He cleared his throat. "And what makes you think you're qualified to know the . . . er *artists'* point of view?"

Elizabeth felt a surge of triumph at his semantic capitulation. Not wanting or expecting anything from this encounter made her tongue amazingly free. "I didn't say that. I only said I cared about music and that *considering* the artists' point of view is vital."

"Well, you're honest at least—I have to give you that. But that's not always enough. Nowadays honest guys finish last."

"And die first."

"Oho! Methinks the lass is trying to tell me something." His smile ceased as he lifted his eyes but he seemed to be looking past her.

"Be off with you now, be off, waste of my time, this sort of thing," the suddenly gruff voice said from beyond the starched collar.

And she had bounded out of his office so quickly that in her haste she forgot to pick up the olive green card belonging to Prestige Personnel which now lay so revealingly on Miss Pryor's desk.

"Well, I'm glad to hear you admit you're surprised too," Miss Pryor said, as she carefully removed a yellowing leaf from a desk plant of African violets and dropped it into her waste paper basket. This office, like Rossiter's, had also been furnished like a sitting room, producing an atmosphere in which even the most finicky would feel at home.

But for Elizabeth this was the antithesis of home: here was where the head was. Or had better be if it wasn't to be lopped off.

Miss Pryor had been retired for some years now; Elizabeth could just picture her walking around a penthouse garden watering her collection of purple and white gloxinia from a long spouted copper can, chastising the slow starters, pinching the decayed heads from their stems, her maroon hat framing her somber face. But duty had recalled her to the battlefield and she now sat staring at a globule of water which sat on one of the fleshy leaves of the plant. "Mr. Rossiter seems to think you've an independent mind. Have you?"

Elizabeth had to smile. It was probably not the first time in the history of the world that impertinence was mistaken for independence—but never so mistakenly. Her very presence in that office at that moment was testament to her lack of independence. The past still held her future captive, let alone the present. But she wasn't going to tell Miss Cash Register that. "I'd like to think that was true."

"True or not, that's why you're here. Mr. Rossiter has always acted on impulse. In fact that's how he started in this business. He had an idea that Yuri Galliuillin might have a yen to play in America. Yuri

Galliuillin—of all people, the pride of the Bolsheviks. He had to beg, borrow and steal to get money for the ticket to Europe but that's what he did. But then you've probably never even heard of Galliuillin, have you? He probably died before you were born."

The woman's high-pitched voice, enunciating each word so distinctly, suggested she was dictating to a dim-witted secretary. There was the briefest pause before Elizabeth replied quietly: "I've listened to his recordings."

The answer spoiled things; Miss Pryor was cut off mid-scorn. "Of course, I see you went to Oberlin," she said, scanning the college transcript before speaking. A new anxiety wormed its way in Elizabeth's consciousness as Miss Pryor turned over the document: what if she called the college for degree verification on that phony name?

Ruth Pryor returned the college transcript into the folder and raised her eyes just as Elizabeth surreptitiously mopped her forehead. "Well, that's fine, of course, but it's still the frosting on the cake. This is a business, not the groves of academe." She warmed to her subject. "We are in business for profit and not concerned about, say, the artisitic influence of the glockenspiel from 1684 to 1700. Do you think you're ready for the rough and tumble of this life? It's not a nine-to-five operation. There are concerts, there are auditions, there's need for caretaker coverage nights and weekends in case something goes amiss with one of the artists on tour, or with a local manager. There are constant crises—I remember when we had to replace Lotte Rosenfield for the opening of the San Francisco season on two hours' notice. They had to hold the curtain for an hour and a half and the audience nearly tore down the War Memorial in their frustration. And the time we booked Gellman in Curacao and he left because there was too much humidity for his Strad. And the many times a favorite piano fails to arrive at the specified concert hall and the pianist either stomps off or has to play on some antiquated mess." She picked up a letter opener and passed it menacingly from palm to palm. "Every day the wires are humming with artists' attacks of nerves, orchestral strikes, overturned buses. From all these equally demanding obligations, one has to learn to prioritize correctly."

Elizabeth smiled, wondering if Miss Pryor spelled prioritize with a *y* instead of an *i*. "It's not funny, Miss Sullivan, every one of these things I'm describing happens time and again. And somebody has had to be on hand to sacrifice herself or himself so that the show could continue to go on. Do you think you'd be ready to sacrifice so much of your time?"

Elizabeth remained silent, her head in a whirl, her blouse drenched in sweat. Her lips moved continually to tell her, no, she was not ready for that kind of sacrifice, there had been enough Guaragna sacrifices at the Rossiter altar, thank you, take your job and shove it. A shudder of apprehension passed through her. Part of her felt she had been led to this place by prophetic instinct: a certitude had brought her here yesterday morning; a certitude made Alfred Rossiter choose her from a group of more than thirty better-qualified applicants. And part of her wanted to jump up and run away as fast as her legs could carry her. Finally, she blurted out, "Yes, I'd be ready to do it—it's in a good cause."

"But that's just the point. It's not a 'cause,' whatever impression Mr. Rossiter sometimes gives to the contrary. We are music brokers—we sell what the public wants. When it wants Bach and Beethoven, we sell them that, when it's a harp ensemble playing *On Wings of Song*, we sell them that. We help to promote good music, because that's what we sell; if we were selling thermal underwear, we'd be promoting human warmth. Those are the side effects. Put the 'cause' idea out of your head. I don't want you harboring any illusions on that score. The sacrifice is needed because the job demands it. I had really hoped to get an older woman with no family ties, instead"—she lifted the card to bang on the table, "they send me a young snippet who barely looks sixteen. And you're such a pretty thing—when one gets past the mane of hair and takes a proper look . . ."

It seemed that Miss Pryor could laugh. "Now don't get offended, I'm very frank and have been all my life. I imagine by the time you begin to learn the ropes and justify your salary, you'll be taking off for greener pastures—And then where'll we be?" She concentrated on the olive card before her as though the entries were holy writ.

"Despite what Mr. Rossiter thinks, I frankly can't see this job working out for you or us. Perhaps we ought to give it a try for two weeks and then reconsider. I honestly think a probationary period would serve us both well."

Elizabeth hesitated before speaking. "Except that I'd have to give notice at my job—and I'd be left without either if you didn't feel it would work out."

"Yes, I suppose so," Miss Pryor said slowly, consulting another paper, half raised by the crease across its middle. "I'd forgotten you were still employed elsewhere. How come you weren't working yesterday?"

"I had some vacation time accrued and I thought I'd like to try my luck here. And I came over now on my lunch hour."

Miss Pryor took the cue. "Then we'd better not keep you. Well, you were certainly lucky—"

She was interrupted by the entry of Virginia Lavin. "George Wentworth is outside. He'd like to see A.R. but can't wait until he's back from lunch. *Now* what does he want?"

"What he always wants. More information. He's decided to write a biography of A.R. That article only whetted his appetite. And A.R.'s taken quite a shine to him. I hope he knows what he's doing, opening up his heart like that."

"Could you see him instead? He says it'll only take a minute." As she hitched up her skirt, she gave a meaningful sidelong glance at

Elizabeth, as if to say little kittens have big ears.

Elizabeth clutched her purse tightly as her adrenalin kicked up. She had once met Wentworth when she stopped in Dalton's to pick up *Transcendence and Tragedy*, his biography of Feodor Konstantinov, and unexpectedly found he was in the bookstore that day autographing copies. A line of people waited when she came into the store, but by the time she bought her copy, nobody was waiting. Feeling sorry for him as he made conversation desultorily with one of the store employees, on impulse—for she was already late getting back to her office—she took her book to him for his signature. "I'm looking forward to reading this," she had politely said, as she handed it to him, "I'm a fan of Konstantinov."

He looked at her dubiously as he opened it to the blank page facing the title. "Did you ever hear him play?"

"I wish I could have. But I've got his recording of the *Hammerklavier* and it's a favorite."

"Mine too."

She would have been perfectly satisfied with just his signature, but he asked for her name so that he could personalize the inscription. When he started to write, his ball point pen refused to function and she handed him her own pen.

"Elizabeth what?" When she told him, he repeated "*Guaragna*" twice aloud, spelling it out the second time. What surprised her was that he didn't ask how to spell the name and got it right from the start. When he finished the signing, he was about to ask her a further question, but a few customers had formed a line again and she had departed. Afterwards she found she had left her pen with him, a grey fountain pen of her father's with his faded initials which she kept as a memento, but it was too late by then to go back for it.

The book—so sensitively and authoritatively written—gave her renewed appreciation for Konstantinov's genius. *Musicians play; others say*, he'd written at one point, in line with his *Transcendence* theme. This was certainly true of her father—in more ways than one.

There was no earthly reason why George Wentworth should remember her, for this encounter had occurred shortly after she had moved to New York a year earlier. Nonetheless Elizabeth was grateful when Miss Pryor excused herself and went to the outer office to see him.

Chastely rearranging her skirt around her, Miss Pryor sat down again in her seat and looked squarely at Elizabeth. After a long moment, she rustled Elizabeth's file and studied it again pessimistically before asking: "Could you start next Monday?"

"I'm afraid I couldn't," Elizabeth said, not knowing whether to laugh or cry. "I need to give at least two weeks' notice. Which takes us to Thanksgiving weekend and I've promised to go to To—"

She caught herself just before saying *Toronto*. No reason for Miss Pryor or anybody else to know the Guaragnas had lived in Toronto, but she would take no chances.

"Two weeks—that will leave us very short-handed. Well, I guess it'll have to do." A smile accompanied this statement, changing her face completely.

They discussed salary. "Was a mistake to list it in the ad but he insisted. 'Want to woo the right sort', he said. I imagine that's far more than what you're getting at your present job."

"Yes," Elizabeth admitted, promising herself the new Richter album of the *Emperor* on the way home in celebration. "It's quite an increase."

She laughed. "I'll bet. Oh well, believe me, before long," she consulted the card again, "Lisa—may I call you that?—if you work out, you'll earn it. Now, before you go, in case I come in later than you do on your first day, I'll introduce you to the coffee-making ritual."

Elizabeth stared. "The coffee-making ritual?"

"Yes, exactly that. This means a lot to Mr. Rossiter. He likes it precisely made. Most days he comes in on the 10:40 from Scarsdale, which gets him to the office at about 11:15. He never orders the limousine in the morning—he likes to walk over from Grand Central. So you should start grinding the beans about 10:45."

She swivelled and reached for the antique hand grinder and a canister of Colombian beans in a cabinet behind her. "He doesn't like electric grinders because they grind the bean too quickly and some of the flavor gets lost. So carefully measure four tablespoons and let it percolate for ten minutes." Her voice slid from word to word like a recording machine. "Better make a note of it, you won't remember in two weeks. I know nowadays, with Women's Lib and all that, they think making coffee for the boss is demeaning. But this means a lot to Mr. Rossiter. And he wants his assistant to make it—not his secretary or anybody else. I did it for years and would continue to do so but I'll only be working afternoons after you start. You must do it exactly as I've indicated and feel grateful for the opportunity. This is like a sacred trust."

Chapter IV

Few, if any, of the members of the Wentworth family, born in the elongated shadow of Horatio Thompson Wentworth, who made a fortune in railroads and steel, were ever able to rise sufficiently to come into the sunlight on their own. George Wentworth tried, but he had other shadows to deal with, for his mother was a Hunnicut, descendent of the famed Bloomsbury literary clan, which made him feel doubly dwarfed. And then there were more shadows, for although he was born in 1948, when the world was said to have been made safe for democracy, the dread of winding up on the rice paddies of Vietnam colored his growing years.

Sometimes, in those vivid moments in the morning when the mind is suspended midway between dreaming and waking, George would see himself grabbing his father by the arm and pulling him into the inferno of a blast furnace. These dreams had started during his years as a Rhodes Scholar at Oxford, where he was a member of the rowing club which, considering he was far shorter than anybody else in the crew, was a surprising concession on the part of the coxswain. On one occasion, after winning a close race with Cambridge, and carrying the boat over their heads triumphantly all the way back to the college quad, the team members proceeded to smash it up to bits. And, as if this weren't enough, that evening the *Chaps* set the pieces ablaze and linked arms to jump through the flames. When George refused point blank to join into these peculiar festivities, he became somewhat of an outcast, or as they put it, he was sent to Coventry.

It wasn't the first time. During his high school days, he never felt able to bring anybody home; although they lived in the understated elegance of "old money," his friends would find out he was a *Wentworth* Wentworth—something he always hid as long as he could. Coventry seemed to be the place into which he had been born. And ultimately, the only place in which he really felt comfortable.

On his way through Central Park to meet his sister for lunch, George wrenched a remaining leaf from a hedge and crushed it between his fingers. The choice of his father to accompany him into these nocturnal conflagrations wasn't difficult for him to figure out. Between his father's rectilinear existence and the bizarre post-regatta rituals at school, were many similarities. Carefully etched behavioral patterns existed in both places. No sign of weakness was permissible by his father for himself or his children. Their futures were as carefully mapped out as was his before them: men and women of taste and education, tireless augmenters of the family coffers, respected after-dinner speakers at Republican fund-raisers, and never, under any circumstances, no matter what they were doing, guilty of losing sight of the wage-price spiral.

The only inaccuracy in the dream was George's pulling his father into the fiery gates of hell, when it should have been the other way around.

About the only time his father had broken out of the mold, as far as George could see, was during World War II when he came back from London with a war bride, to the dismay of his family which had hoped for his alliance with the heiress of another corporate dynasty. The sanctity of Fortune 500 was about to be breached.

But all was forgiven when it was discovered that Iris Hunnicut was the daughter of the essayist Robert Hunnicut; having a prince from the Literati 500 in the family was eventually considered as great, if not greater, an advantage.

George walked past the zoo area and watched the seals jumping high for their lunch. From his sloping shoulders hung an old brown down jacket, the pockets weighted with large gloves and car keys. On his head, pulled down over his ears to shield against the wind, was the battered captain's cap his mother had given him over a decade earlier which had become one of his trademarks.

It was because of his mother that George's pursuit of a literary career and limited participation in the family consortium was finally accepted. But his father still was unconvinced and never missed an opportunity of telling him so. "Thank God for Maggie," he said of his sister, who, as a lawyer—and married to a lawyer—had fit into the family blueprint exceedingly well. "At least somebody in the family has some sense." Whenever George came home he tried to lure him into the latest company project, with rhapsodic descriptions of some super-colossal hotel, condominium or shopping mall scheme. "You wait, nobody'll be able to hold a candle to it. Mark my words."

George, who felt that the main function of architecture should be its suitability to particular human activities, had to keep himself from saying that holding a candle to it was precisely what he felt like doing. George turned east at 72nd Street to leave the park for the wind had driven masses of ragged clouds before it. Golden streaks of brightness were now visible only between the rents. Up above, a row of Canada geese appeared, each coming for a moment in view over a building top as though being created before his eyes. Toward the south horizon stood the towers of Central Park South with their distant glitter; ahead of him, on Fifth Avenue, stood the plutocratic dwellings of the mighty, clearly defined against the sky in blue-grey Cezanne colors.

Standing midway between these two distances, George found it hard to believe that they existed, let alone worlds beyond them. What existed was him, here, five feet and nine inches of feeling bone and sinew, eyes teary from the wind, ears registering the sound of a muffled horn, now standing with his hands knotted behind his back, now reaching into pockets to put on gloves.

On the ground a discarded newspaper, on which a smiling Anwar Sadat was pictured being greeted in Israel by an equally smiling

Menachem Begin, brought George back. Now there was a subject, he thought, as he started again along the path at a fast clip, he wouldn't mind tackling sometime. But he'd begun to carve a name for himself writing about musical subjects and the book on Alfred Rossiter should add a few impressive curlicues when it was finally finished.

Not that it would change his father's mind in any way. Although he made some grudging acknowledgment when *Transcendence and Tragedy* came out, he scoffed at the amount of money it made, as though anything that didn't enable you to declare a dividend was hardly worth the effort. "And I didn't like the implication that tragedy was easier to bear than success," he added. "Sounds like sour grapes. I don't understand that at all."

Oh, come on now, I mean, *pulease*. What planet did he live on? Was the man blind? The results of excessive success were all around him in every walk in life. Everybody in Cleveland knew, for instance, how old Horatio had put a gun to his head one night in 1911 and all he left was a cryptic note, "I've finished what I started out to do." The marble heap brought over from Italy slab by slab was fine for impressing the local gentry with the Sunday evening musicales in the organ room but hardly a place in which to curl up to nurse a head cold. Conspicuous consumption at its most conspicuous. He had lived in it for barely a year before calling it quits.

That it had eventually been donated to the city to house a railroad museum was only fitting. The private parlor car which had once seen him wheel and deal in solitary splendor was now ensconced in the drawing room—to the delight of generations of schoolchildren whose ancestors had helped pay for it through many a livelong day.

Passing an elderly lady seated on a bench in the last remaining patch of sunlight, George politely said, "hello." But it wasn't like England: she didn't respond, just stared at him as though wondering what new mugging ploy he had in mind. The main reason his mother pushed so hard for him to get to Oxford, he suspected, was because it gave her an excuse to spend so much time with her own family in the thatch-roofed cottage in Hampshire during those years. All his recollections of past good times had to do with holidays with his mother and sister in the Hampshire cottage—never with his father.

Although she tried hard to be the very model of a corporate general's wife, his mother never really took to being the honorary president of this or the vice president of that or visiting the old retirees at the company-sponsored senior citizens' home. Like the Iris for which she was named, his mother was all fragility: pale gently dipping lilac petals up against the Wentworth masonry and steel. She reminded George of Japanese paper flowers which magically unfold in a glass of water, except that the operation was in reverse: each time he saw her she seemed to be tightening and drying up.

"Hey, this is good timing, Maggie," George said as he and his sister converged at the entrance to the restaurant. Throwing his arms around her, he enveloped her in a big hug. "Not bad," he added as they pulled apart and he studied her face. It was a mirror image of his own, with speckled green eyes set in against high cheekbones and a wide, generous mouth. But her clothing, by comparison, was immaculate; her thick silver-grey cashmere coat with matching hat guaranteed that any stray wind she felt would be limited to her extremities, if at all. "For a beat up old *hausfrau* from the boonies, not bad."

Margaret poked him in the arm as they entered the straw strewn plank-floored dining room and checked their coats before proceeding to the second floor. "I wish I could say the same for you. Back to wearing that old down jacket. Protective coloration?"

"You betcha. You know me. I'd rather notice than be noticed."

"You're noticed plenty in that rag. I thought Martha got rid of it."

"She tried," George said as the waiter led them to a table. "Lord, she tried. I fished it out of a Goodwill bag twice. Down is for comforters, she said, period. I got tired of arguing about it. "

Margaret smiled. "Yes, she was always dressed to the nines, no matter what the occasion."

"And me, not even to the thirds. She tried to get me to buy myself a raccoon coat once. Boy, did she have the wrong number."

"As the poor woman learned finally. And not a moment too soon, I gather." Margaret sat down in the chair which the waiter pulled out for her.

"About two years too late. But that's water long under the bridge." As he settled into his own seat, he asked: "So how are the kids?"

She made a face. "Delightful, adorable—impossible. Unending headaches. I hate to leave them even for a couple of days. And Peter's not exactly house-husband material when I go away. He's off himself in Arizona now." She became silent for a moment, watching a waiter concentrate on keeping a large planked steak balanced. "Mmm . . . Smell that! I'm famished. Didn't have time to eat before I caught that plane. I thought it was a breakfast flight but all they served was drinks. Let's get a menu."

"You don't need one here. I'm glad you're hungry because we can split one of their monster lobsters then, okay?"

"That should be a no-no." She patted her stomach demonstratively.

"Not lobster, that's a yes-yes. No calories however much you eat. That's their specialty here. They fly them in from Nova Scotia. And the hash browns here are out of this world. Anyway, diet on your own time." After summoning the waiter, he gave the order. "And a couple of White Ladies—" He turned to Margaret. "Or are they only reserved for Christmas?"

"No, we have them at other special occasions too. Like being with you."

George watched his sister with a sympathetic, kindly expression.

Two years younger than she, he could hardly remember a time when she hadn't been his friend and ally. When the waiter brought the drinks they raised and clinked glasses.

"Here's to the English edition," she said, with a smile. "When did you say it was coming out?"

"Late January."

"Well, I hope it's not when we're having that party for mom and dad on their thirty-fifth."

"It is, but I've arranged to go directly from Cleveland to England then. Don't worry, I'll be there. So tell me," he asked, nibbling peanuts between sips, "what's doing in the corporate world these days?"

"Nothing much. Everybody's still talking about Paul Richards—and those false financial reports he gave to the SEC."

"Yes, I read about it." He watched the waiter filling up the water glasses gingerly to prevent the ice cubes from spilling over. "Justice in America. So they fined him a hundred thou and told him to be a good boy from now on. Your friendly neighborhood grocer would go to jail for years for the same offense. Okay, end of lecture. But what's happening with us?"

"Well, you're a director, so you ought to know." She looked at him over the rim of her glass, shaking her short curls. "You still never read your correspondence? You're incorrigible. You and your existential malaise. You really believe you can find your own soul by giving up the world?"

"Cut me some slack, Maggie. I'm a fink. Every time I see that file sitting there, I mean to, I plan to, I try to, but—I'm a fink."

"I know our balance sheet doesn't exactly make for scintillating reading. Still . . ." She shook her head but reached across to pat his hand. "We've signed with the Maruyama Corporation to develop that site in Arizona. That's why Peter's there. Dad's returning from England tomorrow."

"I know—" George paused to allow the waiter to place the lobster ceremoniously on the table. Margaret made the appropriate oohs and ahs as she reached for a claw and sampled a morsel. "He's coming through New York and, as is his wont, going straight back to Cleveland. Can't even spend a day—"

"Well, you know how busy—"

"Yes, I know. And a whole day—my God—he might miss out on a buy-out opportunity somewhere. Every day counts, right? Christ, what will it matter in the end? Forty years down the pike it'll be lucky if it's a blip on the screen of his life."

"You're not going to change him, George. Why try?"

"If mom couldn't, who could? All I wanted was to talk with him about this new book on Rossiter that I've started. Just a little human communication, no heavy-duty father-son stuff . . ." He lifted a claw and cracked it open jaggedly with the nutcracker.

"He'll stop over next time, you'll see," Margaret offered in a placating tone. "You've got him wrong. He enjoyed your piece about Rossiter so much. We all did. But what a change in style from the way you wrote about Konstantinov. You made Rossiter seem like the savior of the music world. I bet some musicians would like equal time."

Leaning a little back from the table, George looked around the restaurant, with its high-powered two-martini lunch tables, its office-outing engagement party, its caricatures of the rich and famous lining the walls in bamboo frames. Legend had it that people sang for their supper in the early days by drawing a caricature of themselves. Nobody in that restaurant had to sing for their supper anymore. He returned his eyes to Margaret to say with a sheepish smile: "I may have gone a bit overboard."

"Who wouldn't? When one meets somebody like that, who can remain entirely rational?"

George shrugged. "I was just trying to tell the truth, elusive though

it may be. To get at the truth of existence, however obliquely it's cam-
ouflaged, is, I should imagine, a universal need."

"Says who?"

"Says I. And a few philosophers too, not to mention psychologists."

"And let's not omit the crooners. Still, George, do you think Rossiter is worth it? You've gone overboard, it seems to me. But then you
always do."

"Maybe so, it's an occupational hazard. A few of my more critical
paragraphs wound up on the cutting room floor at the *Times*. Oscar
Wilde once said that every great man has his disciples but it's usually Judas who writes the biography. I guess nobody could accuse me of that."

"More like Matthew or Luke, I'd say."

"God forbid. As a sworn foe of the righteous, to say nothing of the
wealthy righteous, and especially the wealthy righteous with cultural
pretensions, I need to be careful." He smiled as he speared some lobster into his mouth. "I hope I don't wind up like that biographer of
Robert Frost who started out admiring him and ended loathing him.
Still, it's difficult when you get to know Rossiter to imagine anything
like that happening. Nothing hidden there. What you see is what you
get. And I can't imagine him making too many mistakes. But I'm
aware that I'll need to get a much more rounded picture."

"Dad remembered gossip about him when he married. He was
surprised you didn't get some of that stuff in your article."

George cracked open another resistant claw. "Tell dad I wasn't
writing a gossip column."

"Now don't blow your stack. It was apparently more than just gossip. I'm talking Major Society Scandale. Mom spoke about it too."

"I met his wife briefly one day. She seemed rather bland to me.
Not anybody who would elicit any . . . Unless it's because she's clearly
overfond of the bottle. It seemed kinder not to mention her at all."

She waved a breadstick remonstratively. "It wasn't that kind of gossip."

MOTHERLESS CHILD | 54

. "What kind was it?"

"I think her former husband was a violinist or pianist—I've forgotten which, and she dumped him for Rossiter." She clasped his arm. "I can't believe it. The guy really snowed you. You mean to say you wrote that long piece and he didn't tell you something as important as that?"

George launched a careful probe of the claw in search of any remaining succulence. "Look, don't get your feminist hackles up. The man answered me honestly enough. I wasn't particularly concerned about that kind of thing for the *Times* piece. Why can't I just let sleeping dogs lie?"

"Because sometimes sleeping dogs *do* lie."

"So let them! I detest the current mania to pry into the private lives of celebrities—the psychobabble. It's what they're famous for that matters, not who turns them on and off. It was Rossiter's contribution to music the *Times* was interested in and, in fact, so was I."

"But you'll need more of the personal stuff in a biography."

"Yes, of course. I aim to do a lot of research. It's hard to believe Rossiter would deliberately withhold anything. Perhaps it just wasn't important enough to him. We're speaking of a man who sees the forest, not the trees."

"She isn't a tree, George."

The litter on the serving plate was higher than the original lobster.

"And he isn't God. But, hey, nobody's perfect. You're right, though. I thought I knew the old boy so well." Taking the hot towel the waiter brought, George carefully wiped his hands and face.

Chapter V

When the plane lifted up into the air, the woman next to Elizabeth took out her rosary and missal and began to pray *In saecula saeculorium* softly. Once they were aloft, she whispered a *Gloria* and closed the book, but throughout the flight clutched the beads in her hand in silent exhortation.

Images came to Elizabeth's mind of Grandma Adelina, similarly armored, walking to St. Vincent's to read the missal every morning before Mass began. And images of herself *disarmed* at her First Communion on Trinity Sunday, a raw, wet spring day, the dry crumbly particles stuck in her throat, a supplementary engorgement on the way home when Tom made his stuttered revelations about their mother. From later that afternoon, more images, her father at the piano, hair flying, giving Busoni's *Elegie: All'Italia* all he had, and she afraid of telling him how much she loved it for there were times when he wanted her to hear and times when he definitely did not.

As a prelude to this Thanksgiving weekend, her travelling companion couldn't be more apt.

Elizabeth hadn't been back to Toronto since her move a little over a year earlier following her father's death. Although the city had always been a bustling one, the streets seemed somber after the holiday feeling at Kennedy Airport. On this late November morning the foliage was blighted by cold, and Lake Ontario lay grey and wrinkled.

The mood was more like Remembrance Day, with its two minutes of silence on the eleventh hour of the eleventh day of the eleventh month; a poetic gesture to mark the apotheosis of things unpoetical. *The torch be yours to hold on high.* A decade earlier, as a militant teenager with a red poppy in her lapel, she had marched on that day all the way to Nathan Phillips Square in protest of another war, one from which that country wisely abstained. The Canadian marchers were surrogates for the American resisters seeking sanctuary under their aegis, who, as illegals, were not allowed to partake in a demonstration organized mainly in their behalf.

She loved Toronto; it was home, had given witness to the greatest part of her existence, had split her personality as it did all Torontonians between veneration of its Victorian traditions and fascination with its fast-forward technology.

On Palmerston Boulevard Elizabeth gazed at little hubs of activity in front of two houses being refurbished with new picture window fronts. As the taxi pulled up to the curb, Aunt Ada came running down the porch steps and had her arms around Elizabeth before she could pay the driver. "What a sight for sore eyes," she exclaimed, "what a sight for sore eyes." And then she insisted on paying the driver on the pretext that Elizabeth probably didn't have Canadian money.

"Come," Ada said, bustling up the walk, amethyst beads swirling on the shelf of her bosom. "Wait'll you see the changes." Inside the house seemed the same, but as her aunt pointed out, the books on the bookshelves in the library were no longer doubly stacked. "I donated them all to the library at the Conservatory. Your father wouldn't let me before, but I just had to. Couldn't find anything the way it was."

Elizabeth studied her aunt in her flowered jersey dress and rippled rubber-soled shoes as she billowed about. All yearning was a thing of the past now, the black frizzy hair was almost gray; the gapped teeth more nicotine-stained than ever. But her beautiful black eyes, those big laughing eyes which saw so much and judged so little, were as bright as ever.

She wondered, not for the first time, if Ada repented her generosity in bringing her ravening brother and his family to live with her. For her magnificent gesture she had been stuck with all the disadvantages—and none of the advantages—of wifehood and motherhood.

Often they would have at each other just like old marrieds: she would berate him for the "outbreak of shoes" all over the house whenever he came home from tour; he would complain that she kept using green peppers in everything she cooked even though he'd told her a million times it gave him heartburn.

For a while, when Elizabeth was growing up, every one of the six bedrooms in the Guaragna house was used, but that was when Chris was still alive and Grandma Adelina had lived with them before returning to Italy. Now nobody was left but Aunt Ada to wander about the three story mansion, carrying the portable heater with her from room to room.

Elizabeth barely responded to Ada's effusions. It always took a while to relearn how to behave when she came home, to regain once again the identity she had left in her aunt's safekeeping. And now, with the *Lisa Sullivan* overlay, it was harder than ever to regain that identity.

"I'd like to move to smaller quarters," Ada said, as she moved to the grand piano gleaming in the corner. "I feel like a mouse in a *palazzo*. But I'd have to pay so much more for a new place or for an apartment—it doesn't make sense. Anyway, most of them aren't big enough for this," she said as she ran a finger over the keys of the Steinway. "And the neighbors would have my scalp for practicing at night. So I think I'll stay put. Best thing. On paper, we've all become wealthy. You should hear what houses are going for on this street. Unbelievable. All you have to do is wait long enough and the mountain comes to you." She paused to eye Elizabeth hopefully. "Maybe even you too . . . ?"

Elizabeth, who had sat down on the sofa, jumped up to give her aunt a hug. Over her shoulder, the tiny tables, each bearing Mother's Day jade and china mementos from Grandma Adelina's time—crowded in on her. How she'd like to admit the failure of her New York experiment and return to this normality. At least Aunt Ada would be made happy thereby. Who else did she have in her power to make happy?

On Friday morning, Elizabeth attended her aunt's master class. Ada Guaragna was a born teacher, with a reputation for turning out good technicians as well as stylistic interpreters. Attestations from former students adorned her desk and studio wall.

"Now who told you to play that *scherzo* like that?" Ada asked the student at the piano struggling with a Beethoven sonata. "Not me, that's for sure. Did you dream it maybe? Look," she said, pointing to the music, "more fire here, more defiance. You have to get the right sonority in your mind. And not so much *prestissimo* in that last quaver. You must play *all* the notes. Remember? Like this, poor dreaming *signorina*, like this," and she sat down to run thumb and finger of her right hand in a downward treble run. Sensing the eager expectancy around her, she then continued to the end of the movement.

When she finished, applause, whistles, *bravas, bravissimas*. A beaming smile belied her shake of reproof. Making room on the piano seat next to her, she bade the pupil, "Come now, try it again. You can do it right."

This time the pupil played flawlessly, gliding over the *appoggiaturas* like a figure skater. When she was through Ada planted a kiss on her forehead. "Now you see, *Signorina* Julie, you *could* do it. You only had to stop dreaming."

As the students laughed, Elizabeth remembered the one and only of her father's master classes which she attended, with student after student cringing under the barrage of his cruel mimicry. "No, no, no," he yelled as one of them wrestled with *Scarlatti,* and for a panic-stricken instant Elizabeth thought he'd push the lid down on the piano as he had done with Tom. "Have you no ears? "F—not C—," and he hammered the piano key repeatedly until, fighting tears, the pupil grabbed his music and ran off.

Elizabeth caught her aunt's eyes and, smiling, raised her hands to applaud her silently.

"To take a streetcar on such a day is a sin," Ada said, as they stepped out of the Conservatory gate. "Let's walk home."

Elizabeth agreed. Though faint, more of summer was in the atmosphere than winter. Ada was walking and talking next to her, swinging her wide hips, moving aside to allow a tall man with a barking dog to pass. By the time they reached Spadina Avenue, the two women had caught up on a year's gossip—from the new hirings and firings at the Conservatory to the latest permutations in the Canadian constitutional crisis.

As they crossed over the large intersection to continue along College Street, they fell silent. There stood Rita's Beauty Parlor, freshly painted and sporting a glittering new sign. Elizabeth could see by the way her aunt was studiously averting her eyes that she was thinking of Henry—Rita's son—the boy on whom so many of her hopes for her niece had been pinned, few of which Elizabeth shared.

Stopping at a red light, Ada delved into her purse for a roll of mints, popped one into her mouth and passed them on to Elizabeth. "I always thought you and Henry would—Do you ever have any regrets?" Rita's Beauty Parlor was already safely behind them.

"Regrets?"

"Well I remember that summer holiday when you thought of marrying him."

"Oh, but that was before . . ."

She was going to say before she knew all the facts regarding her mother and Alfred Rossiter but caught herself in time.

"But you were so close. All through high school."

"That's only because we were both too shy to push ourselves into the groups of the more adventuresome. You see . . . together we were an entity, a pair to be reckoned with."

Her aunt smiled. "Exclusive rather than excluded."

"You got it. Something neither of us would have been on our own."

Henry could make her laugh: she, Elizabeth, of the unlaughing face. This same girl with Henry laughed so hard when he did his imitations of poor near-sighted Miss Saunders behind her back that tears would roll unchecked down her cheeks. But some time later, as so often happened after these adolescent pranks, she felt slightly sick, for the jokes were not really funny at all.

Then there was that June night when he pulled her into a dark corner of the veranda of her house and fell on her with breathless kisses. The sudden clang of the piano saved her; as her father began a three-part fugue of Bach, she pushed him away and fled into the house.

"But he loved you so much . . ."

Elizabeth circled her head in mock derision. "Love—what's that?" She thought of her mother and father: one woman's martyrdom at the cross of love; one man's self-imposed asceticism—both dead before they'd properly lived. *Grazie*, but no *grazie*. "Henry only cared for me because of my—He never really listened to me, or respected my opinions."

Ada laughed. "It's funny. When you're young, you want men to love you for your brains, but when you're my age, you'd give anything to have them love you for your body. But you didn't answer my question—any regrets?"

"No," Elizabeth said, carefully side-stepping a jagged break of pavement. "But you do."

Ada didn't bother to deny it. She admitted that both Dominic and she had harbored high hopes for Elizabeth and Henry, had thought him a "fine boy." Again Elizabeth remembered the clang of the three-part invention; had her father seen them? She had sneaked up the stairs past the studio noiselessly, so she never knew for sure. But the following day, looking at her with even more than the customary hurt in his eyes, he seemed to be trying to control himself from saying whatever it was that was on his mind.

"But that's not the real reason you wanted him for me," she said at last. "You were afraid I might follow in Tom's footsteps . . ."

"It's in the blood, you know. Uncle Giusseppe has his heart more in the church than in opera. And Angelo is a priest. Tom is following in their footsteps. But you, I never thought you—Still, you're as much a *studiosa* in your way." She threw her arms up in a gesture of hopelessness. "Ordinarily we'd have never cared. After Chris' death I guess both Dom and I felt like joining some religious order. When Tom first called to tell us, Dom said: 'If I didn't have my music, I might do the same thing.' Me too. *Cara Madre*. So you can't blame us for worrying . . . blood always tells."

"You mean conditioning always tells. I'm hardly the type to take the veil. Besides, you know that Chris' death had the opposite effect on me." Two months before he died he had bought his older brother a tie for his birthday, with money carefully saved from his allowance. The tie had always hung in Tom's room, a talisman over the mirror. When he left to take his vows, the only thing he took with him beside the clothes on his back was that tie. "How could I believe in a God who would allow such a thing? Or a God who would exact the kind of sacrifices Tom makes at Monte Placidus? Fasting every day, not speaking for days at a time, living—"

"I think that's why he went in. Not speaking—it's a boon for him."

"I suppose so," Elizabeth said quietly and fell silent. Tom's stutter, she always felt, was erected as a barrier between him and the . . . She was going to say the world, but thought the reason closer to home. She never had been able to break through that barrier, never in all the years. "But I think he went in because of mother—"

"Oh, my dear." Ada grasped her arm. "Let's not go there. Why can't you leave her alone?"

Elizabeth pulled away. "Why should I?"

"Whatever you think, for Tom it's not such a bad life, if it were why would—"

"Yes," Elizabeth said, putting a protective arm around her aunt's shoulders as they dodged a station wagon at the street crossing. "But none of the priests we've known were likely to ever inspire that kind of fervor in me. Father Luigi is more worried about getting the proper lasagna than the redemption of his eternal soul. All this is beside the point. Henry was just not right for me. Why are you so concerned about me getting married? I'm quite content being alone."

"And that's the other thing we feared."

Chapter VI

For days George had dutifully clocked in at the library researching facts about Rossiter and his early days with the Eagle Broadcasting System—carefully putting the information on index cards. He'd even managed to unearth some old tapes of the *Panatela Tobacco Hour*—the first classical music program on radio—on which every serious piece was sandwiched in between pieces of light operatic fluff, not to mention exhortations from the sponsors to "lighten up, brighten up and heighten up." The next project concerned the Eagle Concert Management and all that its establishment entailed. After a week of absorbing this information—of the hundreds of artists Rossiter had launched and managed from all over the world, of the orchestras, of the chamber ensembles, of the opera companies, of the dance companies—he decided to take a break and start work on some of the man's personal history.

George braced himself. As he'd told Margaret, he hated prying in this area, but their conversation would not let him be. Whether the so-called *scandale* was a sin of omission or commission on the part of Rossiter, was obviously something he must find out. Probably it amounted to nothing—just a lot of media and/or gossip lovers' hyped-up hooey.

But pursue it he must.

Choosing a time when his subject would be at his office and not at home, George dialed Rossiter's Westchester number, hoping he wouldn't have to speak to some housekeeper. If the scandal revolved about his marriage, then obviously it was Dolores Rossiter who he should look up first.

The phone kept ringing. He was about to hang up when a woman's voice came on the wire. "Mrs. Rossiter?" he inquired.

"Yes, this is she."

"This is George Wentworth."

"George who?"

"Wentworth. I wrote that piece about your husband in the *New York Times*. We met briefly at the Colony one day."

"Oh, yes, I remember. What can I do you for?"

Despite her friendly tone, the slurring of the consonants evoked images of lonely corporate wives keeping company with friendly afternoon bottles. Nevertheless, George got straight to the point. "I'm writing a biography now of A. R." Mrs. Rossiter made what sounded like some disbelieving noises. "He hasn't told you? Well, I am, I assure you. Authorized? Of course it is—I'm working in conjunction with your husband every step of the way."

"Every step? Well, lots of luck, pal." The voice was clear enough now.

"Thanks. I'll need all the luck I can get and that's why I'm calling. I wonder if I could come and interview you. I'm trying to get as comprehensive a picture as possible."

There was a pause and a smothered laugh. "Have you spoken to *him* about this?"

Her emphasis on the *him* was unnerving. "Well, no. It's not a secret though. A.R. knows I'll be interviewing those who have been closest to him independently. And this means you, of course."

"Well, I don't know what use I'll be. We lead a quiet life, you know. This is dullsville around here. Besides, you're surely not thinking of writing one of those psycho-histories about him?"

"Of course not, I wouldn't—"

"Well, in that case, what you should concentrate on is his professional life. Mr. Rossiter is a workaholic. If you ask me, I think they invented the term for him. You'll learn much more about him from Ruth Pryor—or even Virginia Lavin. Those dames see a lot more of Mr. Rossiter than I ever do."

The deferential intonation with which Dolores pronounced each syllable of her husband's surname didn't escape George. She sounded more like a servant who had been put in her place than the other way around. And this, thought George, even after *he* called the man by his initials, like everybody else did. "I'll be interviewing them too, of course. But it's not the same thing as you. Nobody knows him better—"

"That's what you may think," she interrupted, "but it ain't necessarily so. I can't see how I'd be able to help you. Mr. Rossiter lives for his work and works to live. It's his colleagues who know him best. I don't know what kind of information you want. He never tells me anything. For Chrissakes, I don't even pay the household bills, he has his accountant do that. Besides, I wouldn't dare say anything without consulting with Mr. Rossiter first. I've got my buns burned before for that."

George changed directions. "You're getting me all wrong, Mrs. Rossiter. I have your husband's best interests at heart, believe me. I've nothing but admiration for the man. It's just that I need a little more background—"

"Like what?"

"Well—I'd like to know when you met, for instance."

"Who gives a damn about that?"

"Anybody who reads the book."

"Come now, pal, you can't be serious. You are? Oh, all right. We met on the Ile de France in 1955. We were both coming back from Europe at the time."

"Were you alone?"

"Yes I was," she said in a tight voice. "Why do you ask that?"

"Well, I thought . . . I mean, wasn't your former husband with you?"

"My former husband?" she fairly screamed. "Whatever are you talking about? I was never married before, who gave you that idea?"

"I—I'm sorry. I was misinformed. I seem to have my people mixed up. I—" George sighed. Definitely not one of his better days. Much better to stick to index cards. So who was Margaret talking about with her *Major Society Scandale*? She and her lying sleeping dogs! Did she have A.R. mixed up with somebody else? It wasn't like her—Then he remembered that she'd only been reporting on hearsay. Perhaps his dad had it wrong. He wouldn't put that past him—a case of the pot calling the kettle black. Obviously he was getting nowhere fast with Mrs. Rossiter and he attempted to put on his best reportorial voice. "I'd appreciate if you didn't tell A. R. about this call."

"Tell Mr. Rossiter?" She laughed with genuine amusement. "Don't worry, pal, I wouldn't dream of it. He never tells me anything, why should I tell him? I don't look for trouble and I suggest you don't either."

Chapter VII

"Oh, my," Ada said, as she stepped into the garden, noting the neat shrubs and the wheelbarrow piled high with leaves which Elizabeth was tamping down. "I was supposed to get Stanley in to do it. On your few days here, you shouldn't have."

"But I loved doing it. I miss the garden so."

"And it misses you. You know how I am. I mean to do it, but I can barely get through the work inside—"

Apart from cooking, Ada hated housework. In the recent past, the chores had all fallen on Elizabeth, including the nursing of her father that last bitter year. Both Dominic and Ada had protested, but the cost of a full-time nurse was more than Elizabeth earned at her job at York University and money had been scarce.

Elizabeth placed a plastic bag filled with crabgrass on top of the wheelbarrow and then added it to the rest of the refuse for removal. The unseasonal summer weather had continued, the air loud with circling sparrows, but the amber sky had suddenly become overcast.

The two women went into the house; Ada brought out a tray of Bel Paese cheese and a bottle of Campari.

They were seated in Dominic's studio, now used as a library and sitting room; on the lidded piano were photographs of him with various conductors—the celebrated celebrating. After lifting her glass toward Elizabeth, Ada ate a cracker with cheese. Then, pointing her forefinger, she tried to conceal her maternal interest with a light tone. "Thanks to you, the garden looks like it's ready to go to sleep for the winter. What a wonderful wife you would make."

Elizabeth settled into her seat. "Oh, Aunt Ada, you're such a cipher—at times fiercely unconventional, at times the opposite. I really don't expect that from you, of all people. Look at the life you made for yourself. It would never have happened if—"

"Well, I *was* married, don't forget that. And it's because . . ." She leaned forward to help herself to more cheese. "By now you must already know what it is to be attuned with another. That's the most important thing."

Elizabeth smiled. "You mean you don't want me to settle for one of these *wham, bam, thank you ma'am* types."

"Do be serious. To be attuned . . . That's the way it was with Pietro and me. I tried with some others, but you know, it's easy enough to get a husband, but a *man*—Don't be shocked." She laughed out loud and threw her head back as if she had cracked a big joke. "As if the young today could ever be shocked! Anyway, with my hot flashes, I'm just as glad to be alone. How the hell are you supposed to enjoy sex when you get a hot flash the minute after you start? It's no fun, believe me, but nobody ever tells you about things like that."

She smacked one palm against the other sharply. "Big mouth! I don't know what the hell started me on that. It's the drink, it's the company, it's not having anybody to talk to anymore. At any rate, after Pietro, it was never the same. I was never again attuned in the same way. If he hadn't died in the war, I'd have been happy to spend the rest of my life where I was."

"But Aunt Ada, how about your playing? You'd never have been satisfied just staying home, you know that." Her aunt lifted her hands in cat's cradle fashion, as though the complexities of life were too much to be discussed. Outside a crack of thunder proclaimed the end of the Indian summer's day of grace. "And if you were as attuned as all that, how come you kept your maiden name?"

Ada put down her glass, clasped her hands lightly between her knees. "Simple. I kept it because the Guaragna name meant so much more in the music world. But if Pietro hadn't died, if he—"

"You and papa. Both clinging to old memories instead of making new ones."

"It was different for Dom. He was bitter. He didn't want to take any more chances. Oh, when I think of the time we were children and planning our lives, everything played *allegro con brio ed appassionato*. How simple it all seemed. We would listen to those Caruso recordings of *Celeste Aida* or *Vesti la giubba* on the wind-up Victrola that papa bought. Papa would sing along with him, and then we all joined in, Mama too. A regular opera company, the Guaragni. And for Dom, this was the beginning. He began to read scores at the age of seven, eight—the most complicated musical scores, symphonies by Mahler and Beethoven—he read them as literature. Nowadays, students come to me at eighteen and have never read a score in their lives."

Ada drew an afghan from the back of the couch around her shoulders. "I didn't marry again because nobody ever was as attuned to me the way my Pietro was. Henry reminded me of Pietro—I guess that's why I like him. Always with the jokes. And now he's a papa himself, with two babies of his own."

"Yes, you wrote me. I'm very happy for him. But I'm glad that isn't me, with two babies already to answer for. Besides—" Elizabeth stopped. She was about to say that the trouble was they weren't attuned. At the beginning she attributed it to their mutual inexperience, but even when they graduated to the back of his Chevy on one moonless night, it never came close to Ada 's description of her experience with Pietro.

"Besides what?" Ada asked.

"He never understood me—like why I wouldn't go to university here, why I had to carve out a life for myself—just the opposite of you—*away* from the Guaragna name."

Ada rose to close the window against the rain. She stood handling the curtain. "Why should the Guaragna name be so difficult a burden?"

"Why?" she repeated, picking her way through the debris in her head as carefully as she had through rose thorns earlier. "You see, it was a case of not fulfilling a role expected of me. With Tom taking vows, with Chris gone, only I was left to carry on the name. I never had the heart for it. You know how much I love music but . . . performing? And how can a *Guaragna* not play the piano?"

Elizabeth lay in her bed and stared at a lopsided moon intersticed through the tangle of branches, trying to rein her galloping thoughts. All weekend she wanted to tell Ada about her new job, but the words never came. How to explain to her aunt that which she couldn't explain to herself?

When she left Ruth Pryor two weeks earlier, she was determined to stop at a pay phone to tell her she had reconsidered and didn't feel up to the job. Instead, before she could change her mind, she went back to the Lincoln Center Library and gave notice, much to the dismay of Mr. Penniweather.

She liked Mr. Penniweather, a throwback to a more graceful era, though he had not yet reached retirement age. With his pocket watch, which he held up to his ear several times a day in Mr. Micawber fashion, and his passion for Pergolesi, he had withdrawn into the impregnable citadel of the early nineteenth century and let the rest of the world go hang.

There was another bond: he had once heard her father play. "Guaragna?" he had asked when they first met. "Any relation to . . . ?" At her delighted response, he said, "I heard him play a recital in Carnegie Hall. I've never forgotten those crystalline articulations of his. Nobody ever played the *Goldberg Variations* like that . . . you should be proud."

He had been the only person who befriended her since she came to New York, inviting her to his home for steak and kidney pie which his wife—another character out of Dickens—painstakingly assembled, and to listen to *I Musici* recordings. "I go for baroque," was his favorite line and though she eventually heard it many times, she always laughed as though it had been newly coined each time.

She had lied about the reason for leaving—lies were proliferating all over the place—a veritable labyrinth with all exits barred. "I'm returning to Toronto," she said in solemn tones, "because my aunt is chronically ill and needs somebody living with her. I must go." And then she went on to attribute some of the grotesqueries of her father's last illness to her aunt.

Nor did she feel one iota of guilt as his face fell. The plethora of untimely Guaragna deaths had made her acutely aware of such possibilities, and the pain she felt as she described her aunt's illness was true enough—merely a rehearsal for the real thing.

Besides, come what may, she had to be ruthless. As Lisa Sullivan, total severance of past connections with Elizabeth Guaragna was a must. And to further attain that end, she had even found a new apartment the previous weekend and would soon leave the draughty railroad apartment forever. The lease was also in her new name; she was due to move in upon her return at the beginning of December.

When she had told her aunt about it, Ada sighed and said: "So now you're never coming back . . . And then she took a pad and pencil to write the address.

"But you'll have to write it in care of . . . Lisa Sullivan—"

"Who's that?"

"She's my . . . landlady . . . and since the apartment is in a brownstone house, she asked—"

Everything was unreal, the only reality now was that of Lisa Sullivan, who was a figment of her imagination. As with murder—the first lie is the hardest. She had forestalled Miss Pryor's calling the library for references by reminding her that since she was giving notice, to ask them for a recommendation was unfair. Ruth Pryor had looked at her with surprise. Since they had already hired her, it was apparent they were taking her on faith and were not going to bother with references. For a minute Elizabeth felt as though she had unwittingly sabotaged herself, but presumably not, for as Miss Pryor escorted her to the door, she again went over the coffee-making instructions as though this were what the job depended on, not perfunctory commendations by some faceless personnel director.

No, none of it made sense. She had always felt that the childhood with which fate had confounded her was but a prelude to . . . This was as far as she usually got in these ruminations. The rest was not at all clear. All she knew was that at some point some unexpected hurdle would appear which would have to be overcome before she could reach the other side. And then past and future would merge into a well-defined present and she would be home free.

She thumped the pillow and turned it over. What was she setting herself up for? She seemed to be acting in some new dimension, as if this grim sortie as Lisa Sullivan would be something out of time itself; and later she could reset herself to Elizabeth Guaragna and stop the infernal flashing on and off.

And when that blessed moment arrived, would she then magically know somehow exactly who she was? Everybody she knew at one time or another had to discover who he really was by himself—or she by herself. She knew who her father and Aunt Ada said she was—but that wasn't enough. Something else was needed to legitimize her existence: perhaps to lie on her mother's grave and flail her arms and pound her head and exorcise once and for all the dancing Camille in the summer garden. Or the Band-aided doll face. Was that too much to ask for? Was she being ridiculous?

If she was, so be it. God was powerless—only knowledge might extend mercy.

But all of this was not exactly conversational material with her aunt. Even on the walk back from the Conservatory, when they had spoken more candidly than ever before, she could not bring herself to go that extra step. Finally, at lunch on Sunday, with her departure time set at four that afternoon, she knew it was then or never. Arranging the cutlery neatly on her plate, she said: "Papa never spoke of Alfred Rossiter. Will you? Did you hear that he started a new concert agency?"

Ada pursed her lips and tipped her head. "Yes, there was a story in *Musical America* that I looked at in school. I also saw a piece somebody wrote in the *New York Times*. And how he wrote—as if butter wouldn't melt in the bastard's mouth. He hasn't done enough harm— he still wants to go on—"

"But why shouldn't he? Regardless of what you may feel about him personally, you surely can't be against somebody just because he's old?"

Ada rose abruptly, shoved her chair in, and her great brown eyes dilated as she stared at Elizabeth. "I'm really surprised at you. Don't you know anything about him?"

Elizabeth picked up a crumb of canoli with her finger and ate it. "Yes, I know about him and my mother if that's what you mean."

"I'm not talking about that. I'm not talking about the way he treated your father either. He wasn't the only person he robbed. All my life I've heard stories about the great Alfred Rossiter. Setting himself up like a demi-God in his principality. He would book people at Lord knows what fee, and then pay them peanuts—a fraction—"

"Oh, Aunt Ada, he couldn't do anything like that. Old concert wives' tales." She picked up her napkin and dabbed her mouth. "There are printed contracts and legal agreements. Even Alfred Rossiter can't put himself above the law of the land. You're probably thinking of Federated Concerts. I recently learned—I know something about that. But they had to charge that "differential," as they called it, to pay for the cost of having a sales staff, of organizing the communities, of—"

"*Ridicolo!*" Ada said, reaching across the table to collect the dessert dishes and taking them to the kitchen. Elizabeth followed her with the tea pot and serving platter. "You've a lot to learn, my child," she said as she scraped the particles of food into the sink and stacked the plates in the dishwasher. "There are twenty ways to have your heart broken in the music world and Dom had all of them. Don't you remember how he used to say, 'Only the music itself saves, everything else destroys?'"

"Oh, I know all that, but we were talking about the *business* of music not—"

"The *scalping* of music, you mean! I remember when Dom first started to play Federated dates before you were born. A $400 fee at that time didn't sound bad to the man on the street, but by the time he paid the so-called 'differential,' manager's commission, transportation for him and his piano, hotels and meals, what do you think was left? She gave a deep moan. *"Madonna mia."*

"But didn't the volume of concerts make up for that?"

Ada poured in the detergent, shut the door of the dishwasher with a bang, set the dial, and in a moment, the room was filled with the hum of surging water. Only then did she turn around and face Elizabeth again, her face pale. "Nothing could make up for it." And then she went on to relate how he would stagger home, after playing sixty such dates, and people would ask him what he was doing with himself these days. *"Niente.* The hostesses at the parties after the concerts, when there were parties—I remember one in Putnam, Connecticut when there was watered-down punch and biscuits—and Dom was starving. You know he never ate before a concert. And the hostess had to consult the program to see who this month's 'piano player' was before she could remember his name."

Elizabeth walked over to gaze out of the window, unable to meet her aunt's eyes. Across the street two boys were tossing a basketball against a backboard bolted to a garage, missing the rimmed circle again and again. At last, recrossing the room, she turned to her aunt: "Still, you can't blame the managers for that. They did try to organize so costs would be lower and there probably were lawyers going over everything with a fine tooth comb to make sure everything was legiti- mate, otherwise—"

"Otherwise, they couldn't have continued!" Ada ran her hand through her hair roughly. "And that's just what did happen. *Legitimo!* That's a laugh. *Mafiosi* every one of them. There was an anti-trust investigation once. Anti-trust is exactly right. They didn't trust the art- ists and the artists didn't trust them. Why didn't the *Times* guy write about that, for God's sake? That's what Rossiter's great Eagle Con- certs amounted to."

"Well, what happened then? They're still going strong, so it couldn't have—"

"Who knows exactly what happened? A little payola here, an en- gagement for somebody's cousin there. Even so, they had to clean up their act, as the kids say. And the head of *Federated* headed for the Vir- gin Islands to sell real estate. But no matter what the courts decided, what fines they paid, most of the concerts booked are still from the lists of big music supermarkets and the small independent manager doesn't have a chance."

Elizabeth wondered what her aunt would say if she told her that Rossiter had also called it a "supermarket." She walked over to a chair, sat down and crossed her legs, dangling the slipper on her right foot. "Well, Rossiter, has now become an independent—"

"Yes, I know. So now, maybe he'll see what it's like being up against the monster he himself created. *Marrone.*" She laughed harshly, mak- ing an obscene Italian gesture. "It serves the bastard right. He'll be— how do you say *hoist . . . ?*"

"Hoist by his own petard." Elizabeth shaded her eyes with her hand and stroked her forehead. A lot of what her aunt had said, she was hearing for the first time. A wave of fear surged and spread. She could feel it in her bowels. How could she have been so stupid? The more her aunt spoke, the more she realized she shouldn't have taken that job.

At the check-out counter the uniformed clerk placed the ticketed small suit case on the ramp. "The plane will be taking off an hour late," she said, tearing the stub from the ticket and inserting a boarding pass in the slot. "You're all set now."

Elizabeth turned to Ada. "We still have time. Let's go to the cafeteria for some tea."

"No, thanks, it's coming out from my ears already. Come away from here and let's just talk."

At the gate for her flight, they sat in moulded plastic chairs facing a window wall and Ada handed her a cassette from her purse. "I found this among Dom's music after you moved away. There was a note which said it's to be given to you. I was going to play it as a surprise last night but I couldn't. He recorded it way back."

Elizabeth looked at her father's tightly packed handwriting on the label: *For Lisa, her Traumerei*. She sat very still, remembering the last time she had heard him play it, a drop of sweat on the tip of his nose gleaming in the light which she would have given anything to wipe off, but couldn't. A fainter, more heart-rending version, she was certain, had never been performed, and played, moreover, with fingers whose every stretch cost. A vision of a faceless hostess consulting her program before she could remember his name intruded. All the necessarily monumental pride of the artist reduced to that. When she could speak, she asked: "What happened to him? Why? How could somebody so great—"

Ada unbuttoned her coat collar and expelled a long breath. "You can thank Alfred Rossiter for that. He saw to it that no manager would book him anywhere. And his arm was very long. There wasn't an American local manager that wasn't scared out of his pants by Rossiter. If Dom didn't have those European concerts he'd have starved. All of you would have."

In the distance, through the window wall, airfield technicians could be seen gesturing with hands and flags guiding a jet into its hold. "But I thought he stopped playing because of his hand, because it hurt—"

"Yes, that too." Her eyeglasses misted and Ada wiped them with the hem of her scarf. "But how did that hand thing get started? I think it must have been here—" She tapped her forehead sharply. "And the cancer? Who knows? He was so heartbroken he had to create some reason why. And he succeeded—on that score, anyway."

The two women remained silent for a long time. Finally Elizabeth spoke. "But he succeeded in other ways too. He had plenty of concerts when he was still playing and—"

"That's how much you know! How can you say that? Don't you remember those years when he didn't have but one or two concerts a season? Trying to hold his head up at the Conservatory? I guess you were too young but—"

Elizabeth did remember. When he went on tour the whole family heaved a communal sigh of relief: they could all breathe freely again. But when he was home there was often hell to pay for these peaceful interludes. Like that February day when the furnace broke down and they all put on extra sweaters, trying to make the best of a bad situation. All except him. He kept railing at Ada, who stood in the kitchen chopping onions for a *chicken cacciatore*, and pointing to the cellar stairs warningly, embarrassed that the repairman would hear him. "Don't you know how bad it is for my hands to get cold? How can you just stand there? Do you realize I can't play? How could you—"

At that moment, Tom, who was sitting at the table, snipping

parsley with a scissors, looked up and asked: "Well, why d-don't you w-wear g-gloves?"

Dominic was so infuriated that he took the dish and slammed it to the ground, garnishing linoleum and wall with minced greens. "You little punk, how dare you speak—"

Tom cowered in the corner, trying to explain, tears bubbling forth. "But I only me-meant like G-G-Glenn G-G-Gould—He always we-wears g-gloves."

Elizabeth dropped the cassette into a zippered compartment in her purse. "Yes, I remember."

Ada pressed the arm of the chair. "But it wasn't only that. Even when he had concerts, they were usually out in the sticks. He never really got into the big time."

"Oh, but I've seen his reviews, he had a lot of success—"

"No, my child," her aunt said, closing her eyes. "He had a moderate success. Failure is easier. You fail, you pick up the pieces, you go on to other things. That's far easier to bear than the continuance of hope, of thinking, maybe, next time will be it, all the stars in heaven will come together and *ecco*, you're made. The overnight success that's thirty years in the making. Success is pre-ordained by the kind of build-up you get before you come to a town. By the size of your fee. Tell the public they're going to hear the greatest artist of all time and they come expecting to hear that. They are at an event—it is an occasion for the memory books, and programs are saved to show to the grandchildren. Everybody wants to talk about the time they heard Horowitz at four in the afternoon. Even Prince Charles. So it becomes a self-fulfilling prophecy. But have an artist come in as a fill-in because the budget couldn't afford anybody else, and that same Horowitz could be doomed to oblivion. To the boondocks. That's what Rossiter did to Dom—he condemned him to a *moderate* success."

Midway during this speech she had begun to speak in Italian; when she came to the word *moderate*, she spat it out. "The Russians can make you an unperson; Rossiter can make you an unpianist. All Dom had going for him was his musicianship and in this day and age it's simply not enough."

"But some of it was dad's own making," Elizabeth said, clearing her voice. "Misery was his gestalt, you know that, he—"

"Is that what they taught you in that great school of yours? Blame the victim for his own troubles? If you had known him when he was younger, before all the trouble, you wouldn't say that."

"Maybe so. I caught glimpses now and then of what he might have been like. But most of the time, he always seemed to me to make a lot of his own misery. And for this you can't blame Rossiter—"

"And how about his recordings?"

"His recordings?" Except for a few cassettes of live performances, she had thought there was no other record of his work. Would these surprises never end? "I didn't know he made any."

"It just goes to show how little you know. He recorded all the Beethoven Sonatas and even the *Diabelli Variations* for Eagle Records—way back in 1952."

"But how come—"

"Because they were never released. Rossiter saw to that. Years of work, between concerts, all down the drain."

The room shuddered as the roar of a departing plane made itself felt. Elizabeth stroked back her aunt's hair and leaned against her arm. "Is there no way of getting them?"

"During that cartel investigation, *Eagle Records* was forced to disband. We were still living in Italy at the time and only heard about it later. Who knows what happened to them? They were probably lost in the shuffle. Or smashed to bits by Rossiter."

"Look, be reasonable. It can't have all been Rossiter's fault. That's too easy. He fell in love with my mother. And he got her. So why would he be so vindictive afterwards?"

Ada sat up straight and was about to say something, then thought better of it. She turned to watch a woman settle down near them with two children in matching jackets. At last she spoke. "Because he's a monster, that's why. All I keep thinking of is the time he sent Dom off on that long Australian tour. Dom was so grateful—the money was good, since it was paid by the Australian broadcasting people. Dom thought he'd reached a new plateau in his career, would be getting the better engagements in the future, the 'straight sales'—the ones not done in package deals with Federated Concerts. And all the while," Ada rubbed her eyes, "all the while . . . The only reason he arranged the tour was so he could carry on with your mother without interference. Just like David and Bathsheba. *Damnazione!*"

Elizabeth felt a prickling behind her nose. "But Aunt Ada,"—her voice was barely audible—"you surely don't think my *mother* conspired with him—"

"No, I don't think that. When Lisabeta and Dom were still together, all they thought about was how to further his career. Career, career, it was an obsession with our generation. I'm sure at the beginning she must have thought she'd be helping his career and the whole thing started innocently enough on her part. But by then she was hooked—he turned her head, he knew how. It was probably overwhelming to be courted by such a famous man, a man who set himself out to win her, come what may. Dom was sent to the Australian outback so he could have a clean field in America. And when he returned, from that day forward, Dom forgot about his career and thought only of her. That became his career." She stopped speaking to light a cigarette and drew on it deeply. "But I guess she was sorry after a while and her conscience got her in the end . . ."

"You mean—her heart attack—"

"Heart attack? Nonsense. I think that's what Rossiter told the papers. Suddenly he was concerned with *delicatezza*. It wasn't good for his image for people to know that one of his—"

The words came out in a flood of Italian and for the first time Elizabeth began to understand the thousand dark years of her implacability. Her heart was beating so hard she pressed down on it as though to prevent its breaking out of her flesh. *Basta! Basta!* The unsleeping blood of her father still cried out for vengeance from the black earth, a marker on his grave reading, as it did on old Roman roadside tombs, *siste viator: stop, traveller.* "You mean, you mean it was—"

She was interrupted by the announcement on the loudspeaker that her flight was ready for boarding.

The two women stood up. Ada took two quick pulls on her cigarette before stubbing it deeply into the sand of the ash tray next to her.

"Aunt Ada—please. My mother couldn't have—didn't—Is that what you think?"

Ada flung a hand up in a gesture that seemed to gather all the woes and sorrows that had befallen the Guaragnas since the beginning of time. "Well," she said, beginning to walk away, "I don't know for certain, but wouldn't be surprised at all, I wouldn't be surprised."

PART II

Chapter VIII

Elizabeth had just finished grinding and measuring the coffee when the door opened and Alfred Rossiter, still wearing overcoat and rubbers, stomped in. "So that's where you are," he said, for she was in Ruth Pryor's office, "it's been so long since your interview, I thought we'd dreamed you up."

Although his tone was characteristically gruff, she could see he was relieved at the sight of her. Not only couldn't she return the implied compliment—as she measured the fourth level tablespoon of coffee according the Ruth's explicit instructions—but after Aunt Ada's disclosures the day before, she was ready to throw up.

Some of the coffee grounds spilled as she poured them into the percolator; she swept them up to deposit in the wastebasket. "Miss Pryor told me you usually come in at eleven-fifteen," she said, placing the lid on the pot. "Otherwise the coffee would have been ready."

"No need to fret." He watched as she plugged the percolator into the outlet. "There's no law in my coming in early, is there? Always keep them guessing—that's what keeps everybody on their toes." Elizabeth winced. "I can wait until it's ready, I assure you. Ruth has an exaggerated view of what's important to me. Like traipsing all over town to make sure she found these authentic Louis XIV chairs—"

He swooped up one of the delicate, rigid side chairs and slammed it down. "It's all for show. Nobody can sit on these damn things except in upright discomfort. Maybe that's what she had in mind—I wouldn't put it past the sly old fox. And now the business of the elevator . . ."

He gave a snort and turned toward the door. "Bring the coffee in when it's ready." A moment later she heard him slam the door shut in his own office.

Elizabeth was quite white when she emerged into the front office and Virginia Lavin gave her a sympathetic nod. She had done her best to make Elizabeth feel welcome when she arrived that morning, telling her who was who and what was what and liberally lacing her instructions with the latest musical gossip. Not that there was much to tell. Besides herself and Ruth Pryor, who only came in the afternoon, there was just Isabel Nagel, who had her own agency on the floor above and was handling their publicity on a free-lance basis. The main thing that concerned them at the moment was to lure proper artists to the firm. Once this was done, they hoped it would have a bandwagon effect, and then they would hire more staff.

Information as to who was or wasn't switching from the Eagle Corporation, however, was a closely guarded secret. "So far the news is bad," Virginia had explained. "George Wentworth says everybody is waiting to see which side their bread will be better buttered on."

And then she had launched into a long diatribe at the "ungrateful beasties" and their deplorable "fence-sitting," her shoulders drooping in exaggerated fatigue. "This is how they repay A. R. after all he did for them. He made them, and now they turn their backs on him in his time of need. And that goes for all the managers and salesmen he trained over at Eagle, too—you can have them, the whole kit and caboodle."

At one time, Virginia told her, she herself had great aspirations to be a singer, but after a devastating review in the *New York Times*, she was glad to accept Rossiter's offer of employment on the other side of the footlights. "You see," she said, lifting the gold chain around her neck to show Elizabeth the two miniature charms of the old and new Metropolitan Opera Houses. "A.R. gave these to me when the new Met opened, the date's imprinted on the back, September 16, 1966. He said if I can't get to the Met, the Met can come to me. And he also gave me this—" she searched in her purse to take out an eyeglass case made of heavy brocade. "They made these out of the curtains of the old Met. Both this and the charms were great fund-raising gimmicks and they've since become collectors' items." She fingered the case for a moment before putting it back into her purse. "But I still work at my music and one day soon I'm going to give a private recital for my friends, just to let them know who I really am."

By the way Virginia had immediately taken Elizabeth into her confidence, it was clear that she, unlike Ruth Pryor, was glad to have her there. Her age notwithstanding, she walked jauntily about the office, swinging her backside, clicking her wobbly high heels, resting her palms on her hips as she spoke. "Enough old fogies around here. We need somebody willing to learn and take instruction without set ways of doing things."

Knowing how unwilling she really was, Elizabeth had felt a stab of remorse and, in truth, could hardly face the older woman.

And she could hardly face the "reading matter" waiting on her desk. Her eye skimmed the Artists' Price List for the previous season from the Eagle management which they would be using as a guide. Sopranos, Mezzo-Sopranos, Contraltos, Tenors, Baritones, Pianists, Duo Pianists, Violinists, Violist (only one), Cellists, Harpists, Special Attractions, Vocal Ensembles, Instrumental Ensembles, Dance Attractions and so on—all carefully categorized, herded, branded, priced, ticketed—so much musical meat on the hoof, wholesale only.

For budgets from $15,000 to $30,000 inclusive, Ljuba Gousseau could be had for $8,000; for budgets $16,000 to $50,000 for $10,000; whereas Monique Henriot's fee, which was only a paltry $5,000, remained the same for budgets inclusive and exclusive. She wondered if Gousseau gave just a bit more of herself for budgets over $50,000 where her fee rose to $12,000: a deeper bow to show more cleavage; a few extra high C's; an extra encore of *Lo Hear the Gentle Lark?* Most likely all of the above.

MOTHERLESS CHILD | 88

Rossiter suddenly loomed over her. She sprang back guiltily, as though he could read her mind. "This kind of mail I can do without," he said curtly, tossing an advertising circular on her desk and imperiously eyeing her as though she were an ambassador from a hostile country. Before she could respond he turned and strode back to his office.

Virginia dilated one nostril in sympathetic disdain. "Don't worry, the old curmudgeon's not always like that. When he wants to, he can be charm itself. It's just Monday morning—he always has a short fuse then. Too much of Dolores." She laughed at Elizabeth's raised eyebrow. "His not so better half. But then I suppose we should all be grateful to her. She's the only reason he started this agency. And I'm not betraying any confidences. He himself tells this to everyone, given half a chance. He'd do anything to get away from her. You'd think in that oversize mansion they call home there'd be enough room for her to keep out of his way. But I guess not."

"Do they have any children?"

"No, no children." Her voice sank to a murmur. "She was well into her forties when he married her. I think he wanted someone closer his age after his second wife died. I guess he thought he'd be getting some peace and quiet." She twirled a pen with thumb and forefinger. "He must have been out of his mind."

Elizabeth waited for her to continue, but she turned back to her work. "What did he mean about the elevator business?"

"Oh, that." She stabbed the air with the pen. "Before Eagle Concerts moved into Rossiter Towers, they used to occupy the top three floors here. That was nearly a quarter of a century ago. Anyway, in those days, whenever A. R. came in, he was scooted up by himself, and all bowed low. No mixing with the hoi-polloi, not for the likes of him. But this building's under new management, and they won't do it anymore. Cost efficiency and all that. Ruth made a big fuss about it."

Virginia grasped the rim of the desk and pushed her chair out as she rose to consult the *Iron Lung*—the name given the large grey fil-ing device which kept the histories of concert series in every city of the nation going back to the old Chautauqua circuit. "I still prefer this faithful old system," she said, giving it an affectionate pat. "At Eagle they've computerized all this information—but I prefer this. Hard to teach old dogs new tricks." For a moment she consulted the map which hung nearby in which red pins indicated all the organized concert series, like the assault plan of a strategic military campaign.

"So that's where Red Creek, Oregon is," she said when she located the tiny dot on the map. "Not exactly the Celebrity Series in Chica-go," Virginia said, "but for Orpov, a date's a date. The work to be done in the building of a new agency is staggering," she added, as she returned to her desk. "So much work, so much detail, yet all Ruth seems to worry about is whether A. R. is elevated exclusively or not."

The buzzer on Elizabeth's desk sounded and she jumped. Although she had her own office, the paint was not quite dry and her desk was temporarily situated catty-cornered to the right of Virginia's. She moved over to answer the phone. "What time is George Wentworth coming in?" It was not so much a question as a bark.

"Three-o'clock," Virginia said as Elizabeth shrugged inquiringly, for his voice was audible all over the room.

Elizabeth repeated the information.

"I'm having lunch at the club—and then, the doctor. Don't know if I'll be back in time. Better make it three-thirty." She could hear him riffle some pages on his desk. "No, I'm due at the club at twelve. I'll be back in time. Let the appointment stand. And by the way, is the coffee ready yet?"

Elizabeth checked her watch. "I was just going to bring it in," she replied, snapping down the button.

"I hope this is how you like it," Elizabeth said, wondering where to set down the tray containing the steaming coffee in a white porcelain pot with matching sugar bowl, creamer and mug, each hand-decorated with a bar of the *Eroica*. She stood uncertainly, not daring to look over at him as he inserted a book next to an ebony-carved head of Beethoven in the bookcase.

"No, here," Alfred Rossiter said, when he turned and saw her heading for the stand-up desk in the corner. After he cleared the round table of books, he sat down next to it in his large leather wing chair.

She was trying to be as careful as she could, but when she set the tray down, the dishes rattled. "Well, it smells all right. Would you like some? I'm sure there's more where these came from," he said, holding the mug aloft and grimacing at its musical motif before filling the cup. "Another bit of Ruth's nonsense."

"No, thank you," Elizabeth said. "I don't drink coffee."

"What do you drink?"

"Tea. Herbal tea. Caffeine doesn't agree with me."

"My doctor tells me I can't take it either. And none of this either"—he indicated the cream which he was pouring with a generous hand—"but when you've reached my age, who cares? There's so much they won't let me take, no this, no that, No-vem-ber. Like that poem. What are they preserving me for? What's the point of existence when your whole life is thermostatically controlled, not too much heat, not too much cold, no ups, no downs, everything at a mean of 70 degrees. And I do mean *mean*. Might as well be living in a test tube." He stirred sugar into his coffee with slow turns and took a sip with almost ceremonial solemnity. "It tastes fine." Then he closed his eyes to absorb it and cuddled the cup, inhaling its bouquet with an expression more appropriate for Chivas Regal. "Very good, very good. Well, sit down, girl. I can't stand people hovering over me."

Elizabeth felt as though the most grueling qualifying examination for her doctorate had just been passed with flying colors. She sat down on the indicated chair facing him. "I didn't bring my notebook, didn't realize you wanted to—"

"You won't need it." He pointed to the stack of letters lying on his desk. "They can keep. It's all bills or starving artists trying to get on our list." He sipped deeply. "Tell me a bit about yourself. You're from New York, right?"

Elizabeth carefully studied his cordovan shoes. "Upstate. But I've lived here for quite a while."

"Who with?"

"I've got my own apartment."

"Where?"

"Well, as a matter of fact, I'm scheduled"—she paused, realizing she had pronounced the first syllable in the Canadian "sh" rather than American "sk" fashion—"to move to a new one this weekend on West End Avenue near Seventy-Sixth."

"Why?"

With his rapid-fire monosyllabic questions, she felt under attack.

"Why do you think? It's much better than the railroad flat I have now which hardly has any heat to speak of—" She stopped again, this time realizing she had said *flat* instead of *apartment*, but in his surprise at her outburst, he didn't seem to notice.

"Harrumph," he said after a moment, sucking the rim of his cup. "Do your parents approve of you living like that?"

"My father died last year. That's when I moved. And my mother died . . . my mother died when I was born."

Alfred Rossiter lowered his coffee mug and looked at her from under narrowed lids. "A motherless child . . ." His voice died away suddenly and she was not sure she had heard him correctly. At last he grunted and said: "Oh, well, mothers today—parking their young at day care centers like excess baggage and then wondering why they wind up in juvenile court."

Crossing her hands over her chest, Elizabeth could feel her mother's locket nestling between her breasts. As he buried his face again in the coffee cup, she scrutinized him. In the bleak morning light, she could see the white hairs in the nostrils of his aquiline nose and each white whisker sprouting from his face. Was this the mind that once conquered and were these the hands that once held and were these the lips that once . . . How could she have stood him? She drew a deep breath before she spoke. "Well, some have no alternative. There's the little worry about the rent at the first of the month." She clasped her arms tighter to keep from saying more.

"Bosh! It's not the rent they do it for. It's 'self-fulfillment', more often than not. Don't get me started on that subject. Least said, soonest mended." Liquid spilled on the tray as he placed the mug down and he mopped it up with a napkin. From the wall opposite, the ormolu clock ticked noisily away, as if ticking his life away from under him as well. "Well, go get your notebook," he said with a sudden change of tone. "We'd better get some work done."

The instructions which Rossiter gave regarding the mail were vague, but since most of the letters were routine, she didn't run into any trouble until she came to the one from Timothy Upjohn, the Scottish tenor. Rossiter had told her to consult with Ruth if she had any questions but when she did so, Ruth had been equally vague, and Elizabeth saw that she would get little assistance from that quarter.

Elizabeth read through the letter again. Too bad the others couldn't share her appreciation of it. Upjohn had written that the George Wentworth article had been carried in the Edinburgh paper and he hoped that Rossiter would be as good as his word—and would run a more "humanistic" agency than the one he had in the past.

". . . the musician feeds the public with the food of love. Managers are there to serve the artists, not vice versa. Yet it's the managers who are more famous than many of the artists. And richer. I remember once bumping into Carlos Antonini and Joseph Suzman on a flight from London to New York. All three of us were traveling tourist class and arranged to sit together. Just as we were snapping our seat belts, my manager, Gerald Wang of Eagle Concerts, came aboard and stopped in the first-class compartment. He tried to avoid us but we saw him."

When Rossiter handed this letter to her, his only comment was: "Just tell this bird where to get off." And all Ruth had said was: "Impudence. Nothing but impudence. I remember when Timothy Upjohn first came over and sat for a whole day hoping A. R. would see him. And now this. Personally I'd ignore his remarks and send him the usual acknowledgment. But use your own judgment, Lisa, that's what you're here for. And you'd better get used to it."

She wouldn't be surprised if Ruth was hoping she would fall flat on her face. Elizabeth looked at the letter. Halfway through, she laid it down and rubbed her forehead. Her judgment! If she'd had any, she wouldn't be in this spot now, working for a man she had every reason to despise, debating how to answer a letter she couldn't care less about.

Or that she cared too much about, if the truth be told, for the letter was one which her own father might have written. Her father: how dim his presence, how light his touch on the *Traumerei* cassette, as though ghostly fingers had pressed ghostly piano keys. He was lucky to be over on the other side now. Her vision of her life divided into two parts returned, the part she was ensconced in so implacably, and the other side, the mythical other side. When the time came, would she have the necessary wisdom, the guts, the seven furlong boots to take that leap?

MOTHERLESS CHILD | 94

She inserted a sheet of letterhead paper into the typewriter with a flick of the wrist. She might as well be fired for a sheep as a lamb, especially since being fired was an outcome devoutly to be wished. The carriage hurtled violently to the left, the keys rattled like bursts of machine-gun fire.

All right, then, folks, you want judgment, here comes judgment.

Chapter IX

"This'll do fine," Rossiter said, handing back the first of the series of letters Elizabeth had drafted. "This one's too flowery—just say we're not holding auditions at this time. The last paragraph can stand. Until I hear from my old artists, I don't want to start up with new ones too fast."

Elizabeth grimaced. Who did he think he was kidding? So far the only artists who had switched to him were a pianist from England; a violinist from Germany; the only reason being, Elizabeth suspected, they were too far away to know which way the New York musical winds were blowing.

"This one's all wrong." Elizabeth was not surprised to see the letter he held aloft was her answer to Timothy Upjohn. "'I hope in time to establish the kind of management that will prove mutually beneficial for artist and manager,'" he quoted in a sarcastic voice and then looked at her sharply. "*Mutually beneficial*, that'll be the day. It's always been a one-way street. We make and they take." He paused to read Upjohn's letter out loud again. When he came to the part about "the food of love," he guffawed. "My old mentor, Colonel Mapleson, used to say, 'If music is the food of love, then the manager is the caterer.'"

"Well, they do provide the food," Elizabeth said. "And the managers *are* often more famous and certainly richer—"

He studied her for a moment and then rose to pace back and forth across the room. "I suppose you're thinking of Hurok. So is Upjohn, probably. Well, everybody knows Sol had a love affair going with himself. Even so, he did a lot for music. I remember when he used to have concerts at the old Hippodrome Theatre. 'Music for the Masses' he called it. It *was* a good idea, I have to give him that. It brought new audiences to music, even if they did bring their lunches in brown paper bags and left orange peels all over the hall. I remember going to one of those concerts when Pavlova danced. Along with trained elephants and Chinese jugglers and assorted other freaks on the same bill."

A cloud passed over the sun outside; the light changed to pure pewter. He stooped to turn on a lamp. "They told patrons if they wanted to leave to kindly do so between pieces, *please*. Music for the masses! A lot of good that did. In any case, I'm not Hurok, as you must know by now. I sell my artists—not myself."

Elizabeth shut her eyes. At least His Eminence was calling them *artists* and not *executants*. He'd got that much right. But when he spoke of selling *artists,* his voice dipped; she felt a halo in the muted colors of an icon descend over the word. *Cultura*—with a capital *cult*. She squared her shoulders and was determined not to be frightened of him. "Well, what about Gerald Wang? He did work for you. Managers live far better economically—"

"Whoa, slow down. There's nothing to compare to the righteousness of the young. Your generation is ready to believe everything it reads. You sure have a lot to learn."

"Maybe so. All my life I've been told that by some grown-up or other, but when it came to being taught anything, I mostly had to do it myself."

He smiled. "You're not the only one. But you've got it all wrong. Look, we don't live better than Upjohn or Suzman, but he's a Scotsman and the other's a Jew so what do you expect? They *would* travel tourist. But they don't need to. Look at Horowitz, he travels with a valet, a cook, a manager, and a piano tuner—not to mention the men who cart his piano around. As for Antonini—well, Italians. They're a breed apart—and always were."

Her face turned pink. "Well, so are managers. For the sake of feathering Gerald Wang's nest, men and women have practiced eight hours a day, risked humiliation at international contests, overlooked empty halls, suffered—"

Rossiter's eyes blinked spasmodically behind his reading glasses. "You've got quite a bit of sass, girl. Ease off. First day on the job and already you're telling me how to handle an agency."

Pulling herself up stiffly, she said: "Mr. Rossiter, I'd appreciate it if you wouldn't call me 'girl.'"

Two large crimson spots appeared on his cheeks as he took off his glasses and stared. For a moment she thought he was going to fire her then and there—to give her her walking papers, as she had once heard her aunt express it when her father was let go by the Royal Conservatory. At the time she thought being given your walking papers was a privilege, an intermediate step on the way to running papers and flying papers.

But Rossiter was going to do no such thing. His eyes were as washed out as sheets hanging on a line and he suddenly looked very old. "All right then. I'll try to remember. I'll call you Sullivan then, okay?"

"Just call me Lisa."

"Lisa, then." He looked at her in a serious, measuring way. "Maybe you think it's always been Easy Street for me. I've paid my dues, believe me. When I began my classical music radio show on what later became the Eagle Broadcasting Corporation, I nearly lost my shirttails. And my suspenders. And everybody else's too. But I was convinced. That was my way of bringing music to the masses, without having the orange peels to contend with."

Elizabeth understood now that the insistence on the coffee ritual was not an echelon-divider and all that signified, but a means to provide this man with the proper setting for his voluminous reminiscences. He was still droning on about his early days in music. Ordinarily these would fascinate her, but at the moment she was far too angry to listen. Rossiter continued without interruption. "During the Depression, if I didn't get a bunch of us to form a merger—that's how Eagle got started, Christ, none of us would have survived. Where would your precious Upjohn have been then? Or Suzman? Or Antonini?"

They studied each other in the reflected circle of lamplight next to his chair. The sky had darkened, casting the rest of the room in shadowed gloom. "You're a young woman, artists seem romantic and visionary, but wait until you see what it's like dealing with them on a day-to-day basis. I've handled them all at one time or another and know what I'm talking about. Casals supposedly would never play in this country because we recognized Franco . . . The truth was he wouldn't play because his former wife would slap back-alimony payments if he ever set foot in this country. And when Rodzinski was conductor of the Chicago Symphony in the days before musicians' unions got so strong, he was famous for firing musicians a few months before retirement so they'd lose their pension. And then there was Oscar Levant, who became so difficult he'd cancel concerts if he didn't like the shape of the local manager's nose. Once he packed his bag and flew back home because a funeral parlor was visible from his hotel window and we ought to have known better than book him into a room with so woebegone a view."

Elizabeth didn't trust herself to respond. When she turned to go he asked her to wait while he read through her letter to Upjohn again, holding it at a distance as if it were contaminated.

"Mmm, well—" He handed her the letter with a gesture of dismissal. "I guess your answer is harmless enough. No sense offending him. But put that line about establishing 'the kind of management that will prove mutually beneficial' in the past tense—or at least the present. I don't have that much time left and he knows it."

As Elizabeth turned to go, Virginia Lavin came in to announce George Wentworth and was followed by a long, loosely built young man, dressed in a turtleneck sweater under a leather-patched tweed jacket, with a down jacket flung over his arm. "My word, A. R., don't you believe in lights?" Tossing his coat on a chair, he proceeded to switch on the rest of the lamps in the room as though lighting up a stage. "It's really coming down out there, but I guess rain's better than snow."

"Now who have we here?" he asked when he saw Elizabeth, and regarded her for a moment with a grave little smile, the same kind of smile she had seen him use that time at Dalton's nearly a year ago. Upon introduction, he moved slowly toward her as if trying to remember where he had seen her before, and extended his hand.

But apparently the name *Lisa Sullivan* threw him off for all he said was "So you're the new assistant I've been hearing about," and sharpened the focus of his tortoiseshell eyes. If it hadn't been for her familiarity with his picture on the flyleaf of his book, she would never have recognized him, so why should she have feared he would recognize her? His hand was cold, but the handshake was warm and firm.

"You're not quite what Ruth led me to expect."

"A snippet, Ruth calls her," Rossiter said, with amusement. "She's not a snippet, but she can be snippety."

Speech trembled on Elizabeth's lips. Old boys' club lingo, ha ha, par excellence. For a moment rage welled up so violently she had to fold her arms to keep from slapping their smirking faces and shouting, *Well, one can't help being snippety with the murderer of one's mother, can one?*

"Snippety, eh?" George Wentworth said with a sympathetic wink.

"Oh, well, forewarned is forearmed."

Snatching the file of letters, she left the room without a word.

"Well?" Virginia asked as Elizabeth returned to her desk.

"Well, what?"

"George Wentworth? What did you think of him? He's the one writing a biography of A.R."

"I know. I've read some of his bowdlerized stuff. The faithful chronicler of the Authorized Version." She dropped the file of letters on her desk with a thud. "No wonder he can write so glowingly about him. He's just like him at an earlier age, success in every undertaking a foregone conclusion."

Virginia laughed. "I suppose you're right. *You scratch my back and I'll scratch yours*—that's their guiding principle. His *New York Times* piece on Rossiter has been picked up by the wire services and reprinted everywhere. When you're a Wentworth, doors open electronically at your approach. He's *persona grata*, in editorial offices as well as to the headwaiter at *Lutece*."

Elizabeth began folding letters and inserting them into envelopes. "I can just imagine the revisionist history Rossiter's feeding him—" She couldn't bring herself to call him *A. R.*, with the mixture of veneration and affection it would imply. "I've heard enough already in the course of only one day myself."

"Revisionist? What do you mean by revisionist?"

"Exactly that. The man thinks managers are God's gift to artists. He forgets what they have to go through. I'd like to remind him of garrets and tendonitis and being on the receiving end of telephone calls which never come and—"

Virginia frowned. "Come on now. He may seem like an ogre, but believe me, he knows all that. And he's aware of his shortcomings, too."

"From what I've seen, even carefully selected shortcomings have become pluses with, according to him, only one goal in mind: to put classical music on America's map."

"And he's done just that! Don't judge him too soon, Lisa. Oh, he's had a few peccadillos, I admit . . . And if somebody got in the way"— she drew her finger across her throat—"well, too bad."

Elizabeth shut her eyes. Her mother—a peccadillo? But she doubted if he ever mentioned her mother: her memory was so entombed, so overladen by later and fresher beguilements, that to unearth it was probably impossible. "Too bad, is right," she wanted to say, but her throat was engorged and for a moment she couldn't speak. When she could, she was surprised at what came out. "But to George Wentworth, all that is probably the stuff of pure macho dreams."

"And it'll certainly help sell the book."

Chapter X

"Looks like you've found quite a girl there, A.R." George Wentworth said as he took his tape recorder out of its leather case. "Reminds me of somebody but for the life of me, I can't remember who."

"Funny you should say that." Rossiter looked up from the official form he was studying. "I had the same feeling when I first met her. And again today. But you'd better not call her a girl. She chewed me out about that one earlier. I don't know what the young are coming to these days. Taking umbrage at all kinds of nonsense."

"What made you hire her?"

"Damned if I know. I've been asking myself the same question. Maybe to get Ruth's goat. She wanted me to hire an old battleaxe who mouthed every cliche in the book. Admittedly, she had the right experience and the right references. But two plusses make a minus, as the old saying goes. At my age, you get tired of predictability. Lisa seems to know her own mind. I like that."

George was fussing with his tape recorder, removing the old batteries and putting in new ones. Now who was it she looked like? That girl in England? He tossed the old batteries into the waste basket. Better not start on that track again. *Fool me once, shame on you; fool me twice, shame on me.* He'd met her on a train from London to Edinburgh, didn't even know her name, and mooned over her for weeks. Martha? No, nothing like that frozen iceberg about this one. Who was it?

After testing the tape to make sure it was working properly, he spread his notebook on his lap and settled back in his chair. Of course, it didn't have to be anybody. Maybe what was familiar was the old leap of recognition he'd felt—not of somebody he'd known but of somebody he'd like to know. Lately the leaps had been rare and, even when they occurred, he no longer did high wire jumps like before. As between a safety net and falling on your face, wasn't a safety net better?

Across the room Alfred Rossiter was finally affixing his signature to the official form spread out on his stand-up desk. "There," he said, with a grunt, putting down the magnifying glass with which he had been examining the small print. "That ought to do it," and he pushed the intercom button to fetch Lisa Sullivan. She materialized almost instantly, approached him warily, pad and pencil clutched in her hand. "This needs to be sent today," he said, handing her the sheet. "Look it over and see if I've skipped anything."

George took another good look at her as she studied the form. She was even better upon closer inspection. Had the biggest eyes he'd ever seen and the shadows around them made them seem even larger and more mysterious. Nothing bad about her skirt and blouse get-up either, which, along with her scrubbed face, suggested little patience with feminine artifice. Though she stood tall and firm and her voice was deep and throaty, he noted something fragile about her as she nodded her head at Rossiter. And something about the awkward set of her shoulders suggested she was on the defensive.

Ruth had also described her to him as a "mere snippet" and claimed Rossiter had been out of his mind to hire her. At first he'd attributed it to intergenerational rivalry but then she'd gone on to explain that she didn't have any experience in the field at all. "And I couldn't believe my ears at the way she spoke to him," Ruth said, lifting her shoulders. "As if she's doing him a favor by coming to work for him. I was certain she'd get her comeuppance, but no—I just don't understand how he lets her get away with it. No respect at all in the young these days."

But then Ruth took a more hopeful tack, saying that "at least she's Irish and the Irish really work."

She looked Irish too—the eyes brought visions of the sea at Shannon where the sudden depth of the water away from the shore is visible from the air. Her hair—pulled back in an old-fashioned topknot—

made you want to pull it down just to see what she'd look like then. Small bells rang in his head but he could not bring what he wanted to the front of his mind. "I'll see that it goes with the rest of the mail," she said and then got herself quickly out of the door, which she shut quietly but firmly behind her.

Rossiter's plume of silver hair appeared golden in the light of the lamp as he took off his suit jacket and draped it on the back of his chair. "Now where shall we start today?" he asked as he lowered himself into the chair with the careful, calculated movements of old age.

"We were . . . let's see." George consulted his notes. "We finished up about Eagle Broadcasting and you promised to tell me about your wife—"

"Oh yes. I guess I should start with the first one—"

"The first—" George started to say and fell silent. Of course, he might have known he'd been married twice. Here he was looking for sinister reasons why Dolores withheld the information about her former husband and it was something as simple as this.

". . . to Phyllis," Rossiter continued, "my first wife. Nothing much to tell there." They'd been childhood sweethearts in Worcester and used to make the long trek to school each day together. Their parents knew each other and it was taken for granted that one day they'd wed.

"Her taste in music was limited but I didn't think that would matter much. Well, it did. It was as though a whole area of my life—and increasingly the larger area—was unknown to her and not to be discussed. We didn't get married for quite a while. I was in France during the war—the first World War, that is—driving an ambulance."

George wondered if that was when she'd married her first husband but didn't want to seem over-curious. He'd take it as it came. "You drove an ambulance? Wow. That must have been quite an experience."

"To put it mildly. It changed my life. We met the wounded as they arrived by train—Christ . . . the screams of the mustard gas victims with their blotched faces. Butcher Haig sent two hundred thousand men to die in the Somme in a single day. And then there were the piles of bodies from the flu epidemic."

His prewar innocence, he confessed, had gone for good. When he returned from overseas, he went back to school and got married by rote, as if standing on the outside watching himself go through the motions. He turned to George and the muscles of his forearms tightened. "There's nothing like war to remind you how finite your life is. I'd sworn over the dead body of one of my friends that my life would have meaning after that. Music was the one thing that seemed worthwhile. But Phyllis wasn't at all happy when I started. I'll never forget the time I went after Yuri Galliuillin—I'd heard him once when I was on leave in Paris—and used up all of what she called the 'rainy day' money. I never heard the last of that. She'd have been happy if I got some job as church organist or something and we'd centered our lives around what the minister told us to do or not do each Sunday. Perhaps if there'd been children, things would have been different but, in her disappointment at not having any, she seemed to shrivel up. I'd wanted to divorce her long before I met Elizabeth—she was the spur."

Elizabeth? George nodded sagely but was feeling anything but. Another wife? The guy was a regular Bluebeard. This, he hoped, must surely be the sleeping dog Maggie had warned him about. He concentrated on trying to sound casual. "How did you meet her?"

"Ah, that." He looked down and studied his fingernails.

The ormolu clock chimed on the half-hour. "Sir?" said George, breaking the silence.

"I hardly know where to begin." Rossiter threw up his arms. "I know it's corny today . . . but it was just like in the song *Some Enchanted Evening*. I saw her across the room at a party and the pull was unmistakable. We looked at each other not as man and woman, but as soul-mates—and the force with which we were drawn to one another was something astonishing. She looked, well she looked, like all the real beauties of that period, cool and exquisitely neat—nothing like your blowsy-hair-all-over-the-place girls of today. And her voice, her pronunciation, everything perfectly clear and correct. Well, I suppose you should know . . ." Rossiter's voice was none too steady and his eyes glistened. "It was the best part of my life. Three years I had her, as against the seventy-seven without, but her scent still flows back upon my memory like balm. The world was re-created for us."

Tears often came to Rossiter's eyes; he ignored them, as if he were too old to care about appearances any longer. A drink may have helped but George was reluctant to interrupt. How more wrong could the gossips get? This splendid old man, who had a genius for relaying the most exalted moments of music into his bank account, happened also to be what they once called an incurable romantic. But now he shrank in his chair, his eyes awash and red-veined, as if to remove himself altogether from his own share of the madness of the twentieth century.

George made a quick note in his pad. *It wasn't only this woman's death that was so smeared all over his heart and liver and guts, but the death of all the ideas and hopes of his far-off childhood when Mozart gave warmth and Beethoven brought in the bacon.* When he finished writing, George waited for more enlightenment but none came. He searched for something to say but, instead, pulled out his handkerchief and handed it over to him.

Rossiter mopped his eyes and then blew his nose loudly. The noise sounded out of place among those plush furnishings which suggested that here, at least, America had done right by its dreamers.

Rossiter returned George's handkerchief to him with a shrug. "That's all past history—nobody's interested in that. The important part is about the artists—Lisa Sullivan makes that clear enough."

"Your new assistant? She said that?"

"Well, not in regard to the book. In regard to everything else, though.

And she's right, I guess. Nobody wants to read the other stuff."

"I don't think that at all," George said quietly. "We need all this personal stuff to bring the biography alive. Otherwise they might as well go read up about you in the encyclopedia or in *Grove's*." Rossiter had slipped off into another reverie and it was with some difficulty that George led his mind back to the present. "So you and she were not together long . . ."

"What is *time* anyway? A few minutes can be a lifetime—or a death time. Our life together was so fragile, we were both mindful of that at all times lest we crush it." His voice had become shaky. "Even as it was happening I knew I had never been nor would ever be so happy again."

Rossiter tilted his head, his face flushed, the tracery of red veins more visible than ever. Much as he wanted to hear more, from past experience George knew it was better to drop painful subjects; the old man would think it through on his own and then impart whatever it was he wanted to say. Better to supplement this information independently than get Rossiter's back up with too much prodding. The tape recorder whirred on, preserving a few of Rossiter's sniffles and George turned it off. He reviewed his notes and made some hasty entries for his own eventual edification. "Phyllis . . ." he said. "What was her maiden name?"

"Lawson."

"And Elizabeth's?"

"Jordan . . . was her maiden name. When I knew her she was, of course, Elizabeth Guaragna."

George's pen paused in mid-air. "Guaragna? You mean G-u-a-r-a-g-n-a?"

"Yes. Her married name. She was married when I met her."

"And her husband's name?"

"Dominic—Dominic Guaragna. And Dolores' maiden name was Norton."

But George was no longer listening.

Elizabeth Guaragna! George sat nonplussed. To have started on that idiotic quest when here, right under his nose—

But, he reminded himself as he pressed his thumb down hard at the top of the grey fountain pen with the faded initials on the side, he hadn't known Rossiter at the time. Six months ago was the first time he laid eyes on him. It had been after that lunch at the Lotos Club that old Geyer gave in March. And that meeting at Dalton's—well, it was a month after publication of *Transcendence and Tragedy* which made it nearly a year ago.

He hadn't thought about that girl in the bookstore since he'd scoured the telephone directories of all five boroughs for her. And had even done a stint with the city directory as well. Although quite a few Guaragnas were listed—especially in Queens—there were no Elizabeths, and the two E. Guaragnas turned out to be Eduardo and—he couldn't remember the second but for all he knew—and now cared—it may have been Englebert. He'd taken her fountain pen and worked his way through all the numbers, calling each one over a period of two evenings, just in case she was living with her parents or something.

But there were no Elizabeths among them. The initials on the pen were faded, the G was decipherable only because he knew her last name—the first letter could have been anything. The pen was a *Parker "51" Special*, issued in 1951 as he later found out, requiring a special superchrome ink which he'd had a devil of a time finding. Anybody using it, he had reasoned, must be doing so for sentimental reasons and he felt it only right that he try to return it. At least that was what he told himself as he set about the search. What he'd say to her if she did answer was another matter. *Miss Guaragna . . . This is George Wentworth. You know—you bought my book. Yes, your pen—you mean you hadn't missed it? I just thought—I found your name in the book . . . well, it really wasn't that difficult, I just—*

Since then the memory of that girl had gone the way of all

temporary aberrations, buried deep down. And what, in truth, was there to remember? He'd hardly gotten a proper look at her face, the features were as blurred in his mind as those of a medallion. All he remembered was the long hair blown every which way in a dark halo surrounding wide-set—but he couldn't say now whether her eyes were blue or black or purple. He had thought of her all that day, could recall the toss of her head—and the way her lips pursed when she referred to Konstantinov's *Hammerklavier,* as if to hold back a flood, suggesting she was either a musician or, at the very least, a real music lover.

The whole episode had been strange. A girl comes in and asks for an autograph—a simple act repeated hundreds of times on his promotional tour, and yet, with the exchange of a few pleasantries—

But that was it. It wasn't just a few pleasantries. You write a book, you put your heart and sinew and embryonic ulcer into it, and all anybody has to say is how interesting they found it or how much they liked it. Or loved it, for that matter but never giving you a clue as to what or why or how or where they did. That is, of course, when they read it, most of the time you sensed they hadn't even gotten beyond the first page.

And the critics, Lord love the bastards, with their once-over-light-lies, settling for such cliches as "high flights of exuberance," or "enlightenment, as well as entertainment," when they were being generous and "a thankless performance" when they weren't. Who in hell was thanking whom?

And suddenly, along comes somebody—starting out just as the others—and then in a few words makes you feel the whole effort was worthwhile after all.

The *Hammerklavier.* It was because of that recording by Konstantin that he'd probably written the book, for the music had played a special role in helping him get through those lonely Oxonian years. Not everybody shared his appreciation. His interpretation of the piece, it was said, was too wild, too careless, too controlled, too mad. And it was wild, careless, controlled, mad. But it was also true, absolute, compre-hended and recomprehended, right on the Beethovenian mark, tragic and transcendental. And here before him had stood somebody who was most likely buying the book for similar sensibilities. On those days when he ripped sheets of paper from his typewriter with disgust and gazed gloomily around his sparsely furnished study wanting to pack the whole thing in and fly back to Cleveland and its waiting sine-cure, the hope for this kind of kindred spirit kept him going on.

On reflection now, he felt it was just as well the girl never answered the telephone. He could hardly ask her to identify the nature of her attachment to the *Hammerklavier*. Besides, no matter what it was, it was bound to have fallen short of his own obsessive expectations.

George watched as Rossiter lit up a cigar and the smoke drifted across his face. Another example of the American dream gone awry. But even dreamers have no immunity from the assaults of fate. And he'd given his all to *art*—not railroads. Over at Eagle they were whooping it up at his downfall. "Where's Elizabeth now?" George asked, as Rossiter squinted through the haze at him expectantly.

"She died, of course—Haven't you been listening to what I've been telling you?"

"She . . . ?" George swung around and looked at him with perplexity. "When was that?"

"On February 20th, 1954."

"But . . ." George rolled his head away from Rossiter's puzzled gaze. Of course she was dead, what was wrong with him? He cer-tainly had made that clear enough. The old man must think him an idiot. "Were there children?" he asked at last.

"Yes, three of them, two boys and a girl."

"But I thought—You told me you had no—"

A frown creased Rossiter's forehead. "They were hers by her previ-ous marriage."

"Where are they now?"

"In Italy. Dominic Guaragna took them over there shortly after— She . . . we . . . never saw them again."

"But—"George began and then stopped. Nothing about that girl in Dalton's seemed Italian—he remembered thinking that when he wrote her name. And there was no accent either—he was sure of it. Which meant . . . what? A coincidence, probably, there were enough Guaragnas around, as he knew only too well. He looked at the faded initials on his pen. *Dominic?* It could be a D. But it could be a B or a C or a J or an O or any damn thing. Still— "Did you say that Dominic Guaragna lives in Italy?"

A vein in Rossiter's forehead began to throb. "As far as I know—it's been a while since I've heard anything about him."

Trace Dominic Guaragna, George wrote covertly in his notebook and then underlined it with a heavy black stroke. If he were able to track him down, it might require a trip to Italy to see him, which didn't seem worthwhile. On the other hand, if he didn't see him, he'd always have the feeling he'd short-changed the book. As Maggie had indicated, he just had to come up with some alternate points of view if the book was to have real meaning. Perhaps he could work in the Italian stopover when he was in England on his upcoming promotional tour.

He could see tears starting up again in Rossiter's eyes and his skin was drawn tightly over his cheekbones. If he left him alone, chances were he'd tell him everything in his own way and in his own time.

George wrapped up the interview with a few more questions, bade Rossiter goodbye, and walked out of the office.

Chapter XI

On the way home after her first day at the new job, Elizabeth bumped into George Wentworth who was huddling at the entrance to the office building. In the driving storm outside, New York was a runny water-color, with red and green lights reflected on wet pavements and on buses dripping in the glaze.

"I'm sorry—"

"Excuse me—"

"My fault, I wasn't looking—"

"I shouldn't have been barring—"

He laughed. "I'm waiting for it to die down a little. My car's parked at the Universal Garage down the street—can I give you a lift?"

"No, thanks, I'm meeting somebody over at the subway," she said, trying to make her voice indifferent, surprised at how readily the lie tripped off her tongue. He had left Rossiter nearly twenty minutes earlier, so what was he still doing in the building? The directness of his eyes made her turn away warily; some subconscious, vestigial faculty came to the fore to alert her to danger. Either he recognized her—which didn't seem likely—or he wanted to get some inside information from her, as both Ruth and Virginia had warned her people would try to do.

Bad news either way.

"Well, let me drive you to the subway at least. It's raining tom-cats and bull-dogs. You'll be soaked through in that thin coat."

"The coat's waterproof, and I'm already late. This'll do me fine." She hoisted her umbrella like a weapon, unfurling it as soon as she cleared the door and, without a backward glance, made a dash into the waiting rain.

But the umbrella offered little protection as the increasingly vindictive gusts came aslant. Within a block, it whipped inside out; after

113

trying to reverse the metal supports for some moments in vain, she tossed the umbrella away.

With the mountains of garbage due to a city-wide strike piled high on the curb, forcing people to walk single file, it took ten minutes until she reached Columbus Circle. When she took off her soaked hat, her topknot of hair fell down. Water ran from the brim of the hat as she folded it to stuff into her pocket. Her stockings were splattered, looking as though they had the measles.

Crossing the subterranean concourse to the east side train, a man in a brown down jacket stepped in front of her. For a moment she thought it was George Wentworth, checking up on her. But no, of course not, no subway rider he. Had he not been waiting in the doorway in knight errant fashion, she could have eaten in the coffee shop next to the building and by then the storm might have abated. Especially since she had been half planning to do so because she still hadn't replenished any food in her apartment since her return from Toronto—and didn't want to since she was moving in a few days.

Instead she had gone off and told the first lie that came into her head. Ever since she had become Lisa Sullivan, new requirements had been grafted onto her life, mendacity topping the list. As if to falsehood born, she seemed to be lying all the time now: she lied to get her job; she lied on leaving her old one; she lied when she signed the lease on her apartment; she lied at the Social Security office when she filled out a new identity form citing *Lisa Sullivan* as her "professional" name.

But was her deception—even to Aunt Ada—in fact, so terrible? If the public had a right to know everything about anybody who took their fancy, from board room to bedroom to potting shed, how about some enlightenment for the private sector? Didn't she have a right to take out and air this thing stored in her heart so long?

She had left Toronto in a deep depression, determined to get to the bottom of this riddle as quickly as possible. But it would take time. She was committed to moving this coming weekend; that was unchangeable. Without the salary increase from her new job, she couldn't afford the new apartment and to renege on the lease would mean losing her security deposit.

Besides, flesh was only flesh. To be a have-not was no great distinction. The difference between the railroad flat and the sunny apartment was so great, she couldn't bear to give it up. To leave that lumpy mattress and the food-encrusted oven which no steel wool and elbow grease could penetrate was no small thing.

Originally, Ruth Pryor had suggested a trial period of two weeks. Perhaps she would hold her to it. By that time she would have unearthed all she wanted—the seed planted so long ago blossoming with hothouse care to its inherent destiny. She could go on looking for a more suitable job on her lunch hours—one in which she could go back to being Elizabeth Guaragna. Soon the interlude as Lisa Sullivan would be erased without so much as making a dent in her alloted span of time.

At the bottom of the steps leading to the BMT line, underneath a teasing poster of *Oh, Calcutta*, a man was sprawled on a bench with the stink of urine pervading the area. Nobody paid any attention to him. Elizabeth walked quickly to the other end of the platform, carefully sidestepping cigarette butts, beer cans, spilled syrupy grape soda. She shuddered. In just a few months, she had become a diehard New Yorker, immured and immune, ready to go to the head of the class.

When she first arrived in the city, she loved the anonymity it offered, loved the fact it asked no questions, told no lies, and she had glided over the pavements aglitter with mica fragments as though they were embedded with diamonds. Millions of possibilities were hers for the price of a subway token.

At home, she had lived in spartan solitude for the first time, with the exaltation of the newly free—no sick father, no overprotective aunt, no prying neighbors. At work too, apart from Mr. Penniweather, she befriended no one. Extraordinary achievement, this isolation in the midst of shore-to-shore people, but there it was. And she reveled in it.

But now the seamier aspects of the city had gotten the upper hand. Breathtaking from afar; breath-suspending from close. Even on her last visit to the newly-expanded Metropolitan Museum, the sheer glut of it deadened the living beside the entombed.

Sodden workers filled the platform; the air was sour with the smell of wet humanity. Fortunately, the train pulled in quickly and Elizabeth was propelled by moving bodies inside. But after the doors closed resolutely, nearly decapitating a frizzed head, the train stood still. Jammed body to body, they avoided each other's expressionless faces, in accordance with ingrained subway etiquette.

Inside, black scrawls of graffiti streaked the walls, thick black strokes of rage—mindless, all-encompassing rage. Adolescent gangs vied with each other for the privilege of leaving these dubious marks of their benighted existence. "What's holding them up?" a withered old man asked. "Who the fuck knows?" came a reply.

Unable to reach a strap, Elizabeth pressed near a subway map to check that she was on the right train. A chill ran through her thin coat—the glass window was also defaced, making the map unreadable.

She recalled the time she and her father had visited the great pianist Igor Brandwein in his country house on the shores of Lake Couchiching. The smell of the lake came back, transcending that of her present surroundings, and the wild joy of being a young girl with everything ahead of her.

However, on the terrace, imposing itself like a cancer, rock music blared from two large amplifiers from the neighboring house. For a while her father and she had pretended not to hear, carefully watching a squirrel scurry back and forth across the lawn with provender for his winter cache in the maple tree. Finally, Dominic burst out: "Igor, don't they realize who you are?"

A quick play of emotions surfaced in Brandwein's once steely but now sunken blue eyes as he jabbed at the flagstone with his cane and surveyed the garden where he had carefully labeled each bush and tree with its name and its date of planting. For a while he gave no answer, but after a time said, "Every few days I go to them and ask them to turn it down. And they do so for an hour or two. Then their children come home and it's on again. But what is there to do?" He spread his hands out as if to free them from the restrictive weight of the arms, in the manner of the great exponents of the tempo *rubato*.

"They're in and I'm on my way out."

Chapter XII

The week that followed Elizabeth's entry into music management proved extraordinarily varied. On the Tuesday morning she had to go down to city hall to file certain forms that Rossiter gave her; in the evening she was asked to cover a piano recital at Alice Tully Hall by an artist who had shown interest in their management. Wednesday was apparently always set aside by Rossiter for board meetings and even though only Ruth Pryor, Isabel Nagel and she were in attendance, the meeting went on as scheduled. Thursday was earmarked for George Wentworth, which enabled Elizabeth to screen the resumes that had begun to arrive from concert executives who were either out of work or disgruntled with their present employers. On Friday, because of her experience with computers at the library, she met with a high tech consultant, for despite Virginia Lavin's preference for the old "Iron Lung," Rossiter was investigating having all this past concert history automated. Even the weekend was full of work-related activities, for she had taken an armful of audition cassettes to listen to at home since she found no time to do so at the office.

By the third week, however, the days had begun to follow a routine. From ten to eleven, Elizabeth consulted with Virginia on routine requests from officialdom regarding a new business, prepared answers to the growing list of young hopefuls, made coffee.

The fact that the artists Rossiter wanted—on whom he felt the success of this new operation hinged—no longer seemed to want him, he began to take with resolute tranquility. He had sent out a batch of personal notes to the most select of them in his heavy-handed script, saying he had started a new management and thought they would like to know. Anything less vague was precluded by his monumental pride. Each post brought some of the replies, most of them apologetic and circumlocutory, but some rather tersely vindictive. Others hadn't even bothered to answer. Occasionally he would point his gold-signeted finger and rail at "the ingrates and infidels," but mostly he behaved as though everything had somehow been preordained, and a whole system of wrinkles would radiate from the corners of his eyes as he pressed his lips together tightly.

From 11:30 a.m. to 1:00 p.m., Elizabeth would join him in his office. Over coffee, using such obsolete phrases as "old geezer, mollycoddle, mutton dressed as lamb," or, her favorite, "you could have seen the Crystal Palace but for the houses in between" (she suspected he had deliberately cultivated the usage of these idioms because of their quaintness), he would become expansive, forgetting the present and talking of the past—the musical lore of the twentieth century encompassed in a few apt nutshells: the time Heifetz had a memory slip in the Sibelius Concerto which made the front pages; the time Rossiter stocked a hotel kitchen with cumin and coriander by the pound to spice up the food for the Dancers of Bali company; the time he had heard the news of William Kapell's plane crash.

"October 29, 1953—a beautiful autumn day," he said, jabbing his fists into the pockets of his jacket. "And then his widow couldn't collect a red cent from the airlines, although everybody from Leonard Bernstein to Claude Frank testified. But tell me, how do you put a dollar and cent figure on the potential worth of a pianist like Kapell?"

Or on Dominic Guaragna, Elizabeth would have given anything to say, but she held her tongue.

Rossiter confided that sometimes he could hardly sleep for remembering and that these onslaughts, far from being cumbersome, were the only compensation given to the old against the losses of time. And then he had stopped for a moment after that, as if not quite knowing where he was and to whom he was speaking. Taking his pipe from his pocket and clutching it like an anchor, he lumbered over to the bookshelf to fill it with fresh tobacco from the canteen. "A little while later that year Cantelli, the Italian conductor, went down," he resumed, after tamping down the tobacco firmly. "For a while many artists refused to fly. The violinist Ossy Renardy was among them. Then he got killed in a car accident out west and they realized that the means of transportation meant nothing. Fate was fate."

On one occasion he talked of the time when Lincoln Center was in the planning stage. "Suddenly performing arts centers became the rage all over the land, each city vying with the next. As for New York, well, of course, the Big Apple wasn't going to be outdone by anybody. Ever notice the portraits up in the lobby of Philharmonic Hall? Not an artist among them."

"That's right," Elizabeth said, but secretly felt that what really griped him was that his picture was not among them. She watched while he lit up his pipe. "I never thought of it. One of the reasons I love going to the Green Room at Carnegie is precisely because of the pictures of the artists lined up along the stairs." What she didn't add was that she often went out of her way to go up those stairs because one of those pictures was of her father in his heyday. Amazing how vivid he still was, at any moment it seemed he might appear out of the quiet wintry day, ready to storm again, to bully—and to console.

"Me, too. But there's not a single artist at Philharmonic Hall. All corporation heads or the like. And the one piece of art is that five-ton sculpture made of gold metal sheets. That's fitting enough I suppose. Gold metal sheets about sizes up the thinking of everybody concerned with the place. Absolutely ridiculous housing all the halls in a single complex."

Elizabeth had thought he was referring to the traffic problem this centralization created but she was wrong. Rossiter began to sound off on one of his pet gripes. "Did these civic planners ever consider, " he asked through narrowed eyes, "the way the removal of the individual artistic centers impoverished the various neighborhoods in which they used to reside? The Old Met gave distinction to the garment district, now it's all frantic messengers pushing clothes racks in and out of gridlock. I finally resigned because of Philharmonic Hall. When they wouldn't put wood in the auditorium, I knew it was doomed. Acoustics was the last thing on their minds—what they wanted was splash. Jackie Kennedy at the opening and all the stops pulled out. Now, millions of dollars and several refurbishings later, the hall still can't compare with most of the old halls—let alone the great ones like, say, the Vienna *Grosser Musikvereinssaal.*"

He walked over to the window, lost in thought, and the light streaming in gave a new sharpness to his craggy head and shoulders. "I remember hearing the *Brandenburg Third* in the church of St. Nichola in Leipzig where Bach himself had played a couple of centuries earlier. I was with my wife—my second wife that is . . ."

The tea cup rattled in Elizabeth's hand and she put it down on the table.

"You throw a stone in the water and the circles keep enlarging. The purity of that sound . . ." He sat down again opposite her. "The same thing in the Royal Opera House in Dresden where Wagner started to compose the *Ring.* But you don't have to go so far afield for examples. Take Carnegie Hall. Or that wonderful hall in Troy, New York, which is now a bank, I believe. The old boys knew you needed reflecting surfaces to bounce the music back so performers could hear themselves. And to reverberate and resonate like that you need wood. Something organic, something that can swell and contract, something real, not plastic and styrofoam. But they wouldn't listen."

"It's one of those things I've never been able to understand," Elizabeth said. "They study the old *Strads* and *Guarneri* to make violins today. Why don't they study and copy the old halls?"

"Good point. But, as you know, they still haven't been able to recreate the elements of those instruments. With buildings, of course, it's different. It would never do today. The old halls would never pass modern building codes. And we no longer have the time for that kind of workmanship. Everything today is condemned to obsolescence, including, my dear, old concert managers."

Sometimes, as Rossiter spun from one story to the next, she had a vision of him as a battered old kiosk with thousands of concert posters slapped over him—a career enfolded in each of them, peel one off and there would be another—pianists, violinists, sopranos, baritones, conductors; gummed deep down, torn and frayed beyond redemption, was a poster of Dominic Guaragna.

But, however resentful she might be at this forced fraternization with the enemy—and hungry too, for sometimes he kept her right through her lunch hour—there was no doubt her curiosity had established a kind of complicity between his need to tell and hers to hear. Who knew when the clue or the insight would appear that would take her to the other side of her life?

She could see similar effects on George Wentworth, albeit for different reasons. He confided to her one day that in writing Rossiter's biography, he felt a partner to another existence, a past which not only seemed more real than his own, but provided some insulation from some of the more gruesome aspects of the present. "Living in an age where people don't even have the courage of their *lack* of convictions, he's a refreshing change." Although she had itched to disabuse him of some of his more rose-tinted illusions, she didn't reply.

Still, whatever Rossiter did or had done to others, with her he played the gentleman of the old school to the hilt, ascertaining her comfort in small things, like buying a hoard of different herb teas for her use. "What's it today—chamomile or lemon verbena?" he would ask, sniffing the air, enjoying the little game, she thought, far more than the situation warranted. Occasionally they listened to sample audition tapes together, particularly when she brought one in that she had already listened to at home that seemed worth hearing, and the two of them sat, he with eyes closed listening to the intermingled sounds of Beethoven and the faint clattering typewriter keys from the outer office, she watching the smoke of his pipe curling around him in the thin rays of the December sun. Often she came across him asleep in his chair, head resting on the side, hands out with curled fingers, as if waiting for absolution.

He told her she brought a sense of peace with her; her "nos" were a welcome relief to being "yessed to death."

A sense of peace? He had to be kidding. And then she would find one of her increasingly frequent headaches coming on. Not only was she unable to share this "peace;" at no time could she let herself forget this was the man who sent both her mother and father to an early grave.

"I guess the best source on Yuri Galliuillin would be in Grove's," Elizabeth said to George. He was sitting in her usual chair, with a speckled spiral notebook on his lap, and the tape recorder placed between himself and Rossiter. She had come into the office to bring some letters for the old man's signature, during one of their increasingly frequent conferences. Occasionally her librarian skills were, as on this occasion, solicited. "I just remembered there was a Russian biography of him that came out a few years ago that's been translated. The writer was Stepanovich and I believe the translation was done by . . . a British writer. I think his name was Hughes but I'm not sure. In any case, it's in the Lincoln Center Library. Ask for Mr. Penniweather, he'll get it for you. He's a walking musical encyclopedia. And he'll tell you a lot about anything else you want to know besides. Somewhere along the way mention Pergolesi to him—that's his favorite composer—and he'll be your friend for life."

"Can I mention your name too?" he asked. "Here, let me help you," he added, a trifle startled, as she made a movement with her arms and scattered the file of letters over the floor.

As they both bent over to pick up the letters, their fingers collided. Noting the tight lines around his piercing green eyes, she suspected his question was neither as casual or innocent as he took pains to suggest. Was he leading her into a journalistic trap? Or was she being over-paranoid again? She didn't think so. At all times he was a reporter, sitting back and making assessments, hearing not only the said but the unsaid. She placed the letters on the table next to Rossiter. Rossiter felt in his jacket pocket. "I must have left my pen at home," he said.

"Here, use mine," George said, handing him her father's *Parker 51* with a flourish. In the lamplight the blue veins in George's right hand were knotted and steely.

But no more so than Elizabeth's stomach.

A cloud of fear hovered over Elizabeth as she took the file of letters from Rossiter and departed the office. First there was the slip about Penniweather; then her paralysis at the sight of that pen.

Although on an easier footing with George Wentworth, it didn't take much to make her stumble and send her sprawling. His job was to pry; hers to prevent him. It was hard enough avoiding potholes but this was a chasm. It reminded her of that time she hid behind the furnace in the cellar when she broke Tom's globe of the world. Closer and closer came the sound of his footsteps, but just before discovery, the footsteps reversed and went back up the stairs.

She glanced at the clock. It was past six and both Ruth and Virginia

had already left for the day. In hopes of clearing out in record time before George emerged, she hastily ran the letters through the mailing
machine.

But she was not fast enough. As she covered the typewriter and locked
her desk drawer, he came into her office to return some old records she
had loaned him from Rossiter's archives. "What's this—half time?"

She did not reply but took the records and filed them alphabeti-
cally. He stood by silently and only moved when she took her jacket
out of the clothes closet. "Don't you ever smile?" he asked as he held
it for her.

"Do you ever not?"

He didn't then, but laughed instead. "It's just that I'm worried
about all that beautiful apparatus going to waste."

The zipper caught the material of her loden jacket; she jerked it
back to release it. "You worry about your apparatus and I'll worry
about mine."

"That's just it—I *am* worried about my apparatus . . ."

With purse and letters in hand, she lifted her expressionless face toward the door. "I'm sorry, but I'm not good at this kind of New York
small talk."

His sandy hair fell loose over his temples. "Okay, fair enough, how
about big talk?"

"Look, George, I don't know what you want. But if it's inside information about Mr. Rossiter or this place, don't expect to get it from me."

"Is that what you think?"

She twisted a corner of an envelope between her fingers. "I don't
know what to think." She could feel his consciousness of her, as palpable as the sleety rain spattering the dark window pane beyond his
head. She spoke suddenly in a different tone, almost inaudible. "All I
can say is I don't believe in starting anything I've no intention of . . ."

The words had bubbled up almost by themselves.

In the silence that fell between them, the sentence completed itself. George's face crimsoned, then paled. "Ruth was right, you are a snippet."

For a moment she felt a twinge, but only for a moment, as she turned abruptly to sidestep him without so much as a backward flicker. Score one for the proles, she thought, his unflappability had finally flapped.

Had he been more mindful of her sensibilities—as it seemed to her she had made perfectly clear—it needn't have come to this.

"Do you also think I'm too snippety?" Elizabeth asked Virginia whom she met at the bus stop.

"Aha, Ruth's been at it again, I see. Not snippety," Virginia said, "cantankerous perhaps, just a little eccentric, maybe. You're not much like your contemporaries, I must say."

"I should have thought that was an asset."

Virginia smiled. "It is, believe me. Still, it's more than that. You're like a being apart, somebody who has to be *explained*—except we don't have any explanations handy."

Elizabeth stepped from the curb staring up 57th Street but not a bus was in sight. "Then they'll come in a convoy, just wait." She stepped back on the sidewalk. "I guess a 'being apart' is your polite way of saying I'm awkward. To sophisticates like you and Ruth, my awkwardness must seem nothing less than a deformity."

"I wouldn't put it that way. But you've got to remember we're used to the vision of the *prima donna assoluta*, bejewelled and begowned . . ."

"With any lack or slack modified by nose bobs, wax jobs and Anderson's Theatrical Makeup gobs."

Virginia laughed. "A poet no less. But A.R. likes your work. That much is clear."

"It's not my work. It's my sympathetic ear—I've no illusions on that score—or what he thinks is my sympathetic ear. If he knew what I really thought, I'd be out on that very same appendage the next day."

"You're much more sympathetic than you admit."

"Sympathetic? Bull shit." She paused, searching in her change purse for her bus fare. "Well, maybe you're right. Who wouldn't be sympathetic with the spectacle of this deposed emperor with no clothes—and nobody even to notice their omission?"

As predicted, a convoy of buses appeared and they boarded one of the empty ones and sat down. Virginia braced herself against the seat in front as the bus stopped short in front of the Rossiter Building where Eagle Management was ensconced. "They notice the omission up at Eagle there all right. That not a single big-time artist wants to switch management to him has them chortling to the skies. Who would have *thunk*?"

Elizabeth looked full face out the window as the bus lurched forward. The image of herself as the avenging Guaragna angel—was it that?—had become ludicrous. Fate was fate, Rossiter always said, and fate had exacted a revenge far more deadly than any she could have dreamed up. And far more appropriate. She turned to Virginia. "But George Wentworth isn't chortling."

"Far from it," said Virginia. "He's genuinely saddened at the turn of events. He sincerely believes the old man has made a unique contribution to music, and, as far as he's concerned, that's what *tells*."

"I re-read his article last night, and I was surprised at how differently it struck me now from my first reading before I met Rossiter." She crossed her legs with care. "Still I think he ennobled him far more than he deserves—still regards his life in heroic terms."

The bus halted and took on more passengers. Virginia said, "As well he should. In many ways, you have to admit, he has been heroic."

"With clay feet."

"Okay, with clay feet. Show me a hero without them. I don't think

George overdid it at all. In any case he made one fact explicit enough: it was A.R. himself who created the monster from which he now has been forced to flee."

"Yes, I suppose you're right." In this, Elizabeth thought, George differed from Aunt Ada not one iota. "But he still softened the picture—one sensed the overtones of a *King Lear* tragedy in the article—the grand old man laid low, done in by near and dear and exiled to the wilderness."

"King Lear? But where's his fatal flaw?"

The bus made the turn from 72nd Street to Riverside Drive and Elizabeth caught a glimpse of the Hudson River beating at the shore. "That George didn't make clear at all, or, what was more likely, never considered."

Chapter XIII

Standing in the wings of the stage at Philharmonic Hall, George watched the conductor urge the orchestra members to rise and join him for a bow. Instead they tapped their music stands with their bows or instruments to offer their contribution to the tumultuous applause.

It was a familiar routine, often performed without real conviction, but George, no less goose-pimpled than those around him, was certain this was one time the tribute was sincerely felt, and he said as much to the assistant manager of the orchestra who had accompanied him backstage.

Lifting his arms in a carefully studied helpless gesture, the conductor then turned to the audience and put his hand to his heart and his lips to another round of bravos, hoot calls and clapping. When the applause showed no sign of subsiding, he turned again to the orchestra and pulled the concertmaster to his feet while motioning for the rest of the orchestra to join him. This time they did, and the applause from the audience was deafening.

Joining the audience in the rhythmic applause, George said: "And no more than they deserve."

"You said it," the assistant manger said. "You could wait for a better performance of Mahler's *Fourth*, but don't hold your breath. A tricky work. It needs a conductor who appreciates its sophistication without losing sight of its child-like innocence."

"In other words, it needs a Gregory Mickiewicz."

"Not *a* Gregory Mickiewicz. *Him*. The one and only. The guys in the orchestra know it too and gave him their all."

After another two curtain calls, the maestro finally came off stage and his valet rushed to place a towel around his neck. Hovering in the background was the conductor's coterie of managers and advisers who now moved forward to accompany him and run interference in case they were needed. "George," Mickiewicz said, slapping him on the back when he spied him, "I'm so glad you're here." After wiping his face with the towel he guided him toward the elevator. "How can I apologize for not seeing you earlier? But what with jet lag and rehearsals and—" He gestured as if he wasn't sure which continent he'd just flown in from. "Come with me to my dressing room. We can talk there."

On the way to the elevator, Mickiewicz affected not to notice the various musicians and hangers-on who had placed themselves strategically on his path. Not that they would initiate anything for, despite the maestro's air of bonhomie, word was out that nobody was to greet him unless he greeted them first.

But this edict had not reached the doorway to his dressing room where another group awaited him—mostly soloists with whom he had performed at one time or another who were now subtly reminding him of their existence. It was *Sensational, Grisha* and *Way to go, Grisha*, and *Fabulous, Grisha* all over the place. Careful note was taken as to which friends rated a kiss on one cheek, which on both, and which not at all. In response to some subtle queries, the maestro coughed up samples of conductorial double talk—promising the world while offering nothing specific. Inside his dressing room he was equally adept in disposing of another batch of intimates, those close enough to him to position themselves in his inner sanctum.

George was familiar with this routine too. A year earlier he had written a long piece on Mickiewicz for the *New Yorker* and as a result had joined the ranks of the five hundred of his closest friends who were permitted to call him Grisha. Even the press referred to him by his nickname, mostly lovingly, but among musicians the name had been transposed into a none too complimentary verb: to be *grishaed* was the equivalent of being *had*.

It was only after Mickiewicz greeted the well-wishers who still waited for him in the Green Room (the bottom of the backstage pecking order), sent manager, public relations representative and valet packing, showered and changed into a Chinese smoking jacket, that he finally could join George for their talk. "My dear friend," he said, sauntering to the couch where he was sitting and laying his skeletal hand on George's shoulder. "Finally, a little peace."

"Yes," said George, "but not for long." He wished he could have met the conductor at some other time for he knew it would be difficult interviewing him about somebody else when he was in a postconcert high. But his schedule was such that it was then or never. He searched for something to say about his own reaction to the concert, but nothing original would come to mind. Everything he might have said had been expressed by the long retinue earlier. Instead he settled on something about the difficulties of dealing with the backstage crowd.

"Yes, it's always like that," Mickiewicz agreed as he went to the sideboard. "But if there's anybody I know who's in the audience who doesn't come backstage, that's even more difficult for me to take. 'But let's talk about you,'"—he repeated the old joke first told about Mischa Elman—'how did *you* like my performance?'"

"I was trying to find a way to say—"

"I know, I know. I can see it on your face. You've got great musical instincts." He filled two glasses with scotch and handed one to George. "I remember you take them neat, just like me."

"I suppose your memory shouldn't surprise me, but it always does," George said, pleased at the royal treatment but enough aware of the conductor's inability to leave any listener uncharmed, on or off stage, to take it seriously.

Mickiewicz asked after his parents whom he had first met at a reception they gave for him when he guest conducted with the Cleveland Symphony.

"They're well and thriving," said George, "and will be celebrating their thirty-fifth anniversary soon."

Mickiewicz lifted his glass in a toast to them. "It's hard to believe—they look so young."

After the statutory time for chit chat had elapsed, George turned on the Record button on his tape recorder demonstratively. "As I explained on the telephone, I'm wondering if you'd share some thoughts on Alfred Rossiter."

Mickiewicz, like all interviewees, stiffened somewhat at the sight of the tape recorder. "Oh yes, of course. Incidentally, I read the piece you did on him in the *Times*. It was excellent, but . . ." He fell silent.

"But?" George prompted. "Don't spare the rod. I want to hear your objections."

"I didn't really have any. It's just that I'd have liked a bit more about the time when he juggled both the orchestras in New York and Philadelphia at the same time. That was quite a feat, you know. There were no airline shuttles in those days. Or chauffeured limousines to drive you back and forth. You know he has a magnificent library at his home. A.R. claims he read every book in the place going back and forth on the train at that time."

"I believe it. He's a regular fount of information. That's why I decided to write the biography. I just couldn't cover enough in the space of an article."

"You're right. We're talking about a many-faceted personality." The conductor whirled the drink in his glass. "But how can I be of help?"

"Well, few knew him from his earliest days as you did. Perhaps we could spend some more time on that. Were Rossiter's musical gifts recognized early?"

"Yes, it was how we met. At Worcester High we were both in the music program. I was still Greg Morgan then. And A.R. was still just plain Al then. We took to listening to any recordings we could get on my father's old Victrola. We sure would have enjoyed some of the classical programs on radio that he was to pioneer later."

"Was he a happy child?"

"Come on, now. What's happy? We're only obliged to pursue happiness—nobody ever said anything about getting there."

George smiled. "What hope is there for the rest of us if *you* say that? Anyway, tell me more about the early days."

"There's not much more to tell. We came to New York about the same time—except he was behind me because he'd been in the war. But of course, our paths diverged when he gave up performing and went in for the business end. Professionally, that is. We still remained friends and I remember the difficulties he faced at the beginning of his career."

"But wasn't it virgin territory at the time? There wasn't much doing—"

"Not as we know the business today. But there was still a music circuit. As a matter of fact, when A.R. came to the business, Hurok and Harshbarger and Harrison had everything sewn up tight. The 3H Club, he used to call it. He had to be innovative. It was touch and go all the way. The gang that now runs Eagle Concerts know nothing about that. Lightweights, these moderns. Got everything handed to them on a silver platter. It was different for Rossiter. If he didn't get a bunch of them to form a merger—that's how Eagle got started— none of them would have survived. Where would we be then?"

George looked surprised. "I didn't expect you to speak in such glowing terms about that. I remember when I did that piece on you, you were pretty bitter about managers—"

"Yes, managers in general—but not A. R. Maybe it's because I never had him as a manager. Business and pleasure don't mix. You see, I'd gone with Hurok before A.R. started. And then A.R. himself didn't want me to change. Felt that Hurok had done right by me, and if he couldn't match it, he'd have felt awful. I'm glad we just maintained the friendship and didn't let practicalities get in the way." He smiled.

"I remember once telling him not to get so hot and bothered over everything. You know how ruddy his complexion is. I was worried he'd never make old bones and die of high blood pressure before he'd had a chance to live properly. I still remember what he said as if it were yesterday. 'It's not high blood pressure. It's fury, pure and simple. It's fury from dealing with artists who think they can manage themselves and their tours better than I can.'"

"Do you agree with that?"

He shook his head. "His temper gets the better of him many a time. Steam seems to rise from his head. And when he became so powerful, he thought he knew everything. But I'll say this, he really cared about music. I remember when he first got back from the war. Music was almost a holy crusade for him. In the early days, I really appreciated what he had to tell me after my concerts. He knew whereof he spoke. Still does. I did rush my Mozart too much. His advice was sound."

"How about his business tactics?"

"Look, business is a competitive sport. A blood sport. Kill or be killed. You can't build an empire without cutting a few corners here and there. And a lot of artists *can* be infuriating. They just don't understand. Some of them think all you have to do is send out a flyer and the local managers will queue up all along 57th Street. And if you get them a date with the Kansas City Philharmonic, they want to know why not with the Chicago Symphony as well. And why not a command performance in the White House thrown in, too? They've no idea how A.R. had to coddle and nurse each prospective date. In the early days, I remember seeing him wining and dining prospective buyers at the Russian Tea Room and trying not to throw up on them when he got the bill."

Mickiewicz seemed to run down at this point, slumping in his seat, obliging George to employ some tactful prodding. "So essentially you agree with him?"

"Well, maybe not at the beginning. I knew what the artists had to go through, too. And though he did too, he had so many of them, he was bound to take them a bit for granted. Every one of them is a pearl cast from the sea, but who can retain that vision in the face of their unceasing demands? The power is in the artist—not the manager. He can only service what the artist initiates. Artists need talent and drive, without drive—forget it."

Mindful that the maestro's time was limited, George veered him back on the main track. "How about A.R.'s personal life?"

"I didn't know he had any. Always worked his butt off from what I could see. I knew Phyllis from our high school days—oh, yes," he paused and shut his eyes for a moment, lost in thought. "How could I have forgotten? There was Elizabeth Guaragna." He pronounced the name in a holy hush.

"Did you know her ex-husband Dominic?"

"Yes, he played with me once with the London Philharmonic. Wonderful artist—and with . . . It's hard to describe. I guess you would call it relentless passion. We did the *Emperor* together. I was wrung out by the end of it. That was before Elizabeth left him. I never forgot that performance."

"What happened to him?"

"He returned to Italy after—" He paused and took another drink. "I lost track of him. Was busy building my own orchestra at the time. I do remember wanting to engage him and asking my manager to contact Eagle for him but they said his schedule was filled. Next time we tried they said he was no longer under their management. After they dropped him, I gave up. Never saw him mentioned again. Out of sight, out of mind."

"How come?"

"Who knows? There always's the latest hotshot to contend with, and if you're not re-engaged, there are five others waiting in the wings to take your place."

"Isn't it unusual for an artist of such talent to just drop out of sight?"

"Not always. Some of them are just a flash in the pan—a seven day wonder."

"Was Guaragna a flash in the pan?"

"No, he wasn't. As I said, I've never forgotten my performance with him. The man . . . embodied the *Emperor*." He gazed past George at the lights over the mirror on the opposite wall. "You know something," he said in a stronger voice, "I just thought of something. I did see him once again. It was at the Information Counter at Grand Central. It was a few years after we'd played together—had to be in the mid-fifties, somewhere in that time frame. He was dressed in black and pounded on the counter for some attention."

"Did you speak to him?"

"No, I didn't. You, see, I couldn't really offer him anything at that particular time. I was between orchestras. Besides, when artists look that bitter and hungry—well—"

George toyed with his glass. "I can well imagine a man being bitter and hungry if his talent was all you said it was and all the doors of managers and conductors banged shut. Small wonder he banged on counters in return. But surely Rossiter didn't—"

Mickiewicz shrugged. "I never said he did. I never heard him bad-mouth him. Never. Despite all that happened. But word gets about when an artist gets too controversial. The music business is damn difficult under the best of circumstances. If there's a breath of scandal, nobody wants to take risks. Especially in those blacklisting days."

George looked at his notes and checked his watch. His allotted half hour was nearly up but he couldn't leave before finding out more.

"How about Elizabeth Guaragna and Rossiter? Did you ever see them together?"

"Yes, only once. We had lunch at Patsy's. On a Friday as usual. On Fridays they have their pot roast special and I never miss it when I'm in town. It's a ritual for both A.R. and me. She was—how can I describe it? Beautiful, but beautiful women are a dime a dozen. She had something different—a kind of . . . incandescence. Still, she was not quite with us that day. A.R. and I had a lot of catching up to do and I guess she was somewhat bored. The reason I remember that is . . ." He laughed and shook his head. "You see, whenever she wasn't eating, she kept peeling off the red nail polish from her nails. Covertly, but I saw her doing it. By the time the lunch was over, she'd picked all her nails clean."

George gave a low whistle. "But I thought they were so much in love."

"I'm not saying they weren't. Certainly he was. Absolutely gaga. Who knows? Maybe she was having a bad day. Maybe they'd had a fight. It doesn't mean they weren't in love. Whatever that is. Love! Everybody talks about it but nobody can really describe it."

"Mahler just did . . ."

Mickiewicz laughed. "Well, he had his Alma. And Rossiter his Elizabeth."

The clock on the wall chimed and their time was up. George finished his drink and got up to leave. After he turned off the tape recorder, Mickiewicz accompanied him to the backstage elevator. "I see you're as much a romantic as A.R. is."

Mickiewicz laughed. "I take that as a compliment. Yes, I am, I suppose. You have to be. In life as in music. You have to provide the wherewithal spiritually to enrich the routine of everyday life. But the young today, with their letting everything all hang out—what do they know? My God, those barbarians—they don't even know what they're missing."

George laughed. "Don't rub it in."

Chapter XIV

Ever since moving into her new apartment, Elizabeth had begun to oversleep in the morning, feeling herself in limbo between old world and new. When she finally did wake up, she had the disturbing feeling her thoughts had been continuous between sleeping and waking. New people had been added to her recurrent dream of her brother Chris and the agony of watching the receding shoreline beyond the mountainous waves of Lake Couchiching. Now large mammals with giant teeth bared floated in the waters; one had the face of Alfred Rossiter, the other of Ruth Pryor.

Having always been an early riser, she found this new affliction hard to understand. Perhaps it was just that after a year of waking to a chilly railroad flat with a rusted fire escape as the only view, the desire to luxuriate in this sunny and well-heated apartment for a few more minutes was too strong. Perhaps it was just that she was loath to begin what she called the tyranny of the hours, the long incarceration from ten to six. Or perhaps—and much more likely—the prospect of going to a job where she operated simultaneously on several treacherous levels was just too much. Every day she promised herself would be her last, and every day she put off giving notice until the next.

Moreover, the levels all leaked into each other; treading them without slippage was increasingly difficult. "Who is your next of kin?" Ruth asked her one day as she was filling out the company insurance form and Elizabeth again said the first lie that came into her head. "Tom . . . S-Sullivan," she stammered, sounding almost like him, but instead of giving the address of his monastery in Quebec, she invented one for him in Buffalo, New York.

Ruth had looked at her peculiarly. But then, Elizabeth kept reminding herself, Ruth always looked at her peculiarly. To have Elizabeth as her successor cast a retroactive pall on her past achievements and she never let her forget it. During her first two weeks on the job, a day didn't go by without Ruth coming into her office holding a letter in her hand with such momentous corrections as a "check" for "cheque" or, on one jubilant occasion, "The Corporation *for* Public Broadcasting." Or she would find a dozen pointless tasks in her garden of unearthly delights for her to do. It was Lisa do this and Lisa do that until Lisa was ready to walk out then and there.

But once their roles became more clearly defined, by tacit agreement, they began to keep out of each other's way. Elizabeth was there to accommodate Rossiter as a Jill-of-all-Trades: a listener, a secretary, a coffee dispenser, and, increasingly, an adviser in all matters musical. Ruth occupied herself with sales, contacting the many clients she had befriended in the past to secure engagements for the few artists already signed up.

They were slow in signing the artists, still hoping for a chain reaction from a superstar. One of the artists, the pianist Percy Quarles, had actually been signed because of Elizabeth. Ruth was still furious about it, and judging from the fact she hadn't booked him for a single concert, it was clear his poor unsuspecting person was now being used as their battleground. When Elizabeth confided this to Virginia one day, she drew her brows together and said: "You're probably right. Of such intramural malice are careers often made or unmade."

Elizabeth's intervention on Quarles' behalf had started innocently enough. As had become his custom, Rossiter had asked her to draft a series of letters, most of them being the usual assortment for neophytes looking to this new management as the salvation of their aspirations. Letters from established artists were still conspicuous by their absence.

Quarles' situation fell somewhere between the two categories. Elizabeth had once heard him with Aunt Ada and the two of them had left Massey Hall in that exalted state of grace which only a great musician can elicit. "He reminds me of Dom," Ada had said. "That Beethoven reminded me of Dom." No higher praise from her was possible. When the letter from him arrived saying he was fed up with his present representation, Elizabeth took it upon herself to invite him to come in to discuss his situation and future management. If Rossiter didn't agree, she had reasoned, he needn't sign the letter.

But before she could bring the letter to him, Ruth had spied it on her desk, grabbed hold of it and stomped into Rossiter's office. "I'd like to know by what authority she writes a letter like this before any of us have had a chance to discuss it?" she demanded of a startled Rossiter. "If this is allowed to go on"—she waved her arm at Elizabeth who by now was standing quietly at the door— "every Sascha, Mischa and Toscha will wind up on our doorstep—a real stampede."

Rossiter looked briefly from one to the other and then read the letter. For a moment he sat in his chair with his hands tented—a gesture barring any interruption. Although his reactions were fast enough, he liked to deliberate slowly, looking at all the complexities before making up his mind. At last, he handed the letter back to Ruth and said: "Yes, it's more or less what I told her to write. Now Quarles isn't your every Sascha, Mischa and Toscha. Not that we did so badly by *them*. He's a real artist. What were you telling me about him, Lisa?"

She dared not meet his eyes. She looked at him sitting there, in his pseudo-sitting room, surrounded by his books, his stand-up desk, his pieces of paper, his Turner seascape, and felt as she often had in her childhood, that there were things she knew just beyond the level where she could grasp them, mysterious things, not quite in her power to understand, but a knowledge with which she was born, resting somewhere in the maze of her brain's circuitry, or between the left and right auricles of her heart. "I heard him do the *Emperor* once," she said, "it reached . . . *inside*."

Rossiter gave her his wide arbitrator's smile. "Yes," he said. "I remember hearing him once too. Look, Ruth, he's worth taking on. And Lisa was right about Weisskopf. I heard his Bloch on the air the other night from Chicago. Fine, really fine. I'm glad now to have him aboard."

"But I don't want to overload on these middle-fee artists before we have the kind who can carry them along."

"We'll get them, too," he said. "But we shouldn't pass up this kind of opportunity either."

If Ruth suspected Rossiter was simply covering for Elizabeth, she was too well-schooled in office politics to give any sign of it. And although she ceased to inspect Elizabeth's letters after this, she gave the impression she was biding her time, waiting for Elizabeth to make just one false move.

Still in bed, Elizabeth sank deeper into her trusty down pillow, the one that had followed her from Toronto to Oberlin and thence to New York. Outside a reluctant December day was just slowly beginning to open up. All too soon she would have to metamorphose into Lisa Sullivan and think about getting through the day without bringing the roof down on herself. The great divide.

One false move, that was a laugh. What Ruth doesn't realize, she thought as she finally dragged out of bed with a big moan, is that *every* move she made was false.

When Elizabeth finally arrived at work, the office was in an uproar. Moreover, Ruth was already there, although she usually only came in the afternoon. At first Elizabeth thought it had something to do with her habitual lateness, but when she saw her beaming smile, she knew she was mistaken.

Isabel Nagel was also there which meant that something very important was up. She didn't have to wait long to find out what it was.

Before she even got her coat off, Ruth came out of her office to say excitedly: "Lipinsky has decided to stay with A.R. and leave Eagle. You know, Lipinsky, the violinist. I dashed over as soon as Virginia called." Her sparkling bright eyes made her look years younger. "I wanted to be here to tell A.R. myself. At least somebody hasn't forgotten who gave him his first break. Keep your fingers crossed, Lisa. This ought to have the bandwagon effect we've all been praying for."

"It can't miss," said Isabel, shaking her beautifully coiffed red hair. "I'd like to take that Polish *wunderkind* in my arms. I can't wait to get this out to the papers."

"And I want the release to go by messenger." Ruth stepped back inside her office to study what Isabel had written on a lined yellow pad. "The sooner we get this working for us the better."

So engrossed did the two of them become in this project, neither noticed that Elizabeth had not had time to respond to the news. She was especially grateful after Virginia gave her the Lipinsky letter to read which, according to what she concluded must be her untutored eye, didn't seem to merit all this excitement.

Written on hotel stationery from Dusseldorf, it was short and to the point: *Of course I'll remain with you, A.R., and let's have a drink to talk it over when I'm in New York in a few weeks.*

"Isn't it great?" Virginia asked as Elizabeth handed it back to her.

A weak smile was all Elizabeth could muster and she went to put up the coffee. Carefully she measured eight tablespoons, feeling certain more cups would be needed than usual, and filled the coffee pot with water from the miniature kitchenette in Ruth's office. The two women were so preoccupied about whether the release should include all the present roster of artists or just feature Lipinsky, that they didn't lift their heads up when she passed by them.

After plugging in the percolator, Elizabeth returned to her own office and shut the door carefully behind her. Depression enveloped her like a cloud, all the more marked in the surrounding air of jubilation. In the vacuum created by the silence from big names, she had begun to believe that perhaps, after all, by default, a new kind of management could be built, with the *medium*, not the trappings, as the message.

Lipinsky was a great violinist, it was true, but all he ever played were the old war horses, he never took risks with untried or less popular works. "What's he ever done for music," she remembered her father once asking. "He won't give a master class, he won't take a pupil, he won't give composers the time of day. When he comes to rehearsals, he makes sure the conductor plays it his way . . . or else."

Perhaps her success in convincing Rossiter about Quarles and Weisskopf had gone to her head. She had enjoyed those little triumphs, there was no doubt of it, forgetting for a while her real reason for being in that job, feeling that amidst all that was wrong, some right was being done. But now it seemed they would latch on to Lipinsky and others like him and all their efforts thereafter would be extended in this line of least resistance.

Wasn't this exactly what Rossiter claimed he was trying to get away from?

Slumping down at her desk, she picked up the Lipinsky letter to read for the fourth time. A big blot on the top showed the haste in which it was written—as did the scratchy script from an antiquated pen probably provided by the hotel. Somehow she couldn't shake the feeling they were acting precipitously. At the very least, they ought to consult with Lipinsky first before sending out this all points release. The letter didn't seem nearly as definitive to her as the others apparently viewed it. But not wanting to risk some dismissive remark, or, even worse, seem to be raining on their parade, she kept quiet about it.

Elizabeth turned to the other mail on her desk. With gusto she tore up the importunings from salesmen of everything from office furniture to computers to room deodorizers. Those from the unknowns with requests for management she would have liked to toss in the waste basket too, rather than write the artful dodges which Rossiter had indicated. Poor misguided souls: they actually believed, as George Wentworth had led them to believe, that the meek were about to inherit the concert stages. His article continued to be picked up by news services all over the world; letters had come from London, Marseilles, Caracas and now, she thought, as she split open a special delivery overseas air letter, apparently it had been printed in Norway, too.

When she saw the letter was from Helge Nielsen, the young pianist who lived in Oslo, her heart lurched. Just the night before she had listened to her cassette. Unless she was very much mistaken—and she didn't believe she was—this Helge Nielsen was a real comer, playing with the sweep and grandeur of somebody twice her thirty years.

Not quite trusting the *frisson* of delight along her nerve endings, she had played the cassette through again. But it was all there, the same fireworks in the Brahms, the same heartwrench in the Schubert.

"Your story has warmed my heart," Nielsen had written and went on to detail how she had chanced on the Wentworth article while waiting for a haircut. "Music is supposed to lift one to the higher realms. But all the emphasis on glamour and publicity distract from the music itself."

Elizabeth gnawed at a fingernail and watched the swirling rain against the windows, a damp living presence in the overheated room. Obviously Nielsen couldn't just jump over from Oslo when, and if, His Eminence got round to scheduling some auditions. She pushed back her chair and went to the window. Across the courtyard a man in an opposite window sat at a tilted drafting table peering down in great concentration.

The hell with it. She would set an audition for Nielsen herself during the time the pianist expected to be in New York. If Rossiter didn't back her on this, she would be provided with that which she had been seeking all along: a good excuse to quit.

Elizabeth had to admit she was surprised by the kind of coverage the release about Lipinsky received. First came the *Times* with the headline LIPINSKY SWITCHES over a long story, not only detailing the contents of the release, but additional information garnered from Rossiter over the telephone from his home where he was recovering from the flu.

Following the appearance of this story, they were besieged by magazine editors and television producers for interviews. The David-Goliath story always appealed, especially when the David was eighty years old, and the Goliath one of his own making. Ruth—always one to rise to occasions—had been forced to come in full time for nearly a week to handle all these requests. Virginia covered the front desk, playing favorites with information seekers in the hallowed tradition of music and theatre management receptionists, while Isabel spent her time enlarging the handouts of Rossiter's history, keeping Janet Kells, the new typist, overtime to finish them up.

From all these festivities, only Elizabeth was excluded; in Rossiter's absence, she was relegated to a secondary role. All routine jobs were left to her, while Ruth kept the more exciting projects for herself, positively aglitter in the glare of TV lights.

Not that Elizabeth minded; had she been asked to comment officially on all that was going on, she wouldn't have known what to say. Or rather, what she would have said was not exactly fit for media consumption.

Time hung heavily. Given the continued sleety weather, she couldn't make up her mind whether she was worried, or secretly hoping that Rossiter would decide not to return to the office at all.

But the following week he was back, hale and hearty, enjoying his return to the spotlight, framing his small witticisms with just the right touch of wry, seeming to grow younger before their very eyes.

All day long he was kept busy catching up, first with Ruth and Isabel, and in the afternoon with George. Elizabeth hardly saw him until she came in at the end of the day with the letters that had accumulated in his absence.

George was sitting opposite him, busy making notes in the speckled notebook he always carried, flipping back pages to study the entries. Ever since their last contretemps, he barely spoke to Elizabeth, always making sure to be occupied with something when she was on the scene. And she did the same, resenting him for further complicating this already over-complicated situation.

Rossiter examined the letters perfunctorily, hardly questioning what she had written before affixing his signature. Even the letter to Helge Nielsen elicited little response. All Elizabeth said was that she had listened to the cassette and felt they'd be making a real mistake not to give Nielsen an audition while she was in the country. Rossiter shifted in his seat to peer at her through narrowed eyes. "If you say so, my dear," he said and then scrawled his signature. "Who knows? Maybe we'll have another Paderewski on our hands. 'Let me have such music dying, And I seek no more delight,' to paraphrase Keats."

They had been discussing Paderewski, Elizabeth knew; earlier she had brought in his biography to Rossiter. "That old blacksmith—that's what George Bernard Shaw called him." He gave a hearty laugh, his silver hair dim in the failing light of the afternoon. "Claimed Old Pad mistook the piano for an anvil—or decibel count for content. Quite an operator, that man. He always gave fifty free tickets to students—even though he was selling out—on condition, well, not to put too fine a point on it, on condition they rush the platform after the performance to cheer him on and strew him with flowers. And they continued the practice until the New York Fire Department, fearing a disaster with blocked aisles, forced them to give it up."

If George was aware of Elizabeth's presence, waiting for the last two letters to be signed, he gave no indication of it. Listening was a tool of his trade and he did it well, priming his source when it began to go dry. "He knew his public relations all right," he said.

Rossiter picked up right on cue. "He invented it. And the ladies—oh, my how the ladies adored him. When he was president of Poland and ran out of money, one of his Santa Barbara inamoratas bailed the *country* out."

George leaned back in his seat and the whirr of the cassette could be heard in the silence. "Wasn't he supposed to have been a great humanitarian?"

"*Balls, picnics and parties, parties, picnics and balls,*" Rossiter cried, as he looked at each of them in turn. "Paderewski was tailor-made for America. Anybody with a foreign-sounding name could make a fortune—the more foreign-sounding the better. In fact, Americans began changing their names to meet the public demand. Like Greg Morgan, who became Gregory Mickiewicz. Like Hickenlooper, a pianist from Texas, who became the renowned Olga Samaroff. Hickenlooper was doubly damned—an American and a woman."

"Who brought over Paderewski?" George asked.

"Well, it was Steinway and Sons. Before they went into the manufacture of pianos exclusively, they had a concert management. They brought over Anton Rubinstein too. Do you remember that essay *How Ruby Played*?" George shook his head; Elizabeth did the same when Rossiter looked at her. "An illiterate wrote it, but with the same kind of eloquence that Sacco and Vanzetti had." With head thrown back in a suitable recitation pose, Rossiter was off and running: "'By jinks, it was a mixtery! He fetched up his right wing, he fetched up his left wing, he fetched up his center, he fetched up his reserves . . . The house trembled, the lights danced, the walls shuck, the sky split, the ground rocked, heavens and earth, creation, sweet potatoes, Moses, ninepences, glory, tenpenny nails, Sampson in a 'simmon tree—Bang!!'"

Rossiter was certainly in rare form; even Elizabeth laughed. *"Judd Brownin Hears Ruby Play*, I think that was called . . . *I knowed no more that evening.* Young ladies for decades memorized it in their elocution lessons. Elocution. Now that's something we could use again today. The way the young mumble, can't understand a word they're saying." He glanced at Elizabeth and poised his pen over the letter in his hand. "Present company excepted, of course."

Elizabeth was busy closing the blinds on the long windows for night had fallen, throwing in clear relief the dark lines of workers being disgorged from buildings along the street. All over New York people were hurrying at this, the most hurrying hour of a hurrying day. So fierce was the wind as it whipped around the street that the stone walls seemed to vibrate. At times like these, Elizabeth would remember that, after all, they were on an island, and just down the street the river gave way to the thudding sea.

The two men were looking at her, expecting some sort of retort, but she didn't know what to say. They had both settled in their respective chairs for a night of serious work; dinner, which she had ordered for them, would be brought later. Rossiter put down the letter to lift the coffee pot with his mottled right hand and poured himself another cup. "As a matter of fact, I keep trying to place your accent. Sounds kind of polyglot. The way you say *about*, I'd swear you were Canadian. How close to the border up there do you come from?"

"Oh, quite close," Elizabeth said quickly.

Too quickly, apparently, for George looked at her thoughtfully, as though wondering what had generated this new disturbance.

She twisted the cord of the blind round a finger and proceeded to elaborate. "We had a Canadian housekeeper when I was a child. So I guess I picked up some of her accent."

Rossiter put down his cup and bent over the two remaining letters. The wind whipped around the building again making moans, real moans, the kind peculiar to New York.

Unwinding the cord from her finger, Elizabeth noticed the red spiral welt. That does it! She must get out of here as soon as she could. What excuse had she to remain any longer? What had she discovered but an almost broken old man—now temporarily on the mend because his fortunes seemed to have taken an upturn—sitting in his wing chair sipping hot liquids all day to ease the pain of a cold heart.

The wind howled again, almost a human voice. Gathering up the sheaf of letters, she made for the door. "If there's nothing else you need, Mr. Rossiter, I'll be going now. Dinner ought to be here by seven. Otherwise," she turned to George, "I've left the phone number of *Patsy's* on my desk and you can call and get them to hustle."

Rossiter shook his head as he glanced at his watch. "You ought to have left before now. The weather's nasty. Take a cab home and charge it to petty cash."

For a moment she stood still, as if weighing the matter. If she quit, there would be no unemployment insurance. And even if he fired her, as Lisa Sullivan, dare she try to collect? "All right, thanks, Mr. Rossiter."

After all his taking, the old man deserved to be taken.

Chapter XV

The personnel director at the New York Cultural Arts office looked at Elizabeth dubiously. "Oberlin . . . York University . . . Not much working experience to speak of?"

Elizabeth shook her head. "But I've much more—" she started to say and fell silent. That she was unable to list her current job as a reference was self-evident, but because Mr. Penniweather thought she was back in Toronto, she couldn't list her job at the Lincoln Center Library either, thereby further limiting her credentials.

"We were looking for somebody with at least ten years of experience in all phases of the arts scene." The green eyes, dilated somewhat, were scanning the application in front of her carefully as if trying to find some important fact she had overlooked.

Elizabeth smiled, remembering Ruth Pryor using almost identical words. Was there a handbook somewhere on how to turn people down? The woman was continuing her explanations. "When the federal funds are allocated, we need somebody who would know just where and how the money would most judiciously be used. It just won't do. Sorry, we'll keep your name on file though, and if anything should come up . . ."

Gathering her purse and coat, Elizabeth left the oak-panelled office and went down the express elevator to the main lobby. After trudging from agency to agency, sending photocopied resumes to every prospect, however far-fetched, she felt increasingly depressed and rejected. Incredulous at first, later in a dull rage, she was ready to pursue any lead, but the jobs were not to be had. Obviously the one she had was a fluke; few were available at her old salary, let alone the new one.

She hated this whole business of job seeking. And particularly the agency people. Though they were honor bound not to use information received confidentially, she wouldn't put it past them to inquire at offices where they knew somebody was dissatisfied on the off chance that where there was employee smoke, there was employer fire. Because of her name change, she hadn't mentioned Rossiter's firm, but she had said she was working for a concert management—and there weren't that many of them if somebody wanted to check.

She consulted her watch. It was nearly two and she was still scheduled to see Emil Schultz, the *Singing Strings* conductor. The agency representative had stressed he was seeking somebody with experience in all phases of orchestral management, but from the pittance he was paying, it was clear why she had been sent to try her chances. Should she or shouldn't she? Nuts—let them fire her. At the corner she hailed a taxi and gave the address.

Emil Schultz turned out to be very different from the autocratic conductorial image she had in her mind. A short bald man, except for a tonsure of thin gray hair which seemed to extend to his sculpted goatee, he wrote background music for television commercials for a living—themes invoking the promise of eternal happiness after solving problems ranging from underarm odor to the heartbreak of psoriasis. From these earnings he managed to subsidize a chamber orchestra which gave three pop concerts a season in Carnegie Hall. "And I do the music for many shows as well," he boasted, "top rated ones too. I use mostly the studio musicians for the orchestra—they're top people, you know—the same musicians playing in the best orchestras."

Although well acquainted with the economic necessities of musicians, Elizabeth said nothing. Abstractedly she noticed the wall of expensive recording equipment across from her. Her experience— at least the experience which she was able to present to him—was a stumbling block, but he was impressed with her knowledge of music. When she told him that her father had been a concert pianist and her aunt a professor of music, he nodded his head enthusiastically as though that clinched it.

He sat there in his knife-creased woolen slacks and double breast-ed jacket and studied her. "You make a good impression when you speak. Sound as though you have the smarts necessary for this kind of operation. It's a small orchestra, but the job is a big one because it needs somebody who knows every phase of it—how to deal with the board of directors, how to handle the publicity, how to contract the musicians, how to book the hall, how to discuss programming. And how to arrange with the board to give enough pre-dinner shindigs to assure we get an audience. Because it has so many facets, I'd want you to take the American Symphony Orchestra managerial training course. They give it periodically. The top orchestral management folks in the country give the lectures, and there's one coming up in a couple of weeks. The course takes a week and I'm willing to pay for it. How does that grab you?"

A feeling of panic gripped her stomach as she groped for control of her voice. A job was being offered to her—one that would at least get her out of the Rossiter office—why was she so hesitant? Since her qualifications were so limited she suspected the only reason he could possibly want her was for her personal background: having the daughter of a concert pianist would somehow legitimize him. He played a portion of a tape made from his last concert—a medley of movie themes—and although the technical proficiency of the orches-tra was fine, the results would hardly further the cause of music. "I'd have to think about it before making up my mind," she said at last.

Her hesitation spurred him on. "Look, if it's the salary—" he be-gan, without looking at her directly, "for somebody with your back-ground, I could up the ante a couple of grand. And your summers would be your own, there's nothing to do then."

He was making it more tempting. She'd certainly like to take that managerial course—and get paid for it to boot. "Let me sleep on it," she said and made her exit as quickly as she could.

But Elizabeth found she did not have to sleep on it. By the time the taxi took her back to 57th Street she'd made up her mind. In the lobby of her office building, she went to a pay phone and called Shultz. "I'm sorry," she said, "but the job's just not for me." She then dialed the man at the employment agency.

"I don't understand you *Ms.* Guaragna, you say you're ready to take anything, but everything I offer you is no good. Here's a perfectly fine opportunity—and Schultz told me he offered to raise the salary— what more do you want?"

"I don't know," she answered lamely. "But I don't think we would have gotten on."

"Well I have nothing else to offer you at present," he said and hung up the phone abruptly.

On her lunch hour, Elizabeth continued to carefully study the want ads in the *Times* and the *Village Voice*, and to call at least one agency each day. She was sitting at her desk one day circling the possibilities, more in grim determination than plausible hope, when George walked in, put a sheaf of folders on her desk and covered them with his hand. She tried guiltily to hide the newspaper in a desk drawer but the abruptness of her gesture had a reverse effect. "Not happy here?" Their eyes met briefly then separated. "Or am I trespassing?"

"Yes, since you ask, you are."

"Maybe so. I know it's none of my business but I do care about what happens with A.R. though."

She straightened the carefully designated *In, Out, Pending* and *Filing* trays on her desk. "Because you're worried something might hold up your . . . book?"

"Now who else is to worry over that?" He smiled and then his mouth tightened. "I'd hate to see A.R. upset. I get the odor of betrayal here, and it's not very pleasant."

"Betrayal?"

"Yes, betrayal. And betrayal is betrayal, no matter how you sugar coat it. If you don't like the man—"

"Why do you say that?"

"You seem to bristle even more than usual in his company. And you've raised the act of bristling to a fine art—it's not hard to see you can't stand him."

She picked up a paper clip and twisted it open. "I wouldn't say that. I'm . . . indifferent to him."

"Come on now, get real. You're not deceiving anyone." He paused. "The person to whom another is a matter of indifference does not go red in the face at the mere mention of a name."

Elizabeth dropped the twisted paper clip on the desk. "Well, no man's a hero to his . . . gopher. Which is all I essentially am."

"From what I've seen you're much more than that." He wrinkled his forehead in a frown. "And it's obvious to anybody with half an eye that he's been darn decent to you."

"Maybe. But I don't share your opinion, let alone your mythification of the man. He said he was going to build a new kind of concert agency—but look what's happened. It's now a scale model of the old. The moment Lipinsky switched, he started the same old star syndrome all over again. The object: to get money and more money—"

"And you think money should be no object. Nice going, if you can get it. But what exactly do you mean by the star syndrome?"

"I should think that's obvious. Veneration of the few—indifference to the many. It's a common enough syndrome in every field."

"For God's sake, Lisa, cut the crap. You obviously don't operate in the real world. I don't know how you got here but you seem to have wandered in from the Victorian age or something. Of such an agency as you have in mind is"—he threw up his hands reaching for a phrase—"the kingdom of heaven made. Or some such. From what I've heard and seen around here, when you don't go off the deep end, A.R. likes your ideas and has been going along with your suggestions. He did take on Quarles and Weisskopf—and now he'll probably take on Nielsen. He told me all about it. He appreciates your sensibilities—and your dedication to music. More than you realize. Despite the way you treat him, he has nothing but good things to say about you."

"I wouldn't take that seriously. He was quite a con artist in his day. Now, well, he's a bit senile. Anybody could convince him of anything. If I were to argue the other way, he'd be equally convinced. And he likes to talk to me because he's lonely."

"Of course he's lonely—ever hear of the loneliness of the long-distance workaholic? Not only him. The whole world's one big lonely hearts club." He brushed his hair back from his forehead. "Senile, indeed. His mind can still outrace anybody. Do you know the background of the man—"

"Yes, as a matter of fact, more than you realize. But I don't see him through your tinted sunglasses. Just because he's old, doesn't make him holy. When has he ever been concerned with real human feeling? Do you know what it's like for musicians? It's not only because they need to pay the rent and feed the children. Music is their life support system. A musician needs—"

"They're not the only ones . . ."

"No, but music . . . well, music is the one art you can't fake. You can throw a piece of clay on the ground, stamp it with saw dust and next month it'll be the latest shlock show on conceptual art at the Whitney. Or you can string a few disparate words together and call it literary abstract expressionism or something. But nobody can fake music—it comes as a trust. And concert managers betray that trust, pandering to the lowest common denominator with group attractions and pared-down classics. And only pushing those that don't need it, while the others get shoved to the back of the line."

In the hush that followed her outburst, the room became still, the faint smell of new paint on the white walls worked on them like an anaesthetic.

George pushed a brass pencil container delicately with his fingers. "But there's plenty of shlock in music too. Some of the new music being written would make Beethoven grateful for being deaf. In any case, A.R. knows all that as well as you. He's a decent man and say what you will, he's put decency above success."

"Oh, sure—and mom's apple pie above caviar roulades. He and his"—she rejected *laughable*—"pathetic simplifications about life—all tied up with a yellow ribbon. Well, I, for one, am not about to nominate him for sainthood—"

"Of course he isn't a saint—I never knew a saint I liked. But I'll take misguided passion over righteous indifference any day. And he's happy about Lipinsky for good reason. Nobody wants to be nailed to the cross of unreachable goals. Do you think you can create a revolution by spouting theories? He has lots riding on this venture, not the least of which is seeing that his staff won't be let down. Yes, he does care, and that's why he's reluctant to sign artists unless he feels he can do right by them. Moreover, he signed the ones up on your say-so because he agreed with you. But Lipinsky, well, you saw the papers. No manager in his right mind can ignore that kind of thing."

They were interrupted by Ruth Pryor who wanted to ask Elizabeth about the audition set for Helge Nielsen. Elizabeth hadn't yet told her about it, but when she explained that Nielsen was only going to be in the city for a limited time, Ruth agreed the opportunity should not be lost.

The contrast in her attitude from what it had been a few weeks earlier was very pronounced. If not exactly mellowed, it was decidedly less hostile. Elizabeth didn't know exactly what wrought the change, whether it was her work, Rossiter's approval of her, or the fact that Lipinsky's coming made prior resentments fall by the wayside.

During their exchange, George had left the office but as soon as Ruth departed, he returned, resolutely taking up his position again across the desk.

Elizabeth didn't want to talk any further. There were four letters waiting to be drafted, three telephone calls from artists to return. She was short of sleep and annoyed with him and herself.

"I'm sorry, Lisa," he said doggedly, "I know you're busy, but I feel you're making a big mistake about A.R. Maybe you'd rather be working among younger people—"

"Not at all!" Her face reddened. Was he prying again? Didn't he ever let his journalistic antennae down? "If there's anything I like about the people here, it's their age, their experience."

"If you feel that way, I don't see why you would want to hurt such a—"

"Hurt *him*? That's a laugh. He'd replace me soon enough. Only his pride would be injured, if even that. You should have seen the roomful of applicants who were here when I applied for this job. Obviously we don't see eye to eye about him. You ought to hear others on the subject. Don't forget you're getting your material from one source."

"What makes you think I haven't consulted others? I've spoken to a number of artists—"

"I don't only mean artists." She squeezed her eyes shut for a moment. "How about the women?"

From the outer office a ringing phone could be heard, like a long wail. George studied her as he scratched his chin. When he spoke, he did not raise his voice, but it held a suffused, restrained quality. "Aha.

Another indictment of male chauvinist pigs, is it?"

"Not at all. But, well, rumor has it—"

"Rumor has it! Give me a break! Rumor be damned. I know his reputation. And I have interviewed some of them. Hogwash, most of what I hear. You should hear how he talks about his . . ." As if further arguments were futile, he pressed his hands to the side of his head, and turned to leave.

Underneath her sweater the locket rested between her breasts.

"Wait," she said. "His . . . what?"

"His second wife Elizabeth, that's who. The love of his life."

She picked up the sheaf of papers on her desk and put it down again. The interval of silence lengthened. "But she was barely cold in her . . . grave . . . before he m-married again . . ." Tom seemed to have taken hold of her tongue.

"Says who? The gossips around here really must have been having a field day. How judgmental the young can be—and callous."

"You're not exactly Methusaleh. Don't forget, as I said before, it's still from his point of view. The women he . . . The women he *buried* should be given equal time but they—"

"I wish Elizabeth were around to prove how shallow *you* are. In any case, contrary to what you think, she comes through very well in what he has to say."

"But how about the children she left behind? You call me callous— what kind of love could ignore all the other lives?"

His eyebrows lifted and he stared at her. "But you're forgetting the custody battle."

Outside it had begun to hail. He's kidding, she thought. It's another of his tricks. In a barely audible voice she repeated: "The custody battle?"

George shifted his position and threw back his head. "Since you claim to know so much about him, don't tell me you've never heard about that. A little knowledge in the hands of the know-littles is a dangerous combination."

He had finally entrapped her. Yet he wasn't gloating but looking at her with concern. He was still speaking but she hardly heard him.

". . . as a matter of fact," he was saying, "I've just finished a chapter about that which would do you a lot of good to read. Might open your eyes a bit. That is if you want to—"

"Yes, I would . . . thank you."

"I'll bring it in with me tomorrow."

Chapter XVI

For two days the chapter of George's book lay unread in her apartment. How could *he* possibly tell her anything she didn't already know? Oh dates, places, names of the supporting cast, everything checked, double-checked and libel-proof in true investigative reportage fashion—all that, yes. Head knowledge, in other words, not gut knowledge.

But the manila rectangle, lying on her coffee table, would not let her be. All weekend it kept staring at her, daring her, mocking her. *A little knowledge in the hands of the know-littles is a dangerous combination.*

Wherever she went in the apartment, the envelope intruded. And what was she doing in that apartment anyway, where the walls were too clean, the furniture she was still paying off too comfortable, the slipcovers and drapes she recently made so cloying an affront? Meant as a refuge, the apartment was now a prison. For these paltry comforts the price had become too damn high.

Finally, late Saturday night, still in an agony of indecision—torn between curiosity and a nervous breakdown—she switched on the lamp next to the couch and slowly drew the manuscript from the manila envelope. Typed double space on high grade bond, with small corrections in George's firm hand in red ink, the sheaf of crisp but somewhat smudgy pages nevertheless had an air of authority and finality about them. For a moment, she stared at it blankly, thinking of Tom, of Chris, of her bereaved Aunt Ada, of her inconsolable father, of her runaway mother, of whether she had enough milk for her cereal the next morning and if this were not so, whether she could switch to eggs and toast.

At the same time, she was considering not reading the thing—pretending she had, and continuing on in negotiable, if not blissful, ignorance.

But that wouldn't do.

Turning away from the manuscript, her eye settled on the accusing picture of the silver-framed Guaragnas on her dresser: Aunt Ada, Tom and Chris standing ram-rod straight, while she nestled in the crook of papa's accommodating leg, under the flowering hawthorn at the Lake Couchiching cottage.

Sometimes, when she used to watch her father play on stage, her eyes would lose focus, and there seemed to be two, or three of him before her, not with two arms flailing away, but four or six. And the sounds she heard did not seem to be coming from one man, but at least three, three giants in unison pounding on the keys, filling every last crevice of her skull with interwoven sonorities, while she rocked back and forth in transcendent time. She would stay unfocussed deliberately until the melodies swelled to the thunderous climax when she would be the first to jump to her feet, clapping and shouting at the base of her throat.

Now, in the same way, she saw, not one, but three pictures on her dresser, a whole army of Guaragnas staring back at her accusingly under the spreading hawthorns.

Pulling her eyes away, she focussed on the words before her. Beyond the initial blur, there they were, each pica letter in fresh-ribboned black following the other to form words, sentences, transitional phrases—seamless, flowing, uncompromising.

And for her, in the end, stupefying.

Afterwards, she had lain back on the couch and stared at the telltale circle on the ceiling where the hole from a fixture had once been plastered over.

Reading for her had always been a secondary love—music came first, its immediacy conveyed from composer to performer to listener making words obsolete. But every now and then, a writer could make her feel he or she was speaking to her heart to heart, and the words became music. "And then my heart with pleasure fills and dances with the daffodils." Like when she first read *Heidi* or *The Little Lame Prince* as a child, or *Pride and Prejudice* and *Jane Eyre* as a teenager, or *The Golden Notebook* and *Middlemarch* in college.

And now, like her reading of the chapter *Less is More* by George Wentworth.

As though cast from some blazing refining oven, each word, solid and prismatic and red hot, imprinted itself permanently in her memory singeing the hair on the back of her neck in the process.

Whatever she had expected to find on the neatly typewritten pages, it certainly wasn't this. That her mother was just one of a long line of Rossiter victims, as in her puritan provincialism she had so long supposed, and so long nursed in cherished resentment, simply wasn't true.

> Maybe it was a trick of the spider-web lighting, maybe it was a bit of black magic, maybe Elizabeth herself had come floating in on gossamer wings, but something extraordinary seemed to happen when Rossiter spoke of her. Instead of seeing the white-haired octogenarian sitting in his carved mahogany chair, I saw instead the young swain, dark, gleaming, a look of confidence and intelligence radiating from his deep set eyes. "When she died, it was my own life dying in my arms. Divine madness, they call that sort of thing. But it was a divine sanity—a sanity supreme."

No, if anything came through in this voluminous vindication, it was that Rossiter had been the victim, victim of a passion which would thereafter make everything else seem lifeless and dull.

She had, to put it mildly, been wrong. From the beginning, she had got it all wrong.

As Elizabeth trudged along a cliff path near the George Washington Bridge, a light snow began to fall. Across the river rose the mighty abodes of the cliff dwellers while down below big chunks of ice shifted patterns on the grey waters. From the distance there was a smell of fire, as if someone wished to warm themselves, however illegally.

The path rose higher skirting the cliff edge and Elizabeth trudged on, unaware of the thickening clouds over the Palisades, the image of the scattered pages on her coffee table before her eyes.

She would have to leave her job now—she had no excuse to linger any longer. Nothing was worth the discomfort this deception had wrought in her life.

Her tingling fingers felt swollen in the woolen gloves and she rubbed her hands together vigorously. When she'd started to read the manuscript, she'd still had a somewhat clear head but the more she read—the more George tugged at her heartstrings in ways he couldn't dream—all objectivity fled. *All right*, she cautioned herself, *take it easy now, get a grip, remember whence it came.*

This was scarcely her first exposure to George's over-romanticizing. Furthermore—a double whammy—that of Rossiter's as well. Unlike the concise and informed manner with which he usually fashioned his prose to suit the editorial specifications of the *Times*, here George had taken a subordinate role, was the camera's eyes and the typewriter's keys so to speak, letting Rossiter's unmistakable words come through on their own, bringing him to life, she had to admit, in a way nothing else could. An Edwardian diamond in the atomic-age rough. And, by extension, bringing her mother to life, her distant, disembodied, callous mother no longer, but a strong and vital woman whose impact on Rossiter never diminished.

They had arranged to meet one day at the 42nd Street library near the stone lion at the right side of the entrance. Always he would remember seeing her honey-colored hair haloed by sunlight as he sprinted up the stairs toward her two at a time. *You know the joke about those lions—that they'll laugh when a Virgin approaches and so far they've never laughed? Well, they laughed that day and I never go by that corner without looking at those lions and remembering that time.*

The snow fell with great steadiness and now hung on Elizabeth's hair and swirled in ghostly patterns over the brambles and headland. She ought to have worn a hat but, after re-reading the chapter, she had run out of the house like a madwoman. Clouds of steam pumped from her mouth and out of dripping nostrils. She bent into the snow unthinkingly, then swerved suddenly, to avoid crashing into another wind-whipped walker. Against the eerie silence, Rossiter's vivid outpouring kept noisily revolving in her head. What a realm those two inhabited, breathing the air of a bygone time, listening to Bach's *Flute Sonata* while the rest of the country was rocking round the clock to an electric guitar. *"Oh, if you could have only seen her as she raised the flute to her lips . . ."*

Elizabeth could imagine him saying it all, every word of it, with heavenward gesticulations of his thick eyebrows, pointing fingers of his mottled hands, gruff voice expostulating, shouting, then sinking to a mere whisper as tears came to his eyes.

And she could imagine an equally impassioned George listening to it all with bated recorder, afraid to monkey with the spinning tape and stop the flow.

Rossiter was aware of how people viewed the whole thing. "'There goes Rossiter again', they said. 'The eternal romantic, passing off lust for love, mutton for lamb.' But I can tell you I know the difference between tricks of desire and the real thing. Being with her was like—well, like moving into a new key in music. All my perceptions changed.

"During those years I was never for a moment without her in a corner of my consciousness—thinking of her playing the flute, walking in the garden, asleep in her bed. And incidentally, she was a superb flutist, she modulated as though the instrument were a human voice. Those were the days before flutists played full recitals or she could have had a big career, not been forced to sit and hide her light in an orchestra."

For a moment the snow came down so heavily it obscured the path and Elizabeth put gloved hands up to massage her frigid ears. Earlier, seagulls had clamored as they circled skyward but now they were mute. With no sense of direction, she was momentarily disoriented but, surprisingly, as she lifted her head to the obliterated sky, she was aware of a total absence of fear.

Like moving into a new key in music . . . Not unlike what she felt today. She thought of her delight the first time she realized how the second theme in the first movement of the *Emperor* suddenly moved from F-flat major to B-flat, stirring up longings which at the time she could not yet name. Or even could now. One grew up, running tall through open fields harum scarum, full of visions of impossible joys.

Snowflakes coated her eyes but when she dropped her head she saw the path and threaded her way. In response to some tough questioning, Rossiter had admitted the experience was not the same for his wife. She had been brought up in a strait-laced Puritan family, had a husband and three children. The obstacles seemed insurmountable.

For a long time after they met, they barely touched each other, protracting their innocence and enabling them to escape temporarily the terrible burden of guilt. "I know it's a cliché, but after a time the whole thing was really bigger than the both of us. And when she lost custody of the children, sad as it was—we nonetheless felt as though this was the price we had to pay for our . . . I was going to say happiness but it was something too ephemeral to be called that."

Suddenly Elizabeth realized she was teetering on the edge of a wide gap and did not know where to go. The silence was total. She laughed out loud; a faint echo carried on the wind. The last time she had come here, in early spring, guide book in hand, she walked clear across the bridge, as minute as an insect against the giant girders. And the two-tiered stream of cars seemed like colonies of vehicular ants juxtaposed against that immensity of steel. But now the entire structure was veiled and she could barely see in front of her. A dislodged stone frightened a flock of pigeons which rose with a loud flutter and disappeared over a promontory of rock.

This was how it was to become blind, to sense everything by feel, by sound, except it would not be a whiteout but a blackout you lived in. It would take all the conviction you could muster to imagine you existed. Just as it had always taken all the conviction she could muster to imagine her mother existed, the phantom lady whirling in the summer garden.

Rossiter and Wentworth—what did they know? Sitting there day after day, staring, glaring at each other, they created these lovers between them, shadows really, no substance, no flesh and blood, no *allegro con brio*—electronic sounds on a tape recorder fed into a typewriter with the deadly printout landing in a manila envelope on her coffee table. She stood quite still until the snow became lighter and the path visible again.

Not surprisingly, the part that most interested Elizabeth had to do with her mother's relationship with her past family. For a long time after George asked whether she saw the children again, Rossiter had sat very still in his chair. Finally he rose and went to the window. "No, never again. Guaragna had flown to Italy with them after the trial and vowed she'd never use her evil influence on them again. *Her* evil influence! She should've known from the start she never had a chance of gaining custody, but she had a kind of innocence that was peculiarly her own.

"Guaragna had blackmailed her into giving up the children in order to get the divorce. And then he had his Weisenheimer Italian lawyer at the custody battle—and worse luck, we had Judge Nebula, also Italian. We were up against a judicial Mafia—everybody was Catholic—and they didn't want the children lost to Protestant infidels. 'You can't have your cake and eat it too, Mrs. Rossiter.' Imagine the gall of Nebula saying that to a woman who until then had been immune from the corruption of the world."

And then he had gone on to describe how the children had been spirited out of the country. "She never did get to see them again. And she never spoke of it. A bargain had been made as the judge rammed his gavel down our throats and she didn't argue about the terms. I wanted to appeal to a higher court, but she was afraid of the effect it would have on the children. After they fled to Italy, she didn't feel we could ever find them again. The only time she ever spoke of her loss was at the end. To each child she wished to send a keepsake. For the boys there were inscribed watches, for the girl there was a locket . . . a gold locket in which she had placed some of the child's baby hair. 'It belonged to my mother,' she said, 'and I want Elizabeth to know it belonged to her mother, too.'"

Suddenly the iridescent sweep of girders reared out of the thinning snow. The bridge base was still shrouded in white but the graceful half circles seemed to hang in space, gleaming motionlessly over the ice-blocked river. Elizabeth felt a sudden surge of freedom eddying in the air, carrying her, suspending her in space, the oxygen she breathed deeply into her lungs was enough to propel her to the outer reaches of the universe.

With the bridge as her guide, Elizabeth regained her sense of direction and began reluctantly to move downhill, using a branch for support. The Little Red Lighthouse was faintly visible. It now occurred to her why they came to live in Canada only after her mother died. And why her father brought them to Lake Couchiching as soon as school terms ended.

No wonder he could never live in any kind of peace with himself.

She had always thought she knew what was brewing in that old head but now she realized she had hardly had an inkling. A man born to plumb the innermost secrets of Mozart and Beethoven . . . But she must not mistake the player for the thing played.

Too bad George couldn't go after her father's secrets with his tong and hammer overkill. Who knew his secrets? Not Tom, not Chris, not Grandma Adelina not . . .

Ada. Yes, Ada knew. She remembered the bitterness in her voice when Chris was drowned—*Now don't blame that on her too.* From the sound of that she must have forgiven her mother—it was Rossiter she had never forgiven.

Elizabeth felt the first stirrings of pity for him. But that was ridiculous. After all, she was reading *his* concept of the whole affair, dipped in moonlight and roses with George's worshipful pen.

What she needed was a little Guaragna *verismo.* Or, at the least, a more objective view. Ruth Pryor? No, she might be more objective about Rossiter, but however she felt about her mother, she would hate anybody who made the precious company take a back seat. Virginia? She would romanticize just like George.

She climbed the hill back to the street slowly, feeling somehow she should be somewhere else; just beyond the blur of white, as in dreams where the place one is trying to reach stubbornly remains unreachable.

Chapter XVII

After standing twenty minutes on the wrong subway platform, taking the wrong train, doubling back, Elizabeth started over again. The IND local to 42nd Street, the subway guard told her, then the IRT crosstown shuttle. This time she carefully followed directions. Finally she arrived.

Her determination not to look at the right stone lion in front of the Forty-Second Street Library didn't do her any good. In her mind's eye, a figure stood there, *haloed by sunlight*, with Rossiter sprinting up the stairs two at a time to come to its side. But then was then and now was now and ne'er could this twain ever meet. She walked determinedly on.

To get the press stories of the custody trial was fairly easy. Taking the heavy 1952 volume of the *New York Times Index* from the bookshelf, within minutes she found the listings cross-indexed under the names of both her mother and her father. Quickly she jotted down pertinent dates and headlines: *Elizabeth Rossiter, Wife of Music Magnate, Sues Dominic Guaragna Over Three Children, Apr. 19/39:2; Dominic Guaragna Seeks Dismissal of Child Custody Suit, May 5/3:6; Elizabeth Rossiter Wins Trial Right, May 9/4:5.* After a series of reports while the trial was in progress came the final verdict: *Elizabeth Rossiter Loses Suit Over Three Children, June 28/5:6.*

What had not been so easy was finding the time to come to the library. Lunch hour was out; no matter what the outcome of the afternoon's expedition, Elizabeth knew she could not come back to the office to cater to Rossiter as though nothing had happened. She pretended to be ill. All she had wanted was to leave at three but when Rossiter heard she wasn't feeling well, he insisted she leave right away. At first he teased: "A stomach ache? A health food advocate like you? How could that be? Now, don't get further upset," he added as his hand reached for the telephone. "Have you a doctor? No? Maybe you should see mine."

"No, no," she said as he began to dial, "really, it's not necessary. All I need is to get some rest. I—"

From the slight flush that infused his cheeks she surmised he probably attributed her illness to what he would quaintly put as *women's troubles*. And the edge in her voice to PMS. "Well, what are you waiting for?" He dropped the receiver back on its cradle. "Be off. No point hanging around when you don't feel well."

To leave him and his paternalism behind, if only for a few hours, was a welcome relief. Her earlier departure had an additional advantage: the awkwardness of seeing George Wentworth that afternoon was avoided. New ground had definitely been established between them, but it was still shaky ground nonetheless. The chapter was no less revealing of George than it had been of Rossiter. Only a bird of similar feather could have focussed on Rossiter's romantic flights as he did. Opening the clasp of the manila envelope she inserted a memo with *I thank you very much* scrawled over her signature and attached it to his manuscript. And then, because she couldn't resist, she'd added: *Did you <u>mean</u> to capitalize 'virgin'?*

Within minutes, the reference librarian produced the cardboard containers containing the requested microfilm. Elizabeth quickly inserted the spool in the holder.

But when she began to unroll the film to attach it, her hand shook so much that the attendant, still standing nearby, came to help. "Here," she said, seating herself in Elizabeth's vacated chair, "you put it under the glass at the bottom, between the two spindles on the left, then through the spindles on the right, and then into the slot of the take-up spool."

In her previous job, Elizabeth had often instructed others in this process but now she stood docilely, allowing herself to be instructed.

The attendant turned the machine so that the printing was right side up. "What are you looking for?"

"I can find it myself, thank you," Elizabeth said quickly, as though she were doing something illegal, and waited until the woman left before reaching for the knob.

In her haste, Elizabeth whirled the film right past April 19th, but then, with a steadier hand, she found it, turned slowly to page 39, centering it on column two. Bingo! The story sprang to life:

WIFE OF MUSIC MAGNATE SUES FAMED PIANIST OVER THREE CHILDREN

A dispute between Mrs. Alfred Rossiter, wife of the board chairman of the Eagle Broadcasting Corporation and Eagle Concerts, and concert pianist Dominic Guaragna, her former husband, over custody of their three children is scheduled to be heard in State Supreme Court here tomorrow.

Under the separation agreement arranged at the time of the marriage between the music magnate and Mrs. Rossiter, the children of her first marriage to Dominic Guaragna, Thomas, 6, Christopher, 4, Elizabeth, 1, were to receive the continued benefit of the companionship and guidance of both parents with custody vested in the father. The plaintiff was divorced from the pianist in Nevada on the grounds of "grievous mental anguish" and married Rossiter shortly thereafter.

Justice Raymond A. Nebula is scheduled to preside in the custody dispute. No decision has been made by him today on whether the case would be heard in public.

When asked whether private negotiations were being carried on with a view toward an out-of-court agreement, Arthur Flint, attorney for the plaintiff, said there "was a motion relating to the care and upbringing of the children. The case did not involve a mother versus the father or the father versus the mother, but a dispute on the proper guardianship of the children."

Elizabeth reread the piece, then placed the article between the designated black lines to photocopy it. Her heart pounded like piano hammers on a sounding board. Face ashen, she twirled the film to the next article.

LAWYERS IN CUSTODY SUIT BATTLE OVER TRIAL VENUE

Arthur Flint, attorney representing Mrs. Alfred Rossiter, wife of the board chairman of the Eagle Broadcasting Corporation and Eagle Concerts, and Steve Spinelli, representing concert pianist Dominic Guaragna, her former husband, appeared in State Supreme Court to argue whether the custody suit launched by Mrs. Rossiter on behalf of the three children of her previous marriage be held in Justice Nebula's private chambers or in open court. The two principals in the case were not present at the discussion.

Mrs. Rossiter's lawyer favored private session "in the best interest of the children," with Guaragna's lawyer sharply in disagreement. When it became increasingly apparent that the proceedings would not be secret, the judge called on both lawyers to consider the problem carefully. The two lawyers wrangled openly then, each alleging "plenty of facts" to support their side and called for an immediate hearing. Mr. Flint deplored the spectacle of a

father of three standing on technical rights and said
that it "shows the kind of parent he is."

Elizabeth shivered. What *were* the "plenty of facts?" What had her
mother thought about all her dirty linen being made public? But she
must have known the risk when she sued. The next article took her by
surprise. Nowhere in Wentworth's article was the substance of it even
hinted at:

GUARAGNA FILES COUNTERSUIT
IN CUSTODY BATTLE WITH
ELIZABETH ROSSITER

Famed Italian pianist Dominic Guaragna has filed
a countersuit to retain full custody of the children
from his former marriage with Elizabeth Rossiter,
wife of Alfred Rossiter, board chairman of the Eagle Broadcasting Corporation and Eagle Concerts.
He cited the fact that a court psychiatrist had examined the two boys at the suggestion of the Supreme Court Justice. The medical examination was
conducted by Dr. Frank Celli in his New York office
and he gave the boys a "clean bill of health."

As a result of this testimony and the countersuit,
Judge Raymond Nebula ruled that the case would
go to trial the following week.

But when Elizabeth turned to the next week's story, she found that
the judge had a change of heart. Citing the effect of adverse publicity, Nebula stated that "since the case concerns the welfare of minor
children, the court rules that it should be heard in my chambers with
the press and public barred. Both sides agreed to the closed hearing.
The court, as *parens patriae* [guardian] of the children, must take into

account the health of the children being adversely affected by allegations as to which of the principals was better qualified to be a parent."

The justice further noted that the divorce judgment Mrs. Rossiter obtained in Nevada had made an equitable settlement, but she now wished to change those custody provisions so that the children would live with her and Mr. Guaragna would have visiting rights. He emphasized that though he was not bound by the Nevada judgment, prior determinations do have great weight.

As Elizabeth bent over to copy the microfilm, her forehead glistened with sweat; in the greenish light from the screen on her face, she looked bilious. She could hardly bear to turn to the next day's testimony which covered the testimony her mother had given for three hours. The testimony was secret, of course, but according to the reporter, Mrs. Rossiter maintained her usual pleasant demeanor and appeared composed after three hours on the stand.

The reporter, obviously a graduate of the *Women's Page*, even described at great length her blue linen suit—speculating as to whether it was a Balenciaga or a Chanel—"so smartly set off by the gold pendant which glinted in the sunlight as she entered the courthouse, with her husband holding her by the arm." Four people testified in her behalf including her pediatrician, a California cousin, and two former neighbors who knew the Guaragnas when they were still married.

The following day was Guaragna's turn; he also testified for three hours in his fight to keep the children. Among the witnesses testifying in his behalf was an aunt of Mrs. Rossiter. Since the press was barred from the actual hearings, all they could report were the names and addresses of the witnesses and a description of their clothing. In the absence of hard news, much seemed to be made of the fact that all the Guaragna witnesses wore strands of pearls, as if this somehow assured them of the wisdom generally associated with those precious beads.

When Elizabeth came to the final story *MRS. ROSSITER LOSES SUIT OVER CHILDREN*, she could hardly go on. Doggedly, she turned the knob forward. Just as she thought. No quarter was given her mother, no judicial fiat to lessen the savage cast of her history. The law was a law unto itself, and in this case it had aligned itself squarely on the side of vengeance and spite.

Citing the fact that it would be a mistake to separate siblings from each other, and the fact that the father had shown the court that he had succeeded very well in caring for the children, Justice Nebula saw no reason to change the original Nevada decree. Unless the court was overcome with persuasive evidence that conditions had changed, the children would remain with the father.

Since both parents were able to provide the children with security, the judge felt that Mrs. Rossiter should abide by the bargain she made when she agreed to give up the children in order to marry Alfred Rossiter. "Neither the health nor the welfare of the children is being compromised under the guardianship of the father, who has succeeded very well in his role and the children are normal, healthy and contented. Moreover, the children are being raised as Catholics and presumably this would be discontinued if they were transferred to the Rossiters, who are Protestants. The evidence adduced does not warrant a change in the custodial arrangement which both parties themselves concluded; the only focal point of controversy and concern here is whether the best interests of the children are being realized under the present situation. Of course the general principle of lodging female children of tender age with the female parent is relevant to the best interest of the one-year-old-daughter. But Mrs. Rossiter had accepted this arrangement in the separation agreement and it was confirmed in the judgment of the Nevada court. Weighing against this is the evidence which overwhelmingly establishes that all three of the children should be kept together as a unit. This is where their great strength lies and it would be a mistake of the first magnitude to separate any one of them from the others."

The reporter noted that the judge, speaking informally after the case was over had said of Mrs. Rossiter that she was trying "to welsh on the deal to which she herself had agreed."

There remained only a schedule of visitation dates—including alternate vacation periods—which the judge duly listed and then, presumably, dusted off his hands and called in the next case.

Fighting tears as she left the courtroom on her husband's arm, in a sidebar, the paper reported that Mrs. Rossiter had been besieged by reporters but was too upset to reply to their questions. Brushing them aside with a terse "no comment," her husband led her to a waiting limousine. But just before she got inside, Mrs. Rossiter turned to say that since Elizabeth was still so young, she did not feel separating her from her brothers would pose that much of a problem. Then her eyes welled up and Rossiter pulled her inside the car beside him.

Only a brief follow-up story ensued but, pictured for the first time, was a photo of the Rossiters taken in the corridor of the courthouse on her final day in court. Mrs. Rossiter had obviously been caught by surprise—her neck was strangely arched, like a flower straining toward the light.

"Oh, dear God," said Elizabeth and shut her eyes.

Even when Elizabeth was a child, imagining her mother whirling in diaphanous splendor, the face was always blank, as though an artist had sketched a picture, filled in all the peripheral details, but waited until the end to tackle the flesh and blood.

Elizabeth Rossiter was shown from the waist up, and although she held her posture erect, it was obvious she was not very tall, for she barely reached her husband's heavy shoulder. The faces contrasted sharply, the one scowling, the other luminous. The caption simply stated, "Elizabeth and Alfred Rossiter leaving the court."

Despite the stiffness of the pose, her natural grace was apparent from her finely accentuated cheek bones to the way . . . but what was that she was touching with her right hand?

So that was the *gold pendant*. Elizabeth's hand now automatically flew to her own chest to make certain it was still there.

That she was beautiful; that her hair was set in a becoming coiffure; that her linen suit—be it Balenciaga or Chanel—was probably hand-stitched—all this meant little to Elizabeth. This was her mother, not an invoked ghost, a face to fill the void she had carried through hundreds of sunlit visions.

What finally became apparent, as her eyes cleared and her mind could function once again, was how little she herself resembled this person. Where she was tall, her mother was short; where she was dark, her mother fair; where her blue eyes were large and almost almond-shaped, her mother's were wide set and, according to the *Times'* reporter, hazel.

Only Tom looked a little like her, the same unblaming, innocent eyes—perhaps Chris too, around the mouth, but Chris she also now only knew from pictures. In any case, there the likeness to her children ended. Nothing in the photograph, nothing she could see at all, remotely suggested herself.

Only after photocopying the page, making her mother's face even more ghostly, did Elizabeth read the short article it accompanied. All it did was speculate as to whether Mrs. Rossiter would appeal the case, and noted that since she had been in seclusion since the trial, she couldn't be reached for comment.

Elizabeth turned off the machine; as the monotonous hum ceased, it seemed as though life itself had ceased. For a while the whole cast and characters had been resuscitated, but now they were gone again. All around her high school and college students were desultorily gathering information for what looked like term papers. She watched them for a moment. *For God's sake, look at me, people, these aren't just dry facts I'm gathering for an examination, but my very life.*

The transformations from infancy to puberty and adulthood were nothing compared with the changes she had undergone during the past three days: from orphaned to cherished child, from not having been loved at all to having been loved and lost.

Carefully she removed the spool and retied the string. Now, finally, the event could take its place in its own sequence, no more to unremittingly haunt the landscape.

What would her life have been like if her mother had had her way? What would it have been like to have been held by her, to have had those soft eyes smiling down at her? What would it have been like raised in the Rossiter home? Would her mother still be around if that were the case?

Two years earlier, their neighbors in Toronto lost their little girl to leukemia. Although mother and father kept vigil at little Tina's bedside day and night during the protracted dying, after she died, the marriage broke up. "You see," the mother explained to Elizabeth, "he thought we'd grieved long enough and should be ready to start over. But how long does it take to get over the death of a child?"

Ada was right. Thank God her mother never lived to find out about Chris. As for Tom, well, he hadn't died but as far as her mother was concerned, he might as well have. Same went for her. No wonder her father had kept her at such a distance at all times—she must have been a constant reminder of his own . . . his own what? Take it that her mother's betrayal, not only of his person but—as he saw it—of his career as well, was enough to justify this bitter battle.

Still, what kind of man would insist on depriving a mother of *all* her children? And, on top of that, despite his own judicial triumph, further deprive her of visiting rights?

Truth, she had always thought, was inviolate, with a life of its own. For a long time after he'd died, she had sat at his bedside, held his cold hand, afraid the dropping of it would amount to yet another betrayal. She had always hoped that one day he'd explain everything rationally to her—how she had acted, how he reacted, how this occurred, how that happened—and with those explanations, she'd know at last where to direct her muddled allegiances.

But there was nothing rational about any of it. One person's truth was another's perfidy.

"Are you finished with these?" the attendant asked. "Yes." Elizabeth quickly folded the photocopies and handed her the tapes. "It's been like looking through a telescope at a time warp."

"I know—it gives me the willies sometimes. Pictures of people caught in limbo. Did you find the story you were looking for?"

"Yes, thank you." A woman in a blue linen suit with a gold pendant, a man leading her grimly to a waiting limousine, an irate Italian desperately intent on *vendetta Siciliana*. "I suppose you could call it a story. It was a court case."

The attendant smiled. "Well, I hope justice was done."

"If this is an example, God help us. People argued and fought, took oaths and pledges, juggled and manipulated and schemed. But no heroes or heroines peopled this story . . . neither did villains."

"Well, isn't that always true? Life itself is usually the villain. Is there anything else I can get for you?"

"No. Thanks. I'm done." *Undone*, she thought privately. Staring at the darkening sky through the tall windows, Elizabeth remembered her brothers on the pier at Lake Couchiching one summer day playing cards while she lay on her side watching the water move softly against the pilings. Below, bright pebbles were embedded in the sand and drifts of algae were visible at the shore; above, weightless flying creatures danced over her face. From the corner of her eye, she saw them flick the cards on the rough boards, laughing and protesting alternately at their fate. She could no longer recall anything of what they said but just this feeling of her being between them, a kind of anchor for both.

The room full of creaking noises came back, projectors being reversed, chairs scraping against the tiled floor. Judge Nebula was right; it would have been a mistake to separate them from each other.

Now that her quest was finished, once and for all she must quit her job and take herself back to Toronto to resume life as Elizabeth Guaragna. The more mileage she put between herself and Lisa Sullivan the better. Nobody in New York would really care one way or the other; to bring some joy to her aunt's life was little enough repayment for all she had done for her.

She unfolded the photocopy to study the approximation of her mother again. Already it had become hauntingly familiar. Had she seen it before? No. It couldn't be. Memory was treacherous, but she'd have remembered that. This is what it all came to, a copy of a copy of a newspaper story, a batch of benday dots.

Suddenly her stomach, which had been queasy all day, heaved. A mad dash to the ladies' room, coat and scarf flying. Kneeling at the cold white china altar, she deposited the remains of her lunch in one giant burst—avocado, tomato, cheese, sprouted wheat bread, frozen yogurt surprise and all. Some tomato residue landed on her mother's photocopied face which she still clutched in her hand. It made her look wounded.

Carefully Elizabeth brushed it away.

Chapter XVIII

"She's not here?" George asked in surprise. It was in hopes of seeing Lisa that he'd made this special appointment to see Rossiter; apparently he missed her by a few minutes.

"Was feeling under the weather," Virginia Lavin explained, watching the effect of her words with just a shade too much curiosity in her voice. "Is there anything I can help you with—"

Before he could reply she said, "Oh, I nearly forgot," and reached behind her to hand him the manila envelope. "She left this for you." She watched him carefully while he extracted and read the note.

George felt he should not be surprised by the brevity of Lisa's response to his manuscript chapter. *Thank you very much.* It was, after all, straight out of Miss Vanderbilt's Office Manual under C for Collegial Relations.

But he was surprised. Writers need to be validated by readers to justify their own existence. *Thank you very much.* He would have liked to thank Miss Topknot very much herself.

The name he privately called her suited her to a T, for the clump on the top of her head seemed to sum up her personality, where every impulse was held in tight check. "Sounds more like Miss Tight-ass to me," Margaret had said when he'd described her one day. He'd argued about that at the time, fueled by the occasional glimmer he detected of a freer soul, or, more likely, wanted to detect. But when he'd tried to voice this, Margaret had given him one of her *chacun à son gout* shrugs and the subject was closed.

"Is that what you wanted?" Virginia asked, her curiosity still set at High.

"Yes. I'm planning to revise this chapter," he tried to explain, "and I want her opinion." Virginia's disbelieving smile was not unlike that of Lisa.

He wished he hadn't come. Lisa's hostility towards Rossiter had had its effect, all right. And the hostility towards Rossiter included himself—if not the other way around. Just as he was returning the note into the envelope, he noticed the scribbled P.S. which his thumb had obscured, and did a double take. *Did you mean to capitalize 'virgin'?* It took a moment for the words to sink in. What they might or might not mean was not at all clear. Yet, what in blazes *could* they mean?

He didn't know. But that this was distinctly out of character for Miss Topknot was something he knew with absolute certainty. It surpriseed him how certain he was, or perhaps, more accurately, the writer in him was, as though all this woman's oddnesses registered themselves on his subconscious even when he wasn't actively engaged in examining them, and this oddness somehow didn't tally with the others.

"Her opinion?" asked Virginia. "Is that so?"

"Yes, that's precisely so," he said, turning away and heading in to see Rossiter.

The telephone rang just as George seated himself in his chair. Rossiter answered it warily and was soon off on a long disquisition to his wife as to why he would not be home for dinner. "I know it's not my regular night with George, but he's leaving town next week for England and we want to clean up some stuff." He shook his head at George who nodded sympathetically. "Look, I can't help it about the McCoys—you never told me they were coming."

George could well understand why Rossiter preferred to work rather than to stay at home. After his first abortive telephone interview, and a couple of others that followed, he'd been piqued with Dolores Rossiter himself. At her age, couldn't she discern the difference between her husband's biographer and a detergent market researcher with nothing more serious on his mind than ring around the collar?

Consideration, if not appreciation, was at least called for.

But as things turned out, he concluded it was probably just as well. The space he had devoted to her in the book was minuscule—reflecting Rossiter's own viewpoint on the role she plays in his life. Less is more is how he described Elizabeth's contribution implying that the reverse was true in Dolores' case. George had been careful to avoid any judgment of this nature, but he could not ignore Rossiter's own testimony about Elizabeth. Dolores' lack of cooperation turned out to be a blessing in disguise. This way, if push came to shove, when and if she read the book, she'd have to admit she'd only herself to blame.

Considering the lopsided space allocation, it was too bad Dolores and Elizabeth hadn't had reverse positions chronologically in Rossiter's marital pantheon. George had really gone to town, so to speak, about Elizabeth, and that section of the book had become his own favorite part. Which made Lisa's reaction to it all the more strange. He opened the manila envelope to ponder the implications—if implications there were—of her P.S. again. An innocent enough remark but from Miss Topknot it almost amounted to a proposition.

Now don't get your hopes up, he cautioned himself, as he noted that the handwriting of the P.S. was less stilted than the note above. It could mean nothing at all, just a hasty scribble added to the more carefully written note above, made in the midst of ringing telephones and barking commands with little thought given to it before or after.

But that wasn't like Lisa at all. Except for those times her temper seemed to get the best of her, she struck him as somebody who thought through everything she said beforehand, let alone wrote. Not that she was one to back off from a fight, the lady definitely gave as good as she got, but set pieces were what he usually got from her. Not the least of which was her still hurtful remark about not wanting to start something . . . et cetera, et cetera.

Given that unequivocal brushoff, this scribble became curiouser and curiouser. If anybody else had written it, he would have thought nothing of it. A brief observation, couched in somewhat provocative terms which he might or might not take up depending on the provocateur.

Was he making too much of it? No doubt it wasn't provocative at all, simply a throwaway line not to be taken seriously. Perhaps Lisa was just exercising her schoolmarmy editorial skills—he wouldn't put that past her.

But that didn't wash either. Even somebody as otherworldly as Lisa couldn't be that naive. It was a provocative remark, no doubt about it. He'd written her off completely but now . . . ?

Written her off? Who was he kidding? He'd wanted to, that was certain, but what with that old tingle in his loins starting up every time he came near her, it was not that easy. In this age of everybody letting everything hang out, she seemed wrapped up in protective tissue paper, to be carefully unwrapped layer by layer at some appropriate moment—if ever—by some lucky devil.

As an antidote to such musings, he'd tried the well-known cure recently of going out with other women, most of them carbon copies of Martha. If you can't have A, try B and C. The truth was, far from effecting a cure, B and C with their sleeked down clothes and spiked up heels only served to enhance the hastily pulled together plaid skirts and crumpled blouses of A. And their hard-edged sophistication only enhanced her vulnerability. He remembered that glance she gave him the other afternoon—it was extraordinarily eloquent in its sadness and came when he started to talk about—

What had brought it on? She'd been her usual combative self until that moment but suddenly—

They'd been speaking about Rossiter, that much he remembered. But then they usually did. What had triggered that sudden transformation?

Yes. It had to do with the gossip about his womanizing. When he countered with his love for Elizabeth Rossiter, he had really hit home. A home run in fact. Not only had her manner altered but even the bone structure on her face became more accentuated.

Perhaps his imagination was doing overtime. Or his so-called sixth sense. After all, people believe what they want to believe and obviously she wanted—for whatever twisted reason—to believe the worst of Rossiter. *No man's a hero to his gopher*— It could be that he was on the wrong track entirely. It had nothing to do with Rossiter's Don Juan proclivities and was only the usual boss-employee antagonism, period.

Rossiter's voice rose. "Look, Dolores, tell the McCoys whatever you want. They can go to the blazes for all I care. I know how much they've helped you. But if they're the real McCoys, it won't matter much, will it?" This last was for George's benefit and was said with a wink.

George smiled. Rossiter's good humor boded well for their session. Perhaps he could clean up the gaps today and finish with Part II. Then all that would remain would be getting to Dominic Guaragna. Another interview like the Mickiewicz one and he'd be home free.

When Rossiter finished talking to his wife, he pressed the intercom button to speak to Virginia. "Did Lisa remember to order in dinner?" he asked. "She did? Even though she was feeling so bad—"

Something jumped in George's head. *Feeling so bad,* indeed. Poor Rossiter, he was the innocent, if it came to that. So solicitous of Lisa's welfare when in all probability she'd probably faked the illness so she could get on with her job-hunting.

Chapter XIX

A week later, Elizabeth sat in semi-darkness, knees drawn up, listening to reports of a blizzard forecast, and looking at the snow piling on the window sill. She wondered whether she ought to go in to work.

But since Tony Arcaro had started the renovations on the outer office, she knew that somebody had to be there to let him in. In such weather, neither Virginia nor Ruth could be expected to show up. And commuter trains from Westchester were cancelled, which meant that Rossiter would certainly not be there.

Bundling up in a ski outfit and high boots—holdovers from her Toronto life—Elizabeth made it to the office in nearly record time. With the subterranean world still unaffected by the storm, the subway trains were largely empty.

When she reached the office, the phone was ringing. She made it to the receiver just in time to hear Tony Arcaro's apologetic voice. "They say they might have to close down the Triboro if it gets much worse—I better not come in."

"The work will keep, Tony. Enjoy your holiday."

"Don't worry, I will."

Elizabeth stood uncertainly as the line went dead and then took off her ski jacket. A stack of work awaited her; she had still not caught up after her absence at the library. As long as she was here, she might as well tackle it.

In Virginia's absence, she decided to sit in the outer office in order to cover the front desk. She had been working steadily for nearly two hours in uninterrupted silence when the door opened to admit a tall middle-aged gentleman with a long coat and fur Cossack hat.

Of course she recognized him at once. What concertgoer didn't know the shape of Rupert Henselt's oval head as it swayed in time to the baton he wielded so forcefully over Beethoven and Bruckner alike? According to many critics—and hosts of music-lovers—the midwestern orchestra under his aegis had become one of the major musical conglomerations of the world. At the same time, stories of the reign of Henseltian terror were no less abundant, provoking many a *do-the ends-really-justify-the-means* discussion in the Ohio flatlands.

As he approached her desk, she saw he was less dark than his photographs indicated, and his hair, as he took off his hat, lying away thinly from his forehead, was shot through with white. He fixed his protuberant blue eyes on her and asked. "Is Mr. Rossiter here?"

"No, I'm sorry, he won't be in today."

Although he feigned a look of disappointment, Elizabeth could see he was secretly pleased by his absence—had probably banked on it. Elizabeth bit her lip wondering what brought Rupert Henselt, of all people, into this office on a day which would even have given a Laplander pause. And then she remembered that his orchestra had given a concert at Philharmonic Hall the previous evening. This, at least, would account for his being in New York. No doubt he had been snowed in, like everybody else, leaving a day on his hands. And no doubt he left his abode at the Plaza to take what his press books proclaimed as his *famous constitutional—which neither snow nor rain could ever halt*. "Tell me, my dear,"—this with an avuncular inflection—"how are things going?"

While ostensibly looking at her, she could see those demonic eyes of his—eyes that struck dread in the hearts of two generations of musicians and which the Ohio Local of the A. F. of M. argued deserved special consideration in their workman's compensation coverage—dart slyly on the papers scattered on her desk trying to absorb everything in sight.

Oh, no you don't, Maestro, not so fast. Quickly she swept the strewn sheaf into a drawer with a click, trying all the while to make it look absent-minded, as she had a few days earlier when the press agent of Eagle Concerts had stopped by on a similar reconnaissance mission. Placing her hand over the remaining pile, she said: "Very well, sir, very well indeed."

"Yes, I read about Lipinsky. How nice for Rossiter." His manner became distracted for his attention had been caught by the piles of debris left by Tony Arcaro and his crew. "Renovations, I see . . . Are you enlarging the place?"

"Yes," Elizabeth said emphatically. This was one bit of information she could give freely. "Have to. We're taking over the adjoining offices and knocking out that far wall. We need room for the new staff."

"I see."

The new staff consisted of Janet Kells, the typist they had hired to help Virginia, but she didn't tell him that. Henselt began to walk around the room, as though inspecting the progress of the renovations, but in fact sidling over to the file cabinet on top of which sat a box with letters ready for filing. Knowing the top letter was just a routine government form, Elizabeth could hardly keep from smiling as he maneuvered his way to the file and, with a quick dart of his X-ray eyes, studied the form.

And he apparently could hardly keep a grunt from escaping his lips, as he edged gingerly around a tangle of copper casing. With a frown he turned and approached her once again. "So you have Lipinsky, how nice." The tone belied the words. His hand closed around his coat lapel and he shook his head. "But tell me, my dear, when are they going to publish their full list around here? How about pianists? Did Serkin . . . ?"

Elizabeth looked up at him blankly as though she didn't understand what he was talking about. But Henselt would not give up so easily and began a new tack. "I know these things are confidential. But, I'm a very good friend of Rossiter, so not to worry, you wouldn't be telling tales out of school." He stopped to laugh, as though what he said was terribly funny, and she was embarrassed for the old goat, preserved on LPs by the hundreds, but still playing barnyard games.

"How about conductors? I guess they must all have come with Rossiter? Right? How about Bernstein . . . Levine . . . Ozawa? Have they switched too?"

Elizabeth pushed back a strand of hair which had escaped the coil at the top of her head and looked at him with distaste. "I'm sorry, sir, but I'm just the receptionist here. I don't know about such things. And even if I did, I couldn't divulge them in any case."

His face fell. The herculean trek from the Plaza had been in vain. As he made a curt bow in her direction and turned to go, Elizabeth could not help asking sweetly: "And who should I tell Mr. Rossiter was asking after him?"

The sharp, sculptured indentation on his upper lip became sharper still as he remained in front of the door for a moment leaning on his arm. Then, without a word, he fled.

Elizabeth was still grinning when George, bundled in his down jacket with the hood over his head, appeared. "Say, was that Henselt I just saw racing down the hallway?"

For a moment she hesitated, uncertain how to behave with him after the sea change she had recently undergone. "It sure was," she said, and then filled him in on the details of his visit. "He came snooping to find out whether he should switch to Mr. Rossiter or not. What a character."

"You didn't really ask him who he was?" He laughed as he untied his hood and then pushed it back. "I pity the poor musician who'll be made to pay for this outrage. You've probably crushed him for life."

"But I think he was sure I didn't recognize him, or he would have behaved differently. Better a blow to his ego, than to have Rossiter find out about his visit."

"Maybe so. But it still was a blow. What a kick his downtrodden orchestra would get to hear this. And wait until A.R.—"

"Oh, but I shan't tell him about it . . ."

"Why not?"

"I wouldn't want to . . . After all, he brought Henselt over from Germany originally and gave him his first chance. I wouldn't want him to know how he came sneaking around to get the lay of the land before committing—"

She couldn't meet George's eyes. If her protectiveness of Rossiter was a surprise, he gave no indication.

"Are you feeling better?" he asked after a pause.

"Feeling better? What do you mean?"

"Well . . . you were out sick the last time I was here."

"Oh, it was nothing serious."

He studied the emotions on her face. "Are you still looking for another job?"

Elizabeth leaned back in her swivel chair, propping her feet on an open desk drawer. If he thought she was out job-hunting on that day she went to the library, she supposed it was just as well. Explanations were so difficult. Yes, she had to get a new job, and in Toronto, to boot. She could feel George's careful scrutiny and lifted her eyes to meet his. "No, I'm not looking anymore. Besides, there aren't any to be had."

George looked relieved but said nothing. "You mean you're all alone?" he asked as he turned from her to poke his head in the various offices. "I can't believe it. Somebody up there must love me after all—" The telephone rang, sparing Elizabeth the necessity of a response.

"Now, don't tell me you came in on such a day," Rossiter's voice boomed over the wires. "I just called out of curiosity. I didn't expect anybody to actually be there. Really, for an intelligent girl—oops, *woman*—don't you listen to news reports?"

"But I was expecting Tony Arcaro—the man who's doing the renovations."

"Did he come? No, of course, not. You see he has much more sense than you."

"But George is here."

"George? He's there now? I didn't expect him today. Thought he'd gone to England already. I can't remember. Well, let me speak with him then."

As she handed the phone over, Elizabeth glanced at Rossiter's calendar which confirmed that he didn't have an appointment with George for that day. He hadn't seen him for several days, since George had been busy catching up at his East Hampton home.

"Yes," he was saying, with a laugh into the receiver, "I'll see she goes home—and that she gets home, too. So don't worry. We'll get together when I get back from England. I thought I told you. It's a promotional tour in connection with the publication of the English edition of *Transcendence and Tragedy*. And I have to go to Cleveland tomorrow. If the planes are flying by then. My folks are celebrating their thirty-fifth anniversary. The chapter on the Philadelphia Orchestra is finished. I've brought it back with me and will leave it for you. I went a bit stir-crazy out at East Hampton. Didn't want to get snowed in there and miss my flight. Yes, don't worry, she'll leave right away . . ."

Elizabeth placed the letters she had worked on in a file and put them in her desk in her own office. As she re-emerged, George hung up the phone. "So," he slid off the desk, "as you must have heard, you're to leave right away. Boss' orders."

"More paternalism—"

"There you go again, Ms . . . Negativity." He had been tempted to say Ms. Topknot but resisted. "I thought reading—"

"Yes," interrupted Elizabeth and her voice petered out. How to gauge herself—let alone explain to him—what laying those phantoms to rest meant? "I'm very grateful that you gave me that chapter. It shed a lot of light on—"

"You were right, by the way. I didn't mean to capitalize 'virgin'." As she flushed, he glanced at his watch. "Have you had lunch? It's nearly one-thirty." Seeing her hesitate, he added: "And don't give me any of that not wanting to start anything routine. Nobody is asking you to start anything except maybe a cuppa kindness or a platter of pasta or some other such. You need some food—good rib-sticking food—to ward off those chills. And I promised A.R. to see you home safely."

With a flourish, she covered her typewriter and banged the desk drawer shut. Taking her ski jacket from the peg and putting it on, she said: "So what are we waiting for? Let's go."

Chapter XX

They were lucky to find a restaurant. With everything shut down because of the storm, New York had begun to look like the wilds of the Northwest Territories. After trudging east to Lexington and then back to Sixth Avenue, they chanced upon The Grotto, a small, unpretentious dwelling sandwiched between two ornate hostelries. When they removed their jackets and shook off the snow, the *padrone*, with an effusion befitting royalty—or the only customers who had braved the storm to grace his establishment—sat them in a semi-circular booth and brought them martini cocktails, compliments of the house.

Inside, the restaurant was surprisingly elegant. But for all its sumptuous accouterments—the linen, the flowers, the chandelier—the pickings were mighty slim. "No deliveries," the waiter explained in his thick Italian accent. "And half-a the kitchen crew no show." All they could get was minestrone soup and lots of day-old Italian bread and cheese. They gladly settled for that.

While they waited for the food, she awkwardly proposed a toast to the success of his forthcoming book. Afterward, they became strangely silent, and downed the martinis in record time.

The woman hugged one knee, molding the ski slacks against her. She looked, or pretended to look, at the wall frescoes, quintessential Italian, aswirl with blue impasto, designed to transport to the grottoed delights of Capri.

The man looked at her.

A party of two, refugees like themselves, came in with much chattering, seating themselves in the adjacent booth. Their own silence was all the more marked, approaching embarrassment. Both spoke at once.

"New York seems—"

"Have you ever been—"

They both laughed. They both remembered an earlier time when they both spoke simultaneously. "You first," she said.

"No, you . . ."

"I was just thinking that New York seems like a small town today." After expanding on this, she said it was his turn but he maintained he'd forgotten what he wanted to say. And he had; he found it much more agreeable just to look at her in the golden glow of a stained glass window, to listen to her without an office desk between them, and note that the only piece of jewelery she wore was an engraved locket resting between her breasts. As though suddenly remembering where he was, he snapped his fingers in the direction of the head-waiter. "Bring us a good bottle of chianti."

Over the experimental sip, he smiled at her. She knew he was again unsure how to proceed and so, in fact, was she. What to do with her eyes or her hands was a problem. "Una salvietta, per favore," she asked the waiter, without thinking, when he brought the soup.

"I didn't know you knew Italian."

She accidentally splashed some soup on the table.

From the adjoining booth the sound of laughter, the constraints of office protocol being tossed aside. No such for them. "I took it in college," she said, shifting in her seat so that the stained glass window now cast her in blue.

"Where?"

"Oberlin."

Well, that's something, he thought. I now know where she went to college. A tiny corner of her mysterious personal history had been penetrated. And proffered by her and not second-hand. But now her eyes were quite closed to him suddenly, as if some light had been switched off. He took a swallow of soup thoughtfully. When she stared at her empty bowl, he offered the tureen but she declined another helping.

Afterwards, he insisted on seeing her safely home. "I promised A.R., you know. Can't let the old boy down."

"God forbid," she replied.

To get his car, which was parked in a garage off Eighth, was out of the question. What traffic was still on the roads was inching its way along, heading for the nearest shelter. Pale spires in the distance struggled toward the obliterated sky.

Taxis were not to be had. Rather than wait for a bus, they began to walk. She again spoke of the transformation of the city and how extraordinary it felt walking along together in the middle of 57th Street, as they might have a century earlier. "This was the upper reaches of the city then, separating the residential areas from the commercial."

"Lisa . . ."

"Yes?"

"See how quickly our footprints get covered up."

They looked back. Only the last two steps were visible, the rest already a dim memory. In a Cockney voice, George sang:

> *"Blow, blow, thou winter wind*
> *Thou art not so unkind*
> *As man's ingratitude . . ."*

And Elizabeth joined in, singing in falsetto:

> *"As man's in-gra-a-a-ti-tude"*

"Fancy you knowing that song," he said.

"Fancy me not."

In front of Lincoln Center, a rollicking group of people were engaged in a snowball fight. They joined in, glad to be alive at a time when snowball fights were being waged again in front of Philharmonic Hall. Again? Probably never, considering that this monolith rose from the ashes of many other buildings and homes. George stared up and opened his mouth to let the snowflakes in. "My God," he said, "I'd forgotten how good the taste of snow is." The time they laughed the most was when Elizabeth spotted a poster of Rupert Henselt, took careful aim and pelted a snowball with all her might right into his demonic right eye. George whipped out his pocket camera just in time to record her look of triumph. It occurred to him that come what may—beggars not being able to be choosers and all that—this spot in front of Philharmonic Hall, would always be associated in his mind with that moment.

At Seventy-fourth Street, Elizabeth stocked up at the grocer's for what she feared might be a "long haul." Other shoppers had apparently had the same idea—the shelves were depleted. Nevertheless, she managed to get a chicken, eggs and bread, while George disappeared into a neighboring liquor store with his own priorities.

At her apartment door, the awkwardness returned. The hall was dim; her mind dimmer. She dug in her purse for the key. At last she roused herself, murmuring something about what a pleasure the day had been.

They stood looking at each other in the musty gloom. He seemed mildly amused and allowed the pleasure had been his. When she again fell silent, he cocked his head and narrowed his eyes questioningly. "Lisa, for pity's sake, cut the crap. You're not going to send me home on a night like this?" He thumped one of the paper bags with his glove. "I have champagne here lady, open up."

As she fumbled with her key, he set his packages on the floor, took it from her, inserted it into the lock and threw open the door. "Voilà . . ."

"I never knew you knew French," she said.

"I took it in high school."

When Elizabeth returned from hanging wet jackets over the bathtub, George was busy examining the series of watercolors of Lake Couchiching. "They transmit the exact moments and feelings of the beholder."

"The beholder was my grandmother."

"A.G.?"

"She was my maternal grandmother: Alice . . . Gordon." At the wall of books and records, he immediately spotted the copy of his own book *Transcendence and Tragedy*. "Definitely what no self-respecting library should be without." Remembering the inscription to Elizabeth Guaragna inside, a serpent of fear slid through her bowels when he partially removed it from its niche.

But then his eye lit on the family photograph on the dresser, and he moved away from the bookshelf to pick it up, the better to study the shadowy figures standing by the cottage. "Is that little thing really you? What a nice family." She saw he assumed Aunt Ada was her mother, was about to explain but then checked herself. No point in telling more than she had to. "Where are your brothers now?"

"Tom, the one on the right, he's a Benedictine priest. A member of a Quebec order where he's a specialist in Gregorian chants." She stopped, suddenly remembering she told Ruth he lived in Buffalo. "The other one, Chris . . . he was drowned about a week after that picture was taken."

"And your parents are both dead too?" He placed his hand on her arm for a moment. "I'm sorry."

Placing the picture carefully back on the dresser, he then followed her to the little kitchenette to help unload the bags. Afterwards, as she moved from refrigerator to cutting board, she could feel his eyes watching her, a glass of Campari with soda in his hand.

She minced the onions and green peppers with great precision.

Dinner was a success, the air sparkling over the *Pollo Napolitano* and *Pouilly Fuissé*. Between mouthfuls they found they both loved Jane

Austen; George had visited her haunts in Bath and Steventon when he went to Oxford. "And I spent a day at her house in Chawton. Picnicked in her back yard, visited the church nearby where her mother and sister are buried—saw the estate where her brother lived. The one that was adopted by his rich uncle." On the tape recorder, afterwards, Elizabeth played the cassette sent by Helge Nielsen, her pulses pounding to the staccato fury of the Appassionata Sonata.

"You know, it wasn't Beethoven that named it but his publisher Cranz—or somebody else in the office. Whoever it was, he/she was right as rain. It is Appassionata incarnate."

"How did you like the pianist?"

"I can see why you flipped over her. She certainly seems like a great prospect."

Outside, the city was reduced to the isolation of a snowbound village. For George to go home that night was impossible. Both of them behaved matter-of-factly about it; George, she suspected, to reduce her embarrassment at being forced into such unwanted intimacy, for the studio apartment had only the one large room, with two day beds on either side.

Obviously her taunt about not wanting to start something she didn't want to finish had cut deep; several times during the day he referred to it obliquely.

But perhaps his circumspection was on his own account and had little to do with her. If rumor was correct, he had already had his own share of troubles in this area. After he left the woman he lived with for some time, she had threatened to sue him for breach of "a promise he never made." She had learned this last bit from Virginia, who had gone on to roll her eyes meaningfully and add: "Once that gold digger got her hooks into a Wentworth, she wasn't letting go, nohow."

Elizabeth had attributed the story to Virginia's often florid imagination, but George himself had corroborated it to some extent earlier in the day. "Martha seemed to know about so many things, the best restaurants, the best shows, the best movies. But if you happened to disagree . . . Once burned," he added with a cautionary display of his spread palms, "forever shy."

She had listened to his story with mixed feelings. Such confidences made him too real, and she did not want his reality. Dealing with her own was more than enough. Just like their footsteps in the snow, soon she would be vanishing without a trace to Toronto.

George was staring out the window when she returned from the hall closet with sheets and blankets piled in her arms. "Come and look at the wilderness, Lisa. An entire city lies still before us."

She stood beside him, dazzled by the white. The snow fell steadily; the silence was absolute. "It's hard to see where the snow on the street and the whirls above it separate."

"Yes. Mother Nature wants to let us know who's still boss. From somewhere came the low whimpering of a dog. "This is one night you have to appreciate what man hath wrought. I love the feeling of being warm and sheltered with the weather shut outside."

She dropped the bedding into his arms. "You take the bed on the left. There's another blanket in the hall closet, if this one isn't enough."

By the time Elizabeth emerged from her bath in her old terry cloth robe, freshly-shampooed hair wrapped into a towel turban, he was in bed reading a magazine. When she crawled into her bed, it was already warm. "Thanks for turning on the electric blanket."

"Not to mention." He watched her for a moment over his reading glasses. Then he closed his magazine, dropped it on the table beside him, and turned off the light.

What with the wine and champagne and exertions of the day, she was exhausted and immediately lay back and closed her eyes. Nothing could have been more eloquent than the extraordinary silence in the room. From across the room came the sound of George turning on his side and a soft "good night." His discretion, she saw, she could take on trust.

Something about the night was strikingly familiar but her mind seemed to shy from it. Was it her father, bending over her, smelling of tobacco and after shave—

And then it came to her all at once. When Chris was still alive, he always slept in the same room with her. No matter how much they might have fought earlier in the day, they always wished each other good night. With prayers such as "I pray to God my soul to keep" as their nightly ritual, even at that early age, fears for their mortality were already strong. Particularly with Elizabeth, as if she were born with a prescience that one day his body would be fished out of the slime of malevolent waters.

But on the night before he died, she hadn't wished him a good night, because after dinner that evening he had tattled on her when she spilled grape juice on a piece of music, bringing down her father's wrath and Aunt Ada's well-intended but, as usual, futile intercession. For a long time she worried desperately that it was this omission which had caused his death. Tom, she later found out, had been plagued with a similar worry: it had been his assigned task to watch over them at the lake—at the fatal moment he had gone into the house for a drink of water.

After Chris' death, she always slept alone. At home because Tom already had his own room; at Oberlin, except for her freshman year, by choice.

The swirling bright snow at the window made the night unusually bright, but within five minutes she was sound asleep.

Chapter XXI

Outside the blizzard still raged, with gusts creating a wind-chill factor of twenty-five below zero. George gazed at Lisa for a long time. The sense of for once being in the right place at the right time overwhelmed him. "The gods always seem to provide for me," he said. "But prodigal as this, they've never been before."

Across four inches of pillow he smiled, but she didn't smile back.

"My grandmother always used to tell of a contessa praying, 'Please God, provide for the already provided, the poor are used to their lot.'" She shook her head. "I don't trust this luck as much as you do. What the gods usually provide for me doesn't make for unshakable belief."

He rested his head on his hand, thinking how much he could love this woman if she would only let him. The already provided may have been provided for—pleasure had engulfed them both like a dance of exploding atoms—but he felt uneasy: the whole thing had come about almost by accident.

If he hadn't awakened when she was having that nightmare about her drowning brother and come over to comfort her, it would probably never have happened. One minute he was patting her shoulder like a loving brother; the next he had plunged his hands into her still damp hair and put his mouth to hers blindly, almost blunderingly.

What with any other woman would have been a perfectly natural train of events—almost inevitable, given the circumstances—with her seemed . . . It was hard to pin it down, but somehow he felt he was in her bed under false pretenses.

Not that what he felt for her was false. Far from. Nor was there anything false in the way she had dissolved when they fell back on the bed together, meeting passion with passion, as though both had been moving toward this place all their lives. At first he'd wanted to go slow,

savoring each step, comparing them to the images he'd long fanta-
sized over, but she herself had prevented that. And when he went in,
for the first time in his life he felt all the missing jig saw pieces of his
life come together at last. Perhaps, it was true, some special dispensa-
tion from above had come to enable him to spin out these hours of
happiness.

And if it scared him to see how open and ready for love they were—
how different the whole world suddenly seemed—he could imagine
its effect on her. Ruth Pryor had told him how "stand-offish" she was
with everybody—especially young men. "Won't give them the time
of day," she had confided with a shake of the head, "not that any of
them would ever have the audacity to ask. A young girl like that, I
can't understand it."

He looked at her face, at the mad tangle of her Vitabath-scented
hair, at her ringless hand with the chewed down nails. Two women
seemed to inhabit that body, the one infected by his own urgency a
little while earlier, and the one that was now wrestling again for supremacy, with a large sign reading *Trespassers will be prosecuted.* An
alien force sometimes seemed to descend on her. Christ, he wouldn't
be surprised if she got up and put her hair in a damn topknot again.

He lay back in the faint morning light, just making out a plastered
patch in the ceiling. It had happened too quickly, he supposed, two
starvelings in *terra incognita* struggling with an unfamiliar tongue.
Nor was there any compass to point the way further. "'Divine sanity,'" he whispered, quoting Rossiter, as she tentatively strained her
body toward him.

She pulled back suddenly. "I prefer what *you* said—more like Mother
Nature letting us know exactly who's boss."

He ran his fingertips gently up the soft surface of her cheek. "Much
as I'd like to be with mom and pop on their anniversary, I hope the
planes are still socked in today."

"Come now, you wouldn't really want to miss that. You don't know how lucky you are. I can't even begin to imagine what it would be like being part of a family with father, mother, sister—even living grandparents intact. When I was a kid I used to dream of a father who worked from nine to five as an executive at Eaton's and then came home to my mother's splendid four-course dinners straight out of the Ladies' Home Journal—"

"Eaton's . . . What's that?"

She looked at him quickly with wide eyes and checked whatever she'd been going to say. "It's a store in the town where I grew up. You see my dreams were modest—I never dreamed what it would be like to be the daughter of the *owner* of Eaton's. Just the simple nuclear family was all I imagined. Nuclear family—that's an appropriate term all right. What's a nuclear family but a sleeping bomb waiting to be ignited?"

"What did your father look like?"

"Well . . . you saw the picture. He was dark, brown eyes, small moustache, he was tall and rather stocky—except at the end."

"What did he do?"

"He was a . . . postman. I used to see him come home, walking in the rain, a big . . . mail bag under his arm . . ." A tear escaped from underneath her lid and fell on the pillow.

"Now what?" he whispered, moving closer, bending to kiss her forehead. "I want to make you smile—and there you go again. Why does Lisa-bella cry?"

"I guess if I knew that—" She reached for a tissue and he pulled at her, feeling her face wet on his shoulder, as she burrowed in for a moment. "With your background, you're probably immune—"

"*Balls, picnics and parties, parties, picnics and balls,*" he said, lifting his hand and looking over imaginary horn-rimmed glasses in a perfect imitation of Rossiter. "I must say you have a peculiar idea as to what constitutes a proper immunization system."

"Well, maybe not immune. Exempt is a better term."

"Exempt from what?" He shook his head. "Would it help if I jumped into some fiery pit to prove—"

"It's just that . . . why *me*?" The words came out bare, unschooled.

He turned her toward him and stroked her head and shoulders. "Why *not* you? There are limits to brotherly restraint, you know. Given your obvious discouragement, I've often asked myself the same thing. But there was this—I guess you could call it *Lisa-monium*—inside me when I saw you which I couldn't exactly ignore."

"You never take me seriously."

"Wrong, lady, I've taken you seriously from the first time I laid eyes on you." He pinned her outstretched hand under his own and studied her. "Woman of mystery, that's what you are. There's precious little of that commodity around. A beautiful mystery, from a life in some enchanted forest or something—"

"Enchanted forest—oh my God, if you only knew." She caught her lower lip in her teeth, biting hard.

But he had dropped back on the pillow and did not hear her. "And then there's that righteous indignation of yours, you don't come across that very often either."

"I don't believe this docudrama view of me for one minute, and I wonder, in fact, how you can. *Righteous indignation*. I have enough of that, I suppose, but I'm usually much too chicken to show it. It's only in relation to Mr. Rossiter . . ."

"Why him and nobody else? Because you see him as being above the fray?" At her head shake, he continued: "Because you want to quit the job anyway and don't give a damn?" Still no response. "You sure have a blind spot there. Funny how differently we view him. I see him as one of the grand old men of music management. A man for the ages. Oh, he's made his share of mistakes, sure. I told you, saints and

I don't get on. If you believe in God, you also have to believe in the Devil. So a saint he ain't. But when he begins to talk about the old times—especially his second wife—there's an aura about him—you know, it's funny. When we were working on that chapter, you kept coming in and out, and I began to imbue you with the soul of the woman Rossiter was describing. What's wrong?" he asked sharply.

"Nothing . . . why?"

"You looked so strange, it scared me." He turned her to him again, studying her, as if her swift alternations of mood were too much for him. Assuming her quickened heartbeat for something paralleling his own need, he tightened his clasp. Although they again dissolved together, time out of mind, he sensed her terms of surrender were no longer what they had been before.

"You see, the gods don't always listen to me, Lisa," George said after he checked with the airport and learned his flight for Cleveland would leave as scheduled.

"You should be glad, your parents would have been so disappointed. Besides, you said we shouldn't argue with Mother Nature."

George opened the curtains all the way to bring light into every corner of the tiny apartment. As often happens after a blizzard, the sun had come out in full force, reclaiming its sovereignty in the universe, gilding the snow-blanketed city with dazzling color.

"How beautiful," Lisa said, as she came to stand beside him.

George looked at the glittering snow and the melting icicles above the window frame. Deep inside him, icicles had melted too, but now a keen awareness of imminent change engulfed him. It was coming to an end, this interlude of belonging, of enclosing and being enclosed, of the temporary deliverance from his own recent special brand of segregation. And from hers. There would still be belonging, but it would never be quite like this. He took her hand to hold in his own and lifted it to his lips. "A.R. talked about the brevity of his three years with his second wife—I've only had one day. I can't bear the thought of that whole month in Europe without you. I've nearly five days free on my itinerary between Paris and Vienna. How about joining me?"

"I could never take time off just now. You know how much Mr. Rossiter depends on me."

"Well, how about for Washington's Birthday weekend? He'd surely not object to that. We could stay in Paris, or better still, we could stay at my grandfather's cottage in Hampshire. He's a grand old man, you'd love him. And the countryside's gorgeous there. Even at this time of year. Crocuses sprouting—"

"How could I explain at the office? I don't want them to know. . ."

"Why not, for heaven's sake? They'll all be bound to know soon enough."

"Look, George, it's all happened so fast. We both need a little time now—a little space. Let's just keep it between us for the time being. I want to be certain—"

"Well, I'm certain. I don't need any time. And we'd have such a great time in Europe together." She had backed away from the window and in the glare of the sun, her freckles stood out sharply against her chilled skin. "All right, Lisa-bella, but it's going to be a damn misery without you, I already know that. I was so excited by the English publication of that book—but now—"

Lisa turned to look at him for a long moment. "You'd better go shower if you're going to make that plane. I'll make the eggs."

Soaping himself, he sang *Blow, blow, thou winter wind* again and felt his own body's lightness as never before. And never before were his apprehensions so sharp to everything around him, the sound of the water beating on his head, the smell of the pine soap, the rough texture of the towel with which he dried himself.

In the tiny tiled bathroom, he dislodged a clothes hamper, and from the back where it had fallen, an envelope appeared. He stooped to pick it up. *Elizabeth Guaragna, c/o Lisa Sullivan . . .* The return address was from an Ada Guaragna and the postmark was from Toronto. "Lisa," he cried as he flung open the door of the bathroom, "I didn't know you knew Elizabeth Guaragna."

Arrested in mid-motion in the process of reaching out for the knob under the boiling kettle on the stove, steam accidentally penetrated her hand. She gasped. He strode over to turn the faucet handle to let cold water gush over her hand.

"I didn't mean to startle you," he said, clasping her shoulders. "Why, you're trembling. Are you okay?"

She stared tightlipped into space while drying her hand with a dish towel.

"I saw this sticking out from behind the hamper," he said, showing her the envelope. I didn't know you knew her."

"Know her? Why? What does it matter? I didn't know it was important." Turning from him, she took a sponge to rub hard at a spot of egg which had hardened on the surface of the stove. When she finished he was still staring inquiringly at her with the envelope in his hand. "She's just somebody I knew in college. She visited here a couple of weeks ago and stayed over."

"Well, I'll be darned. But you never mentioned you knew her."

She wrung the sponge and then dropped it in the sink. After covering the serving plate with the scrambled eggs, she placed it on the warming tray on the table in front of the bay window. "I didn't know the connection until I read your chapter but that was after—And I don't know if she's the same Guaragna."

"I see the postmark's Toronto—it might be worth a trip—"

"But this Elizabeth comes from . . . Chicago. She may have been visiting—she can't be the same Guaragna. It's a pretty common name in Italy. Almost like—Smith."

He gave her a dubious look. "That may be so. And A.R. told me that those Guaragnas live in Italy. Once a girl by that name asked for an autograph for my book. At the time the name meant nothing to me either. She forgot her pen. Before I got a chance to return it, she'd slipped away. I tried finding her in the phone books, but no luck." He looked at the envelope again. "Still I'd like to find out if she's the same one—"

"Well, she never mentioned any such connection to me."

"Did she know where you were working?"

"Yes, she did . . . She picked me up there one day when we went out to lunch." Lisa pressed two fingers to her forehead.

"A headache?"

"Yes. I get them more and more. Come, let's eat."

"I guess it *must* be another Guaragna. But what a coincidence."

Again her eyes looked as if some light in them had been switched off. After a moment she took the envelope from him and tossed it into the trash bin. "You'd better hurry now. Your eggs will get cold. And the plane won't wait."

In Cleveland, he had the family all agog with hints at big doings in his personal life in the near future. "You don't say," Margaret teased. "Miss Topknot is it? I rather suspected you had a soft spot for her."

"That's not the adjective I would have chosen."

"But she can't be all you say she is. You're just the last of the big time romantics. Remember Martha—"

"It's precisely because I do that I'm so drawn to Lisa."

"But you said she was a tight-ass bitch—"

"You said that. In any case, all that's before I got to know her better."

"Okay, so what's she really like?"

"True-blue. Straight as an arrow." He thought of her sudden reti-cences, the unsureness in the midst of surface sureness. "Of course, there are some things about her that I still don't understand—"

"Which probably sweetens the attraction."

"No doubt." He grinned. "And if it takes the next fifty years to really get to understand her, I can imagine no better way of spending it."

His mother and sister exchanged wary smiles at this but said noth-ing. His father made some comment about it being high time for him to sow a few wild oats.

On the drive to the airport, however, his mother introduced a cautionary note. "Listen to me, George," she said, placing her hand on his. "From everything you *haven't* told us about her, I gather she's something special. I'm not prying. But I want to say something now, before you go any further, which is very hard to say later. If you find you've made a mistake, cut your losses fast."

Outside the car, the sky was closed to the sun, a pallid airport was bound by February cold and ice. She screwed her tiny head inside her big fur collar and gave him a long look. "You waited two years with Martha, so you had a taste of it. But it gets even harder the longer you wait, after you've too much invested in the thing. When you marry Ms. Wrong, you pay and continue to pay forever."

There was barely time for a quick call to Lisa from Kennedy Airport before embarking on his overseas journey. "I tried to get my publisher to postpone the tour but he hit the ceiling. He has all these TV dates and interviews set up. They're beginning to use as much hype over there as we do here. Of all the times when I don't want to be away from New York."

"The month will be up before you know it. And you'll be so busy traipsing around. London, Paris, Vienna, Berlin—how lucky can you get? Are you going to spend those free days in Hampshire?"

"No, I've decided to go to Italy."

"Why Italy? Is there an Italian edition of the book too?"

"No. It's all your fault. Since you won't join me during that time I thought I'd go there to do some research on the Rossiter book."

"What kind of research?"

"I thought I'd try to track down some of the Guaragnas there. Maybe Dominic Guaragna. It would add a lot to the new book if I got some insights from some of Rossiter's adversaries. If I'm not to be accused of writing a glorified puff piece, I need some alternative opinions."

There was a long silence before Lisa spoke. "I think it'd be a wild good chase. Who would know—"

"There's bound to be somebody who knows. After all, we're talking about a famous pianist—or somebody who once was a famous pianist. Mickiewicz raved about him. There's sure to be records of his whereabouts. It's worth a try and I'd like to hear the story from his point of view."

"But he's . . ." Her voice had a strangled quality. "For all you know he may no longer be living."

"I doubt that. He's a relatively young man. And then there are the children. It'd be interesting to meet them." A faint noise at the other end of the receiver. "What did you say, I can hardly hear you? This is a bad connection."

"I said my buzzer rang. Mr. Rossiter is calling. I must go."

"He can wait a minute. Listen, I've mailed you a list of my whereabouts—please drop me a line. And by the way, when I get back, I'm also interested in getting in touch with your friend from Chicago. Maybe there is a connection between the two families. The fact she didn't know who Alfred Rossiter was doesn't necessarily mean anything. I'd want to interview her—no matter what. On my return, perhaps we could both spend a weekend in Chicago. But don't breathe a word of any of this to A.R. He doesn't have to know about my independent research. When I get back, I'd like to see her. Do you think you could arrange it? Ask her—"

"George, Mr. Rossiter is getting frantic. I really have to go now. Goodbye."

Chapter XXII

"Lisa, A.R. just called to say he'll be late getting back from his doctor. He didn't want me to interrupt you. My God, you're white as a sheet! Like somebody walked over your grave. What's the matter?"

Elizabeth looked up to find Virginia standing across from her desk. Thought had stopped. Should she laugh or should she cry? She couldn't believe what she had just heard: George Wentworth was going to look for her dead father. And after he returned he was going to search for Elizabeth Guaragna. *For her dead father. For Elizabeth Guaragna.* She had wanted to scream out: "Don't go, stay with me. Don't go for God's sake. I don't give a damn about your book."

But instead she had hung on to the receiver and got all tongue-tied. *Tongue-tied?* Hog-tied was more like it.

In her continuing silence, Virginia came around the desk to take the receiver out of her hand and replace it on its base. Then she bent over to put a hand on Elizabeth's shoulder. "Steady, steady, now. What is it, Lisa? Bad news from home?"

Elizabeth shook her head. Despite its pinkish underglow and barely perceptible pencilled eyebrows, Virginia's face at the moment seemed to her the very picture of sanity. Good, solid, down-home-folks sanity. When the watcher felt herself being watched even more closely, she lowered her eyes.

"Man trouble? Is that it?"

Elizabeth nodded, plucking at a tuft of wool that had loosened on her sweater to push it inwards. Virginia's definition of man trouble and hers were far from the same thing. The sense of being hunted was stronger than ever. "Oh, damn," she said as she tore the tuft. "I've made it worse."

Virginia whistled softly under her breath. "Anybody I know?"

MOTHERLESS CHILD | 220

"No . . . nobody you know, somebody I met at a party. He's—"
With a desolate moan, she cast herself as far back as her swivel chair
went and covered her eyes with her hand.

"Married?"

She shuddered. Would that the situation were as conventionally
complicated as Virginia imagined. Staring at the deadly telephone receiver on her desk, she could picture George in some telephone booth
on the other end with that puzzled frown which brought his eyebrows
together. As sensitive as he was, as empathic, as full of a sweetness she
had never before suspected, he really didn't know her much better
than Virginia. Like her, it was the non-person Lisa he knew and cared
about—not Elizabeth.

"Don't say anything if you don't want to, Lisa, but it might do you
good to get it off your chest. And you can trust me, I'm like a tomb."

"It's just all been so fast," Elizabeth finally got out. Her voice rang
out; Virginia instinctively threw a look round and then went to shut
the door. "I don't know how it happened. For the pre-emption he's
so quickly achieved—it's like being set at fast-forward while I'm still
struggling to catch up to yesterday. I've swung from nothingness to
everything and back to nothingness in four short days."

"Sounds like he's quite a fast worker. He must be something for you
to go overboard like this. But if it had to fizzle, it's better it was fast."

"You're right. Cruel April-mixes of memory and desire are not for
me. If I have to give him up before my body's even been able to as-
similate the idea, it's just as well I didn't have the time."

Virginia smiled. "Lord, you sound like—a young girl like you—it
must be some atavistic wisdom of the species coming to the fore."

"Oh, Virginia." Hands twisting themselves together, she gabbled
at speed. "It was like that time when my boy friend Henry and I went
to a high school dance just for fun and Howie Peters, who later went
on to become a professional dancer, took me out on the floor as the

rock band started up. When the other dancers saw him, they began to cheer him on with 'Way to go, Howie,' and cleared the floor to watch. I'm a real klotz on the dance floor and wanted to die right there. 'Don't panic, just let go,' he said and to my astonishment, there we were, moments later, dancing to beat the band."

She unknotted her hands and splayed them out on the desk. With George, a deeper symbiosis, a parity of electrical charges, flares bursting throughout the room. Had she really told him not to stop, not to *ever* stop? The *insaziati*; she no less than he. Her mother's daughter, after all.

Her eyes filled with tears as she remembered how he had lifted her two breasts in his hands to bury his face between them as in a baptismal font. In that moment they had both felt everything the other was or could be. And she had felt his love at once a benediction and a sacrilege. A benediction for Lisa Sullivan; a sacrilege for Elizabeth Guaragna. Or was it the other way around? "You see, it was all so different from what I'd always imagined: you think one thing, you skip something else."

"You have got it bad," Virginia said. "When I see this kind of thing, I'm glad all that's behind me. But if he's given you the gate, why should you care? You're young, you've got everything going for you, why mess with a married man? I know it's easy for me to say, but I've been there, believe me."

"He hasn't given me the gate—that's not it—"

"Then what's the problem?"

"I don't want to get tied down. I may be confused about many things but at least I know this: I'm a loner and I like being a loner—"

She stopped short and closed her eyes. Her mother's example must not go for naught. On the strength of such illusion she had blithely relinquished her right to her children—and where had that brought her?

"Well, I've been a loner most of my life," Virginia said, "not wholly by choice. Oh, I had chances, but I guess something in me wanted my

freedom. Besides, there was somebody . . . But he, too, was married—
Still, if I were starting out today, I don't think I'd do it that way again."

"Well, I am." Elizabeth crossed her arms tightly over her chest and
laughed harshly. "It's back to my life of *dos* and *don'ts*, mostly *don'ts*."

"You can say that again. And the *don'ts* undergo a qualitative
change as you get older. From don't succumb, don't overdo they become don't expect, don't hope, don't give, don't receive—those are
the keys to the loner's kingdom."

"You sound like Rossiter. But I wouldn't say that. Things are different today. There's no stigma to being alone. A neighbor back home
once told me that when she was a child, they didn't allow married
women to teach in the schools and how sorry she always felt for her
spinster teachers. 'At home,' she said, 'my father used my mother as
a punching bag and there wasn't a moment of peace, but still, every
time I thought of those *old maids*—as they were called in those days—
having to go home to an empty house, I'd cry. That's what believing
in all those happily-ever-after fairy tales gets you.'"

Virginia said nothing for a moment. "You don't have to explain
the term *old maid* to me. Sticks and stones . . . But no matter by what
fancy names they want to call it today, an onion's still an onion. I
know marriages aren't made in heaven, but at my age, it becomes
damn hard being alone." She picked up the gold charms of the new
and old Metropolitan Opera which hung around her neck and twirled
them around her finger. "Well, I guess I'd better be getting back to the
salt mines. I really hope you know what you're doing."

With great effort Elizabeth heaved herself out of the chair and went
to the mirror on the back of the door to straighten her hair. *Omerta*,
the Sicilian code of silence—she was as bound to it as any Mafioso.

Smoothing down her sweater, she looked at her curves and planes, all newly appreciated by George's adoration. *Proibito*, as Grandma Adelina would say whenever she brought up a touchy subject (i.e., her mother), *proibito*. Don't go there. Now George had joined the ranks of the *proibito* subjects too. And her body seemed a thing apart from her now.

As though etched in acid, the image of George standing with the accusing envelope in his hand returned and she put her fist into her mouth. This frail edifice, erected on such shifting sands, could dissolve in thin air—and she along with it—if she were to continue seeing him.

She had vowed she would quit her job—she had vowed to return to Toronto—but now some deeper assertion of life made it impossible for her to do so. Even though she had already found out more than she bargained for, she was far from content with the outcome. The *insaziati*—in more ways than one. Okay, so on a sunny Thursday in June of 1952, three children remained in custody of one Dominic Guaragna, defendant, instead of being awarded to Elizabeth Rossiter, plaintiff. So it was ruled, written and done.

But what happened when the locket-fingering Elizabeth Rossiter in her tailored linen suit stepped into the limousine with her husband and sped away from the prying reporters? How had she really borne the news? Did she cry, did she laugh harshly, did she lift her hands and beat Rossiter on the chest for having brought her to this? Did she wonder whether the switch from cramped apartment and diaper pails and baby sitting pools to Westchester mansion and limousines and a staff of servants was worth it? Was the status change from wife of struggling artist to concert world king worth it? Did she stick it out for three years and then, as Aunt Ada suspected, call it quits? *Mama, mama,* tell me, tell me.

And how had Rossiter taken it? How had he felt seeing what his great vaunted passion had done to the so-called love of his life? How had he felt seeing the sweet golden dream they shared turn black and sour? She had to know more, she just had to. Monster or not, Rossiter was the key source of further vital knowledge.

So far she had just nudged the tip of the iceberg—banked around the shore, more jagged and jutting tips loomed. To further explore these mysterious salients, she *had* to stay at her job. She had no choice. Or rather, this was her choice. George was a way station, an enchantment of the heart—on the road to the other side of her life. His quest and hers were diametrically opposed. He wanted to find Elizabeth Guaragna; she had to make certain he never did.

It was different with Rossiter, though. He had somehow taken possession of her so that she felt his presence all the time. He took up all the room. Even George—though he had been able to cut straight and clean through—was not able to displace this primacy.

Chapter XXIII

"And would you believe it," Ruth Pryor said, pointing to the upper left-hand corner of the page in her leather-bound album, "that's A.R. with Galliuillin in that canoe."

Elizabeth leaned over to stare at the snapshot so carefully ensconced in its four glued corner tabs. Breathing became difficult. The wildly-maned Russian in his embroidered peasant shirt and Rossiter in his vacation garb of Hawaiian shirt and tattered sombrero were barely glanced at. With some difficulty, forcing herself to sound casual, she asked: "Who's the woman with him?"

"That's his wife Elizabeth. His second wife, that is. She died shortly after that, totally unexpectedly. She was such a radiant creature."

The description surprised Elizabeth. But then everything about the evening surprised her. They were sitting in Ruth's early American-furnished living room overlooking Central Park after having a lively discussion over one of Mrs. Todd's famous Friday roast chicken dinners. In order to keep a full-time housekeeper busy, Ruth had these weekly dinners; Elizabeth had been invited several times before, but this was the first time she accepted. On the grand piano opposite her, a lovingly inscribed picture of Gregory Mickiewicz was set in an elaborate silver frame. As a young woman, Ruth had worked for the conductor; it was during the time that Rossiter managed the Philadelphia Orchestra that he had lured her away to come join him in New York.

Elizabeth surmised she sometimes regretted the decision: the way Ruth looked at the picture was not unlike the way she had taken to gazing at the one of George on the fly leaf of his book.

It was because of George that she was there; the evening was one of several in which she had forced herself to go out. Anything was better than staying home alone all weekend and yet again reading his lovingly scribbled post cards from Europe. And then coming into the office on Monday morning and having her own voice startle her, reminding her of warnings of a *use-it-or-lose-it* nature.

Ruth began to turn the page, but Elizabeth slapped her palm on it to prevent her. "Just a minute, I want to take a better look." She bent over to hide her own face. "Yes, she does look radiant. Where was the picture taken?"

"On Lake Lucerne. We were at the festival there when Galliuillin played. I'd just flown over for the performance—it was the world premiere of a new concerto by Ilanovich—but the Rossiters came from Italy—"

"From Italy?" In the sudden silence, the start of the defrost cycle of the refrigerator in the kitchen could be heard distinctly. "What were they doing in Italy?"

Ruth gave a long sigh. "It had to do with her children. She'd been married before and lost custody of them. Her former husband had taken them to Italy. But she never did get to see them. He'd taken them somewhere for a holiday—or so some grandmother said. She was all broken up about it."

Elizabeth sat very still. Nobody, she'd always thought, ever seemed to give a damn whether the Guaragnas lived or died; now it seemed everybody had converged or was converging on Italy in their hot pursuit. "You never could tell, looking at that picture."

Ruth shrugged. "Well, pictures—they do lie, you know. She'd never have married him if she hadn't—"

A phone rang in the adjoining room and Ruth excused herself to answer. Elizabeth took advantage of her absence to study the picture more closely. Her mother was wearing a light jersey top but the locket was there nestled between her breasts.

"God," Ruth said when she returned. "That was one of my spies over at Eagle. They've hired such nincompoops over there. Some local opera company wrote saying they were putting on *Die Meistersinger* and asked if they had a *Hans Sachs* for it. You know what one of their new young hot shots answered? 'I'm sorry but Hans Sachs isn't under our management.'"

Elizabeth would not be diverted; she pointed to the picture of her mother in the album. "You said she'd never have married him if she hadn't—Hadn't what?"

Ruth gave her a puzzled look. "I don't really know, but I think she expected to get custody. I don't know if she'd have married Rossiter if she knew she was going to lose the children."

"But didn't she give them up when she got divorced?"

"I suppose she did. But she never expected her ex would want them himself. I know nowadays it's a much more common practice—but in those days it was a rarity for children to be taken from the mother. Poor thing, she never did get to see them, though they ran all over Italy on the off chance they'd catch up with them."

"So that's how she spent the last months of her life . . ."

"And earlier, too. She never gave up trying to get them back. And then, suddenly, she was gone."

"Did you see her before—?"

"I'd no idea she'd been ailing. It came as a shock."

"How did Mr. Rossiter take it?"

"A romantic like him? As you can imagine. He was terribly broken up about it. They really were so much in love. She'd been married to one of our pianists—a very gifted one. I don't know what happened to him—never heard of him again."

"How could that be?"

"Well, maybe he wasn't up to a career. Some artists start out great guns but they can't sustain it. I've seen that happen often. I never did get to hear him myself. In any case, what with the scandal and everything—I guess nobody would touch him with a ten-foot pole.

Especially with A.R. involved. Most of the conductors were under his management." Ruth bent to look at the picture. "There was something ethereal about her. I've never known A.R. to go so completely wild about anybody. He was besotted over her. After she died, he took a leave of absence to recuperate, and to the amazement of everybody at Eagle, he came back with Dolores hanging on his arm. His new wife."

"I've never met her—what's she like?"

"She was quite attractive when he first married her. Took him in hand—he needed it—and mothered him a bit." She turned the page in the scrapbook and pointed to a picture of Rossiter, sitting in a deck chair on a liner, smiling up at a woman handing him a drink. Ruth snorted. "That's probably the only drink she ever passed up. She probably has her own hidden behind her back. She's promised to go on the wagon so many times—but what can you do? And she won't go to A.A. or anything like that. It's a tragedy—I don't know why he puts up with it."

Elizabeth took a deep breath. "Probably because he wouldn't want to have two suicides on his conscience—"

"Suicides? What are you talking about? Are you out of your mind? What makes you think that? Elizabeth had a heart attack—they do come on suddenly you know."

Elizabeth turned her head. "I don't know what gave me that idea." But she remained unconvinced.

At the office, Elizabeth was kept busy with a series of auditions; now that word of Lipinsky's switch had spread, several artists had followed suit and even Ruth agreed it was time to give the newcomers to the field a break.

After listening to a so-so singer, a violinist beset with memory slips, and a pianist who approached the piano as though it were an enemy to be overcome, she had become somewhat discouraged. The more so since she had done the original screenings through cassettes and only chose the most likely candidates. Obviously a live performance and a well-doctored cassette were two very different things.

It was therefore with some trepidation that she drove with Rossiter in his limousine to Town Hall one afternoon to the audition of Helge Nielsen, for she had seemed the likeliest candidate of all. Elizabeth hoped they were not in for yet another disappointment.

When they entered the darkened hall, a young man was practicing scales at the piano and Elizabeth wondered where Helge Nielsen was for only she was scheduled that afternoon. When the pianist saw them, he welcomed them with a slow arpeggio, sustaining it ceremoniously with the pedal. To her astonishment, he turned out to be Helge Nielsen, whom she had always assumed—and led Rossiter to assume—was a woman. "It's a man's name in Norway," he explained with a laugh and from the way he looked at her, left no doubt of it.

As Rossiter led her to seats in the back of the auditorium, Elizabeth's apprehensions returned; the blonde and blue-eyed giant sitting on stage in no way corresponded with the tiny Larocha-like figure she had in mind when she had listened to his cassette.

But as his fingers stretched to new octaves and the massive harmonies of the *Appassionata* unfolded, she relaxed: it was clear *his* cassette had not misled, they were in the presence of a real artist, absorbed and dedicated to music to the exclusion of all else. From the corner of her eye she could see Rossiter equally transported, the gruff lines softened with slack.

"This is the state of the art—the language of music—old compositions made new, new old," Rossiter whispered between pieces. "A language beginning where others leave off."

When Nielsen stood up to bow at the end, Rossitter came to the stage to shake his hand. "You reminded me of something Arthur

Schnabel used to say: 'safety last.' You'll be hearing from us."

Nielsen wiped the sweat from his brow with a clean handkerchief and beamed.

As Rossiter went to speak to the manager of the hall, Nielsen covered Elizabeth's hand with both of his. "I know it was you who arranged it all." He spoke quietly, looking owlish behind his glasses, the more so since his protruding teeth prevented his mouth from closing completely.

On the way back in the limousine, Rossiter related another of Arthur Schnabel's famous statements: *The notes I handle no better than many pianists. But the pauses between the notes, ah, that is where the art resides.*

"You see the race is also to the not-so-swift."

"That reminds me of something I read somewhere—that human beings are nothing but amalgams of chemical matter, what is human are the spaces between them."

He almost smiled. "You've got good spaces, Lisa. And good instincts. This Nielsen knows how to pause all right. His instincts are all there too. Stick with them and you won't stray far. Learn to trust them."

Her instincts! She cringed at the thought. These instincts had brought her exactly where she was, sitting beside this man under an assumed name, in an assumed role, in an assumed affinity, forced on his account, like her mother before her, to sacrifice love and honor. As for Nielsen—anybody with the least musical discernment would have chosen him. George had been equally impressed when she had played his cassette for him.

"Go ahead and book that recital at Carnegie for him."

"But he doesn't have the money for it, I've already ascertained that. And I've spoken to the Norwegian Embassy. Nothing doing there either."

He looked at her and gave a big sigh. "You worry too much. Have you been eating enough? Your face is thin almost to gauntness. And your eyes have deep shadows. I hate to see an old head on young shoulders. Is there anything wrong?"

"I haven't been sleeping well lately."

He gave her another searching look and placed his hands on his knees. "I founded this business by a simple formula. The artist pays for every stamp, every telephone charge. That way we reduce the overhead and take no risk."

"How about their risks every time they come out on stage?"

"Don't we put ourselves on the line every time we start a business? Look, we don't take monthly retainers for our services. Lots of managers do, you know. Otherwise they wouldn't survive. You can't allow yourself to get emotionally involved in a business. We mustn't mollycoddle artists. Learning to finagle is as much a part of the concert world as playing the right notes."

"He's not the kind to finagle, you can see that. And don't forget, you left Eagle precisely because of this kind . . ."

"Ah, too clever by half, you are." He stared out the window at the traffic jam. They had turned up 57th Street and across the street stood Rossiter Towers, the building named for him at a time when his reign there seemed as solid as the brick and mortar which held it up. Ironically, the Eagle management was still ensconced there in stately fashion, with three-sheet posters advertising the forthcoming annual concert of the Lithiemberg Boys' Choir. "You know we used to have a recital division over there." He dipped his head to the left. "It really was mostly a service organization—booking the hall, printing the tickets and flyers, etc. We never made money on it."

"Did you pay for the recitals?"

"Of course not. It's not exactly a growth industry. I told you, we couldn't afford such indulgences or we'd have been out of business in a week. If word got out we'd sponsored a recital, every stage mother in the land would have demanded it."

Elizabeth shifted in her seat, gripping the handle of the side door as the car moved forward with a jerk. "But you want to start a new kind of management. And here's an opportunity. Why not reinstate the recital department? A Nielsen doesn't come along every day. An artist like that—his heart served up whole on a silver platter . . ."

"I envy your conviction. But there'd be no end to it if we sponsored him. To establish a precedent—"

"Look, you could have a committee to audition those that should be awarded with a recital—an honorary committee. Made up of artists and teachers. If we did something like that, we'd be making a real contribution to music—"

"Hold on now, girl, er—Lisa—don't get carried away." He sat silently mulling over her words. Through the narrow gap of the building opposite, majestic skyscrapers lit up like giant firecrackers were visible. At last he said, "There are contests for that sort of thing, of course. No commercial management has ever stuck their neck out like that. But I've been thinking of setting up a foundation—don't know what to do with my money, Dolores is well provided for and I have no heirs. Might as well make a virtue out of a necessity. That would be the only way to do it. The business couldn't afford to take such a financial beating, if it's to survive." He sat back in the seat again and closed his eyes. "You know, it's not a bad idea. Perhaps we should do a feasibility study. I think you've hit on something."

As they came through the revolving doors of their building, Rossiter put a hand on her shoulder. "Okay, we'll do it. Forget the feasibility study—it'll never wash. You can call Nielsen and get the thing rolling. I'll give you a list of prospective judges. Get Ruth to tell you how to paper the house, she's past master at that. And call Isabel first thing in the morning to draft a release."

The atmosphere at the office was full of plans and counterplans the following week as Elizabeth tried to infuse Ruth and Isabel with her enthusiasm for the foundation project. But they both felt they had a gold mine in Lipinsky and could see little reason to start promoting unknowns when other superstars were beginning to trickle in on the strength of his name. "Look," Isabel said, in her scratchy chain-smoking voice, "I've done the release about it that A.R. asked me to do, but that's it. I've got my hands full with Lipinsky's upcoming concerts with the orchestras here and in Washington. You can be sure they won't do anything to promote them over at Eagle, though they booked those concerts. Not after his switch here. He's a lame duck for them now."

The biggest disappointment was Rossiter himself. Having given Elizabeth the green light, he now seemed to take little interest. "If it works," he said, "it works, if not, no skin off our nose."

Elizabeth was determined to make it work. Before she vanished to Toronto, she wanted to leave at least this little legacy behind.

The complications were endless. "But Mr. Weintraub," she argued with Rossiter's lawyer. "Of course, not just everybody who comes knocking at our door. There's going to be a panel of judges to decide."

"Made up of whom?"

"Of artists and music teachers and the like." She didn't go on to tell him how difficult it had been to get that panel together. "You mean Alfred Rossiter?" the conductor of the New York Symphony had said. "And no ulterior motive? I don't believe it." She'd heard similar statements from other artists. And then she could almost hear their minds clicking as to whether joining the panel would be good or harmful for their image.

This hurdle, however, had been as nothing compared to the nitty-gritty of filling the hall. Papering the house—sordid facts of fledgling concert artists' lives. Gritting her teeth, she stood in the lobby of the Juilliard School one evening, tickets in hand. "You won't want to miss this—you'll kick yourself if you do." Everybody had exams coming up or conflicting engagements. But in the end she felt a deep satisfaction at palming off over fifty tickets in less than an hour.

Afterwards she checked to see that enough leaflets were on display in the lobby, and surreptitiously tacked one on every bulletin board she could find. She did the same everywhere she went, including The Russian Tea Room, where she had struck up a friendship with one of the waiters for the sole purpose of making sure the leaflet rack was filled with Nielsen flyers at all times.

In the office she scoured the yellow pages until there wasn't a school, hostel, music club, union, fraternity or senior citizens' organization which she hadn't contacted.

Eventually the large piles of tickets on her desk had dwindled down. Not that she expected to fill Carnegie Hall, just enough people to keep the occasion from the special kind of bleakness of an empty house.

Chapter XXIV

Ian McMasters, the name of George's English publisher, was exactly what the name had led him to expect. He was dressed in a brown worsted double-breasted suit that was strictly Savile Row, a button-down white shirt with French cuffs, and—the only departure from his upper-classness—a wine-colored bow tie. His hair was as clipped back as his speech, while over his tight lips a small and well-tended moustache reigned.

Meeting new authors was not something he generally did, he gave George to understand, but as his grandfather Robert Hunnicut had once been one of the authors on the McMasters & Company list—"in my grandfather's time, of course"—he was making an exception. "The tour has been going splendidly," he said to George the day after his return from the reading he had done in Edinburgh, "we've been getting great reports from everywhere."

George was relieved to hear this. Ordinarily he took such junkets in his stride, but his mind had been far from Konstantinov during the past two weeks: he still had not heard from Lisa. Whatever the silence betokened, it was hard to imagine it could be anything good.

The tour, however, was a pleasant surprise. His London talk-show hosts seemed to know much more about his book than their American counterparts did. The press interviewers also seemed to have more than a passing acquaintance with it, except for the woman from the *Guardian* who was more interested in discussing his illustrious antecedents than *Transcendence and Tragedy*. But the antecedents were from his mother's side, not his father's for a change; George enjoyed delving into their Bloomsbury past.

"But my dear Wentworth," McMasters now said, leaning back in his brass-studded leather chair, "I was sorry to hear from my secretary of your reluctance about that Russian engagement. We worked hard to get it for you. I should've thought you'd be pleased to have that empty period filled in. And since Konstantinov was Russian, I would think a few days in Leningrad would be very welcome to you. We'll certainly be able to do lots with the publicity from there. The Soviets may be our nemesis, but any news out of there is given a big play here—especially news of a literary nature."

George tapped his fingers on McMasters' desk. Everything on it was vintage silver, the inkstand, the letter-opener, the photograph frame with a picture of his smiling wife and children inside. The diagonal angle enabled their glowing faces to be seen—and admired—by persons on either side of the desk. "Ordinarily, I'd love to get to Russia. But I did have my heart set on doing a private little investigation in Italy in connection with the book I'm now writing on Alfred Rossiter. I'm searching for the man who was once married to his second wife."

"You mean the first husband of Rossiter's second—" McMasters made a show of counting on his fingers.

George smiled. "You could put it that way. But I'm afraid there's nothing funny about it. He absconded with the children so that the mother could never see them again."

"He must have been very vindictive. I suppose he had his reasons. Couldn't she sue?"

"There was a custody battle. He won."

"So why then bolt?"

"Exactly. That's what I'd like to know."

McMasters paused in the act of lighting a long-tipped cigarette. "The chap does sound intriguing. Perhaps our Rome office could help you locate him. I could get Carruthers there to do it for you."

"Who is Carruthers?"

"Our man in Rome. He's general manager and glorified dogsbody there. Speaks Italian like a native and that would facilitate things in any case. What did you say the name was?"

"Dominic Guaragna."

Sunlight sparkled on McMasters' horn-rimmed glasses as he looked at George sharply. "The singer?"

"No, he's a pianist."

"Oh yes, he accompanied singers—all the great ones. But that was fifty or sixty years ago. We've a book out on La Scala on our lists this year and I remember noticing that name." He turned his swivel chair around to reach for a volume of Grove's Dictionary of Musicians and flipped the pages to the G section. "Guaragna, let's see. Yes, here we are: Dominic Guaragna. Born in Naples 1890. Studied, bla, bla, bla . . . I see he was a chamber musician in the ducal chapel there, too."

George frowned. "Born in 1890? That family lives in some kind of time warp. I met an Elizabeth Guaragna last year—learned recently she's been dead for over twenty years. And now it turns out there's another one. The man I'm seeking was a well-known pianist—at least at one time. I don't know that he accompanied singers."

"Here we are—this explains it. Married Adelina Coppolini 1916, daughter Ada born 1918, son Dominic—there's your man—born in 1920. But there's nothing else here on him. Of course, this is an old edition—it's got whiskers. There's a new edition coming out soon again—you could find out there. Hmm." He read further silently. "It doesn't give his address. You won't have the time to track them down. I'll get hold of Carruthers—"

"No, hold on. I just don't know if it'd work. You see the whole thing is just a hunch of mine. I wouldn't want anybody else speaking to him—don't even know whether he'd agree to be spoken to. And I've no idea where he lives. But I do remember Rossiter saying something about Naples. So that ties in with Grove's."

McMasters looked over George's itinerary which lay on his desk. "Sounds worthwhile, all right. And it'd certainly pep up your book. I read the piece you did on Rossiter and think he's a fine subject for a biography. It's something we'd be interested in doing over here, too, eventually. A musical robber baron—we never tire of that kind of stuff. A bit like your robber baron grandfather, wouldn't you say?" He laughed. "No offense intended."

"None taken. *Great*-grandfather. You're right, Rossiter is made of the same stuff."

"You could stop in Naples at the end of your trip—if you don't mind delaying your trip home a few days. Meanwhile Carruthers could at least track him down for you. He knows his way around everywhere, since he's half-Italian. It would work out well, and you could get a flight back from Rome."

Reluctantly, George agreed. The last thing he wanted was to delay his return trip, but McMasters confirmed his own feeling that the Rossiter book would be improved immeasurably if he were to get an interview from Guaragna. Not only about his former wife, but about Rossiter's business tactics in those days from somebody who obviously would be disgruntled about the whole operation.

Not that he hadn't already gotten to hear many a tale from those— apart from Mickiewicz—he had recently interviewed, but it always sounded like sour grapes to him. With Guaragna, it might be different. Here was somebody who, by all accounts, had been quite a pianist. Those reviews he'd looked up in the *New York Times* certainly attested to that. But suddenly there'd been a complete halt. Nobody ever heard of him again. A sudden nonentity. Why? He was sure to hear an earful if he managed to track him down.

Of course, when it came to negative viewpoints, he had no further to go than Lisa. Her antipathy to Rossiter was strange; he couldn't understand it. And the old man was crazy about her—she could wrap him around her little finger if she tried. Not that she'd ever do that. It was precisely that kind of thing that she held against Rossiter. What she couldn't—or wouldn't—see was that those that could be wrapped no longer did any wrapping.

The rest of the tour went by quickly though no letters from Lisa awaited him at any of his known stopover points. In Russia, where he received the full vodka and caviar treatment by the writers' association, he didn't even look in his mailbox. He knew she didn't know where he was. He sat glumly in his hotel room, staring out the window at the squalid trolley cars winding their way under gray, wintry skies, sipping Slivovitz in a tooth-paste glass, and remembering the feel and taste of her hair across his mouth.

Always, before this, whenever he was away, he willfully tried to blot the absent from his consciousness, to match spiritual with geographic boundaries. This time the absent dominated, the rooms and scenes he inhabited were rendered void. The Bolshoi, the Winter Palace, the Kremlin, *nyet, nyet, nyet.*

What he did try to blot out was the memory of that smile she gave him when they parted, the one without warmth, as if she had already gone away and left him. This was the withheld part of Lisa, that other being he had gotten to know so well in her office.

The withheld part must have gotten the upper hand for it now withheld letters too. He turned over the possible explanations in his head. Maybe she'd been terribly hurt by some bastard in the past and was wary. Maybe he'd rushed her too much. Or maybe it was something simple, like getting the dates of his itinerary screwed up. But she was too efficient for that. He concluded that it was all the fault of the damn mails—the French, Austrian, and German ones as well as the one back home.

He was less sanguine when his continued calls went unanswered. Of course there was the time difference, but several times he'd timed it to catch her before she left for work in the morning. Then, since he'd given the operator the number from memory, he went through information to confirm his recollection. The number was correct, but to make sure, he had the operator dial it again. Still no answer, only the steady ringing which meant she wasn't home, or wasn't answering. Her silence reverberated with disconcerting echoes, but his mind shied away from whatever they were.

He wanted to call her in the office, but knew she'd balk. With his snapshot memory he remembered how red in the face she'd become when she said she needed to keep her two lives separate. God, he was tired of trying to sort through the contradictions of this elusive woman. You'd think they were doing something illegal the way she carried on. But, of course, she was a very private person, and it was she, not he, who had to face those people every day.

Disheartened, he tried to rouse himself again by exploring the city. After an afternoon of trudging through the Hermitage and seeing her face in every Titian and Fra Angelico, he decided to chance a phone call after all. He called Rossiter, hoping she'd answer first, but she was out; Virginia Lavin put him through immediately. "I visited the Galliuillin memorial," he said, "it's quite an impressive sight." The old man guffawed. "If he falls out of favor tomorrow—like Shostakovich did over cosmopolitanism or some other trumped-up charge, it'll be dismantled before you can say Jack Robinson." After filling in the conversation with a few more desultory remarks, he asked after Lisa and learned she was off at the printer's getting the Nielsen flyer out.

"Nielsen? Quite a pianist, that girl."

"Not a girl—a man," Rossiter said with a chuckle. "Name had us fooled, too. Where did you hear him?"

"At—It must have been over the radio somewhere over here."

"We're giving him quite a build-up. Or I should say Lisa is—she's running herself ragged over him. I don't blame her. If he comes through, he could make her career for her. Like Pavlova did for Hurok in the old days. And he's a good-looking son of a gun. Where did you say you heard that broadcast? She'll be interested to know."

A pause. "I don't remember, maybe it was . . . in Paris one night."

"Hey, this is costing you a bundle. Was there anything special you needed Lisa for? Can I give her a message?"

"No, nothing special," George said hastily, "tell her I was asking after her."

And afterwards, as his imagination raced frenziedly on, he even worried about that, for Rossiter had given a sympathetic snort, as if he sensed he wanted to say much more than that.

Nielsen, eh. Damn. You never know the damage that is done by going away. After the jet takes off or the train rounds the bend or the ship sails beyond the horizon, the here and now has center stage and everything else is shoved away. Hell, it becomes non-existent.

George tried to quell his misgivings but what did he really know about her? She was still a stranger—with her wild changes of mood, from one persona to the next. The way she'd looked at him when he went—

The thought came like a sudden door banging open. He had said something about her not proving to be a figment of his imagination and for a moment she hardly appeared to see him; then her eyes had gone dead. He had the reporter's gift of prescience—or at least he thought he did—but not this time. And in the door came another picture of her earlier that last morning at breakfast, pushing the eggs around on her plate, barely eating.

A figment of his imagination? No, no—a sharp thrust in his mind cried.

Still, the longer she kept up this bloody silence, the more he was beginning to think she was just that.

Chapter XXV

Monte Placidus was set on the side of a Laurentian mountain in a heav-ily-wooded area at the top of a steep rise. The bus wound upwards, carefully following the sudden dips and curves, and swerving around the spattering of boulders dislodged from the steep cliff face. As it neared the crest, it came upon the sharpest of the many hairpin turns which punctuated the journey. After pausing a moment as if to catch its breath, the bus moved first to the left, then careened sharply to the right, spitting up gravel from the shoulder and unseating an elderly pas-senger at the front. Elizabeth woke with a start and yawned deeply.

A long unprotected stretch loomed ahead, without an inch to spare, a sheer drop on the right of five hundred feet.

Under her knitted wool hat, Elizabeth sat tensely erect. Through the muddied windows she looked down at the tops of petrified pines, branches sagging under the weight of grey snow, and the frozen lake far below, as remote as childhood memories. On wintry days such as these, she and Tom had sometimes skated hand in hand on the rink on Bathurst Street, coming home to Grandma Adelina's hot choco-late with marshmallow fluff. And she would gather them in her arms and cry out in Italian her thanks to the heavens for bringing them back safely. When they laughed, she would tell them of her private little chats with God each day, thanking him for helping her and her loved ones get through another day unharmed.

What, Elizabeth thought, was the nature of the talk she had on the day Chris drowned?

As the bus rocked Elizabeth against the clouded windowpane, the reek of tobacco and salmon sandwiches assailed her. Having risen at dawn to catch the early morning flight to Montreal, and making a mad dash from Dorval to the inner city to catch the bus into the Quebec heartland, she was beyond tiredness.

Her decision to visit Tom for the long Washington's Birthday weekend was a consolation prize after turning down the chance to join George. The man in the aisle seat opposite grinned at her, as he had several times before when he caught her eye. With his sandy hair and aquiline nose, he reminded her of George.

But then everything and everyone reminded her of George. *I meet people,* he had written, *I think of you. I make speeches, I think of you. I catch airplanes, I think of you. All at the same time.* He took the words out of her very own heart. Arranging her camel hair coat tightly around her, she turned to stare at the telegraph poles struggling their way up the mountain. It was all very well to issue injunctions to her traitorous flesh, but she had no more control over these lapses than she had over the way her hair grew.

At night his pale rounded smiling face hung over her. She was determined not to think of him. *Get real,* as George once put it, *Elizabeth cum Lisa!*

He defeated her at every turn.

The bus skirted as far to the right as possible, halting to allow a dangerously swift station wagon go by, its motor screaming in protest. In its wake, came a man on a yellow snowmobile. The abyss falling away toward the valley below pressed against Elizabeth's chest and along all her nerve endings. Ice sculptures had adorned many of the steepled villages they'd passed, but none could compare to the celestial crests of the bluffs ahead, glinting like the entrance to Hallelujah Come.

The sight did not raise her spirits. Spectacular though these views were, the fact they were the only ones Tom ever saw or ever would again, intensified her sadness. Even their father's funeral had not been sufficient reason for him to leave the monastery.

As the bus trundled tortuously forward again to ascend another steep rise, her ears plugged up.

"Do you think the ears adjust when you live in these altitudes?" the man across from her asked.

The woman in front of her responded. "Probably. But then they're used to having part of their consciousness permanently blocked."

George's look-alike laughed. "No wonder they built the monastery here—the choice of location was probably deliberate. An aid for the zealous to diffuse reality."

"And to *defuse* it," thought Elizabeth as the bus approached the great abbey on top of the knoll. A tangle of juniper and arborvitae were banked on the left, carefully pruned by some unknown devotee's hand.

As disappointed as Aunt Ada was that she wasn't coming home to Toronto, she had been appeased when she heard she was visiting Tom. The visit was long overdue. With their father gone, Tom should be the first to understand her desire to find out more about their mother. She wanted to tell him everything, from the beginning, how it began, how it grew—everything pent up for so long. A true confession. Not for absolution—she was way beyond that, just a little understanding from somebody who'd had to wrestle with similar demons.

But a sinking feeling swept over her as the bus swung past the wrought-iron gates when she saw a column of brown-robed monks file by on their way to the domed chapel. Suddenly she remembered the cold-shower letters she used to receive in college, those letters written in Tom's backward slanted script which somehow seemed to characterize his whole personality since he'd taken his vows.

She could feel the nick in her skin when her thumb once tore a jagged slit through the envelope.

As always when Elizabeth entered the visitors' gallery in the chapel, she was overcome with guilt, the plaintive voices below stirred a blend of confused longings and regret.

It had to do with Tom, of course, with her inability to ever reach him, with his shackledom in expiation of other peoples' sins, with the sins of those other people, if sins they were. And it had to do with her discomfiture in these surroundings, her apartness even in the act of receiving communion. "I've never seen you here by choice," Tom once said to her, "only by circumstance."

They were just beginning the Office of None as she took her seat, and the chant—*God come to my assistance, Lord make haste to help me*—with its distinctive tonality—so different from that of major or minor keys of modern music, made her heart stop still. It took time for her eyes to adjust from the bright sunshine outdoors to the semi-darkness and she could barely make out the pulpit and font with the elaborately ornamented lamp suspended high above the gleaming pews.

What wouldn't she give to join in the chanting of this sacred litany—the very essence of her past—in fullness of heart, like those around her? Or in believing the gentle homilies, drawing sustenance from every phrase. From behind the choir loft screen an *Alleluia* supplemented the Gradual-respond and the music floated higher and higher, beyond the crenellations, beyond the uppermost reaches of the gold and lapis lazuli speckled dome, its beseeching message of *joy in being* transcending earthly cares.

All around her the women had sunk to their knees and a fragrant cloud from the burning censers settled over their prostrated bodies. *Pietus*, Elizabeth thought, as she also fell to the floor. She could not betray Grandmother Adelina, she told herself, she could not betray her who was now beside her, behind her, and in front of her, praying for the dead, the living dead, the future dead.

In these hallowed precincts, how easy to become a real Guaragna, a Guaragna of Napoli, a Guaragna who could surrender to the icon of the Virgin, trusting her to transform the seethe of her emotions to the simplicity of the *cantus planus*.

But the air thickened with the helpless cries around Elizabeth; the smell of the incense, previously so soothing, now cloyed and made breathing difficult.

Anger, not peace, surged as she threaded her way to the exit: anger at the betrayal of her own convictions, anger at having to wait until Tom completed his daily fast before seeing him, anger at the five hours of the day he gave over to repetition of the liturgy, chanting the Matins, the Lauds, the Sexts, on and on until eternity.

Her hand fumbled in her purse to withdraw a few dollars for the collection box on the table at the back of the basilica; then she changed her mind and walked on ahead.

Her anger was not appeased when she finally saw Tom in the visitors' lounge shuffling along apologetically like a nursing home inmate, peering through half-averted, half-glazed eyes. *You're only thirty-four years old, for God's sake! Stop it, stop it now.* His figure in the brown monastery-woven wool was gaunt, his face deeply lined—all the punitive aspects of the catechism made flesh, or rather, made skin and bones.

She tried to hide her alarm, but the carefully couched questions she did get out didn't fool him. He gave her a long slow smile. "All we're trying to do is regulate and foster asceticism and mysticism." His dimple faded into his cheek. "Outside is anarchy, I don't have to tell you that. It's been the dream of man since the beginning of time to find a higher meaning. The world grows meeker and meeker and the soul dies. We need this more than ever before, more than ever before." He moved away abruptly to stand at a window, stooped and grayed, his glasses held behind him. Then he crossed back to his chair and hung his glasses on his ears as he read the letter from Aunt Ada which she shared with him.

They spoke of his work for a while. Around them everybody spoke in whispers and they did too. Tom sat forward pushing back a lock of hair with the side of his hand, revealing his fragile fingers and satiny dark eyes. His trick of clicking off his thoughts was more pronounced than ever and half the time his eyes looked blindly ahead of him. "I'm still working on the *Antiphonal*, trying to get it back, always trying to get it back—"

"In what way?"

He opened and shut the ear rests of his glasses which he held in his hand. "Well, you know how the plain-chant was debased in the past, when they introduced those harmonies, making the plain-song less and less plain. Most of it has been restored to what it was but a lot still . . ."

"It certainly seemed restored from what I heard."

With the descent of the sun, the room became increasingly dark and the tall shrubs outside wrapped in protective sacks looked like figures huddling in the snow. Not unlike the column of monks she'd seen earlier. As the Vesper hour approached, the room emptied and for a while the silence closed around them.

Something about Tom was different but she couldn't figure out what it was. If she didn't hurry up, he'd have to go to the chapel soon and she'd lose her chance. As she turned on the lamp between them, he blinked and looked frightened, bringing back that time at the piano when the lid nearly came down on his hands. He had run away from home after that, trying to put as much distance between him and his father as he could, but two hours later the police found him at a drug store on the outskirts of Sunnyside Beach, reading Captain Marvel comic books in a corner. When Aunt Ada opened the suitcase with the belongings that he took along with him, she found one undershirt, one sweater, his well-thumbed copy of *The Lord of the Rings*, and the green and blue tie Chris had once given him.

Elizabeth wanted to speak but was unable to do so; the words were trapped inside. "What's wrong?" he asked. When she shook her head his face was so full of understanding, understanding beyond *words*, that she hardly felt the need to say anything.

But as she studied him more closely, she saw something new in his face, a serenity it hadn't had earlier, a serenity born from her disturbance, a vacuum filled by her troubles. She pulled her open cardigan tightly across her chest.

Nevertheless he had this gift now, no question, he brought peace, a kind of universal peace, which the mere recital of particulars could not alter, and which his hand, now stroking hers, confirmed. She wondered if he still kept Chris' tie over the mirror in his room. But then she remembered there were no mirrors in his cell.

The chapel bells rang again calling the faithful; as he started to edge crabwise toward the door, she put a restraining hand on his arm. He stiffened. He had to go now, his eyes pleaded, couldn't she see that?

But she couldn't bear to lose him again so soon. "Tom, dearest Tom, wait just a minute. I've got to tell you something—I'm working for Alfred Rossiter, Tom."

"You what?" His large fist closed over the glasses in his hand and the frame snapped.

She regretted the words the instant they were out but seeing him withdraw into his usual light trance had touched off a fuse. Now it was too late. "Alfred Rossiter. I'm working for Alfred Rossiter."

Opening his palm, he held up the frame of his glasses, the metal of which was twisted irreparably. "Are you mad? I don't understand . . ."

She drew back from him as her heart filled with fright, the way it used to when her father was alive, forever guilty of crimes neither of her making or doing. And it came to her for the first time how much Tom looked like him, the same collected fury in the dark eyes, the same lips squeezed tight, fighting for control.

With his arms folded inside the sleeves of his habit, Tom looked at her, not as his sister, his friend, but as some mysterious creature from the outer regions of space. "Why would you do such a thing?"

"But, Tom, I thought *you* would understand. I'm trying to find out more about mother. We've only known what papa told us. I wanted to have some other knowledge. Can you imagine a man depriving a mother of all her children—"

"Why shouldn't he?" The spasmodic tic in his right cheek started. "Wages of sin"—he articulated the *sin* with all his force.

The phrase infuriated her. "Of course, I should have known you would take this view." She opened her sweater to close her fingers around the locket on her chest. "Dominic Guaragna and his trusted son, sitting in judgment from on high, full of wisdom and mercy, sprinkling music and incense on the faithful. But for the unbelievers and the heretics there are other liturgical resources—right?"

"What's come over you, Lisa? You're getting to be as blasphemous as she was." Tom stepped as if to go, the halo of light fell over his shoulders and down to his hand where the ruined glasses still lay.

"But did you know," she exclaimed at last, playing her trump card triumphantly, "that she fought to regain custody of us, this blasphemous mother of ours?"

Suddenly, ferociously, he turned, waving the twisted glasses. "Not us. Just you. All she really wanted was you." And he turned on his heels, filling the room with the sound of his footsteps clicking furiously on the wooden floor.

In the guesthouse, Elizabeth took down a book on medieval history from the bookshelf, a pious tract called *Why I Believe* by some of the more famous converts of the twentieth century, a study of the great abbesses of Central Europe. After thumbing through them for a while, she replaced them in their allotted spaces.

Concentration was impossible. She had spent a sleepless night, going over and over in her mind the conversation with Tom. Where did Tom get the idea their mother had fought hardest for her custody? The opposite was probably true. She was used to them, had tended and nursed them through their formative years, whereas she had been a newcomer with little emotional investment for her attached.

Pulling on her coat and tucking her hair into her wool cap, she went outside, bending her body into the wind. On one side the land dropped sharply; no house or road was visible, nothing to indicate the existence of humanity. Only the snow capped peak of the neighboring mountain loomed in the distance, looking grim and forbidding, the rock and shale just discernible in the early morning light.

How she'd hoped things would be different with Tom, as though the barriers of a lifetime could magically disappear. Well, *arrividerci* to that dream. To the right a panorama stretched, with the road winding down to the villages below. She had a mind to run down it as fast as she could, but this was one time she knew she must stay. Tom had gone to great lengths to obtain special permission for her visit and even though visits to the abbey lodge were restricted to only a few hours of the afternoon, he would be expecting her and she couldn't bear to disappoint him.

Disappoint? *Controsenso, bambina.* Probably he'd be as relieved as she would be if she disappeared.

To part on that distressful note, however, would be too painful. Who knew when—or even if—she would see him again?

A faint sound of voices could be heard from the chapel which meant they were probably finishing the Matins. In soul-damning clarity she recalled the priest intoning beside Chris' open grave, "Holy Mary, Mother of God, pray for us now and at the hour of our death. Hail, Holy Queen, Mother of Mercy, accept this boy in Heaven and forgive him his sins . . ."

What, pray tell, were *his* sins?

Once again Elizabeth was forced to wait until the late afternoon to see her brother. But she was less resentful than the previous day for her long walk through the woods surrounding the monastery had been invigorating, and she had awakened from her afternoon nap feeling refreshed.

She was happy to see that Tom also seemed to be in better spirits. His erect posture and crisp steps as he strode toward her bespoke some kind of new determination. On his ears hung his glasses, the frames straightened and strengthened with duct tape.

He greeted some people he knew at the couch in front of the window, acted the thoughtful host with others, jumping up, rearranging chairs.

"You're still confused about me," he said when he settled into his own seat.

Elizabeth leaned forward to remove a thread from the sleeve of his habit. Again she tried to figure out what was so different about him, but she could not pinpoint it. "Maybe so."

"You think I've chosen to be here out of some escape. What you can't seem to understand is that for me—this is the true reality. Everything else"—he made a large sweep with his arm—"has just melted away since I've been here—all the guilt that I'd been burdened with for so long—all of it just lifted when I surrendered."

"Even about . . . Chris—"

"Yes, even about him. Or, especially about him. What else was there to feel guilty about?"

This was delivered with such force that for a moment Elizabeth could say nothing. "How about mother?" she asked at last.

"No reason for *me* to feel guilty about *her*. The other way around I should say. You don't remember her but I do. She used to tuck us in each night and tuck "Message of the Day" notes into our lunchboxes—I'd read them to Chris. The idea of the messages, I suppose, was to give us a laugh as well as build up our confidence. And to let us know that whatever happened, she would always be there for us. Ha. Those messages are my most vivid memory of her."

"What were they like?"

"Oh, nothing profound, or anything like that. She tried to be funny, that's all. It was the deed not the words that I remember. She'd dash them off on the spur of the moment. I remember one that went something like this: 'Your road to heaven you will pave/ if you remember to behave.' She should have taken her own advice."

"What else do you remember?"

"Not anything concrete. Oh, yes, I remember the gladioli. She loved them and always had a great burst of color around the room. But that's what made her going so terrible, no messages ever came again, nothing could bring her back. And no gladioli."

For a while Tom sat in silence, shifting his legs and adjusting his robe around them, his face contorted with the effort to continue. At last he got rather unsteadily to his feet. "It took me by surprise, what you told me yesterday, but I got to thinking about it and could see why you would want to find out more. But I know as much as I want to about that sord . . . sad story. What's Rossiter like?"

"About what you'd expect. Full of self-righteousness—thinks he's been God's gift to music. And that artists are a dime a dozen."

He asked, "Does he speak of mother ever?"

"Well . . . not to me. But he loved her, I'm convinced of that. Perhaps more than she— I don't really know about that, of course."

Tom lifted his shoulders and paced back and forth for a moment. He turned toward the window, stared at the pond covered by a sepia glaze in the distance. "How does Rossiter feel about you working for him?"

"Well, you see, that's what I wanted to speak to you about. I assumed a false name—"

"So that's it." His voice had a caroling quality to it and he looked relieved. "I wondered why—I mean, I didn't think he'd want a Guaragna in his *sanctum sanctorum*. But isn't it illegal to have a false name? It seems to me you're asking for a lot of trouble. Does Aunt Ada know?"

"No, she doesn't. And please don't tell her. I don't want her to. I'm planning to quit soon and she doesn't need to know a thing about it. It'd only worry her."

"You're right. I think the whole idea's mad. And I advise you to get out of there as fast as you can. I don't know what possessed you in the first place."

She hesitated for a long moment, gazing beyond him. Day had darkened over the garden, the skyline invisible. "There's another complication. I've . . . there's a man I met—" She could hardly get the words out.

"What does he have to do with it? Does he work there, is that what you mean?"

"No, he's doing a biography on Rossiter. As a matter of fact, he's in Italy right now trying to find some Guaragnas to interview."

Tom's face, which in the gathering dusk had held unearthly beauty, now tightened. "My G-God Lisa, what kind of me-mess have you g-gotten us all into? In Italy—who knows wha-what he'll turn up there. How could you stir up-up this hornet's nest? Have you no lo-loyalty at all?" He encircled his hands tightly around the sleeves of his habit. "You'd be-better get out of there at once. P-promise me you'll d-do that r-right a-a—"

With the force of a blow she now realized what had been so different about Tom and could hardly breathe. Her hand twisted her locket in remembered pain. It was his stutter, totally absent earlier, but with the utterance of a few loaded words, now was returned full force, just like that, as if a switch had been turned on.

His stammered "P-promise me you'll d-do that r-right a-a—" seemed to ricochet from several points in the room all at once. Her own voice tensed, waiting for him to expel the word trapped on his recalcitrant tongue; she wanted to finish the sentence for him—just as she did when they were children—but knew better than to dare.

What was she doing there—instead of getting help as she had hoped, she was shattering her brother's hard-won serenity.

She turned from him and fled.

Chapter XXVI

Clutching her chest as though it might split apart, Ada cried "Lisa, I don't believe it. I thought you were visiting Tom. What happened?"

Elizabeth deposited her small overnight case in the foyer and stepped inside the living room. Rancid cigarette smoke had settled over the music, and books were tossed about on coffee table, piano, and couch. "I couldn't spend another day waiting for him to finish the homilies of the Gospels before seeing him. I still had a day left, so when I got to the airport I changed my ticket to Toronto. I had to see you."

"What is it? What happened?"

All previous self-exhortations to the contrary, Elizabeth blurted out: "How come you never told me about the custody fight my mother had put up for us? How come?"

Ada subsided into a chair; her face went gray. "You mustn't do this to me, Lisa. You must never surprise me like this. I want to see you—I count the days till you'll come, but I can't take this kind of shock anymore."

"How about my shock? How about that? How come you've never told me about it? Don't you think I should know about my own mother?"

"How did you find out?"

"Never mind how I found out. I just did. How could my—how could *your precious brother* have done such a thing to her? Never to let her see us again . . ."

Having never before spoken like this to her aunt, Elizabeth knew she ought to soften her stance, especially since, after all, she too had been a victim. But she was unable to do so. "And you're no better— Knowing all this and never—"

A long silence followed a sharp intake of breath. Finally Ada cleared her throat a few times and said: "You know I don't believe we should—how you say—spoil an artist. They have to answer like every other human being when they do wrong. But do you know what it takes to be an artist?"

"Of course I do, don't start—"

"Look, every time they go on stage, they have to go a little mad. At all times they have to be mindful of the whole piece—and every part of it so that not one note is lost. Then, like a space ship they have to lift off and go on to another world, to the world the composer inhabited."

"Don't get off the subject. I know that. I want—"

"This is the subject. Listen, I remember once in the early days of television they had a special with Mary Martin and Ethel Merman called *Ninety Minutes is a Long, Long Time*. And everybody marvelled how two performers could carry a show that long all by themselves. Well, a concert artist does that at every recital, and doesn't have a whole army of stage managers, producers, make up men, coaches, and the whole might of a television network behind him."

"Why can't you give me a straight answer?"

"There's no such thing as a straight answer. Life's too complicated for that. Let me finish. I tell you Lisa, re-entry isn't that easy from those heights. Astronauts aren't the only ones who need a debriefing, decompression period. Artists need it too—for if he's done it right, something did happen out there, he *has* transcended into another plane, and it's not easy to come back to earth so fast and remember to pick up a bottle of milk for breakfast on the way home. Ninety minutes of remembering every detail, every *pizzicato*—and every *pizzicato* of each instrument in the orchestra as well—"

Elizabeth felt a deep stab. When she was very little, she remembered her father giving her and Chris what he called *pizzicato kisses*, quick little kisses all over face and head. She had forgotten all about them; after Chris' death, they, along with any other such demonstrations, had abruptly ceased.

"Why *he* always? Mother was an artist too. Why not give her the same benefit of the—"

Ada dragged a fist slowly across her eyes. "Yes, she was. That sonata recital they once gave together, I've never forgotten. The purity of her tone. You're right. I never said Dom was justified, never. It's only that lover of hers I condemn."

"Must you be so evasive? You still haven't said anything about the custody battle. Neither would Tom. What is it with the Guaragnas? Why can't I ever—"

"You spoke of this to Tom?"

"Why shouldn't I? He's my brother, isn't he? But then I had to leave him because I saw he couldn't take it. The last thing I want to do is to take away his peace, too. Or what he calls peace. But I'm different—for better or worse I need to know these things. I'm tired of going round and round in my head trying to figure things out. I want to break out and I can't. I've a right to know and nobody ever tells me anything. Isn't it bad enough I never had a mother—do I have no right to know anything about her? You said she committed suicide. Well, I don't believe it. She loved Rossiter and he loved her. Why should she do that? I just don't believe it."

"So don't believe it. I never said she did. I only said I thought so. And I still think so." Ada picked up a piece of cellophane wrapper from the table and tore it into pieces. "Maybe I should've told you about the custody battle. But I thought these things were better left in the past. I don't know why you can't just leave these things alone. What's the point of raking it all up and spoiling your life with it?"

"But it *has* spoiled my life, down to the last details. It has poisoned it, ruined it, tainted it. That's the whole point, don't you see that?"

"Now look here," Ada said, rising to her feet. "Is this what I get for all I've done? I had to be *in loco parentis* to all of you—not only the children but my brother, too—"

"I know, I know. It's not your fault." Her eye ran over the piano standing mute in the corner; the music rang in her head, it and nothing else. "There's a Guaragna curse on all of us. I know it, I feel it, I can't get out from under it. Why? Why? Why?"

"Keep this with you whenever you leave your seat," the train conductor said as he punched a hole in a ticket and inserted it into the ledge above. Elizabeth nodded her head as she closed the railroad magazine and placed it into the pocket of the seat in front of her. Because of a sudden blizzard, all flights had been cancelled and she was returning to New York by train.

Immediately upon leaving Union Station, the train wound its way to the left of the CN Tower. In dull red letters on the gray stone background encrusted in ice, a sign said: *THE TOP OF TORONTO.*

On this day, however, the top of Toronto was obliterated, as was the bottom, all lost in the whirling whiteness.

As lost as her father and Chris. And now as lost as Tom. From now on he was on his saintly—she on her unsaintly—own. Henceforth, and from a distance only, they could wish each other godspeed—and that was final. The same for Aunt Ada—she didn't know how she could face her again.

And ditto George.

Windows in a passing town sprang into distant illumination as the day wound down, street lamps, enmeshed in drift, cast their dull glow. But mostly it was now black outside, the landscape disappeared and all she saw in the black glass was her own despair. She could feel the cold seeping through the window sash and pulled the collar of her jacket around her neck. The train had barely left Hamilton when it came to a screeching halt. The generator went off, shutting the lights. Broken up like a puzzle, the fragments of her existence lay scattered over her mind in the silent darkness. But it wasn't like a holograph, where each fragment contained the essence of the whole—all were disparate pieces with no connection to each other. The night before, dashing out of the house to escape Ada's omnivorous presence, she had walked blindly through snow-covered streets, not knowing what she was thinking. Ditto now.

The train started up again with a lurch. The foothills rose silver to the east, the denuded trees sharp black against the white backdrop. "Where do you live?" a customs official asked suddenly. She wished her answer was as simple as the reply she gave when he handed her a form. "Fill this out and give it to the immigration inspector at the border."

"Why does the train keep stopping?" she asked.

"Why do you think? We have to get the tracks cleared before we can move on them, especially the switches, and the only way is just a short ways ahead—otherwise there's no point."

Elizabeth filled out the form, then sat back and shut her eyes. There was something otherworldly about train travel. No music, no movie, a little like going back in time. The train which had cautiously started now stopped again. Start, stop, start, stop. She looked out and found they were midway over the Niagara River, suspended high in the air over the gorge that separates the borders of the two countries. For all the appearance of solidity, in the eerie moonlight the train seemed too dangerous a weight for the slender bridge, which was nothing more than a steel casing.

Elizabeth looked down at the expanse of fiercely swirling waters below bracketed by mountainous icy cliffs. Either the river was on its way to the plunge up ahead or had just taken it, she wasn't sure. She could easily see the train taking the same plunge and she plummeting through space knowing no more than that her terrible thoughts had suddenly ceased.

If only she could see her mother just once, it wouldn't have to be up close, she wouldn't have to touch her. Was that too much to ask? But her dancing Camille of a mother would never agree to such terms. She would seize her hands and pull her in a wild waltz until the waters rushed up to meet them.

Chills ran in ripples along her chest and between her shoulder blades and she shut her eyes. *All right, God, listen to me: if the train has to topple, please don't let it be here, please let it be on the other side, that's all I ask, please let it be on the other side.*

A hand came down on her shoulder. "Sorry, but I need that immigration form. Did you buy anything in Canada?" The train had begun to creep again, was on terra firma again, through the window Elizabeth saw an American flag. "No, nothing," she said, handing the inspector the form.

"What was the purpose of your trip?"

"Pleasure."

Chapter XXVII

Item: Lisa had predicted it would be a wild-goose chase and she was inclined to be right about these things. Item: Carruthers, the hail-fellow-well-met representative of the McMasters Publishing House, had told him there was no Dominic Guaragna to be found; neither was there a Tomaso, a Christophoro, or an Elizabeta . . . "Only some old bloke by the name of Giuseppe Guaragna who claims he never heard of him."

So why the hell had he headed for Naples, even though he couldn't get a seat on a plane there when he wanted to and had to wait until the next day?

He couldn't say. Or yes, he could say, but it made little sense: fine tuning your material was one thing; trying to fit an alien set of strings on it was another. And there was this nagging feeling that he wasn't doing right by Rossiter, sneaking off behind his back trying to pile up some dirt. The old man would know a Judas when he saw one. Lisa wasn't the only person he'd been darn decent to.

Lisa's attitude had definitely undermined his confidence in the man. He had a good mind to ignore her and go to the next part of the book, finish it up and write paid to the whole project.

But try as he might, he found it hard to discount what someone who worked for Rossiter day-in and day-out had to say. What she had to say was not exactly crystal clear; still, the very fact she had such misgivings was proof of a kind in itself.

And anyway, for God's sake, this was the twentieth century—no bloody, big-scale heroes existed anymore. Even the small-scale ones who start off on the right side fighting tyrannies, and winding up in prison, establish tyrannies of their own once they're out. Rossiter was no better or worse than any of the entrepreneurial primitives of his generation. And if their slice of the American dream came with a bad smell, tough. There was always a monogrammed hand-stitched linen handkerchief to place over the nose to shut it out. Or somebody else's nose. And an image maker/transformer like Isabel Nagel to do even that for you.

But was his much-vaunted generation any better? After a brief hiatus in Haight-Ashbury or at the feet of some guru in Boulder riding around in a Rolls Royce, many of his friends in Shaker Heights had returned to the family mansions—or the guest houses thereof. Time was when they'd scoffed at the valet parking service at country clubs for those not yet chauffeured in their own limousines. Now they were emerging from these Audis and Bentleys themselves, a couple of bills discreetly folded in their hands to pass along with the car keys.

He stared glumly at the mauve haze over the Italian hills that dotted the landscape down below. The plane crossed over some forests and a river spanned by a bridge; in the distance he saw the pale mouth of an estuary. Wild-goose chase though it might be, he was glad he was making this stopover. Even apart from the Rossiter connection, it would be interesting to meet Guaragna. Not easy for an artist—tunnel-visioned, single-minded, egotistical creature that each of necessity was—to throw over everything in one mad act of revenge. And then to renounce his music too—as he seemed to have done. In the post-breakfast somnolence of the giant 747, the thought was like an outrage.

Vendettas, however, he reminded himself, were a famous local product. Alongside olive and orange orchards, crops of them in all shapes and sizes were raised for generations in those islands in the sea below.

But the chances of meeting Guaragna were slim, he had to keep reminding himself. And if he did succeed, perhaps mentioning the biography of Rossiter right up front would be the wrong tactic. Perhaps he could dig up some old Guaragna recording and make that the basis for his search. *I heard your Diabelli and never heard anything like it. How did you get that sound?*

Provided, of course, he ever played the *Diabelli*. Or that any recordings existed. Plenty of topics came to mind that he could invent: the peculiar psychoses of conductors, the outlook and psychology of contemporary composers, the effect of continued exposure to hard rock on the unsuspecting young, the cost of getting your tails cleaned during stopovers in Machu Picchu.

All this was predicated on meeting him. If he hoped to get somewhere, first he had to tackle Giuseppe Guaragna and lay on the charm. As he fastened his seat belt for landing, something from his gut seemed to be working its way upward, pressing heavily on his chest.

From the airport, he took a taxi directly to the address Carruthers had reluctantly provided. It got bogged down in a series of traffic jams, but by mid-afternoon the driver found the street. At the corner building, a woman was hanging out two pairs of jeans on a clothes line strung between two second storey windows. George paid the driver off at the corner, wandered in search of number sixteen. As he approached the blue-shuttered villa overlooking the sea, he imagined a tail-coated figure with flying hair and a copy of a *Mozart* sonata clutched under his arm climbing the same steps.

All at once, jet lag seemed to overtake him. What was he doing here? Looking at the heavy oak door before him, it was all he could do to direct his feet to carry him forward. At the front window, a face flickered behind the curtain. A moment later, even before he rang the bell, the door opened.

A plump and placid lady stood in the doorway. When he told her who he was and why he was there, the placidity vanished. She remembered the visit of Signor Carruthers and she thought she had explained to him very clearly that they had no relatives by the name of Dominic. All this was accomplished in her broken English and his broken Italian.

"Is your husband here, Signora? I know this is awkward but maybe he knows. I just want him to tell me where he is—or anything else about him. Perhaps I could see—"

It was even heavier going than George had expected. She said she was sorry but as she had also explained to Signor Carruthers, her husband wasn't well enough to see anybody. He sensed some reluctance in connection with the Guaragna name itself and hastily considered what other subjects he could bring up which might soften her up. None of those he had imagined on the plane were remotely appropriate. Despite his decision not to bring up Rossiter at all, he was certain the chance of her having heard of him was unlikely.

"You see, I'm writing a book on an American impresario who once managed him . . . I only wanted to meet Guaragna in connection with that. It has nothing to do with him except as it relates to Alfred Rossiter."

He was prepared for some reaction—anything from a glint of recognition to a look of disgust, but not the gasp that came at the mention of Rossiter's name. The inside surface of his skin tautened. "I take it you know who I mean."

"I knowa nossing." She stepped back in the shadows and stared at him for a while, creating a chiaroscuro as the hall light fell on her dark eyes. "I tolda you my husband will see nobody, the *doctore* forbid— You will learna nossing—"

Not if I can help it came into his head as if she had transmitted it directly into his brain. In an effort to quell what amounted to ripples of hysteria, he said gently, "I only need to see him for a few minutes, at most. I've travelled a long distance especially for this. I promise not to tire him."

From inside, a Rossini aria could be heard on the radio; the volume was suddenly turned down. Panels of sweat ran down the woman's nose and across her brow. Crossing her arms over her chest, she stood in the center of the doorway barring the whole house. "Nossing,

nossing—you will learna nossing."

As she spoke, a dark shadow flickered in his mind for an instant. "I see, I see," he said finally and turned around to go down the steps, cursing himself for his clumsiness and for having paid off the cab.

For a moment he leaned against the wrought iron gate. Now what? *Folle, bloody folle!* It was all very well to hop on a plane and arrive in another country because somebody might have something to tell you. But what if that somebody didn't wish to tell it? Since when did people rearrange their existence obligingly to suit yours?

As he began to walk away, he saw somebody move away from the curtain in the front window. The dark shadow flickered again in his mind, like both the past and present were intertwined. What was going on here? From the glimpse he had of the man's white-cropped head and the speed with which he moved, he didn't look all that disabled to him.

Chapter XXVIII

On the last weekend in February, Elizabeth rented a black Ford, got into the car, and headed for the Golden Heights Christian Cemetery in Westchester. Anybody witnessing the resolve with which she went about doing this would hardly guess that earlier that morning she had stared up at the ceiling of her bedroom telling herself: "You don't really need to go. Really, you don't need to go."

The day was sunny but bitter cold; the car needed the heater on at all times to keep the windows from frosting over. From the West Side Highway, Elizabeth could see the Hudson River down below; swollen and angry-looking blocks of ice, like monsters of the deep, drifted in the blackness. It reminded her of the suspension of the train over the Niagara River the previous weekend and she shuddered. On the leather seat beside her were six gladioli, their translucent spikes of pink and blue a constant reminder of their own evanescence.

It was her mother's fifty-sixth birthday, a fact Elizabeth had discovered on a return trip to the library in order to read the obituary of her mother's death and was rewarded with the date of her birth too. Not a big fact, but solid, concrete: not open to differing interpretations. Beyond a shadow of a doubt, Elizabeth knew that if her mother had lived, she would have been fifty-six years old on that day.

The trip to the library, the result of a brainstorm following her return from Toronto, also clarified the reason for her death—thereby permanently laying that particular ghost to rest beside her. The obituary stated: "Mrs. Elizabeth Rossiter, wife of concert impresario Alfred Rossiter, passed away at the Matthew Donnelly Memorial Hospital following acute congestive heart failure on February 20, 1954."

The hospital could hardly have been in cahoots with Rossiter to invent that story. The article had gone on to list her husband and three children as survivors. Interment was at the Golden Heights Cemetery in a private ceremony; friends had been requested to send memorial gifts to the Musicians' Benevolent Fund in lieu of flowers.

Elizabeth made two copies of the obituary, one of which she sent air mail, special delivery, to her aunt in Toronto. In her accompanying note, she had simply stated: *Now we can really let her rest in peace.* No more the fire and brimstone of the suicide's lot.

Carefully Elizabeth steered the car into the left lane to pass a slow-poke in front of her and then eased back into the right. She loved to drive, to be enclosed in an environment of her own in the midst of the larger one beyond. It had taken three driver's tests before she obtained her license but that seemed to be par for her every pursuit. Nothing came to her easily.

Once she left the Sawmill River Parkway, Elizabeth found Ridge Road—Route 23E on her map. After several miles of discount shopping plazas and fast-food restaurants, the heavily-scrolled wrought iron gates she had been told to look out for loomed ahead.

The gates were attached to two massive piles of red brick, more like the entrance to a fortress than a cemetery. A quick check with the custodian in the gatekeeper's cottage gave the approximate location of her mother's grave between Azalea Lane and Lilac Path and she headed north toward it on the salted roads. When she reached the location and parked the car, she found she was nowhere near it, and wandered for ten minutes in circles past large slabs of marble, looking like petrified incarnations of the humans whose last resting place they identified. The only other people she met were a family of four, but they were leaving as she came up the path.

At last, after doubling back beyond a big square crypt, she finally spotted the shoulder-high tombstone on which *ELIZABETH ROSSITER* was carved across the top in a simple typeface. The stone itself was also simple, with none of the gimcrackery embellishments favored by its neighbors.

Quaking with a trespasser's fear, standing three feet from the stone as though at the edge of a nightmare cliff, she stood transfixed. The hour was getting late and a curious light that was something between silver and gold lit the valley in which she stood. Only a flock of pigeons disturbed the intense stillness as they splashed in and out of a nearby thicket.

She seemed to recognize the place, but knew that was impossible. But just because things were impossible didn't mean they couldn't happen. It was quiet around her, a complete and comforting silence. When she rubbed the bits of snow and ice from the stone, the inscription read:

IN LOVING MEMORY
ELIZABETH ROSSITER
Nee Jordan
BELOVED WIFE AND MOTHER
Born February 28, 1922
Died February 20, 1954

SHORT WAS HER SPAN
LONG WAS HER REACH

Elizabeth fell to her knees to fling the six gladioli on the base of the tombstone, her senses awakening as from a long, troubled sleep. *"Mamma, mamma mia,"* she cried and clenched her eyes, feeling her mother's spirit about her as a received presence. *At last I've found you, at last I know you.*

Peace, a real peace seemed to envelop her; some warm flesh was hushing and humming next to her own. A stranger was at her side. She herself was the stranger.

In the distance church bells rang their Sunday reminder to the faithful. She counted the bells, one per second. Somebody else counted, too. Afterward silence again, all-encompassing silence.

Elizabeth didn't know how long she knelt there, one arm clinging to the lettered slab, but suddenly she heard footsteps crunching the tightly packed snow. Lifting her head sideways, she saw Rossiter, carrying a bouquet of gladioli, coming up Azalea Lane. His head was bowed and he hadn't seen her. Heart madly thumping, Elizabeth moved stealthily on her hands and knees to hide behind the large neighboring crypt.

Until then she hadn't noticed how cold she was—feet and hands were numb, nose was running, breath was steamy—but it was too late to do anything about it. She didn't dare move from the spot. An icicle, suspended from the arms of the stone angel above her, plunged down, missing her by an inch, and scattering slivers over her boots as it hit the ground. She tightened her scarf and shook herself deeper into her coat.

The footsteps came closer and then ceased as Rossiter reached the grave site. Two pigeons plummeted onto the crypt and she prayed he wouldn't look over in that direction. She heard Rossiter clear his throat. Crouching painfully on the frozen ground, she remembered how Ada spoke to Dominic at his grave site. She hoped Rossiter wouldn't do that—*please, God in whom I do not believe, dear sweet God, let him not do that.* For him to be as maudlin as in fact she herself had been a few minutes earlier would be too much.

But Rossiter didn't speak, all she heard was a big sob. *We think we are stronger than the dead, but they are stronger than we are. They preside over us in all their immutability.* Her mother was there. She could not see her, but she had seen her. Rossiter's baffled exclamation, "Who in damnation?" brought sudden tears to her own eyes. Cold drips of water trickled down her cheeks. He must have seen the gladioli she had accidentally left behind.

But it was no accident, she had a right to leave gladioli, too.

Chapter XXIX

What George expected Lisa to say he didn't know, but certainly it was not, "of all people," not, "my, what a surprise," not, "how was the old mother country?"

And this after he had raced straight over to her office the minute his plane landed, retaining the cab while he dumped his suitcase in his apartment, not even bothering to pretend to Virginia Lavin that his visit was of a more official nature.

Of course, he should have known it would be regarded as inappropriate behavior. Raised eyebrows from Ruth Pryor, a long "harrumph" from Rossiter, a knowing twinkle from Virginia. As Margaret had once warned him, he seemed incapable of learning the lessons of his own history.

So all right, it was inappropriate. But what in blazes was appropriate? When was the last time he had experienced the same kind of delicious anticipation? When was the last time he had luxuriated at the thought of seeing someone with such intensity? The way his heart hammered when he saw her was also inappropriate. Not to mention the way (against all logic because he'd changed his return flight) he kept looking for her face among the people waiting up in the airport gallery while he was going through customs.

He had half a mind to take her in his arms and start all over again, but her cheeks, caught in the glare of the high-intensity lamp on her desk in an embarrassed flush, warned him against it. "You don't seem very pleased to see me," he finally said, when he could find the words.

"Oh, but I am," she replied, "but I'd no idea you were coming today. I've made other plans."

"Like what?"

"I'm going to see *A Chorus Line* with Helge. Give him a taste of pure Americana," she said with a nervous laugh.

"Helge?"

"Helge Nielsen, the pianist." She lifted one of the Nielsen leaflets from the piles on her desk and handed it to him. "Anyway, you're going to be far too jet-lagged to go out tonight. What you need is a good night's sleep."

Of course he was jet-lagged, but he'd envisioned a far different cure for it. Although she pretended she didn't, she goddamn knew it, too. At last, after the silence between them became untenable, she began to straighten the leaflets into neat piles and said: "George, I just need more space, more time. We've got to go more slowly."

Declarations of this kind produce moments of terrifying silence: a giant step to oblivion. Nor can the moment ever be re-reeled, the words unsaid. He crumpled the Nielsen leaflet in his fist. So much strangeness—all at once, the particular strangeness emanating from particular intimacy. "How much more slowly? Christ, we've just been apart over a month."

She managed a smile at that, but only just, her hand flying to her head to secure a bobby pin that had loosened her topknot. How he longed to loosen the tightness, feeling a kind of mirror pain on his own head, as though invisible hands were pulling his hair back too. They spoke for a while longer, covering a variety of subjects and then there was another silence, which neither of them wanted to fill.

Nossing, bloody *nossing.*

Two characters in a play, he thought, doing their set pieces with equal aplomb, which is to say, none.

"I was right proud," George Wentworth Sr.'s voice boomed over the telephone. "Imagine coming across my son's book in Hong Kong. And then on a stopover in Gander."

George made a wry grimace. At any other time he'd have relished his father's comments, but the timing was off. "Now I know where I can send friends to get it. You sure can't get it here. McMasters has gone all out in the distribution. Much better than the American publisher."

"You don't sound very happy about it."

"It's not that—" He wasn't sure whether he should satisfy his wounded heart by making the most of his meeting with Lisa, or escape the implications by making as little of it as possible. Besides his father was the last person to whom he usually confided. But before he knew it, out the whole sorry saga all came, he was sick and tired of dissimulating any longer.

To his surprise, instead of a round of *I told you sos,* his father chided him for being melodramatic. "Oh, come on, George. You're being hypersensitive as usual. Just because she didn't fall down for you. She was in the office after all. Be reasonable."

His guffaw over the telephone sounded shrill and George moved the receiver away from his ear a notch. "But why didn't she come with me?"

"Look, you arrive a day early. She's going to the theater with another man. So what? It's not exactly a capital offense."

"She could have seen me afterward—"

"From what you describe, the girl works her tail off in that office. And just because you're ready at the drop of a hat—"

"You've a distorted view there. I'm not that ready at all. If you only knew how dependent I am—"

"Dependent? You're a Wentworth."

"A *Wentworth!* Don't judge everybody by yourself. Of course I'm dependent." He thought of the way her eyes met his across her desk and then veered quickly away. His image of Lisa was of roundness itself, circles interlaced upon circles, but she was certainly all sharp angles at that moment.

"On what?"

"Not everything is economics. On trust mainly. It seems to me sex is all bound up with trust. I'm beginning to wonder if I can trust her anymore."

"Stop making such rash judgments. You're a big boy now. First it's all gung ho—now it's gung bah. I have a policy—one tested by time—of sleeping on things—no pun intended—before jumping to conclusions. A code of my own, as it were. Give the poor girl a chance to explain—"

"What's to explain? She's not what I thought she was."

"And what was that, pray tell? Some cross between Cinderella and Florence Nightingale?" His gravelly voice sounded amused. "What did you see in her in the first place?"

Frown lines creased George's brow. *What indeed?* The way her long graceful neck moved from side to side as though not quite able to find a comfortable resting place? The way she held down the Nielsen leaflets protectively on her desk as though he was going to toss them in the wastebasket? "I guess I don't know. How to explain chemistry? But I can't believe you're taking her side. You don't know her. Margaret called her a tight-ass bitch. She was right. She's an ungrateful, bad-tempered, spoiled brat. Rossiter lets her get away with anything she wants and she behaves as if he's Genghis Khan on the warpath. She's—"

"I see you've got it really bad. Give yourself a break. What you need is a good dose of sulphur and molasses."

If he wasn't to spend the next few days breaking off dialing her number before completion, he had to put some distance between them. After unpacking his suitcase from his European trip, he repacked his manuscript, accumulated mail and shaving kit and left the apartment.

George pressed the button and waited for the elevator. As the doors opened and he stepped in, he felt bereft. So many emotions surged that his knees nearly buckled. Most of all, he was angry at himself for failing to realize how his precipitousness would affect somebody as protective of her privacy as Lisa. There would probably be office jokes and insinuations which she would hate. And they both knew enough about office realpolitik to discern jokes that said one thing and meant another.

At the entrance to his building the doorman lifted his cap. Seeing his overnight case, he said: "Leaving us again so soon?"

"Can't be helped," he said as he stepped out on the street and headed for his garage.

Outside the air was brisk and he felt unsteady on his feet. "Where's the fire, buster," a man asked when he nearly bumped into him. "Sorry," he answered.

His father had told him not to jump to any conclusions. Okay, so he'd walk. Crawl, if necessary. But even if the remedial scenario he'd constructed for Lisa and him was out, did that mean they were now back to formalities? The mind champed at what would be next. Moreover, no gap in her defenses presented itself—all the barricades were solidly entrenched. And Nielsen ones at that. His father didn't have a clue as to what he was up against. He thought he was getting somebody like his mother: a hothouse plant which, with the proper tending, would grow any way you wanted it to, one which would—

Come to think of it, so had he. Of course, Lisa resembled his mother. Too bad he hadn't thought of that when his father asked him what he saw in her. She was Irish, but it was undoubtedly her English reticence that attracted him. Yet she wasn't quite English either. Not with her snippitiness. Olean, was it? As far as he knew her home town was a small upstate New York town with the usual complement of white clapboard houses, a steeple church, the village grocery. Or supermarket chain.

She didn't seem to go with that either.

What did all that matter anyway? Lisa was probably right. No promises had been made by either of them at any time. No promises given and none taken, thank you. And her all-too apparent reluctance to begin anything, spelled out in large indelible letters, surely adumbrated the difficulties that were to follow. The moratorium when she had ceased to be Miss Topknot was over. From the start she had made the whole episode seem like a recess, with that schoolmarm side of her warning that the bell would eventually ring and he'd again have to return to parsing French verbs and toting up columns. Recess was over. Time had stopped—that was precisely the way it was when he'd put his lips to hers—but it was sure making up for it now.

He couldn't fathom her. But he never had been able to. The best he'd come up with before was that she seemed to be two people, with the cool and cryptic one fighting for supremacy over the—

Perhaps he'd been kidding himself, there was no other one.

George passed a big trailer truck on the Long Island Expressway, then moved back to the right lane and reduced his speed. He'd been driving at seventy-five miles per hour all the way and his stomach was in knots.

A whole convoy of army trucks were up ahead, each with their lights on indicating they wanted to stay together. George moved to the left lane again. One truck overtaken, on to the next.

Compulsively, he kept recalling his conversation with Lisa earlier, going over it to see if he could make things connect. Apart from her personal rejection, the most maddening thing was the way she had smiled when he told her the trip to Italy *had* been a wild-goose chase, just as she had predicted. It wasn't exactly a smile, but there was no doubt her need to be right was more important than his success.

And when he added his only remaining lead was her friend

Elizabeth Guaragna, her mouth had gone tight, as though after his Italian fiasco, he should have known better. Then she picked up a leaflet and he noticed her hands trembling so badly she had difficulty closing her finger and thumb on the page.

Was it because it was a Nielsen leaflet? Was that it? And if it was, so what? He was getting weary of trying to second-guess the woman.

The speedometer advanced to eighty as he pictured her across the desk, hair coiled into that punishing knot, face strained and rigid. "I spoke to . . . her while you were gone," she said. "She never heard of a Dominic Guaragna. She asked her folks and they never did either. So there's no point in . . . seeing her. You'd be wasting your time again. Besides, she's gone abroad for an extended vacation."

"Where to?"

The silence was suddenly deep between them and she did not look up or meet his eye. At last she said, "England."

Had she been anybody else, he might have thought a little jealousy had come to the fore, so strongly did he feel her reluctance for him to pursue that possibility. But with Lisa that was hardly the case. A callousness was more like it, a callousness—or perhaps indifference. What did she care that such a meeting might enrich his book? Whatever it was, it could only mean humiliation for him. You didn't have to be a goddamn musician to detect a false note.

When they'd first made love, he'd whispered to her, "You're wonderful." And she'd replied, "No, you're wonderful. Or rather, *we're* wonderful. It takes two to tangle." And they were wonderful, he thought, remembering all the things they managed to do in that narrow day bed.

All right then, dammit to hell. If she was going to withdraw to that secret dark schoolroom behind her face every time she saw him, then let her. There was nothing he could do about it. He'd just have to improvise as he went along. It was his mother, not his father, he should heed. She had warned him to cut his losses fast and she was right.

The trucks in the army convoy were uniformly drab, with leaded grime covering doors and windows. He felt covered by similar grime, weary beyond recovery. Anyway, he had to acknowledge that his bubble picture of Lisa and him together could use a reality check. You couldn't make things happen, you had to take them as they came. Happiness is serendipitous, coming by itself, fluttering like a moth's wing—by grace of a summer's bounty—or, even more serendipitously, by grace of a blizzard. But to expect it, plan it, invite it—was to scare it off forever.

Okay, give it a rest, George. If *slow* is the way it's got to be, then slow be it. If finis, then finis. This kind of behaviour was more like a case of involuntary seizure than love between a man and a woman. Perhaps pills existed for a person thus stricken. Little pink capsules taken three times a day guaranteed to bring results or your money back.

Passing the leader of the convoy, he turned on his right signal to cross to the slow lane.

Chapter XXX

Elizabeth looked around the private ball room at the Plaza Hotel. Apart from the office staff and Isabel Nagel, all of whom were occupied in greeting the guests, she hardly knew anybody. At least to speak to. Plenty of celebrities were scattered about, surrounded by little enclaves of accommodating admirers. At the doorway, Marguerite Hoffman was bedecked from head to toe in glittering gold mesh; she billowed into the room—an effect created by tugging at the chiffon panels of her dress to send them afloat. Several people rushed to greet her, including George.

Always Elizabeth felt alien at other peoples' good times but never more than this evening. She hadn't wanted to come but since Rossiter threw this party in honor of Ruth Pryor's seventieth birthday, it was unavoidable. Everybody was busy circulating and, depending on your point of view, seemed either overdressed or underdressed. She wished she knew how to work a room as George obviously did, laughing, drinking, delivering just the right bon mot to the right ear at the right time. At the far end of the room Virginia Lavin was popping a pig-in-a-blanket into her mouth, while Janet Kells was looking suspiciously into her glass.

Marguerite Hoffman enveloped George in a bear hug, her twisted gold pendant earrings swinging to and fro, and Lisa turned away. She tried to mingle with people at the bar, but neither they, nor her campari and soda, did anything to dispel the queer, aching feeling that had settled below her heart.

George had been avoiding her, and not only this evening. First he had spent a whole week in his East Hampton house; then, having convinced Rossiter they could get far more done away from the bustle of his office, they had taken to conferring at the Oxford Club.

At first she was grateful for what she had deemed his consideration. Short of a formal renunciation she had, after all, done everything to discourage him. But when Rossiter told her the neat set-up he had at his club, having appropriated one of the private rooms and set up shop, she began to suspect the arrangement had little to do with her.

As he was having little to do with her. When she arrived earlier, not only was his greeting constrained, but he hardly made an attempt to be civil. When his eyes did meet hers, so distant were they, so caught up in some other vision than the one she presented in her decorous black crepe—bought especially for the occasion—with the string of Grandma Adelina's seed pearls around her neck, that she might have been on Mars.

Not that she expected a single excursion into intimacy to bind him to her forever. But what had caught her by surprise was that the termination of their closeness also meant the termination of friendship.

Through the several layers of materials, she could feel her heart beat. *She wants to have her cake and eat it too*, Judge Nebula had said of her mother. Was she any different?

She lifted her drink and placed her lips on the rim of the cold glass. George didn't seem to want to have anything more to do with her. Even when, as happened on one occasion, Rossiter had directed him to her for some specific information about Galliuillin, he never approached her, apparently preferring other sources rather than risk a confrontation.

People pressed against her, trying to get closer to the bar. She could feel a headache starting up, centering right over her eyes. Only one cure existed for it: as soon as the Nielsen recital was over, she was leaving town. It was hell making these promises to herself and then backing down again and again. Having promised her brother Tom as well, this time she meant to make good on her intentions.

"Is that Campari and soda?" Rossiter asked her, coming up from behind."No herbal tea?"

Elizabeth turned to him gratefully. Her feelings toward him had undergone a sea change since her discovery of the custody suit. The unbeaten and undaunted Rossiter of her imagination, now seemed both beaten and daunted. Heresy, her aunt Ada would say. She looked over the milling throng trying to spot his wife. "Is Mrs. Rossiter here?" Rossiter lifted his drink to his lips. "No, she couldn't come. Wasn't feeling up to it. But then she never does—"

"What happened to the famed Rossiter powers of persuasion?"

"Ha," he said, raising one eyebrow skeptically. "Reports of my powers have been greatly exaggerated. As you, my dear, should be the first to know."

Not the first, she thought, *not even the last*. Elizabeth gazed beyond him to the swarming crowd. Formidable, it seemed formidable. Her headache was worse. She felt even less able to cope with the deceits and deals and defamations surrounding her than when she arrived. When Isabel Nagel came up to speak to Rossiter, Elizabeth took advantage of the interruption to go to the buffet table.

With her plate heaped with shrimp and hearts of palm, Elizabeth looked around for a place to sit. When she turned, she saw George sitting on a settee, still with Marguerite Hoffman. When he spotted her, he shifted his body involuntarily, although clearly there was not enough room for the three of them. A childish elation rose within her; she turned away quickly in search of another spot.

Not until that moment did she realize the extent to which she craved such a sign from him.

But afterwards, as she jabbed away at her shrimp, she remembered Grandma Adelina's expression, "A thin blanket for a cold night," and wondered whether her heart hadn't been playing tricks on her, leading her where it wanted to go. She put her plate down on the table beside her—she wasn't hungry anymore.

"So that's where you're hiding," Helge Nielsen said, sitting down next to her. "I've been searching all over."

Although she made a big show of welcoming him, she hardly listened to a thing he had to say. "Yes, of course I've invited everybody from the Norwegian Embassy, they were the first people on my list, you can be sure of that. Don't worry, the concert will be great. I just know it."

Marguerite Hoffman, doing her *noblesse oblige* bit to the hilt, came over to give a small hello, having expended her bigger ones elsewhere. "How are you, my darlinkk," she asked, sniffing the air through her reconstructed nose. But before Elizabeth had time to reply, she spotted Ruth Pryor over her shoulder and was off for bigger game.

"If she had half a brain, she'd know that you're more important than she is—at least as far as getting some real work done," Helge said.

Elizabeth smiled. He was such an innocent; he didn't realize that he was a very special case. Not only because of his talent, but, as the first concert presented by both the new management and foundation, many other factors came into play. As if they could afford to give this much attention to every aspirant—

Once she left to return to Toronto, nobody would take up this aspect of her work, of this she was certain. She must get Rossiter to arrange a meeting for the panel judges to establish ground rules—that way they'd have to come up with *something* from time to time, if only to save face. If they were committed to sponsoring two new debuts each season, at least that much would be assured. She turned to Helge. "Yes, *my darlinkk,* but it's Ruth who does the bookings. Every artist needs her on their side, believe me. It's different for you right now, but you'll see what I mean once you get launched."

As soon as Elizabeth felt she had put in enough time at the party, she got up to go.

"But you've only just come," Helge argued. You're always running away."

"Nonsense! But I've a headache. I've been here for—"

He wanted to accompany her, but she urged him to stay on and get to know more of the guests. "A lot of them have heard of you by now, and it's important that you circulate and get acquainted. Virginia," she called as the older woman passed by, "take Helge around and introduce him. It'll mean more people at the concert, Helge," she lifted her hands to cross her fingers, "and we want every seat filled."

When she went to take leave of Ruth, she was standing at the doorway deep in conversation with George, with her back to Elizabeth. Trying to get her attention, she placed a hand on Ruth's arm to interrupt. When she did so, she could see George give a corresponding start, as though her touch had been for him. Communication by proxy.

Like children playing statues, they both stood motionless for a moment, their blood remembering, even if the rest of them made a point of not.

Chapter XXXI

When the registered, special delivery came for Rossiter from Lipinsky marked *PERSONAL AND CONFIDENTIAL*, Elizabeth's stomach tightened. Somehow she knew the news within could not be good.

She had begun to sense something amiss a few days previously, when she heard him play the *Beethoven Violin Concerto* with the New York Philharmonic, sitting with Rossiter in the private viewing room of Avery Fisher Hall. Instead of being met by Lipinsky's wife, as they had expected, they were greeted by an orchestra official, who escorted them through the labyrinthine back stage corridors to their seats.

Rossiter, however, had sensed nothing untoward and sat, as usual, with his eyes closed after the music began. This had served to reassure Elizabeth; she began to attribute her queasiness to the feeling of voyeurism which sitting in the dark enclosure of the viewing room engendered. The *sanctum* was located to the left of the auditorium on the first mezzanine level. From its plush vantage point, one could look down at the audience and the orchestra without anybody aware that they were being watched—bringing to mind stories of certain bordello arrangements.

But when the orchestra official ushered in a reigning movie couple and Rossiter and she were shunted off to the side to make room for their majesties, all her former apprehension regarding the violinist returned. Especially since they were told after the performance that Lipinsky wasn't seeing anybody in his dressing room because he "wasn't feeling well." Judging from his spectacular performance, which Rossiter termed as "sublime music played sublimely," and which brought six curtain calls and a standing ovation from the usually staid Friday afternoon luncheon-ladies' audience, this had simply not rung true.

Lipinsky's letter now seemed stuck to her hand and she knew with a certainty that the news it contained was bad. "Looks ominous to me," Virginia said. "I'm glad I don't have to give it to him."

"Perhaps it's not—" Elizabeth began but the crawling of her skin could not be denied. "I can't do it now. He's in there with George and told me specifically not to disturb him this afternoon."

"Yes, I know—George told me they're at a crucial part of the book. Getting close to the end."

An added upsurge of apprehension: the timing of George's arrival during her lunch hour was not, she suspected, accidental. Elizabeth peered at the post-office date and time of registration on the letter. "It was sent yesterday. Which means just before he left town for Washington. He's scheduled to appear there with the National Symphony this week. And the address is typewritten which means that he went to the trouble of finding a typist or a typewriter—and all this between major orchestral appearances." She tapped the letter on the desk half expecting it to explode. "I wish Ruth were here. Of all days for her to be sick. It's only two-thirty. If the news is bad, the whole afternoon's work will be shot. You know him."

"Why don't you call her?"

"I hate to disturb her. She may be asleep. But maybe, you're right." Crossing her fingers, she moved the telephone closer.

Ruth fortunately was not asleep when she reached her. "Go give it to him immediately, Lisa," she said. "You don't want to take responsibility for something like that. And what makes you think it's bad news?"

Elizabeth's uneasiness must somehow have communicated itself for then Ruth's voice wavered and she added: "I suppose you're right. Good news doesn't come by registered mail . . . Go give it to him right away."

The two men had obviously been working well; half a tape was already used up and filled pages with George's descriptive phrases hung from his notebook as though he hadn't had time to fold them under. She took a deep breath. *Mi scusi se la disturbo,* she started to say and stopped abruptly in the doorway. Another throwback from childhood—lapsing into *Italian* at home was always a way of softening the atmosphere.

Fortunately both men were preoccupied and noticed nothing. Waving the letter in her hand, she began again. "I'm sorry, but this came in and I thought you would want to see it right away. It's marked personal."

"Now what?" Rossiter scowled as he tore open the envelope roughly, nicking his finger in the process.

"I don't—" Lisa began but stopped. Rossiter's tangled eyebrows nearly touched as he began to read. He looked like a huge old bear, sitting in his oversize wing chair, tie loosened, white hair falling forward, peering through the lower half of large horn-rimmed glasses.

George took advantage of the break to go over his notes and didn't acknowledge her presence by so much as a nod. As she hesitantly turned to leave the room, Rossiter stopped her and thrust the letter at her. "Here, read it yourself." Panic seized Elizabeth. To have brought the letter in to him in George's presence had further compounded the man's humiliation, and she ought to have anticipated that. Why hadn't she asked to speak to him privately? The letter in her trembling fingers shook so badly she could scarcely focus her eyes.

> My dear A.R.:
>
> This is not an easy letter to write. When you wrote me about your new management, I thought you meant you were just shifting divisions around again at Eagle. I had no idea you had abandoned your old company and had started a new one. I hardly glanced at the stationery, so I didn't see the different address. Nor would I have noticed the change even if I had looked, since it was still on 57th Street.

As a result, you can imagine my surprise when clippings from the New York press were sent to me announcing my "switch" to your management. As you can understand, I have had many friends over the years at Eagle, and certainly didn't realize I was getting myself involved in an imbroglio of such proportions.

Accordingly, I must withdraw myself from consideration by your management. I have sent a similar letter to Eagle Management also. In the future, I will be managed by Terry Nicholson who, as you know, has been my personal representative for many years.

My lawyers tell me my previous note was not binding and that the release sent to the papers by your management was, in any case, premature.

I regret the rift between you and your former management but I am sure you understand that there is enough advantage taken of artists by management in the general course of events without such extra-curricular exploitation.

Elizabeth could find nothing to say when she finished. A small lump closed off her throat. *Extra-curricular exploitation.* Once she might have agreed with that; why should the phrase now strike her so hard?

Rossiter bade her to give the letter to George and it fluttered between them as it was passed from hand to hand. After reading it through quickly, he passed it back to Rossiter and pressed his fingertips to his eyes.

Rossiter reached in the breast pocket of his twill jacket for a cigar, lit it and then withdrew behind a cloud of smoke. It was an unnerving gesture, since smoking had recently been absolutely forbidden to him, and in the past few weeks he had rarely succumbed.

In the shaft of light from the window, the trail of smoke turned golden. At length, George said: "I'm sorry. I know this is a blow—" He folded his notebook with a snap and his eyes narrowed just perceptibly. "Do you want to wrap it up for the day?"

Rossiter, utterly spent, looked dead, his face sagging like an old mattress with the springs all shot and stuffing oozing from the yellowing seams. For a moment Elizabeth thought he had fallen asleep . . . or something . . . and felt heavy as stone. As George bent to take the dangling cigar from his hand, he opened his red-veined eyes and squashed the cigar in the ash try. "No, none of that. I've had far worse and survived. We'll survive without Lipinsky."

Taking the letter from the table, he crumpled it up and tossed it in the wastebasket. "But I'd better tell Ruth. She's got several holds on him from different orchestras."

He went round to the stand-up desk, leaned heavily against it, grasping the top for support. The Turner seascape was in front of him and he stared at the yellow, blue and gold slashes. At last he slammed his fist on the desk and dialled with a palsied hand. "Ruth, A.R. here," he bellowed into the receiver.

"Now, are you happy? Out with it. Did you have anything to do with that?" Elizabeth's hands crashed on the typewriter keys, causing them to tangle and stick together. She hadn't noticed that George followed her into her office. "What are you talking about?"

"That phrase '*extra-curricular exploitation*' sounded like one of your diatribes. I wouldn't put anything past you. Quit if you must, but breaking an old man's—"

"I can't believe you're serious. Why would I—"

"Who in hell knows why? You're a goddamn riddle at the best

of times. You weren't happy when they took on Lipinsky. And you looked guilty as all hell when you read the letter—you dislike the old man, you've made that clear enough—isn't that true?"

"However I may feel about Mr. Rossiter, you can be certain I wouldn't have done anything like what you suggest. The only reason I didn't share in the general jubilation about Lipinsky at the time was . . ." Her face squeezed shut. "Well, you remember. We spoke of it. I thought this management was going to be different. Some *different!* And if I looked guilty, it's because . . ."

"Because?"

"Because I did feel they were being a bit hasty when they sent out a release on the strength of his note."

"Why didn't you say so?"

"Because I didn't want to spoil their fun, that's why."

"Fun?"

"They were so excited—I know they'd have resented any interference and were in no mood to listen. Look, I'm a novice here, and was even more so then. I thought maybe I was wrong. And I certainly felt I was wrong when I saw what a play the release got in the press. What were my misgivings . . ."

"Well, you ought to have expressed them." With his arms folded over his chest, he looked dubious. "I wish I'd seen the letter at the time. It would have saved a lot of trouble."

A long silence ensued with the only sound in the room coming from the squeak of her chair as she revolved from side to side. "Well, you know what they say about hindsight—"

"You're right, it isn't worth a damn." Their eyes, drawn irresistibly, met for a second only. Then his face contracted as he abruptly made for the door. Hand on the door knob, he said over his shoulder, "But that's the only thing you're right about."

Chapter XXXII

On the night of Nielsen's debut concert, snow again blanketed the city, badly enough to discourage all but the most intrepid concert-goers. As Elizabeth made her way through the drifts to Carnegie Hall, she remembered another snowy March night in her fourteenth year when Aunt Ada tried to buoy up her father before his performance with the Toronto Symphony. "It's still early, Dom, wait and see," she had said as they peeked through the curtain back-stage into the cavernous and largely deserted hall. "The crowd will still come. The hall is almost sold out by subscription, so they'll be there—"

"That's the point," he cried, as they made their way through the back-stage obstacle course, "if they'd bought the tickets for *me*, there might be a hope. But subscribers aren't going to budge on a night like this. Most of them never heard of me. It seems as if my whole life has been spent waiting for a crowd to arrive which never does."

And it never did for Nielsen either. The hall was pitifully empty, even though they had closed off the two upper balconies. Elizabeth stood at the back of the auditorium counting heads. Where were the college and conservatory students, the union members, the club and auxiliary members—all of whom she had chased after so diligently?

So much for her great satisfaction at seeing the ticket piles diminish on her desk, as though the job were over. Her father was right. Unless they paid for the tickets, waited their turn in the queue at the box office, cash on the line, on a night like this you were dead—stuck with thousands of no-shows. And no stand-bys waiting at the gate either.

She could hardly bear to face her colleagues. Since she did most of the papering after hours, she doubted if anybody knew the extent of her effort. Instead of surprising them with a nearly-filled hall, as she had hoped to do, chances were they would think the job wasn't done properly.

The mezzanine usher greeted her profusely, as if she, too, had a stake in the concert. "Aren't you the brave one though?" After peering at her ticket, he unlocked the door of Box 19, and handed her a program.

Inside the tiny cloak room, Virginia was taking off her ancient beaver coat to hang on a peg. "Look at A.R.," she whispered. "It's so good to see him back in that seat. That's the same one he sat in all through the years when he managed the Philharmonic. They used to play in this hall before Avery Fisher was built."

Elizabeth glanced into the box at Rossiter's monumental back. On one side sat Ruth, looking prim and proper in her black concert suit, and on the other sat a tall, thin woman, the facets of her diamond necklace catching fire from the chandelier over-head. "That's his wife, I take it. I forgot she was coming."

"Yes, his one and only. The one and only reason he keeps working so he can get away from. God, she's reeking, I think I can smell—"

"How do you know she doesn't feel the same way when the door is closed behind him in the morning?" Elizabeth asked snidely, as surprised at her own words as was Virginia. "And when did she start to take that one too many to help her get through the day? He isn't exactly a teetotaler himself."

"My, we are touchy tonight." Virginia stooped to take off her boots. "Anyway, she's not about to miss playing the grand dame at the reception. They've booked rooms at the Plaza so they can stay on there until the weather clears up. No way they could go back to Westchester on a night like this."

Because of a last-minute cancellation in Texas by an ailing pianist which had kept Elizabeth late trying to secure a substitute, she had not had time to go home to change before the concert. Not that she would have even tried in this weather. In the tiny dressing room mirror she looked without enthusiasm into her wind-whipped face.

After smoothing down her plaid skirt and blouse, she rummaged in her purse for a comb to bring some semblance of order to the strands of hair which had escaped from the topknot, but with little success.

"Oh, there you are," Rossiter said to Virginia, when she entered the box. "I thought maybe you'd stay away too . . ." As Elizabeth appeared from behind her, he added: "Oh, sorry, I was afraid the weather might keep you—"

Elizabeth said nothing. More and more recently things had begun to come to her as though images in a dream, or like those that reel by in a jumble just before sleep. Somewhere, sometime, she had been in Box 19 before. She shivered, could almost see her mother's wavering ghost before her—no, not before her, in her, a part of her, she *was* her mother. The past lost its chronology, it was 1953, 1954 . . . Why shouldn't the vanquished in the fullness of time be given another chance? Her legs felt weak as the image faded.

Meanwhile, Ruth was berating Rossiter. ". . . don't know how you can even think that. Lisa's been stuck at the office trying to salvage that date with the Houston Symphony for Quarles. And you know how much work she put in on this concert. Nielsen has been her pet project—"

Elizabeth gave her an appreciative nod: the last thing she would have expected a couple of months ago was for Ruth to go to bat for her like this.

"Sorry. I should have known." Rossiter shifted and took his wife's arm. "I don't believe you've met Mrs. Rossiter . . ."

The smell of liquor interlaced with Sen-Sen hung in the air as Dolores Rossiter turned to extend her calf-gloved hand. "Pleased to meet you," she said thickly, a little red smile playing on her lips, as though she were privy to some private joke. Despite the spangled velvet hat perched on top of carefully set hair and the hand stitched green brocade enclosing the tiny frame, the woman looked every bit of her sixty-eight years. Her oddly protruding blue eyes, veined in red, were circled by large pink-lensed glasses.

"Likewise," Elizabeth said, giving her hand a sympathetic squeeze, then withdrew her own slowly.

Mrs. Rossiter gave her a lopsided smile, as if inside she were not smiling at all. "Too bad about the weather," she said, as Elizabeth sat down.

"Who're you expecting?" Virginia whispered in her ear.

"What do you mean?"

"You keep looking at the doorway."

"Was I?" She felt the absurdity of the response and gave an upward jerk of the chin. "I'm so tired, I don't know what I'm doing." An elaborate show of studying the program followed, *Beethoven . . . Chopin . . . Poulenc . . . Schuman . . .* She flipped the page for she already knew the program by heart. *Born in Norway in 1949 to musical parents, the father a violinist and the mother a cellist with the Bergen Philharmonic . . .* The door to the box clicked and Elizabeth wheeled about swiftly, but the usher apologized; she had opened the wrong door and closed it shut again.

I wouldn't miss it for the world, George had said to Rossiter a few days earlier when he'd invited him to the concert. His voice on the telephone was audible all over the office and he'd gone on to say that he was nearly as big a fan of Nielsen as Lisa was.

But it now looked as though the world would keep him away. He was out in East Hampton and nobody could be expected to drive in such weather.

It was just as well. She hadn't seen him since that afternoon when he accused her of . . . Lipinsky it was that time. Not that she was fooled. George's argument had little to do with Lipinsky. In any case, even George on the warpath could hardly hold her responsible for the nasty newspaper accounts that followed his defection. "Who Needs

Managers?" the caption over the article by Bruce Andrews, the *Times'* music chief, read. A sentiment which she would have at one time applauded, but which at the time had made her retort: "Who needs music critics?"

Everybody waited gleefully for the fall of the mighty, the public lifting the favored to the heavens the better to enjoy the eventual crash. An acquired national taste—carefully nurtured by repeated samplings—one enjoyed by gourmet and glutton alike.

The words on the program swam before her eyes. *Under the tutelage of Mathilde Cahn at the Oslo Conservatoire, at the age of eleven Nielsen made his debut . . .*

Elizabeth shut the program and sat back. On center stage, the piano stood patiently biding its time, as it had for nearly a hundred years. The hall itself was a presence; embedded deep in the moldings of gold leaf was the essence of hundreds of thousands of glorious moments, their sounds wafting from the walls with measured emanations. And embedded with hundreds of thousands of prayers and hopes too.

Her father's and mother's among them.

"The *Carnaval* . . ." Rossiter was saying, studying the program. "The way Rachmaninoff played that . . . Remember that tour we booked for him, Ruth? We sold it out so fast we made enemies all over."

Elizabeth only half listened. How many times in her life had she listened to this kind of musical gossip in her home in Toronto, and even more dimly back in Italy. Thus did each generation provide the proper veneration and musical link for the next. She came back from Aunt Ada and Dominic to hear Ruth describe Rachmaninoff's gold and ebony cigarette case. "The doctors limited the number of cigarettes he smoked to eight a day. So he carefully cut them in two. 'That way I smoke sixteen times,' he would say, 'instead of eight.'"

"But the cancer won in the end." Rossiter stretched his large frame backward and interlocked his fingers. "'Farewell my poor hands.' Those were his last words. Artists, they're all children."

"Who isn't?" Dolores lowered her head when she saw the frown her remark raised on her husband's face.

"Right on, Dolores," Elizabeth ached to say. Though she was less angry with Rossiter, it didn't take much to make her blood heat up once again.

The sudden arrival of George, guiding a tall and tanned woman into the box, brought all such thoughts to a halt. "I'd like you to meet my sister Margaret," he said to the assemblage at large. "She's in town from Cleveland for a couple of days, just in time to swell the ranks here."

Of course she was his sister. Elizabeth hoped her relief was not too apparent. You could see it in the way she stepped imperiously into the box, her sleek blond hair smoothed back from her face with a diamond clip, secure in her hierarchical privileges. And you could see it in the way she spoke to each in turn in a lilting even voice, the product of the right finishing schools and Junior League chairpersonships.

When she came to Elizabeth, she looked at her with open interest. "Mind if we join you?" Sitting down in the second chair to her left, she left the one between for George.

A stilted little minuet followed, convincing Elizabeth that the seating arrangement had been purely accidental. Yes, she'd been fine, thank you. Yes, she'd enjoyed her visit home last month. No, it wasn't Buffalo—it was Olean.

"I never thought you'd make it," Rossiter said. "Thought you'd be stuck out in a drift somewhere. How's the book coming? Have you finished the first draft?"

"I still need to get a few facts straight. A little more research at the library, a little rewriting and it'll be done. Sometimes, the more I work on it the worse it gets. But you know I wouldn't have missed this concert. I heard his cassette—" He bent to pick up his program which had slipped to the floor. "But who ordered this weather? What a lousy break."

"Oh well," Ruth said, "at least it's not as bad as that blizzard in January. Be grateful for small mercies."

Elizabeth scarcely heard what else was said until she realized Margaret was speaking to her. ". . . so hoping he'd play Bach—something like the *Well-Tempered Clavier* . . . A perfect night for that kind of music. Don't you think so?"

Elizabeth was grateful when Rossiter jumped in to explain that most people play that on the harpsichord nowadays."Ever since Landowska. She always used to say, 'You play Bach your way and I'll play it *his* way.'"

"I'd forgotten that," Dolores Rossiter said."And then she completed the picture by setting the stage like a living room and wearing an old cloak and slippers."

Her voice trailed as George rose to inspect the audience, his jacket brushing against Elizabeth as he leaned over the balcony. "I'm surprised even this many turned out. Tough luck. I sure wish—"

"'If wishes were horses,'" Rossiter said, "'beggars would ride.' That's the music business. You can't let these things affect you. Just hope the critic makes it."

"Oh, here he comes," Ruth said as Helge Nielsen emerged from the wings and took a deep bow. "But I do wish he wouldn't look so serious."

Rossiter harrumphed. "What's he supposed to look like? Like he's about to do a vaudeville turn?"

After adjusting the piano stool, Helge sat down, coattails flung behind him, small face haloed, the air of expectancy a palpable thing. He waited, hands at his side like obedient soldiers, until the sound of a cough ended and absolute quiet prevailed. "I sure hope he doesn't disappoint," whispered Virginia to Elizabeth, as the first notes of the *Hammerklavier* filled the hall.

Not only did he not disappoint, but to Elizabeth's mind he was even better than at the audition or at the run-through at the Norwegian Embassy two nights earlier. From the moment his steely fingers bore down in a brilliant crescendo, atoms went off, spinning, dissolving into thin air. It was apparent that those who braved the slush and ice were to be rewarded with an evening of musicianship of the highest order.

And later, the incredible contrast during the *Largo* of the Chopin Sonata. Everybody seemed to stop breathing, lest one note of the *pianissimo*, in all its dying gradations, pass them by.

Elizabeth's skin was tingling. Sitting so close to George, she warmed to, and was warmed by, him. Surreptitiously she gazed at the angle of his cheek, the lines of his shoulder and arm, his beatific smile.

Music had done it again.

At intermission, George congratulated Rossiter, who pushed him away. "Lisa found him, not I. Congratulate her. But he's some talent."

"More than that, A.R. You know what they say—you possess talent, but genius possesses you."

This last was said for Elizabeth's benefit. They were standing in the corridor; George looked at her over Margaret's shoulder. It reminded her of the way he had glanced up from the street that Saturday morning and kissed the air in her direction. Now the look meant something else entirely: he realized he had been wrong about her that last time. Wrong about Lipinsky, that is.

She ought to be grateful; it became increasingly clear as the evening wore on that he now wanted their friendship, at least, to continue. Just as well. Looking at Margaret, so sleek and svelte in her slitted black velvet skirt and green silk shirt, she saw how many worlds they were apart. Shadowed in the eyes of brother and sister were untold experiences: young children running, heads thrown back, a world teeming with grass, leaves, flowers, all creatures great and small in pursuit of their own preordained destiny. And a mother and father to boot, at home to greet them. Oh, there were knee scrapes, mind scrapes, heart scrapes, peals of thunder, strokes of lightning, but they'd calmly come through it all, making light of the bad, heavy of the good. She tucked her own blouse into her skirt, trying to keep it from bunching at the back.

"Reminded me a bit of Konstantinov in that *Hammerklavier,*" George said, turning to Elizabeth. "Didn't you think so?"

Elizabeth froze. Once again there was in his voice, in the way he stared at her challengingly, a sense of knowing more than he was letting on. "Konstantinov? I think . . . I mean . . . I suppose—" She strove to keep her voice light. "I never heard him."

He eyed her for a second or two before saying: "The recording, I mean."

"I don't know it."

Returning to her seat before the others, she flipped the pages of her program rapidly, but her eyes saw nothing.

At the end of the concert, after being recalled by the audience three times for bows, Nielsen again sat down at the piano. "What's that he's playing?" Margaret asked.

Rossiter looked blank and Elizabeth said, *"Deux Petits Riens.* It's by Rossini."

Rossiter pointed his head in Elizabeth's direction. "She's got an inside track. He even tells her what he's going to play for encores."

"But—" Elizabeth stopped as she saw George's eyelids tighten. Beyond him was Margaret's look of inquiry as well. Mohair prickled deeply into her elbow as she slid further into her seat.

She felt misunderstood on two counts, for he hadn't told her about this encore at all. The piece was a favorite of her father's who had played it for her nearly as often as Schumann's *Traumerei.* She watched Nielsen lift his hands high to achieve the whimsy the work called for and felt as though she were again watching *him*, with the smell of candles flickering fitfully in a misty dining room beyond.

Music never lets you down, Papa used to say; she wished she could quote *him* to this party and see how that anecdote would go over.

Chapter XXXIII

Despite the lengthening of the days, the last of the light was going; what remained was drab and grey under a sky heavy with undischarged rain.

Following the freak storm on the night of Nielsen's concert, the weather had turned somewhat balmy. Although the trees were still bare, the season of fruitfulness was beginning to make itself felt in the swelling buds along the branches and the newly awakened life beneath each step on the soggy earth.

George parked his car in the garage area below the house and walked up the hill to *Bellemore*, the large Tudor mansion in the Westchester hills that housed Alfred and Dolores Rossiter and their staff of three.

Built in the tradition of English country homes made to last through all the winds of change, the house stood safe and secure, its leaded windows framing muted scenes of privilege and position. A hedge of Japanese yew surrounded it; atoms of remaining light quivered through the clumps standing in the corner like sentinels.

George took off his cap and let the evening mist envelop his face and hair and eyelids. Nearby a robin was perched on a hedge looking sleekly beautiful. He watched it without moving, afraid to scare it away, until it flew off into the murky twilight in a perfect arc.

At the top of the three steps of the quarry-tiled entranceway he pressed the doorbell. Rossiter must have been waiting for his arrival because, as soon as the butler opened the door, he came out of the library to help bundle him out of his brown down jacket and to take his captain's cap. "Here, Percy," he said to the butler as he handed over the garments, "put these away."

In the foyer, a grandfather clock ticked resonantly near the curving, polished stairs. So deep was the carpet on them that Dolores' feet, as she started down from the landing above, made no sound. Dressed in a flowing orange satin caftan, she held on to the rail tightly to steady her step. On top of her dyed blonde hair sat a coiled braid which, although carefully matched, was clearly not her own. "I'm so glad you could finally visit us, George," she said in her flat, dispassionate voice. "We've been looking forward to it for so long."

I'll bet you have, George thought. Aloud, he said: "Not nearly as much as I have." When she extended her hand to him in greeting, he noticed the scrubbed look of the fragile skin, as though all the essential juices of her body had dehydrated.

"That's nice to hear. Why don't you both go in the library for drinks. I'll join you later. I need to check up on the dinner."

George mumbled a response. On the few occasions when they met, he always felt that Dolores Rossiter was acting a role, as though she deliberately distanced herself from everybody, preferring as little real human contact as possible. Or was it a matter of her distancing herself to forestall being distanced from? And now, when she walked by them gracefully, he didn't imagine her going to the kitchen, but walking off into the wings of the stage, a moment before the close of Act I.

George followed Rossiter into the library where a smell of roses mixed with beeswax polish. The room exuded good cheer, the drapes were drawn, the lamps lit, the light from the roaring fire was reflected in the boulle and marquetry furnishings and gilt-framed mirrors. In a corner was a game table with an ivory chess set, with two comfortable club chairs on either side. At the bar Percy stood near whiskey and sherry decanters and glasses set out in readiness. "It's all right, Percy," Rossiter said, "I'll do the honors. I think you'll be needed in the dining room."

George headed for a chair near the open fire, still feeling chilled.

He had tried to reach Lisa that afternoon, hoping he might see her as he passed through the city from Long Island on his way to Westchester. He wanted to tell her how much he'd enjoyed Nielsen's concert and how right she had been about him. It had been impossible to do so after the concert because Nielsen had been with them when they'd gone down to the *Times* building to get the reviews. And then the review had never appeared. In their dejection, putting in his two cents' worth hadn't seemed right.

But Lisa hadn't been at home when he called. She never seemed to be at home anymore, God alone knew what she was up to. This business of trying to efface herself by vanishing whenever their paths crossed had reached new heights. Still, it hadn't kept him from deliberately driving by the brownstone apartment building where she lived, in hopes of . . .

But there was no sign of anyone around it either. Just as well. He couldn't afford another rebuff. Then even his fantasy life would be kaput.

"Want some soda in this or do you take it neat?" Rossiter asked, his hand on the decanter. "Neat," came the reply. After he handed him his glass and poured one for himself, Rossiter joined him in front of the fire, loudly sighing with gratification as he sunk into his armchair.

"It's quite an establishment you have here," George said. "Isn't it a little big for just the two of you?"

"Well I bought it when I married Elizabeth. We thought we'd be getting the children then. When we didn't, we just remained anyway, still hoping we'd see them for holidays and such. When she died—" He broke off abruptly, then held up his glass in a silent toast. "Count your blessings George, to be unencumbered and footloose."

"I'm footloose, if not fancy free."

"And what pray tell is your fancy? Some beautiful and mindless china doll?"

"Hardly." He was sorry he had given him this opening. This, of all uncertain times, was not the time for confession. "I've been there though. Better believe it."

Rossiter studied George's taut face in silence for a moment. "You look peaked, George. What's eating you?"

George shifted restlessly in his seat. "I haven't been sleeping too well."

"You young folk, I don't know what's wrong with you. Same thing with Lisa, girl's wasting away to nothing before my eyes. I know it's the fashion to be thin as a rail these days, but I don't understand it at all."

"I've been meaning to ask you—" One hand balanced George's glass on the arm of the chair, the other hung to the floor, as though vaguely searching for something. The two men had such rapport between them that he hated to spoil it with intrusive queries, but nonetheless he continued, "How's Lisa working out?"

"Lisa?" Rossiter rose suddenly to stand by the hearth, his elbow resting on the mantel. When he turned to look at George, he seemed to stare through him. "Better than I could have hoped for. She's got a real knack for the business, is right on target most of the time. I tested her on this Nielsen thing. Let her go ahead and do it on her own. And she made quantum leaps. You see what a triumph it was, despite the untimely storm, and the goddamned no-show critic. Yet, she wasn't as happy about the outcome as I expected her to be. Instead of coming into her own and strutting around a bit, she seemed, I don't know, sort of saddened by it. And now she's been hammer and tongs at me about getting the *bona fides* of that foundation project all in order, making sure the board has to meet regularly twice a year to consider the applications. Wants it all made foolproof as if I won't be around long enough to see it through."

George got up abruptly, bumping against the coffee table and knocking over an ash tray. He bent to pick it up and then sat down again. "Or maybe *she* won't be around long enough . . ."

"What's that you say? I don't think that— She's doing a terrific job with us."

"Yes, but that's not really her doing it . . ."

"What does that mean?"

George looked at the leaping flames to keep from looking at Rossiter. The truth was, he didn't know what he meant. The words had come out by themselves. He supposed it had to do with that vision he had of that other Lisa lying on the pillow next to him. The night before he'd dreamed of her standing at a bus stop and when he went to speak to her, he couldn't remember her name. He was sure he knew her name, but for some reason, it kept eluding him. What was her name—what was it? Now he turned to throw up his hands at Rossiter and waved his fingers in a gesture of helplessness.

"Nonsense. She's got a fine future with us and I think she knows it."

Feeling slightly heady, George gazed at the fretwork of broken veins in Rossiter's cheeks. "Our Miss Topknot? I don't think she does."

"Miss Topknot? Is that what you call her?" He laughed briefly.

"Poor girl can't win. You should have seen what she looked like when I interviewed her. Hair all over the place."

"Are we speaking about Lisa?"

"Of course, I'm speaking about Lisa. Ruth spoke to her about it and the next time I saw her, the hair was all pulled back. I hardly recognized her. But she looks much better that way. Don't tell me she'd go to all that trouble if she didn't know she's got a good future with us. You must be mistaken. There's been no slackening in her work—on the contrary. Still . . . I have been worried about her. Seems more than usually wan these days." His fingers rose and fell on the mantelpiece, like those of a flutist. "Women! I'll never understand them. I've tried to put my finger on what's troubling the girl but I don't get anywhere. She has a chip on her shoulder and gets riled over the strangest things. Like a high voltage wire. She fights it a lot, I can see that, but it's there."

George looked down at his hand grasping his glass, the knuckles showed white. A chip on her shoulder? Why, for God's sake, why? What was wrong with her anyway? More and more their time together was like a speeding ocean liner further and further out of reach; it was all but swallowed up by the trail cut behind it. "I know what you mean. As I said before, I sometimes get the feeling there are two people there."

"Well, aren't we all guilty of that? Not two, but several? Your Sunday self, your workday self, your family self, your IRS inspection self— All pieces of a puzzle that don't quite fit."

"'Not two, but several,'" George echoed softly. The multiple split personality. So which of the several had he made love to? Certainly not her Sunday self, her workday self, her family . . . Which one dammit? Which Lisa was real and which was the façade? Or was that yet another self—the passion flower self which bloomed only on major blizzards?

Rossiter stood with his feet planted firmly on the Oriental rug beneath him, the heavy marble mantelpiece containing its array of pre-Colombian art behind him. Glancing at the portrait above the mantelpiece for a moment, Rossiter drew his breath, as though coming upon it after a long absence and seeing it with new eyes.

George followed his gaze to the pale woman in a large picture hat, the impastoed face softened by the sadness in the clear, limpid hazel eyes. "Who's that?"

"That's Elizabeth. Painted by Frank Kessler right after we were married. Before all the—"

"Elizabeth Guaragna?" George stared at the portrait with renewed attention: as far as he could remember, there was no resemblance to the girl he had once seen.

"No, Elizabeth Rossiter—the one who gave me three short years but left me with a life sentence. A long one. This is the only room in the house that's remained exactly as it was in her time. Except for the attic that is."

"The attic?"

"She had it done over so it looked like the inside of an ocean liner. Portholes for windows. Horizon beyond . . . It was to be the playroom for the children. And they never even saw it." He pointed to the music stand in the far corner. "That was hers. And that's her flute in that case on the bookshelf. This room is where I live, Dolores can have the rest of it. But you think that's enough? I still can't mention Elizabeth to her. She still gets jealous."

Through George's glass, Rossiter appeared as a blurred shape as he slumped back into his chair, almost as remote as the woman in the portrait above the mantelpiece. He sat cross-legged, gripping his trousers at the knees. The room held such positive, intense quiet that it seemed separated from the rest of the world. He studied the portrait again cataloguing all the stories about its subject: star-crossed lover, beloved wife, courageous mother, enchanting musician—Even her portrait kept the old man still in thrall. No wonder Dolores was jealous—how can you compete with a ghost? Could such a paragon really have existed? The woman in the portrait gave him her *Mona Lisa* smile—but was it a smile? "Your feelings must be contagious. She does weave a spell. It feels likes she's warning me now how brief it all is—"

"That's right . . . Portholes for windows! The eager heart with its readiness to fill in the empty spaces. By then she should have known that life holds no guarantees."

It was not until he heard the clink of the decanter that he realized that Rossiter had risen and was refilling his drink. He'd barely begun on his own. When Rossiter sat down again, George asked: "You're sure all her children live in Italy?"

"Yes, I'm sure. Why do you ask?" His voice was harsh with impatience.

"I met—I thought—I was just curious."

Again George felt the force of not being seen as Rossiter seemed to look through him. The whirr of the clock as it chimed the hour seemed to rouse him and he gestured briefly at the portrait. "I just thought of something. Damned if I know what it means. On her birthday last month when I visited her grave, there were gladioli on it when I arrived. First time I've ever seen them there. I've racked my brain. She did have an aunt—one who was against her when she left Guaragna, even testified on his behalf—but she lives in California now, as far as I know. But there they were, big as life, and still fresh. Gladioli."

George put his glass down on the table next to him and supported himself with his palms on the armrests. "Maybe they'd been put there accidentally, or maybe the wind blew them over or something—"

All the time Rossiter made his long speech, he had been using his formal, dull voice, but his next remark was snapped out: "But they were gladioli—don't you see? It was her favorite flower."

Chapter XXXIV

The review didn't appear for three days. By the time they got it, it was five days after the event. Every day Elizabeth had searched every edition early and late but the concert seemed not to have happened.

Purely by chance somebody saw it in Hartford and sent it to Rossiter, for it only appeared out of town and not in New York. This was a big disappointment to Ruth and Virginia, for it meant that nobody at Eagle saw it.

As far as Elizabeth and Nielsen were concerned, the review was such that it didn't matter. So used to disappointment was Elizabeth that she was quite unprepared for the galvanic rush of success. *HELGE NIELSEN: A SENSATIONAL DEBUT*, read the headline, over a three column spread, including a picture: *his Beethoven was monumental; his Schumann had grace and vigor; his Chopin was pure poetry . . . superb technique at the service of each composer's style. Some romantic mannerisms, some overlong ritards, but even these were forged with his own style and expressed with a unique personality. A pianist's pianist . . . welcome to the hallowed club, Nielsen.*

Though always suspicious of good fortune, this time—because it was, after all, Nielsen's good fortune—Elizabeth hoped it wouldn't fizzle out. When she called him to come in to the office and showed it to him, he looked at her as though it was all her doing. For an unguarded moment, she allowed herself to enjoy the vision of herself as a kingmaker, the power behind the panoply.

Elizabeth read the review again and again, feeling the ripples of excitement proliferate. It made up for the disappointment of the early morning hours after the concert, when George and Margaret drove them to the *Times* building after the party. The death watch, George quipped, he and his sister trying to bolster flagging spirits as they huddled in the car on 43rd Street, with the engine going full blast to keep them warm.

They had waited over two hours—everything was running late because of the storm—but when the paper finally was available, no review appeared.

Helge had been crestfallen, his fingers shook as he went through the newspaper twice, page after page. He had changed from his tails for the party earlier; in the dim light he looked like one of the employees coming in for the graveyard shift at the newspaper—a shadow of his concert self.

"Don't worry," Elizabeth said, trying to hide her own desolation, "there'll still be one—on a night like this, the critic probably went home first and the review will appear later."

But she feared, as Rossiter had, that the weather provided adequate excuse for the critic not to come at all. It wouldn't be the first time an artist had pinned all his hopes on a review and the reviewer didn't bother to cover the concert.

But she'd been wrong.

This time he had come.

Another surprise awaited Elizabeth later that morning. It was a congratulatory letter from Bruce Andrews, the critic of the *Times*, to Rossiter, telling him "you've covered yourself with glory" for sponsoring a recital award contest and launching it with Nielsen. A sharp contrast to his recent *Who Needs Managers?* article.

A messenger had delivered the letter while she was conferring with Isabel. When she returned, Rossiter came into her office and handed it to her. "Bruce and I have been in an adversarial position for a long time, given our jobs. Years ago, however, before he went to the *Times*, when he was still a musicologist at Columbia, we were friends. But this letter—" his voice faltered—"rightly belongs to you."

The review and its aftermath decided her. Elizabeth could leave now. It was back to Toronto for her as soon as she could make the arrangements. It was a close call the other night when George had asked her about Konstantinov and the way it set her heart racing was a wake up call. Get out, woman, while the going was still good.

Had he deliberately tried to trap her? She didn't think so, but who knew when he might? Unless she left the city, it was just a matter of time before he would. Not for anything could she risk having this whole house of cards come tumbling down on her. Tom had been vociferous enough about that danger and Tom was right.

Besides, she would learn nothing new anymore by staying. Given what she had already discovered, she had, in a sense, completed her job. Whatever her other regrets, she had to admit her expedition to the 42nd Street library justified everything else. As the weeks slipped by, she had found she had been rewarded in ways she could not have foreseen: from the diminution to what seemed to be the restoration, if not the establishment, of her feelings of worthiness. There were no more blank spaces, empty shapes, unfilled vessels, fragments of herself scattered in different places. Those few precious sheets of photocopy might just be part of the technological superfluity which photocopying machines had created the world over, or might just hold the very source of being—at least her being—in their closely-packed script.

Chapter XXXV

The great war to end all wars was over. Alfred Rossiter, not yet twenty-five years of age, was determined to make up for lost time. Only one good thing had come out of his wartime experience—the concert he attended on leave in Paris one night at the Salle Gaveau when he heard Yuri Galliuillin play. He had hung onto the velvet-covered balustrade in a trance as the Russian pianist, hailed alternately as the Pride of the Bolsheviks and the Apostle of Pianists and

And what?

The lean mean piano machine?

George had run out of ideas and paused to look at what he had written. The chapter had been revised three times already and still wasn't right. He crossed out "in a trance" and substituted "mesmerized." Or would "hypnotized" be better? No, the whole thing sounded wrong, back to stet. *Rossiter gripping the velvet covered balustrade . . . Rossiter pawning his wordly goods on the off chance he could get Galliuillin to come to America . . . Rossiter—*

He wanted the reader to feel the urgency, the commitment, the fever, the road that had to be taken. But none of it would go. His images lacked authority. The golden-haired pianist had sat at the piano and the young lieutenant had wanted to leap over the balustrade to get closer but nothing he wrote had made this come alive. He pulled the paper out of his typewriter and tossed it into the wastebasket.

George was obsessed by voices. Rossiter's voice, Elizabeth's voice, Mickiewicz's voice, Galliuillin's . . .

No, not Galliuillin. He couldn't get his voice. That was the problem. He couldn't hear it. Other than the few recordings he'd listened to—which should have been enough but somehow weren't—he hardly knew a thing about Galliuillin other than what Rossiter had told him. Other impresarios had tried to lure the pianist to America, seasoned impresarios, lucrative impresarios, contract-waving impresarios, world-promising impresarios—what possessed him to choose a young "whippersnapper" as Rosssiter put it, who offered no guarantees?

Rossiter had suggested he consult with Lisa on the subject but after her reluctance to help him on the Guaragna search, he'd been loath to do so.

Suddenly he remembered Lisa's mentioning a biography about Galliuillin that might be of help. He took a draught of the coffee and stared at his desk covered with three by five cards, numbered cassettes, and volumes of musical texts with red flags in them. She'd told him to check with somebody at the Lincoln Center Library—

Now what was his name? Quickly he flipped back in his notebook but he could find no reference to it. That meant it was in the earlier one and, after extracting it from the desk drawer, he began to turn each page carefully. Sure enough, there it was, Stepanovich. Way back in December was when the notation had been made. But Stepanovich was the name of the biographer. What was the librarian's name? He remembered she'd told him to mention Pergolesi to him—Pergolesi—if he remembered correctly the man's name also began with a P. Next to Stepanovich he had a doodle of a coin . . . Penny—Yes, that was it: Mr. Penniweather.

It was a warm morning, but a dense fog had come in over the water creating a primordial cast to the landscape. George stepped out on his patio and felt like he'd walked into a swirling steam room. Knowledge, the quest for knowledge, from Guaragna, from Mickiewicz, from Dolores Rossiter, from whichever and whatever source, would it never end? On the far side of the house, the earth was walled in white, with occasional trees poking their heads through the ceiling.

All around him was silence, except for the lapping of the invisible waves, and even they sounded muted, as if reluctant to disturb the quiet. In the distance the wail of a foghorn could be heard warning any would-be sailors to think twice.

He could call the library, have them reserve the book and pick it up when he went into the city the next day. But somehow, he didn't feel he wanted to wait that long. A strong gust of wind blew his hair and flattened it against his forehead. Call it an evolved sense, call it another wild goose chase, call it a hunch to which he could not even put a name—nor did he want to, lest he jinx it—he found himself putting on his jacket and cap, grabbing the ignition keys from the hook near the back door, and sliding into his car. He gunned the engine and pulled out of the dunes into the road. Not a great day for driving, but what the hell. He'd had a lousy night, kept dreaming he was trying to get up a flight of stairs but tripped every time he came to the fifth step. When he awoke, he could swear he felt tremors up his foot where he'd banged it.

The streets were shrouded with fog and he had to drive slowly; the white lines were indistinguishable in the surrounding whiteness. Nevertheless he made good time from East Hampton to Manhattan, since on this off-hours weekday morning, advisory warnings kept most people home watching *Donahue* and sipping hot chocolate.

By the time he crossed the 59th St. Bridge and parked his car in the subterranean garage at Lincoln Center, the fog had somewhat lifted; as he walked west across Rossiter Court, the sun was struggling valiantly, if vainly, to make its appearance.

Within minutes he had located the department where Mr. Penniweather worked and entered the door marked Rare Books. Inside, the air had a lifeless quality—as though the entire office was coated in the acid-free covering used to protect yellowing manuscripts.

"How can I help you?" asked the receptionist.

For an instant he was perplexed to find himself there, hardly remembering why. And when he responded, he found out Mr. Penniweather had just gone off to lunch. It was five minutes after twelve.

Of course, he could get the book without Mr. Penniweather, but
Penniweather was who Lisa had suggested and Penniweather was
who he wanted to see. "When do you expect him back?"

"A little after one."

No two-martini lunch here. Not even designer water. A day in the life
of a faithful retainer. He smiled at the receptionist. "I'll be back then."

George recrossed the courtyard and watched the play of the fountain. Without the backdrop of blue sky and sunshine, pearls cast before swine. He was undecided as to what to do next. Perhaps Rossiter
was free for lunch? He'd been neglecting him lately and a few amends
wouldn't be out of order. But if he went to his office there was Lisa
. . . The thought made him uneasy somehow.

Inasmuch as it was Lisa who told him to see Mr. Penniweather
what could be wrong with that?

He walked over to a coffee shop. Despite the blandishments of
a corned beef on seeded rye, his vague unease, which he was hard
put to explain even to himself, increased. The clock over the counter
ticked and he timed the consummation of his sandwich according to
the minutes he still had left to kill.

At exactly one-fifteen he was back at his post at Rare Books and within minutes the receptionist introduced him to Cyril Penniweather, a
craggy gentlemen in a pin-striped three piece suit, with handkerchief,
watch and spectacles all in their designated pockets. George offered
his hand and gave his name.

"George Wentworth? The author of *Transcendence & Tragedy?*"

"Guilty."

"Well, this is indeed a pleasure. I enjoyed the work so much. I heard Konstantinov many times in my youth. There are only a handful I've heard who were his equal. In fact, come to think of it, perhaps only one. But I shan't bend your ear about that. Miss Graham told me you came earlier and just missed me. I don't want to take up any more of your time." He beamed at him. "What can I do for you?"

"I'm writing a book about Alfred Rossiter."

Removing his spectacles from his pocket, Penniweather unfolded them slowly, placed them on the bridge of his nose and stared at him. "I read the piece you did on him in the *Times*. But I never met the man. What brought you to me?"

It was *deja vu* time and George couldn't understand it. Penniweather had decidedly cooled toward him at the mention of Rossiter's name. Dammit to hell, he was just like that woman in Italy. And why was it so, why? After all the man had done for music—outside a courtyard named for him attested to his contribution—you'd have thought people would be more grateful. "There's a girl who works for him who used to work for you. She told me you could help me with a biography about Yuri Galliuillin. It was Rossiter who first brought him over here."

"He did, did he? Well, even a stopped clock is right twice a day. I heard Galliuillin too. Another of the greats. But not in the same class as Konstantinov. Yes, there's the Stepanovich biography which has been translated by Peter Hughes. That's your best source." He turned to the receptionist and put in a request for the biography. After he was through, he pocketed his glasses, turned to George and asked: "A girl who used to work for me, you say? Who would that be?"

"Her name's Lisa Sullivan."

"Lisa Sullivan? I never heard of her. Are you sure you've got the right person?"

George stared beyond Mr. Penniweather to a pointillist painting on the opposite wall of a young woman. From where he stood she looked whole, lips, eyes, breast, hips all in place and accounted for—but take one step closer and poof—she would dissolve into a million separate dots. "Of course, I'm sure."

"I don't remember anybody by that name. We don't have much of a turnover here. When did she say she worked here?"

"Until she came to the Rossiter agency. That was last November, shortly after it opened."

"I don't remember anybody by that name. Maybe she was a temp—we sometimes have them in when we're rushed. Last November, you say. We had a substantial acquisition from Berlin then and hired extra people to help with the cataloguing. That's probably the answer."

George frowned. A temp? She didn't sound that way when she spoke of her last job. An awkward silence ensued in which they drifted toward the window. He could see Penniweather wished to leave but was too polite to do so. The fog had lifted enough for them to see the rush of traffic over on the West Side Highway. Seeing the cars crawling ant-like bumper to bumper, lane beside lane, the wonder was more in the amount of traffic accidents that didn't occur, than in those that did. Each vehicle in its prescribed space, one foot too much forward or backward, right or left, and it could create a chain reaction for miles. "I can't believe she was only a temp."

"Must have been. I don't flatter myself that my fame has spread much beyond this department. Yes, she must have been a temp. My memory's not what it used to be. I just can't keep track of all these people any more. Ah, here's Miss Graham with your book." He handed the black and yellow plastic-covered volume to him. "Peter Hughes. He's a fine translator. I'm sure you'll find what you want in here. And if there's anything more you need, I'm sure Miss Graham can help you."

Chapter XXXVI

Elizabeth's decision to return to Toronto was postponed again, this time by illness. Lying abed with the flu, telephone bell turned to off, she felt the hours run together in stereoscopic images. First there was her mother's picture retrieved from the microfilm depths at the library; then there was Rossiter handing her the letter from the critic Bruce Andrews; then there was George and her together at the Nielsen concert.

But superseding that, alas, was the image of him asking her about Konstantinov and the *Hammerklavier* with that crafty smile. Elizabeth tried to gather her thoughts. Was it indeed crafty, she wondered for the umpteenth time, or was she again imagining others doing unto her what she was doing unto them? If George was on to something, he would have confronted her about it; his book, if nothing else, would have demanded it. But if he wasn't, what else could that question mean?

Not that it mattered any more. For over a month, ever since that evening in fact, she hadn't seen him. After he'd completed his research, conferences with Rossiter were done by telephone and he was sequestered in his East Hampton home.

Only the drip from the kitchen sink faucet disturbed the stillness, but she was too tired to get up to tighten it. When she looked at the blinking dial face of her clock, she didn't know whether it was six in the morning or six at night. The unrelenting grayness from the window gave no clue.

As George—whom she had once thought transparent as glass—gave no clue. Not about things that didn't matter and not about things that did. In the car after the concert, he'd been careful to give the impression to Margaret and Helge that they were good friends. So why should she complain? Wasn't that precisely what she wanted? To be friends and nothing but, so help them God? Wasn't that the only thing left for them?

True, the intensity of her feelings for him had caught her off guard. But this too would pass. Already the painful removal process had begun. Body was removed; mind would come later. Once the book was finished, opportunities to see him would cease. As would this particular rat-run of her mind, if she had anything to do with it. Perhaps she should contact Infatuates Anonymous, quit cold turkey, and then have former sufferers talk her down whenever she began to backtrack.

On the table next to her was a teacup which she kept refilling whenever she could gather the energy, ignoring the scum on the bottom. In between, she went to the bathroom to take anti-histamine tablets, forcing herself to swallow again and again when her throat balked. In her feverish drowsiness, she had no idea if she was waiting out the full four hours before repeating the dosage; she only acted when the blockage in her nostrils prevented breathing. Once she woke with a start, imagining herself back at the microfilm enlarger, Rossiter standing over her as she unrolled the tape.

Or was it her father?

After a long week under tangled blankets, Elizabeth felt her strength returning. She was going back to Toronto, she was going back to Toronto. This was all she could handle now, any thought of her future once she got there put her in a panic. She took a steamy bath, soaking her battered limbs in the bubbly froth up to her chin. Across from her was the hamper behind which that damning letter had once lain. She stared moodily at it, thinking of George's start when she touched Ruth's arm at the Plaza party.

It was tyrannous, nothing less, the way that tiny infinitesimal moment kept imposing itself, suspended in time and quivering like a hummingbird, blotting out everything that followed, including the way his iron mask descended more steely than ever a moment later, shutting her out.

At the time, she'd had to control herself from grabbing him by the arm violently and shaking the living daylights out of him.

As he no doubt felt like doing to her.

What was going on here? It was inconceivable that the relief of touching or holding each other was now closed off to them forever. Hadn't she been punished enough by fate, must she be her own executioner?

Except for the giveaway of that little reflexive lurch—as though something inside him had given way briefly, she would have thought George's foreclosure complete. *Giveaway*—only a hungry soul would call it that.

She couldn't wait to be in Toronto with the charade safely behind her. It would be so good to be with Aunt Ada again—fellow feeder on such frugal fare. It would be so good to be able to come home of an evening and hear her sympathetic *Wanna tell me about it?*

The Toronto reservation which she had to cancel because of the flu must be reinstated. She'd stop by at the travel agent's as soon as she went back to work. No backing out this time. How much longer could she go round feeling a traitor to her real self?

The waste, the gigantic waste. Her mother, her father, Rossiter—now she and George. In her head, she wrote letters to him:

"I'm sorry to have to disappear like this, but if you knew the circumstances, you'd understand."

"You must understand I'd never have left if I didn't need to—you must see that."

"If I have one regret, it's not being able to tell you why I had to leave."

"If you knew what I've gone through, I know you'd forgive me—"

Fatuous, simpering, corny claptrap.. Better to write nothing. Better to deal him a *fait accompli* and let him make of it what he wished.

Shuddering, she turned on the faucet to raise the water temperature. It reminded her of the week after her father died when sexual fantasies assaulted her in her darkened bedroom and she would try to purge the images by hot baths. Why then, of all times? She scrubbed at her heels with a pumice stone.

Off, off, damned dead skin.

Chapter XXXVII

"Over at Eagle," Ruth said, referring to a story about the Rossiter Recital Award Foundation in the morning's paper, "they're calling it the senility syndrome." Her mouth was full of tuna fish but that didn't stop her from shaking her head in disdain.

"No matter what he does, he can't seem to win with them," George said. He had come directly over to the Rossiter office from the Lincoln Center Library, still trying to make some sense of what he had learned there about Lisa, or rather, what he had not learned.

"And there's no need to try. It's jealousy, if you ask me. Especially after they saw that leaflet we printed about it with the Nielsen review on it. That gave them something to think about, I'm sure."

"But I thought you were against it—"

"I wasn't exactly against it. Just lukewarm. At my age it's hard to take on new risks. I think Lisa was right about it though. I have to give her that."

"By the way, where is she? Still out to lunch?" Although he had come over to the office on the pretext of checking further facts on Galliuillin, it was Lisa he wished to see. Surprisingly, he had not been sorry to find her out. Part of him was itching to confront her with the fact that Penniweather, whom she had described—if memory served him correctly—as a close associate, had never heard of her; part was cautioning him to just let well enough alone for the time being.

"No, she's been out for a couple of weeks with the flu. A nasty case of it. That's why I'm here. I usually don't get in until later. But she called to say she'd be back tomorrow."

"The flu?" Another ploy to go job-hunting? He hated to find himself suspicious of Lisa's every action but what choice had he? "Did you visit her?"

"No, I'd have gone but I have to be careful about exposure myself. I hate to think of her all by herself with a temperature of God alone knows what. Poor thing."

After a while he asked, "Still think she's a snippet?"

Ruth smiled. "Oh, that. Yes, she is. And I still can't understand how Rossiter takes all that guff from her. But all things considered, there's no doubt she's been one of his better hunches." She slipped him a sidewise smile, enjoying her own candor. "Stays on all hours getting things wrapped up around here. A real go-getter."

"But she couldn't have just been a hunch." He patted the coffee cup he held in his hand. "She must have had fine references . . ."

Directly he said that, George could have kicked himself. If Lisa had come to this office under false pretenses, he didn't want to be the one to give her away. Still, he was curious. If she hadn't worked at the Lincoln Center Library, where in blazes did she come from? Perhaps he'd get to the personnel files on his own one night when he was working late with Rossiter. But the book was nearly finished; he didn't think there would be any more late nights.

Ruth studied him for a moment. "References? I can't remember. She must have." Reaching into the file drawer at the bottom of her desk, she began sorting through the folders until she found the one with Lisa's name. "Hmm," she said, looking over the documents, "not much here." Inside was an olive green card, of the sort given by employment agencies, some Social Security information and a photocopy of some sort. She lit a cigarette and temporized in the air with it. "I can't find anything. That's strange . . ."

It was on the tip of his tongue to ask how they could have hired somebody without references in this day and age, but he held back. Though Ruth clearly had begun to like Lisa, she would not be above having her prior opinion proven right after all. He was not about to undo the hard-won gains Lisa had made on her own merit by exposing her to—

To what? That was the point—he didn't quite know. Nevertheless, whatever shenanigans she was up to, he unequivocally was on her side. The least he could do was change the subject. "So you think Eagle will come up with a similar—"

But Ruth would not be diverted. "Now I remember," she said, shutting the file. "I didn't bother with references. She was still working at Lincoln Center Library, and didn't want to jeopardize her job. And since Rossiter was so set on her, I didn't bother. I was sure she'd fall flat on her face soon enough." She shook her head. "Just goes to show you how wrong this old lady can be."

The following morning George was at the library door when it opened. He had needed some unpressured time to get all his questions—whatever they were—properly answered and he didn't want to run into the lunch hour hiatus again.

After a short interlude with the receptionist, he was accompanied this time directly to Penniweather's office.

"Mr. Wentworth," Cyril Penniweather said with rumpled lips. "What brings you back so soon? Don't tell me you've read the book already?"

The man was clearly annoyed at the disturbance but George was not to be deterred. "Yes, I read it last night and it was a real help. But I haven't come about that. It's about Lisa Sullivan. I'm trying to trace her background. I know she told me she worked here."

"Trace her background? What for? Is she under some kind of investigation?"

"No, nothing like that. It's for something . . . I'm writing which I have to confirm."

"Well, I can't see how I can help you." He regarded George seriously, as if unconvinced with his explanation. "But if it's that important . . ."

He rang the intercom on his desk. "Miss Graham, do you remember a Lisa Sullivan working here? No? Perhaps in that rush when we got that consignment from Berlin—? Yes, do that." He switched off the telephone. "She's gone to check the files. But I don't understand, why can't you ask Miss Sullivan about it yourself?"

"Well, you see . . . I wouldn't want her to think I was prying. She seems to have a very strong sense of privacy. Doesn't want her . . . space invaded."

Penniweather's spectacles slipped down his nose and were pushed up again slowly. "I see."

But from the look he gave him, George didn't think he saw at all.

Neither, for that matter, did he.

Mr. Penniweather took out his pocket watch as a nearby bell in a church tower began to peal the hour and held it to his ear. "It looks like this needs cleaning again. I don't like it when it's not synchronized." The buzzer on his desk sounded. "No record of such a name, you say? How far back did you go? Last five years. Well, that certainly does it." He turned to George. "Well, I'm sorry I can't help you further in your investigation—"

George rose to go, the interview again setting up disconcerting echoes of that villa in Naples when he had also accomplished zilch. He took out his pen and wrote his name and telephone number on a pad. "Here is my telephone number. Perhaps she worked in another department. If anybody has any further information, I'd appreciate if you'd give me a ring."

Mr. Penniweather took the slip. "I'll be glad to," he said, but his intonation suggested otherwise. "That's a nice pen you've got there. They're a hobby of mine. I still use my trusty old fountain pen too. Could I look at it?" He turned it over in his hand when George gave it to him. "A Parker 51, eh? Don't often see one of those anymore. A real antique now. Come to think of it, I knew somebody else who had one like it."

"You did?" said George quietly, feeling a strange pricking at the base of his neck. He knew without asking but asked anyway. "Who might that be?"

"A young lady who *did* work here. Name was Elizabeth Guaragna."

"*Did?*"

"Yes, she left some time ago."

"Well, it's the same pen. It belongs—Wait a second, now I remember. At least this trip doesn't have to be a total waste. Lisa told me she had a friend here by that name, so she must have worked here."

Penniweather's face lit up. "Well, she was right on that score. Elizabeth? Of course she worked here. Now you're talking. A real prize, that one. Had a marvellous head for details. And her musical sense was impeccable. Not too surprising considering who her father was."

"Who was her father?"

"Dominic Guaragna—a marvelous pianist."

George's heart pounded in his throat. Dominic Guaragna's daughter? But Lisa had said the name Rossiter meant nothing to her. How could that be? Surely the daughter of Dominic Guaragna would know that. Why did Lisa lie about it? Why did she lie about working at the library? Why should she deprive him of the very thing he needed for his book? It didn't make sense. "Dominic Guaragna?" he asked stupidly.

"When I said yesterday that Konstantinov had few equals, I was thinking of him. Gave one of the best recitals I've ever heard."

"Is that why you don't like Alfred Rossiter?"

"Who said I didn't like—" He shook his head. "Well, yes, to be blunt about it. I thought he treated Guaragna shabbily. Not that Elizabeth ever said anything—"

"What was she like?"

"A darling girl. A little otherworldly—like she's been plunked down in the wrong century. But, as I said, brilliant. I was sorry to lose her. How's her aunt doing?"

He turned to Penniweather: "Her aunt? Which aunt?"

"The one in Toronto. Is she better? Any chance Elizabeth might return?"

"Toronto?" According to Lisa, her friend Elizabeth lived in Chicago. But that postmark on that letter that day—wasn't it Toronto? Yes, of course it was. He remembered the Canadian stamp. He stared at Penniweather. What was wrong with the man? How in hell could he remember Elizabeth and not Lisa? George had a gut feeling that would not let him be. "She told me to ask you about Pergolesi—"

Penniweather's face wreathed in a smile. "Now I know Elizabeth sent you. She told you, eh? How I go for baroque?'"

George continued to stare. "Oh, I nearly forgot, this is what I came to show you in the first place." Taking out his wallet he showed Penniweather the picture he took of Lisa throwing snowballs in Lincoln Center. "Here she is. Now do you remember Lisa?"

After adjusting the spectacles again on the bridge of his nose, Penniweather took the picture and examined it closely. "You must be mistaken. That isn't Lisa Sullivan."

"Who is it?" George asked.

But again he already knew the answer before Mr. Penniweather got the words out.

A spring was released. It came all at once. He'd once read that people dream of many things simultaneously, rather than chronologically, which explains why dreams seem so long and in reality are only a few seconds. Like lights in twenty rooms opening up all at once. Continuum time. Suddenly he saw Lisa that day in the office, speaking with so much more passion about A.R. than her situation ought to warrant. And he saw her that time dropping the file in her hands when A.R. mentioned her Canadian accent—he knew that day she was lying but couldn't see why. And then, finally, he saw her again . . . that time in bed when he spoke of A.R.'s second wife.

Her mother. In other words, she was her mother.

He was not one for self-congratulation but one thought kept reverberating in his head: By golly, he'd thought she was two people and he was right.

Chapter XXXVIII

Elizabeth was well into packing for her return to Toronto when the outside buzzer sounded.

"Lisa, I must talk to you. May I come up?" George's faint voice came over the intercom.

Elizabeth pushed the button to release the catch in the front door to her apartment house. Hastily she zipped up the suitcase and stashed it out of sight under her bed, and shoved the cardboard carton being sent by UPS into the closet. Since she was only dressed in a short nightgown, she quickly put on her flannel robe, wondering what would suddenly bring him calling at this late hour.

Probably it was some last-minute information in connection with the book; she knew the deadline for turning the manuscript over to the publisher was coming up soon.

At least that's what she hoped. With her plans to return to Toronto on Sunday all set, she didn't want any new complications.

Steeling herself, she opened the door to greet him, determined to set just the right kind of friendly tone. But, as he emerged from the shadowy stairs into the bright foyer, she saw he had lost weight—his green eyes were more prominent in his drawn face—and her mutinous heart rose in her chest. She said nothing.

"Sorry to come barging in at this hour," he said, handing her a bouquet covered with wrapping paper. "I waited all evening until I saw you were home."

"How kind," she said, taking the offering. "I was working late. I've been out sick and had a lot of catching up to do. We're getting ready to announce the addition—"

"Yes, I heard. You needed a couple of good salesmen for the road.

And the choices are excellent."

He was referring to the two personnel additions at the office, one of whom had been manager of a midwest orchestra, and the other the public relations director of the Los Angeles division of Eagle Concerts. Ever since the Nielsen debut, the office had taken on a new lease on life, and Elizabeth could hardly keep up with the demands. Now that these two new employees were almost broken in, she felt her departure would hardly be felt.

"Can I get you a drink?" she asked as she went to the kitchenette, turned on the cold water and filled a vase.

"Nothing, thanks. This is a no-frills visit."

Unwrapping the cone, a rainbow mix of rose, blue, and yellow gladioli greeted her. Her heart started what had become a familiar rat-tat and she gave a sharp glance at George. Who was this larger than life photograph surprisingly revolving three dimensionally before her? A coincidence, she thought as she arranged the spikes haphazardly in the vase, then placed it, dripping, on the coffee table. Just a coincidence. She tried to say how lovely they were but her voice wouldn't come forth.

"I need to speak to you. Tell me, Li . . . what is your real name anyway?"

She understood the question well enough but suddenly didn't know the answer. Tying the sash of her robe tightly, she began to speak but was still incapable of getting anything out. Feeling her legs giving away, she lowered herself carefully on the day bed.

He pulled a chair near her, sat down, and pulled her father's pen from his suit pocket. "This is yours, I believe, Elizabeth. It is Elizabeth, isn't it?"

She rose abruptly, turned on another light, plumped a pillow, straightened an afghan. Alternative responses passed before her but one look at his face and she knew the ridiculous jig was up. She sat down again and took the pen from his hand.

With her continuing silence, George rose to pull out *Transcendence and Tragedy* from the bookcase and opened it to the flyleaf to study the inscription. "If I'd done this the last time I was here, I'd have saved myself a lot of headaches. To say nothing of heartaches." He replaced it on the shelf. "I thought you looked like somebody I'd met when I first saw you, but . . ."

Leaning over as he sat down beside her, he took her hand in his. "I was in such a panic all day. Afraid you might have already skipped town or something. But I didn't dare see you in the office."

"How did you find out?" she asked at last.

"You don't have to be an investigative reporter to smell something fishy. I didn't really believe you. Didn't believe you at any time except, perhaps, the last time I was in this apartment."

"Was there such a . . . difference?"

"'*Was there such a difference,*'" he mimicked, giving her a brooding look, "lordy, lordy. Anyway, in the end it turned out to be easy. I had one of my *aha* moments," he said with a smile and went on to describe the events of the two last days culminating with his foray into the inner sanctum of Mr. Penniweather. "Can you guess the rest?"

And then his arms were around her and he was saying her name unintelligibly into her hair. *Elizabeth* that is, he was saying *Elizabeth*.

Elizabeth pulled away and considered the wall for a minute. Although the room was well-heated, beads of cold sweat rolled down her forehead and stung her eyes. All through the recital of his meeting with Mr. Penniweather, she kept wondering if it was indeed she he was talking about. She was twenty-six years old now, had lived over a quarter of a century, but the world had no logic she could see; it was just an amalgamation of souls each of whom was trying to outwit their own special brand of *sfortuna*—lousy luck.

Fate, the demon seed, was fate, Rossiter said, and so, too, she had always believed. Either you pursue it or it pursues you—take your pick. The Harris' lose their only daughter to leukemia; the virtuoso Brandwein is condemned to rock music on his patio. Capricious fate. Father, mother, Rossiter, Tom, Ada—crippled spirits all. Nobody's record remains unspotted. She, who had once wished above all things to diminish the pain of those around her, was increasingly becoming the instrument of its enlargement.

"You can still call me Lisa. It was my nickname. Or perhaps my father wanted to differentiate my name from my mother's."

His two hands spread over her cheeks. "Lisa, then. I love you, Lisa. I'm sure you must know it."

She leaned against him, her face hidden in his shoulder. They were so good, those old words, newly coined with each usage, so simple and so good, though they had grown up in an age when they learned to mistrust such simplifications. He held her to him without speaking for a long while and then confided his fantasy about her being two people. Even at his most angry, he knew which was the real person. "Only I didn't know she had another name."

She turned from him and, on impulse, put the cassette of the *Traumerei* on the tape recorder and turned it on.

"Your father?"

She nodded. There it was again, the opening notes, open heart-strings coaxed. Her eyes filled up, as did a familiar lump in her throat. The years stretched backward, like a vast continent, with lakes and rivers and carefully tended farms, and, dividing one crop from the other, rows of Russian olive trees.

"Now I see what Penniweather meant," George said when she turned off the tape recorder, "it is reminiscent of Konstantinov. Oh, what a tangled web—" He withdrew a handkerchief from his pocket and wiped her eyes. "Tell me, what gave you the idea to take that job?"

"In a way, it was you who let the genie out of the bottle. When I read the piece you did on Mr. Rossiter—you see, you must believe me, I never expected him to hire me. I didn't have any qualifications. And I didn't really want the job. I just wanted to see him at close range. I knew so little about my mother. Thanks to you, that's all changed. I *know* her now, I don't have to speculate any longer. Knowing is life—not knowing—death. So I applied for the job—and for some reason, for some crazy, unaccountable—"

She stopped short. With George's scent of after-shave cologne, the room enclosing them felt warm and safe. Slowly her taut shoulders relaxed and her fingers uncurled. There was a reason there, but she was so exhausted. It would come in time and she would have it, but not quite now. It must wait.

But George would not wait. "He hires a *snippet*. That's what you've got to understand about A.R. He's an old horse trader. Likes to play long shots. Why didn't you tell him after he hired you?"

"It became increasingly difficult." She tried to explain how everyone she knew hated this man. How mythological a monster he was to her all her life. "You complimented me on being 'able to pick them.' Growing up in that household, listening every morning in my bed to one of the greatest pianists that ever lived—well, if that doesn't train your ear—and he was the greatest, make no mistake. I wish I could play something more than just the *Traumerei* for you. But with no breaks—look how the career of Helge is off and running. Given those crucial breaks, given a helping hand instead of a . . . a shove—" her voice choked on the word—"the career can become self-sustaining. But, by the same token, take away those breaks, and the greatest pianist would die on the vine."

"I can't believe—" He spoke as much to himself as to her. "I can't believe Rossiter deliberately tried to subvert your father's career—neither did Mickiewicz. Unless he wanted to get even because he ran off with all of you to Italy. Not very nice, I agree—but he is human, after all."

"It wasn't because of that. It happened before that." She went to the dresser to show him the picture with Aunt Ada and to explain that she was also a pianist. "She could tell you plenty about Rossiter. You see, even if he didn't subvert him deliberately, it's enough for somebody like that to wrinkle his nose—and then his *cosa nostra* would blow it for him. I know I shouldn't have stayed on. I kept hoping he'd fire me. God knows I gave him enough reason."

George laughed. "He knew the real thing, too, no matter what blarney you tried to superimpose on it." At her head shake, he continued. "He's not as bad as you make out. Believe me, he isn't. You must tell him and find out for yourself—" He stopped as her face darkened. "What's wrong?"

"I couldn't do that."

"Why not?"

"Don't you see? If he found out who I was, it would just add additional complications. Look, the kindest thing I can do is to leave him now to live out the rest of his life in whatever peace he can find. Besides, I feel as though I'd be unfaithful to—to the dead if I told him."

"It's the living you have to worry about now, Lisa."

Chapter XXXIX

It was decided. At some time in the early morning, both had agreed she must tell Rossiter. "For your peace of mind," George said and promised to come to her aid in the afternoon. But it was one thing to decide, another to do. Instead of going to work, she had gone for a walk in the park but couldn't remember what path she had taken or what she had seen. All she remembered was seeing a flight of Canada geese flying in formation overhead, heading north, and wishing she were among them.

When she finally did arrive at the office an hour and a half late, determined to say her piece immediately and then clear out, Rossiter was not there. He had gone to his doctor's office straight from Grand Central and had still not appeared on the scene.

She worked in fits and starts, mostly clearing her desk for what she hoped would still be her imminent departure. Ages went by between eleven and twelve, eons between twelve and one.

If only the day were already over, she kept repeating to herself. Just another day among the multitudes, in the world's scheme of things, nothing of importance. If only it were over. Although what "being over" would be like she had no idea. One doesn't simply get over the hatred of a lifetime—it was inconceivable. What could she "tell" Rossiter and what "peace of mind" could she ever have again?

But whatever it would bring—just let it be over.

She had just finished putting Rossiter's letters into three neat piles when George came into the room. "How did it go?" When she shook her head he took both her hands in his. "He's not such an ogre, you know."

"But what good will it really do? I've been thinking it over and—"

"*Stop thinking. Do.* He'll understand. And I've a hunch he'll be grateful. I'm becoming a horse trader myself. But, Lisa, you've got to tell him—"

"Tell him what?" Rossiter had suddenly appeared in the room noiselessly. As they both wheeled around guiltily, he gave them a mischievous smile, then hung his coat in the closet and placed his hat on the shelf above it. "That you two are goofy about each other? Come now. I'm not blind you know. I recognize a mutual adoration society when I see it. And I'm all for it. Glad to have been the unwitting catalyst. You're well-matched. True minds and all that sort of thing."

"Thanks," George said. "That means a lot coming from you. But that wasn't what we were discussing."

Elizabeth was feeling as if she might have to vomit right on Rossiter's beautiful antique Tabriz carpet. George looked at her expectantly, cornering her. *Stop thinking. Do.* "I'm not Lisa Sullivan," she blurted out, "my real name is Elizabeth Guaragna."

But Rossiter didn't understand, for he was speaking simultaneously, straightening back a lock of hair. ". . . well, what is it? Has she been dipping into the till again?"

George took a step forward; for a moment Elizabeth thought he was going to leave the room. But he only went to stand next to the old man. "I'm Elizabeth Guaragna," she said, lifting her immense and resolute eyes, "not Lisa Sullivan."

This time he understood. His face went scarlet but the half smile remained on his lips, as though transfixed, nothing could change it. He took several short breaths and said: "You can't be, you're twenty-eight—I saw that on your application."

She could no longer see him, could no longer see anything.

This was not at all how she imagined she would feel at this moment: always it had been in terms of triumph, revenge, redemption.

Instead she wanted to behave as George was doing, standing staunchly by Rossiter's side, to reassure, to help, if necessary, to smooth his brow.

She clenched her fists. Time flowed around her while she remained a large boulder in a raging sea. She was, after all, Elizabeth *Junior.* Reaching slowly inside the neck of her sweater, she drew out the locket, unfastened it, and held it up for his inspection. He stared uncomprehendingly at the glittering heart-shaped pendant in her hand.

"I lied about my age. I'm only twenty-six."

The change in him was sudden and total. One moment a jovial grinning old man, the next doubled over, face creased in pain, unscrewing the lid from a bottle which he withdrew from his suit jacket. With a shaky hand he took two pink capsules and popped them into his mouth.

George's fingers closed comfortingly around his arm. "Are you all right, sir?"

"Of course, I'm all right," he answered, but as he straightened up, very slowly, he moaned. It was as if the whole room moaned, the Turner seascape, the three neat piles of correspondence on his desk, the music parchment lamp, the African violets.

Turning from them to stand next to his desk, he appeared only in profile, but what Elizabeth could make out from the set of his face and shoulders was not a look of anger, but one of regret so deep as to make the whole day darken around them. He took off his glasses, wiped them with a handkerchief and put them back on. "So you've been here all this time under false pretenses—" He rattled the desk top with the tips of his fingers. "Just the sort of thing I could expect from somebody raised by Guaragna."

Elizabeth blanched. "Just what *you* could expect—how dare you speak of him that way? After all you did to him—"

"*I did to him!* What about what he did to me? And to your . . . mother?"

"She brought it on herself, didn't she? *You* brought it—"

"What are you talking about?"

Though Rossiter seemed in command, all power seemed to have drained from him. But for Elizabeth there was no turning back. "She gave up her rights to the children in order to divorce him, didn't she? So she could marry you?"

Rossiter's jaw slid out, his scalp reddened where the hair had thinned. "Is that what he told you? She didn't give up the right to *you!* She never dreamed when she signed that paper in Nevada it would include an infant child she was still breast feeding. What did your mother know about life? And then he ran off to Italy so she couldn't ever see any of you again. By what right—"

"By a father's right," Elizabeth burst out, standing tall and slim, the avenging Guaragna angel at last. "By a deeply hurt father's right. We were his children, too, remember?"

"*You* weren't—"

Their eyes met like a wild clash of arms. Whatever horror imagination could wring was less horrifying than the implications of that single, uneradicable word *you*. In one swoop it cut through everything.

"I don't understand," she started to say but there was this business of breathing. Rossiter gazed at her in ashen dismay, as though he would give anything now to take back his words, and then rushed out of the office. Gazing after him, she felt as though she were seeing him for the first time.

All of it became clear, just as in the parallel dream which George had described: the guilty looks between Ada and Dominic; Tom's strangled cry "All she re-really wanted was y-you"; the strange way Dominic treated her after Chris' death, as though he had somehow brought the whole thing on.

The big circle closed; she had reached the other side.

"Please, sit down," Rossiter said. "You know I don't like people to hover."

It was later that afternoon. When George and Elizabeth returned from a late lunch at which both said little and ate even less, Rossiter rang for them to rejoin him in his office. As they settled in seats across from him, they could hear the clock's innards gather momentum before beginning to toll the hour.

"Would you like some coffee?" George asked, breaking the silence that possessed them.

"No," Rossiter said, "I need whiskey."

After pouring a shot into a glass and handing it to Rossiter, George looked at Elizabeth questioningly. She shook her head.

"He ought to have told me," Elizabeth finally said, articulating what was in all of their minds, but of a sudden her father's haunted and pleading face passed before her as it was that day in High Park when they spoke of cotton candy. What could he have told her? That he was cuckolded and then fled with the issue of that cuckoldry? For the first time the magnitude of his fear hit home.

But he wasn't her father. Every thought brought a new onslaught of pain. On the table lay a book called *Hemidemisemiquavers*. She kept re-reading the title, sounding it in her head like a tongue-twister, anything rather than dwell on the complicated set of new equations the past two hours had cast on her history. All the while Rossiter sat stone still, his eyes half-closed, his hands circling the glass which George had given him.

"The gladioli," he said, and took a long pull of brandy. "It was you, wasn't it?" She nodded. "I should've known it was you. There was something that reminded me of somebody . . . And now I see it."

He stood up and moved toward her, cupping her face in his two large hands. "I thought I was the last of the Mohicans, but here's another. You look a bit like my mother did. And my sister Penelope. Some genetic quirk about the eyebrows. They're both gone now. It was that look that must have drawn me when I hired you, of course." He studied the locket and then moved away. "If you knew how often—but I still thought you were in Italy. With a life of your own and—I even thought—" A few more stabs at sentence beginnings.

He laughed suddenly, startling himself. "More recently with needing to get my will into—remember, George, I told you about that."

"Yes," George said. "You said something about one never being able to complete it, even on the deathbed—but I thought you were speaking in generalities."

"No—I meant Elizabeth. But how to find her? And here you were right under my nose. But then I thought I couldn't do that without leaving something to Tom and Chris and—"

She told him about Chris. Heaving himself back into his chair, he covered his face with his hand. "Ignorance isn't bliss but I'm glad Elizabeth never lived to hear of that." George refilled his glass and he lifted it with trembling fingers. "I looked at that date of your birth on your application almost automatically—I always did it with girls of your age. Not that I was consciously thinking anything. I often studied the faces of young women just to picture in my mind what Elizabeth might be like. My *daughter* Elizabeth, except I never allowed myself to think of her—you—in those terms. I never really expected to find—"

Elizabeth watched him, this world-renowned ravener of artists, creator of broadcasting networks, defendant in anti-trust suits, spoiler of her childhood, thief of her mother, maimer of her fa—she gasped at the pain that tore her—of *Dominic,* now dwindled to a doddering old man whose Adam's apple painfully twitched with every gulp of drink.

"You realize I'm going to have to rewrite my last chapter, don't you?" George said with a laugh.

"I expect we're all going to have to do that now. But that isn't necessarily a bad thing." Rossiter turned to Elizabeth. "What are you going to do now?"

"I'd planned on giving notice today and returning to Toronto at the end of the week. Now I don't even want to wait that long."

"And you, George?"

"I'm going with Lisa. I'm not leaving her out of my sight ever again."

Rossiter smiled. "I don't blame you. I feel the same way." He turned again to Elizabeth. "But why Toronto?"

"That's where I lived until coming to New York. I have to see Aunt Ada and do some serious repair work." She conjured up a mental picture of her aunt as she had last seen her, beaten down by Elizabeth's unending questions, her pale face quivering. "I've been beastly to her and now I appreciate her more than ever."

"Your Aunt Ada. You mean Dom's sister? Well, in that case, there's something I'd like you to take to her for me." He rose and unlocked the side door of the cabinet along the far wall. From the far corner of the bottom shelf, he extracted a large brown parcel tied in frayed string and brittle tape. "Here it is," he said, straightening up and blowing away the accumulated dust.

"What is it?" Her heart had started up again.

"They're Dom's recordings of all the Beethoven sonatas. They were supposed to come out just about the time I married your mother. But then Eagle Records decided not to release it—"

"Why was that?" George asked. "Because of your marriage?"

"I urged them to release it—I didn't think our personal and professional lives should get mixed up. But they wouldn't listen. In those days we didn't capitalize on scandal as is done today, on the contrary, we tried to sweep it under the carpet. I had copies made from the master. And then I meant to send them on—but it was like the will—too many loose ends. I didn't know where to send them. You see, by that time there was the custody trial." Taking a handkerchief from his pocket, he dusted off the package carefully and handed it to her.

"They're wonderful recordings—perhaps we could have them released now, Elizabeth."

The package was heavy and cumbersome. Both men looked at Elizabeth who sat still looking at the package on her knees. Lifting it sideways to her chest like a breastplate, she put her arms around it and shut her eyes. To have her father restored to her playing all the Beethoven Sonatas—and even the *Diabelli Variations*, as Aunt Ada had put it—tears rose to her eyes and fell. And he had called her Elizabeth, he had called her Elizabeth, just as George had. It was all too much. The two men were still looking at her but she couldn't speak. What she wanted was to go home and listen—but even that was too much for her now. "I can't think," she said at last. She turned to George. "This weighs a ton. Would you help me bring them home?"

Chapter XXXX

"All right, if I've been guilty of foolhardiness, of poverty of perception, of stubborness, well, okay, I'm guilty."

"Give yourself a break. How could you have known?"

Only now, riding back home with George, was it all finally beginning to sink in. "I should have known. But even in my wildest fantasies, I wouldn't have thought of this. Alfred Rossiter, the feared, the hated, the loathed, the suffered, and, more recently, the grudgingly liked, is my—" She could not bring herself to complete that sentence. "Do you realize what this means? I don't know how to begin. All the known and fixed points of my life have to be altered to accommodate the shift in the terrain."

George said: "And knowing you, all the little red pins will soon be stuck into other places."

She studied her hands. Then she leaned over to kiss his cheek and said, "No more of that, I promise."

"A few fixed points of my book will have to be altered too. It is a bit much. What I still don't understand is why Giuseppe Guaragna wouldn't see me in Naples. And why his wife gasped when I mentioned Rossiter's name."

"Giuseppe Guaragna is my great uncle. He's the conductor of a small opera company. He must have known my father had broken the law when he absconded with my brothers and me. I guess there was always a cloud of fear hanging over the whole family that Rossiter might have us extradited and my father put behind bars. And everybody connected with him considered accessories. Rossiter must have been anathema in a lot more ways than even I suspected. God, I see it all now. No wonder Aunt Ada was so fearful of my move to New York. Now I can really understand her horror at my defense of him."

George swerved around a pothole as best he could but the under-belly scraped against a jagged edge. It was still light outside—the low-ering sun over the Hudson coated the windows with pink. "But what did your aunt really have to do with it? From what you've told me she was an innocent bystander and, as with innocent bystanders every-where, plenty of collateral damage came her way. It sounds like she was just trying to keep the heavens from falling down on everybody."

"I suppose so. I begin to understand so much. The *Traumerei*, don't you see, that's all he could do. Even though he so wanted to reach out to me, my father never dared."

"Your *father?*"

"Yes, my father," she said. "He *was* my father, will always be, noth-ing could change that. Rossiter? Well, he's . . . he's my *blood* father. He's still my mother's lover to me. Perhaps I'll feel differently with time. But for now—"

The traffic light changed; George upshifted his white Porsche around Columbus Circle, inching his way as slowly as the bus had around the curves of Monte Placidus. The lampposts, swathed in pink, gave a Venetian cast to the fountain in the center. Elizabeth grasped the door handle as the car swerved to the right. Poor Tom, he had known, somehow he had guessed . . .

"I still can't get over it, either. What made you apply for the job? Was it really only the thirst for knowledge?"

Elizabeth took a deep breath. Somewhere, in the depths of her psyche, was the answer, but what was it? Aloud she said, "On one level, yes. But now I see it was beyond that. And it was beyond the thirst for vengeance, beyond the thirst for justice. Something impelled me, something beyond vision or comprehension."

He smiled. "Something taken on faith."

"I wouldn't go so far as to say that." She was beginning to feel giddy. "I really don't know. From a soggy grave came those impulses—and now from two."

She looked at George's strong hand, finally ungloved, after the long, bitterly cold winter, as he pressed the switch to lower a window. The scent of spring possessed the world, inevitable and tyrannical, forcing thoughts of renewal and blossoms whether you were ready for them or not. Nature was ready for another turn around the track. A police car, lights flashing, siren screaming, whizzed by and George pulled over to the right. In front of them brake lights were aglow all along Broadway and Central Park West.

Shell-fragments were whizzing past her head. She remembered the way Rossiter shut his eyes as she clumsily reached for his proferred hand when they left him at Grand Central. She remembered seeing dust particles on it, still remaining from the package of recordings. She remembered realizing that the hand that held hers had once held her mother's hand. She remembered she no longer felt revulsion at the thought. She remembered him trying to stanch tears, then seeing them run down his face as he stumbled past the gate to the train.

No need to speculate what he was thinking. She had taken this job to find out more about herself; what she found out was as much about him as she would ever know about herself.

She wondered if Dominic might have wished for the secret to be finally found out. She guessed not, he covered up all his tracks too carefully for that. The truth is always so much larger than one can foresee. It was only after his death she'd been able finally to move to New York, though she had certainly wanted to earlier.

Rossiter had asked her to reconsider her notice—and, of course, she would. She already had. There was no reason for her not to continue at her job anymore. Strange that Rossiter—could she ever stop thinking of him as Rossiter?—should never have known she lived in Toronto. "But I suppose you could say it was willful ignorance," he had said. "After Elizabeth went, I just wanted to erase the whole episode from my mind. Ha."

Her heart had given such a lurch at the *Ha*. She and George had exchanged looks between them and there was nothing more that needed to be said.

The line of cars began to move again and George made the tricky right to Broadway. She leaned back and took a long breath, looking at the marquee at the Regency, which advertised a Cary Grant Festival. One way to keep time standing still, playing the same pictures over and over again. And old people going in to see them, trying to recapture their young selves alongside images frozen in time.

"It seems fitting," George said with caution, "that the two of us should now be making our way up this route, covering the same ground which we did in the snow a little over two months ago."

"Was it only two months ago? Even this morning, when I still woke as a *Guaragna*, seems a century ago. My God, it's been difficult enough trying to get used to being called Sullivan, but now it'll be a tossup between Guaragna, Sullivan and—pinch me, pinch me—*Rossiter!*"

Stopped behind a double-parked truck, George took her left hand in his and put it to his lips. "There's a way to avoid that, you know."

She had to smile at his way of putting it. He smiled in return, but he wasn't being funny, he was serious. Very serious. And attuned, attuned, yes, yes, yes, even Aunt Ada would agree.

She stroked back his hair. There was an earlier declaration, his "You don't seem very pleased to see me" when she had, of necessity, had to seem remote. And earlier still, his worry about his apparatus. Now it came to this.

An idiot joy swept over her—a lightheadedness, something almost holy. But at the same time she had to fight her craving for bitter, hot tears. "I . . ."

But she could not find words.

Postscript, 1981

The sides of Monte Placidus were covered with bursts of yellow and white daisies, day-lilies, scarlet poppies. Black and white lowing cows—occasionally rust and white—could be seen grazing in the meadows and bleating lambs cavorted to and fro. High above geese flew in formation and swooped down to a lake below.

Inside the wrought-iron gates of the monastery, in contrast to the wildness outside, butterflies flitted over a carefully-tended garden ablaze with red and yellow roses, foxgloves, irises, phlox, Queen Anne's lace and creamy white stars of Jerusalem. The smell of newly-cut grass mingled with that of freshly-baked bread coming from the kitchen area.

For such a day as this are bleak wintry months gladly endured.

A man and a woman walked up the path, she with a wide-brimmed hat covering her long black hair, he with an old captain's hat, as they drank in the warm smells. Their figures were not hard-edged, each was molten by the surrounding color. The woman walked gingerly, accepting the support of the man's arm gratefully, for she was heavy with child. But when she saw the young priest in a brown robe emerge from the visitor's lounge to greet them, she broke away to dash ahead and embrace him as tightly as her girth would allow.

After stuffing his hat into the pocket of his jacket, the man greeted the priest in a more subdued fashion. "I'm happy to finally meet you," he said, shaking his hand.

"Not half as much as I you," the priest answered. "I can't tell you how much your letters meant to me." He smiled at both of them. "But I didn't understand how you two signed the visitor's book—how come it was Elizabeth Guaragna and George Wentworth?"

The fact that he could make this longish statement without any speech impairment was not lost on the woman. Thinking about it, she found it difficult to speak herself. At last she gently said, "You've been away from the world too long. Nowadays, married women retain their maiden names if they choose."

"And you chose . . . Guaragna?"

"Yes, I especially chose that."

The priest responded to this by lifting her hand and putting it to his mouth. When he spoke, it was to change the subject. "Can you imagine what it meant to me to hear those recordings? It brought papa back like nothing else could. And Aunt Ada wrote that they're selling marvelously."

The man said: "They've developed quite a cult following."

"Ada's donating half of the royalties to the monastery. Some to the Royal Conservatory. How did it all come about?"

The woman said: "George remembered hearing Dinu Lipatti's records, which were also brought out posthumously. But that was another time. With the commercialism of today, no record companies were willing to chance it."

"So what happened?"

The man looked to the woman to answer. She hesitated for a moment, then said, "I guess we must thank Alfred Rossiter for that. As he put it at the time, 'it helps to be a big stockholder at Eagle Broadcasting.' He even offered to fund it with his . . . now, my foundation, if they didn't want to take the risk. 'Who's to say,' he asked me before he died, 'that we can't bend the rules a bit?'"

He had said something more at the time, something about her being his immortality, and now her own immortality gave her a vigorous kick in her belly as if privy to her thoughts. She shut her eyes for a moment, remembering a shrunken body propped against a huge down pillow in a four poster bed, its distorted image visible in the water carafe and inverted drinking glass stopper on the bedside table.

She had held his hand, even as she had once held another father's hand, and it occurred to her that each of these men had been stead-fastly faithful to her mother in their own way.

And his wife Dolores, unable as she was to witness pain and in-sisting until the end that his illness was temporary, was surprisingly grateful for her presence.

After a pause, the priest turned to the man, and asked: "How's the book doing?"

"It's doing well, for a biography. And part of the reason is con-nected to the chapter on your father. There's talk of a movie sale. The release of the recordings helped the book enormously—"

He stopped speaking to enable them to listen to the distinctive trill of a cardinal coming from the willow nearby.

"Another plainsong," said the priest.

The light altered and the landscape changed. From a nearby arbor, the priest gathered some purple grapes hanging from the roof and of-fered a bunch to them. After that, they began to walk down the lane, each with their own thoughts, each accompanied by absent others of their own choosing, each experiencing the healing grace of rectification.

Reading Group Guide

1.   Discuss the factors that lead Elizabeth Guaragna to apply for a job with Alfred Rossiter, even though she has a good job that she likes.

2.   What are the reasons, both psychological and practical, that impel Rossiter to hire her?

3.   The author writes about Dominic Guaragna (in Chapter II): "Grievance was holy, second only to music. But whereas with music he was both slave and master, with grievance he was only slave." Keeping those lines in mind, discuss Dominic's character and his relationship with Elizabeth.

4.   The tension between overpowering silences and sound—in particular, music—comes into play in several parts of the book. Elizabeth's childhood home is "a house of silences upon silences," and certain names were never to be uttered. But it was also filled with music, which, in her father's words, "unfreezes the imagination." There are other silences in the book, particularly when Lisa's deception about who she is threatens her relationship with George. Discuss the roles that silence and music play in the novel.

5.   The piano piece *Traumerei* (usually translated as "Dreaming"), by Robert Schumann, comes from a longer set of pieces called *Kinderszenen*, or "Scenes from Childhood." Listen to *Traumerei*; there are numerous recordings that one can hear on the Internet, and it lasts only about three minutes. What is the significance of the piece in Elizabeth's life, and why might Dominic have chosen to play it every night?

6. What role does Ada Guaragna play in Elizabeth's life? How do her revelations about Rossiter (in Chapter VII) affect Lisa? How did they affect you?

7. What factors in George Wentworth's personal and professional background might explain his adulation of Alfred Rossiter? What causes Lisa to repel George Wentworth's advances from the outset?

8. What are the similarities and differences in the two major sibling relationships in the novel: that of George and his sister Maggie, and that of Elizabeth and her brother Tom?

9. Discuss the other women in Rossiter's life: Ruth Pryor, the imperious loyalist who comes out of retirement to help him get the new agency started; Virginia Lavin, the one-time singer who had hoped for an operatic career, went into music management instead, and frequently wears a Metropolitan Opera necklace that Rossiter had given her; and Dolores, his third wife, who spends most of her time drinking to escape her loneliness and misery. Discuss what we know about Rossiter's feelings toward each of these women. What has inspired such extreme loyalty by Ruth and Virginia, and such extreme dissatisfaction by Dolores?

10. Discuss the business side of the classical music world as described in the book. What are the struggles of the musicians, and what are the challenges of the managers? Why does Elizabeth work so hard to help establish the career of Helge Nielsen? What might have happened to her idealism had his concert never been reviewed? How have business practices changed since the 1970s?

11. The book is about two interlocking quests: Lisa wants to learn about her mother by getting to know Rossiter; George wants to learn about Rossiter, in part by tracking down some of the

Guaragnas. How do these two quests affect each of the main characters in the novel?

12. The book is also about a deception: Lisa changes her identity to get the job with Rossiter. Discuss the role of deception in other aspects of the novel. Who else deceives? How have deceptions affected and shaped Lisa's life? Rossiter's life? Other members of the Guaragna family? How does Lisa's sense of her own identity—both as Elizabeth Guaragna and as Lisa Sullivan—shift as the deceptions are revealed? What questions does the novel raise about deception, identity, truth, betrayal and love?

13. Toward the end of Chapter XVI, Elizabeth walks on a snowy afternoon near George Washington Bridge, thinking about the chapter she has just read in George's manuscript about her mother and Rossiter. What might the bridge that disappears and reappears in the snow convey symbolically at this point in Lisa's life? What bridges does she need to cross? Similarly, when she and George walk in the snowstorm in Chapter XX, how do their disappearing footprints evoke the history of Rossiter and his wife that they are searching for?

14. After Lisa visits the New York Public Library (Chapter XVII) to find the articles about the custody battle, she says to the reference librarian, "But no heroes or heroines peopled this story . . . neither did villains." How has her perspective changed from the outset of the book?

15. What impact might the phrase "motherless child" have on Rossiter and on Elizabeth?